Love Is Usually Where You Left It

Gary Locke

Also by Gary Locke:

Congratulations…..you're having ~~a baby~~ *twins*!

! – For when full stops aren't enough and question marks aren't appropriate

The Paul Day Chronicles Comedy Series -

The complete days of 2006 –
Paul Day Chronicles – Happily After *Ever*!

Short Stories from 2006 –
Paul Day Chronicles – Love Is Like Fireworks!
Paul Day Chronicles – The Stag Do.
Paul Day Chronicles – Football Is Like Sex!
Paul Day Chronicles – Fate… Bloody Fate!

The complete days of 1992 –
Paul Day Chronicles – Goodbye B.M.X., *Hello S.E.X.*

Short Stories from 1992 –
Paul Day Chronicles – Love for the Very First Time.
Paul Day Chronicles – Dead Legs, Exam Dreads and Fun Behind the Bike Sheds.

Cling and Grow Publishing

Cover Design by Andy Tiplady – Freelance Graphic Designer

First published in Great Britain in 2019 by Cling and Grow
Publishing

LOVE IS USUALLY WHERE YOU LEFT IT LOVE IS ALL YOU NEED LOVE IS IN THE AIR LOVE IS LIKE OXYGEN LOVE IS A STRANGER LOVE IS A BATTLEFIELD LOVE IS LIKE A BOMB LOVE IS WAR LOVE IS A WONDERFUL THING LOVE IS ALL AROUND LOVE IS LOVE REFLECTED LOVE IS LIKE FIREWORKS LOVE IS BLINDNESS LOVE IS AN OPEN DOOR **LOVE IS USUALLY WHERE YOU LEFT IT** LOVE IS ALL YOU NEED LOVE IS IN THE AIR LOVE IS LIKE OXYGEN LOVE IS A STRANGER LOVE IS A BATTLEFIELD LOVE IS LIKE A BOMB LOVE IS WAR LOVE IS A WONDERFUL THING LOVE IS ALL AROUND LOVE IS LOVE REFLECTED LOVE IS LIKE FIREWORKS LOVE IS BLINDNESS LOVE IS AN OPEN DOOR **LOVE IS USUALLY WHERE YOU LEFT IT** LOVE IS ALL YOU NEED LOVE IS IN THE AIR LOVE IS LIKE OXYGEN LOVE IS A STRANGER LOVE IS A BATTLEFIELD LOVE IS LIKE A BOMB LOVE IS WAR LOVE IS A WONDERFUL THING LOVE IS ALL AROUND LOVE IS LOVE REFLECTED LOVE IS LIKE FIREWORKS LOVE IS BLINDNESS LOVE IS AN OPEN DOOR **LOVE IS USUALLY WHERE YOU LEFT IT** LOVE IS ALL YOU NEED LOVE IS IN THE AIR LOVE IS LIKE OXYGEN LOVE IS A STRANGER LOVE IS A BATTLEFIELD LOVE IS LIKE A BOMB LOVE IS WAR LOVE IS A WONDERFUL THING LOVE IS ALL AROUND LOVE IS LOVE REFLECTED LOVE IS LIKE FIREWORKS LOVE IS BLINDNESS LOVE IS AN OPEN DOOR **LOVE IS USUALLY WHERE YOU LEFT IT** LOVE IS ALL YOU NEED LOVE IS IN THE AIR LOVE IS LIKE OXYGEN LOVE IS A STRANGER LOVE IS A BATTLEFIELD LOVE IS LIKE A BOMB LOVE IS WAR LOVE IS A WONDERFUL THING LOVE IS ALL AROUND LOVE IS LOVE REFLECTED LOVE IS LIKE FIREWORKS LOVE IS BLINDNESS LOVE IS AN OPEN DOOR **LOVE IS USUALLY WHERE YOU LEFT IT** LOVE IS ALL YOU NEED LOVE IS IN THE AIR LOVE IS LIKE OXYGEN LOVE IS A STRANGER LOVE IS A BATTLEFIELD LOVE IS LIKE A BOMB LOVE IS WAR LOVE IS A WONDERFUL THING LOVE IS ALL AROUND LOVE IS LOVE REFLECTED LOVE IS LIKE FIREWORKS LOVE IS BLINDNESS LOVE IS AN OPEN DOOR **LOVE IS USUALLY WHERE YOU LEFT IT** LOVE IS ALL YOU NEED LOVE IS IN THE AIR LOVE IS LIKE OXYGEN LOVE IS A STRANGER LOVE IS A BATTLEFIELD LOVE IS LIKE A BOMB LOVE IS WAR LOVE IS A WONDERFUL THING LOVE IS ALL AROUND LOVE IS LOVE REFLECTED LOVE IS LIKE FIREWORKS LOVE IS BLINDNESS LOVE IS AN OPEN DOOR **LOVE IS USUALLY WHERE YOU LEFT IT** LOVE IS ALL YOU NEED LOVE IS IN THE AIR LOVE IS LIKE OXYGEN LOVE IS A STRANGER LOVE IS A BATTLEFIELD LOVE IS LIKE A BOMB LOVE IS WAR LOVE IS A WONDERFUL THING LOVE IS ALL AROUND LOVE IS LOVE REFLECTED LOVE IS LIKE FIREWORKS LOVE IS BLINDNESS LOVE IS AN OPEN DOOR **LOVE IS USUALLY WHERE YOU LEFT IT** LOVE IS ALL YOU NEED LOVE IS IN THE AIR LOVE IS LIKE OXYGEN LOVE IS A STRANGER LOVE IS A BATTLEFIELD LOVE IS LIKE A BOMB LOVE IS WAR LOVE IS A WONDERFUL THING LOVE IS ALL AROUND LOVE IS LOVE REFLECTED LOVE IS LIKE FIREWORKS LOVE IS BLINDNESS LOVE IS AN OPEN DOOR **LOVE IS USUALLY WHERE YOU LEFT IT** LOVE IS ALL YOU NEED LOVE IS IN THE AIR LOVE IS LIKE OXYGEN LOVE IS A STRANGER LOVE IS A BATTLEFIELD LOVE IS LIKE A BOMB LOVE IS WAR LOVE IS A WONDERFUL THING LOVE IS ALL AROUND LOVE IS LOVE REFLECTED LOVE IS LIKE FIREWORKS LOVE IS BLINDNESS LOVE IS AN OPEN DOOR **LOVE IS USUALLY WHERE YOU LEFT IT** LOVE IS ALL YOU NEED LOVE IS IN THE AIR LOVE IS LIKE OXYGEN LOVE IS A STRANGER LOVE IS A BATTLEFIELD LOVE IS LIKE A BOMB LOVE IS WAR LOVE IS A WONDERFUL THING LOVE IS ALL AROUND LOVE IS LOVE REFLECTED LOVE IS LIKE FIREWORKS LOVE IS BLINDNESS LOVE IS AN OPEN DOOR **LOVE IS...**

Love is usually where you left it…

CONTENTS

This Is... *Love Is...*

Love Is ....
Company No. LI57535117SB
CEO: Jeremy Corden

(Our Mission Statement)

Love Is ....

Love is all you need – *John Lennon (1967)*
Love is in the air – *John Paul Young (1977)*
Love is like oxygen – *Brian Connolly (1978)*
Love is a stranger – *Annie Lennox (1982)*
Love is a battlefield – *Pat Benatar (1983)*
Love is like a bomb – *Joe Elliott (1987)*
Love is war – *Jon Bon Jovi (1988)*
Love is a wonderful thing – *Michael Bolton (1991)*
Love is all around – *Marti Pellow (1994)**
Love is love reflected – *Steven Tyler (1997)*
Love is like fireworks – *Paul Day (2006)*
Love is blindness – *Jack White (2013)*
Love is an open door – *Kristen Bell / Anna (2013)*
*Inspired by / Stolen from Reg Presley (1967)

Many people over many years have attempted to describe what *love is*. Intriguingly, a large percentage of them seem to have been singers, as if holding a microphone in your hand gives you profound insight into the great mysteries of the matters of the heart. And their opinions vary greatly. Love is described as being like *oxygen* and yet also like *a battlefield*. It's *an open door* and yet it's *blindness*. Is it a *wonderful thing* or is it *war*?

So, which one of these singing love philosophers is right?

Well, actually *all of them*; but, at the same time, *none of them*.

Because love can't be described as just *one thing*, because love is *everything*.

It's the cause of those unusual, exciting butterfly feelings in your stomach and also the reason you sometimes feel like you could cry until the end of time. It's responsible for those goose bumps that appear for no

i

reason and is the cause of that permanent, ridiculous, face-aching smile that you wear without even realising it. And yet it's also the explanation behind why your heart aches uncontrollably and sometimes feels like it's been torn out and ripped into a million pieces.

But here is the *one thing* about love; *true love*, that most people don't seem to be aware of.

It is *eternal*.

If you fall in love; true, head-over-heels, heat-racing, can't-eat, can't-sleep, can't-think-about-anything-else love; then it lasts *forever*.

Why then, especially these days, do so many people seem to break up?

Because love can get *lost*.

Maybe mislaid because of the pressures of modern life. Pushed into the shadows by the stresses of work, and mortgages and bills, and responsibilities and feelings of underachievement.

And because of its absence, people *give up* on love.

But before *you* give up on love too, why not allow *Love Is...* the chance to help you find it again.

Because do you know what?

For that real, true, *eternal* variety that I just mentioned; turns out *love is usually where you left it...*

Introduction.

If she wasn't crying already, then this latest turn of events would certainly have driven Gayle to tears. It was a Sunday afternoon (you know, the nice, easy, lazy, *relaxing* time of the week?) and she was lying face-first in a muddy field in biblical-style wind and rain; her head squashed and sweating profusely inside a helmet that was way too tight, her £250 knee-length *Kurt Geiger* boots (her only *ever* footwear indulgence) were stuck in the mud twenty metres away, and now two impossibly large men were firing increasingly painful paintball pellets at her from dangerously close proximity. She wasn't just a sitting duck, she was a dead duck, in the mud, and yet they still continued to shoot at her.

And yes she was paintballing. *Paintballing!*

Not because paintballing had somehow made its way onto some kind of desperate-to-try-new-things-before-I-die bucket list type thing because, for Gayle, the only list paintballing would make it on to was a things-I-will-never-never-never-never-never-do-as-long-as-I-live kind of list; but because she had agreed to do absolutely *anything* this weekend. After the disasters that had gone before for the last day and a half she wished that she'd stuck the heels of those now-ruined *Kurt Geiger* boots in about this one and refused to take part.

As each new paint pellet painfully struck, and Gayle realised that she was going to be more bruised than an apple that had bounced down the entire staircase of the *Empire State Building*, whilst thinking that her dying wish right now would be something as simple as being able to enjoy one last hot bubble bath, she accepted that this was one of the *worst* moments of her life.

And then it happened.

The type of event that maybe only happens once in a lifetime for just a few, very lucky, individuals.

A moment that literally changes the world.

And that one-of-the-worst-moments-of-her-life became, for Gayle, in the space of a heartbeat, without doubt, one of the *best* moments of her life. Because just as...

Wait a minute. This isn't the best way to start a book is it? By giving away the ending? No, I think it's best to start somewhere more appropriate; somewhere like the beginning...

ONE: *That's That Then.*

"That's that then!" said Gayle out loud as she, Clive and Mr Dennis watched Jack's car slowly drive to the end of Percival Road before turning left and then passing out of sight.

"The end of an era!" she added dramatically, almost in that over-the-top, emotional way that soap actors do in those, rather pointless, special "live" episodes. (Nothing like a live soap episode to separate the bad actors from the, well, *really* bad actors.) She began wiping a couple of tears away from her cheek, cursing the fact that she'd put her make up on *before* waving Jack away to his new adventure at university. She turned and walked back into the house so she could check the severity of her "panda eyes" in the hall mirror before having to leave for work. The last thing she wanted was to give the boys from the warehouse the opportunity to call her *Chi Chi* all day again, as they had on the day that Jason Orange announced he was leaving *Take That*. (She had always been a bit "meh" about Jason's part in *Take That*, reasoning that he was her fifth favourite member of the group, but the day *he* left the band had brought all those memories of Robbie's departure, in 1995, flooding back. To Gayle *that day* was possibly the most traumatic day in history.)

Gayle smiled to herself as she focussed on the fact that Jack had set off on his new adventure in life quite a bit later than he had planned to. He was hoping to be on the motorway before being caught in any of the rush hour traffic but things hadn't gone quite to plan. And that was because he was just like *her* in that respect. They never *intend* to be late, but it just *happens*. She sniggered a little as she thought about how mad their being late made Clive, who likes to *boringly* be on time for everything. She tried to kid herself that she and Jack were too cool, maybe *too Zen*, to be restrained by something as trivial as being on time but, in reality, it wasn't that. It was because time just seems to evaporate and mysteriously vanish into thin air sometimes. You're doing just fine getting ready and then, *boom*, fifteen minutes has just disappeared in the blink of an eye. Where the hell does it go? Gayle had always thought that someone, preferably from a scientific background, should definitely look into this strange time-disappearing phenomenon.

As his wife headed back inside, Clive, still standing next to Mr Dennis from over the road, sadly nodded his head in agreement. Watching your only child heading off to begin a brand new life, hundreds of miles away, was certainly an emotional event. Maybe not quite as emotional as feeling like you had to be on suicide watch as your then-new-girlfriend struggled to cope with the "utter horror" of Robbie-bloody-Williams leaving *Take That*, but it certainly brought a tear to his eye also. Clive couldn't believe that Jack had left home and the sadness of that fact seemed to press down on his shoulders and he could feel himself physically slouching.

Where had the time gone?

It seemed just like yesterday that Jack was a little baby, crawling around, all cute, big-eyed, smiley and cuddly. Or a little toddler when, as a family, they started to go regularly to the park on Langley Lane; just around the corner. Clive smiled as he remembered the exciting games they'd play on the park, pretending to be pirates and space heroes or even *space-pirates*. He remembered they even pretended there was a wishing well in the park that had a genie that lived there. It was certainly handy knowing someone who could make wishes come true. They were the days. Wow, it seemed a long time ago that *wishes came true*. Clive didn't want to think about that and so tried to steer his mind back towards happy thoughts of Jack as a child. Although admittedly back then, in the *early* days, there was all that drooling and projectile vomiting everywhere to contend with as well. Clive's smile slowly turned into a grimace as thoughts of drooling and projectile vomiting reminded him of one of the clearest childhood memories of his son: *Jack losing his first tooth*. You know, that monumental event in your child's life that signals them progressing from toddler to genuine, bona fide "kid". That moment when, after wobbling and twisting and cajoling a tooth that hangs at impossible angles and appears that it may never leave the mouth, it finally does fall out and they are introduced to the "magic" of the tooth fairy. They then leave the said tooth under their pillow at night and find, the next morning, that it has been magically exchanged for, increasingly inflation-busting, monetary coinage. The problem, though, was that somewhere in between breakfast and cleaning his teeth, Jack's first tooth; the *really* important, monumental one, somehow got *lost*. The evidence suggested that there was a 50/50 chance between the tooth being spat out, and lost to the sink plug hole as part of the teeth cleaning process, or having been swallowed along with breakfast. Clive did what any loving parent would do, hoping it was the latter of the two scenarios - meaning the tooth could be retrieved, and vowed to check for it "on the way out". For six days he sieved through seemingly unlimited amounts of child "poo", cursing the fact that Jack always insisted on having "crunchy" peanut butter on his toast each morning, because the number of times that *success* turned out to be another tooth-shaped, half-digested peanut was completely heart breaking. But Clive had promised to try and find that tooth because he would do *anything* for Jack, because you really do try and do anything for love. Although, after nearly a week of sifting and retching, searching for a tooth that was probably *never* even there, Clive was pretty sure he wouldn't do *that* again. Maybe that's what *Meatloaf* was singing about all those years ago?

The tooth never did turn up and, to add insult to injury, it turned out that Jack didn't even seem that bothered about losing his first tooth, claiming "*I'll just keep next tooth!*" Clive also learnt how the smell of shit can linger on your hands for days – even if you do "double-marigold" your faeces-scrutinising hands.

Clive resisted the urge to sniff at his finger nails, which he usually did out of habit when he thought about that incident, you know, just in case they needed another good scrub with hot water and industrial strength Carex. Instead he allowed himself to bask in his internal feeling of immense pride for the boy that he and Gayle had produced and raised. Jack had left home, because his time to leave had arrived. And he was off to university – something that neither he nor Gayle, or even *anyone* that they knew very well, had ever achieved. And, weirdly, Clive even accepted that Jacks gap years had just been his mature way of recharging and broadening his horizons before continuing with his studies, which was so different to what other kids doing similar "study breaks" are: *lazy, social parasites*. But going to university was just one of a million amazing things about Jack, who had grown into a good, honest, sincere, selfless, *beautiful* <u>man</u> that Clive was incredibly proud of. Including the fact that he had recently passed his driving test, at the *first attempt*, with not one single bit of "professional" tuition; but only Clive's own "patient" lessons. Even here today, Jack had started off down the road without the merest hint that he may stall the car. What a boy!

Inside the house, Gayle stared into the mirror, satisfied that the mascara damage was fairly minimal, but a little alarmed by how evident her crow's feet wrinkles appeared this morning. At work, Jennifer and Janine's (her two teenage colleagues) recent assessment that they were "*just* a couple of laughter lines" that "*just* show you're a happy, laughy person" had only served to heighten her concern about how she was beginning to look older all of a sudden. Why can't people respond to a simple question about wrinkles with the obvious and *correct* answer: "wrinkles, *what wrinkles*?"

Gayle was now also having to dye her hair every couple of weeks, knowing that if she didn't she could very soon be mistaken for Mary Berry. She wasn't old enough to begin looking *old* yet; shouldn't these signs of aging wait until she was, at least, forty-plus before revealing their ugly heads? She sighed and realised that she should have probably dyed her hair the previous night or, at the very least, washed it - it was greasier than a lay by port-a-cabin fry up. There was no time for any of this now though as she should have set off for work at least ten minutes ago; she would now be stuck on the by-pass with all the lazy losers who had pressed snooze on their alarms one time too many. She instead took out the can of dry shampoo from her handbag.

(*Dry shampoo* = best invention *ever*. Sure *the wheel, sliced bread* and even *the internet* are all pretty good. And then there are mobile phones these days, or *smart phones* as they are so aptly named, that are *so smart* that they have calculators, diaries and cameras / video cameras built within them. They can even access the internet and have therefore meant that people no longer need to remember, or even *know*, anything anymore. Yep, smart phones have replaced the need for people to actually have a *brain* – something that more and more people seem to be taking advantage of. Even so, having said all that, can *any* of the above inventions turn greasy, couldn't-be-bothered-washing-it-again hair into something just about socially acceptable in a couple of quick sprays? No. Case closed.)

Just to be clear – this is the opinion of Gayle and not (necessarily) the writer.

Gayle shook the can vigorously then gave her hair a major blast, as if she was applying hairspray in the 1980's, and then scraped it back into a ponytail. If would have to do, besides if she could get her ponytail tight enough if might just pull back some of those "happy, laughy, laughter lines".

She grabbed for her car keys, from the hideous key rack that Clive had put up in the hall, and walked into the kitchen. There was no particular reason that Gayle had walked into the kitchen other than out of a habitual tendency to do so before she felt she was ready to leave the house. (It was possible that it was this type of thing that allowed time to "mysteriously vanish into thin air".) Whilst in there she noticed, on the work surface by the bread, the certificate and badge she'd just received for giving her tenth blood donation. It was something that she'd been put off doing when she was younger due to her trepidation about needles and she'd always thought it was ok not to because other people were donating. But more recently she'd felt almost a duty to donate. There will always be someone out there who needs blood and to know that you've helped, now *ten times*, and even potentially *saved someone's life* completely outweighed any squeamishness about needles. She took in a deep breath and felt a little better about herself.

Outside, Clive began to manoeuvre his conversation with Mr Dennis towards something of an exit strategy.

"Well, can't stand around here all day chatting..... things to do an' all that!" he said beginning to walk towards the front door. Undeterred, Mr Dennis followed him and continued to witter on with whatever he had been wittering on about.

"Yes, that's why *I* didn't even consider university – all the bloody silver-spoon brigade. I remember....."

Clive tuned him out again and began to contemplate what the hell Mr Dennis was even doing here; out in the cold, on a Friday morning waving a young man off to university; a young man who he'd only ever communicated with fleetingly, whilst shouting at him during the times that his football had gone into his garden.

Mr Dennis was probably well into his 80's and was comfortably within the *eccentric* zone on the "loon chart". If every street had a crazy neighbour, then Mr Dennis was definitely Percival Roads undisputed title holder.

Clive temporarily cleared his thoughts of Mr Dennis hoping to think a bit more about Jack but, instead, he couldn't stop his mind focussing on the last words that Gayle had used outside:

"That's that then..... the end of an era."

Maybe "end of an era" may seem something of a far-fetched statement just because your son had left for university but, whilst for the planet as a whole this event was not quite up there with something like the extinction of the dinosaurs, for Gayle and Clive this was *exactly that*.

Eight years earlier Clive and Gayle had made each other a vow. Their feelings for one another were changing and they began to question whether they should actually be together any longer. They had originally met at high school and fallen deeply in love but their lives were changed forever when Gayle became pregnant with Jack whilst they were still at

6

school. Educational plans, career dreams and aspirations and, for all intents and purposes, carefree teenage life was put on hold so that they could focus on becoming a family. Love, even the deepest, strongest love, when not cherished and cared for properly, stands no chance against the shadows that grow out of bills and mortgages, and mundane dead-end jobs, and monotonous routines, and the resentment of those plans and dreams slipping ever further out of reach. Clive and Gayle didn't break up though because they wanted to give Jack, unlike both of them, the chance to grow in a happy, healthy, loving home environment; with a mum and dad who both loved him dearly. They agreed, though, that when Jack left home they would go their separate ways and go on with their lives in *different directions*.

And Jack had just left.

So, just as Gayle had said earlier: *that's that then*.

TWO: *Jack.*

Jack pulled his car into the lay-by by the park on Langley Lane. He got out and checked how close he had parked to the kerb. Pretty good, really. He'd got near enough that any passenger wouldn't have needed a plank to step across onto the pavement, but not so close that there was ever any danger of scraping his wheels. His driving "skills" were quite an achievement seeing as the only tuition he'd ever had was from his Dad, Clive. He smiled as he recalled Clive's (mostly patient) lessons and some of his "nuggets of driving wisdom". *"Once you've passed your test - that's when you <u>really</u> start learning", "a car can be like a weapon - it's a huge responsibility to be behind a wheel" and "use your <u>breaks</u> - not your <u>horn</u>. Horns are for emergency and extreme situations only, or if you see attractive women!"*

Jack realised that his driving lesson memories maybe summed up how life in general was with his parents. They had always been there for him, teaching him the important lessons in life, but had always complimented everything with a sense of humour and fun.

Maybe learning to park his car close to objects was helped by the fact that, since passing his driving test, he'd been through the McDonalds drive through on numerous occasions. You only accidentally park too far away from the payment booth once. Having to pretty much lean your whole body out of the car window to be able to pay for your Big Mac Meal, whilst the queue behind you stares and sniggers, means you up your parking game from that moment on.

Jack looked at his car before walking into the park. It was just a blue, three-door, eight year old Ford Fiesta but was a source of pride for him and he took great pleasure in washing it and keeping it clean and tidy. It had been paid for by the savings from his part time job working with a local window cleaner and a contribution from Clive and Gayle. It's amazing how you appreciate how special things are when they've been paid for by genuine hard work. Jack smiled as he remembered the day that Gayle proclaimed: "Everything in life is so much better when you've had to save up and *pay for it.*" She thought about what she said before hastily adding: "Except *sex*. You don't need to pay for that – that's much better when *love* is involved." Despite being around the time that she and Clive had felt Jack was old enough to talk to above love and sex, saying this had obviously embarrassed Gayle. Jack laughed to himself as he remembered her face turning a deep shade of red before she hastily exited the room they were in.

Jack looked over to the playing fields, beyond the green metal fenced off play area, and several memories flooded into his head. Endless days playing on his bike with his friends to, more recently, spending times there with his girlfriend and, of course, from when he had joined the local under elevens football team, *Norbury Rovers*. It was here that they played their games, mostly on Saturday mornings, and it was Gayle who brought him because Clive was, almost always, working. He smiled again as he remembered his Mum running up and down the touchline shouting encouragement at him and the odd bit of embarrassing abuse at the poor referees, who had all generously donated their time to help officiate youth football, but many had, as Gayle loudly observed now and again, appeared to have "left their glasses at home".

Jack chuckled to himself. They were good times. Especially the Saturdays when Clive wasn't working because everything felt extra special when the three of them did things together; as a family. Jack breathed in the air as he remembered the warm, "three-way" hug he'd had with Gayle and Clive just before leaving this morning. It's something that they used to do regularly when he was younger and it had felt good. A few tears formed in his eyes. Not through sadness of leaving home or leaving his memories behind, not because of the excitement of starting a new adventure, not because of the unknown nature of change, for him, *and* his parents; but probably a combination of *all* those things. But, as he thought about it, it was probably mainly because of his thoughts for Clive and Gayle; and it was those thoughts that had led him *here*, to the park.

He smiled broadly again as he remembered the many times they would walk right down to the stream and skim stones across the water. It was one of those things that seemed impossible at first but, with lots of tuition and practise, you finally master that flat, spinning trajectory that's needed and you have the enormous satisfaction of seeing your stone skipping across the surface of the water. Jack laughed to himself again as he remembered the time that, when down at water's edge skimming stones, Clive had *punched a dog in the face*. Clive had always said it was an accident and he hadn't seen the golden retriever jumping in front of him, seemingly thinking he was going to throw a ball for him. It was just his throwing action follow-through that had meant he'd caught the poor dog on the jaw. Jack and Gayle hadn't bought the whole "accident" excuse though, seeing as Clive *hated dogs*. He said they were an *occupational hazard*. For, while dogs are *Man's Best Friend* they are also <u>*Postman's Worst Enemy*</u>. (Well, joint worst enemy - along with rain, wind, sleet, ice, snow – a.k.a. *typical British weather*.) So, while Clive claimed "accident", Gayle and Jack thought it was more likely that Clive had seen an opportunity to land a sneaky right hook on the poor pooch. Although that golden retriever did have the *last laugh*. He skipped off happily down the stream non-plussed about Clive's "assault", while Clive himself ended up in A&E nursing a couple of broken knuckles, lamenting the fact that the dog "had a chin like a young Mike Tyson".

As Jack continued laughing he realised he was, as usual, running a little later than he wanted. But he felt it was really important to stop off here for a few minutes before continuing his journey towards university life. He was enjoying replaying some memories in his mind but, in particular, he was here because he wanted to visit the *play area* one more time. It was perhaps this small part of the park that represented his *earliest* memories. Taking the short walk from their house, he, Clive and Gayle would often make a full day out of a visit; bringing balls and Frisbees and picnic lunches. Jack remembered playing on the slide and swings and the roundabout and, especially, the climbing frame. The large red metal structure that became a space ship or pirate ship (or space-pirate ship), or a moon base or treasure island; depending on what adventure they were having on that particular day. He remembered the characters they played as: *Long John Skywalker*, *Captain Han-beard* and *Princess Leia – The Lioness of Brittany*. Jack had friends who had bigger, fancier houses and went on exotic holidays, to unpronounceable places, but he didn't know anyone who'd had the same kind of fun adventures that he'd had with his parents. But as Jack looked around, memories of space travel and encounters with blood-thirsty pirates happily dancing around his head, it was the object in the far corner of the fenced-off section that he completely focussed on. The <u>real</u> reason he was here: the cylinder shaped, concrete *bin*.

The fact was, during their many adventures here, the Ford family had *discovered* that this wasn't actually a *normal* bin. It was also a *wishing well.* It was home to a genie named *Shelli Bwingwing.* (The best name-anagram of *"wishing well bin"* the family could come up with – it narrowly edged out their second favourite name: *Eli Wing Winshib*). *Shelli Bwingwing* specialised in wishes and dreams; a place where you could leave notes if you wanted to wish for toys or bikes or maybe send any messages to Father Christmas. And, not always but, fairly regularly, *Shelli Bwingwing* would make those wishes and dreams come true.

Jack took the piece of paper out of his back pocket and opened it up. As he read through the words he had written the night before, he laughed at the silliness of the whole thing. But, as he laughed, he also thought that it fitted perfectly with his upbringing that had been full of fun, invention and imagination; and lots of love. He closed his eyes and held the paper close to his face, kissing it slowly. He then followed the "wish ritual" that he'd not done for many years but remembered so clearly. (Well, after making sure that there was no one around near enough to see what he was doing.) He gently folded the paper as small as he could before holding it low behind his back. This part was as awkward as it had always been, as if he was squatting on a toilet; as he carefully threw the folded paper from between his legs and into the "wishing well", chanting (quietly) as he did.

"Shelli Bwingwing, Shelli Bwingwing,
Read my words, please do your thing,
Shelli Bwingwing, Shelli Bwingwing,
Read my words, please do your thing."

Jack laughed to himself one more time before slowly looking around again, relieved there was still no one around. (Especially anyone with a phone – you do something a little *odd* these days and you're an instant *Youtube* star for all the wrong reasons.) He then walked back to his car. He started the engine, checked his mirrors, saw the road was clear and...... *stalled* the car. He restarted, checked again, and this time moved out of the lay by and onto the road – feeling thankful that Clive hadn't seen him stall. Clive would have made a jokey reference to that until the end of time!

He glanced at the clock, cursed his lateness slightly, and then pressed gently on the accelerator and headed off towards his brand new life.

Dear Shelli Bwingwing,

It's been a long time, but I want to request one last thing from you. This time it's not for me but rather my Mum and Dad (you know them – Gayle and Clive Ford) – the best people in the world. They gave me the greatest childhood and upbringing that anyone could ever dream of, or even <u>wish</u> for. I know now that they made many sacrifices in their lives; just for me, and yet they never, ever let me know or made me feel like they had.

I'm sure that they still deeply love each other, although I'm not sure that <u>they</u> know that anymore. I'm also sure that they're both unhappy in many ways and, unfortunately, I'm pretty sure that they <u>do</u> know that.

My wish is that you can find a way so that they can <u>both</u> be happy again – <u>whatever</u> that means for them both.

Please do your best.

Thank you,
Your friend,

Jack Ford.

THREE: *We Did It Together.*

Gayle finished her aimless, and rather pointless, meander around the kitchen and took one last look in the small mirror by the door. She decided she looked about as presentable as she was going to be able to, and took the deep breath needed to convince herself to step out of the front door and off to work. Before she could head towards another day confined to the tiny dimensions of her humdrum office existence, her eyes caught sight of the picture of Jack, at the age of eight winning the school sports day sack race, that sat in a frame between the microwave and the toaster. It seemed like the perfect opportunity to allow some more time to mysteriously vanish into thin air as she took her mind on a little trip down memory lane; observing several moments of Jack, the boy that she and Clive had nurtured so lovingly, as he grew over the years. Her thoughts arrived in a neat montage, similar to how a carefully designed medley of images would signal the imminent climax in a Rocky movie. First up was that *first tooth* episode (that Clive still annoyingly insists on talking about even now – and usually when people are eating), then Jack's first day at school and then his first *girlfriend*. She laughed a little to herself as she remembered his awkwardness when bringing *Sarah Cunningham-Chapman* round for dinner for the first time. Or how she and Clive had been impressed by her never ending, posh sounding double barrel surname before learning that her surname was just the sad result of her parents divorcing when she had been younger. At least she and Clive hadn't put Jack through that.

Gayle moved her shoulders round uncomfortably though as she remembered one of the strongest memories of Jack of them all: just how freakishly strong and vigorous he was whilst breast feeding. Wow, at the age of two months, that boy could have walked into a job as a *Lockets*

Throat Lozenge tester. As a result Gayle had been left with nipples that were more sensitive than a sunburnt bunion. It also meant that, ever since, wearing any material harder than silk was completely uncomfortable and painful. She had spent a period in her life when she vowed to never wear a bra ever again but there are only so many times, when she had to walk through the warehouse area at work, where the temperature is always at a level that Eskimos would find challenging, that you can take half a dozen guys saying "watch it – you'll have someone's eye out with one of those, love!" Of course there's the old gravity factor that also needs to be taken into consideration when deciding to never wear a bra again, although, once again, something that shouldn't be a problem until well *after* forty years of age, thank you very much.

Damn you early signs of old age.

Gayle freed her mind of thoughts of nipple tenderness but that only led her to a different contemplation of discomfort – namely the fact again that her little baby had just left home. And with that thought came the overwhelming realisation that life would never be the same again.

Clive was now within reach of his front door but still hadn't managed to rid himself of Mr Dennis and had dangerously and unwittingly began to allow his mind to again try to address the riddle that was "Dennis the Menace". As usual, his aging neighbour was wearing his faded avocado coloured dressing gown that looked like it could be as old as he was. (It most probably came as part of one of those hideously coloured bathroom suites from the 1960's/1970's)

Mr Dennis' dressing gown had long been a thorny subject for the residents of Percival Road, primarily because of an event that occurred some years ago that Clive and Gayle refer to as the *Marilyn Monroe Incident.* Can you picture that iconic image of *Ms Monroe* having her white dress blown high into the air by that "breeze from the subway"? Well, substitute that with the image of an old man having his avocado dressing gown have the same thing done to it by a freak gust of wind during the *Queens Diamond Jubilee* Percival Road street party. Oh yes, and add to it the fact that, at that moment, came the disturbing revelation that the primary street pest likes to live his life *commando*. Yep, underneath that retro-coloured bath robe, Mr Dennis felt no need to wear any underwear whatsoever. It created an image that, once seen, *always* appears whenever you close your eyes. The kind of image that, for everyone unfortunate enough to be a witness, leaves irreparable scars. Clive, for one, had never been able to look at cocktail sausages and dumplings again without feeling instantly nauseous. And no one who lived on the street had *ever* mentioned it to each other since. In fact, no one who lived on the street had ever been able to look each other in the eyes ever since. Nobody wanted to look at eyes that had seen the *same horrors.*

Clive kept his eye level up and hoped for a calm morning. Trying not to blink and give his mind the opportunity to place those unsettling images in front of his eyes, he instead focussed on the fact that, as per usual, Mr Dennis was carrying a mug of tea in his right hand. Actually, now he thought about it, Clive had never seen him *without* a mug of tea in his right hand. He's the only person Clive has ever seen washing a car with just one hand. If he's so dependent on having access to tea at *all times* perhaps he should contemplate having a PG Tips intravenous drip attached? Clive wondered whether he was so paranoid about putting his mug down because he was scared that someone may steal it. Either that or maybe he'd been the sad victim of an unfortunate, fast-setting superglue accident sometime in the past. One second you're gluing your favourite set of false teeth back together when, without realising it, you've dribbled some on your fingers, have innocently reached for a sip of tea, and are left with a mug stuck to your hand for the rest of your life. Perhaps he'd been too embarrassed to go to A&E, probably not realising that the staff there wouldn't bat an eyelid about *his* accident because they were too busy laughing at the freaks who had "accidentally" got plastic dog bones stuck up their arses.

Clive concentrated his resolve and finally reached out to open his front door despite Mr Dennis still shadowing him and still ranting about something university related.

".....and they don't call them university *snobs* for nothing now do they?"

Perhaps now realising that Clive was about to enter his house and leave him waffling on to nobody, Mr Dennis decided *he* would end things.

"Well, I'd love to chat, but I've got things that need doing..... goodbye Clifford!"

He turned and walked off at great pace, no doubt heading back to his own house to get his deck chair ready for today's couple of hours' worth of watching the new by-pass being built.

"Bye" said Clive through gritted teeth, closing the door behind him. He had told Mr Dennis that his name was *Clive* more times than he cared to remember but, no, it was always *Clifford.* It was almost as annoying as when Mr Dennis would address Tony, who lived next door, as *Anthony.* And not just Anthony, but actually *An-th-ony*, because Dennis the

Menace was one of those people who insisted on pronouncing the silent *th* as loud as he possibly could. At least, thankfully today, he'd not been subjected to the sight of a tiny, wrinkled penis and ball set underneath a fluttering old, avocado dressing gown.

Clive looked round and noticed that Gayle had taken her car keys off the slightly skew-whiff key rack that he had erected about six months earlier. Sure it wasn't the prettiest key rack ever made, slightly off centre on the side wall of the small hall area they had, but surely that was a small price to pay for no longer having to remove all the settee cushions and coverings every time you wanted to go out in the car? Gayle, upon hearing Clive enter the house, walked out of the kitchen finally ready to face up to the day ahead. Their eyes connected as she entered the entrance hall area.

"You managed to shake him off then?" she asked, referring to Mr Dennis.

As Clive nodded, she added,

"How *windy* is it out there?"

Clive laughed.

"Not windy at all. Everything managed to stay out of sight today, thank God!"

They both gave each other a mock disgusted look before smiling.

"Do I look ok? Can you tell I've been crying?" asked Gayle.

Despite her having more than a passing resemblance to Jack Black in *Kung Fu Panda*, Clive said.

"No you look fine."

Fine is one of those strange words that can either describe something as *mediocre* and *just ok*; almost *beige*-like, or can mean something pretty special, like *a fine wine* or you look *damn fine*. Clive had meant the latter for, despite her (slightly) dark, make-up stained eyes and her hastily styled ponytail, Gayle still looked like she usually did – which was pretty *damn fine*. He wished that he added that all important *damn* which makes it clear which version of *fine* you were using for the occasion, but he hadn't and had to make do with Gayle believing he meant she looked *just ok*.

"I need to go..... I'm going to be late." Gayle said, her eyes now showing signs of moisture again. Clive sighed as he gazed at the sadness that was shining through Gayle's damp eyes and he could almost feel her emptiness. His heart began to melt a little.

"Hey," he said "He's not gone *that* far away. He's not gone to the moon, or to Mars!"

16

Gayle smiled a smile that looked like it took all the effort in the world.

"We'll still see him a lot," added Clive "You'll probably get sick of him bringing his washing round, or coming to see you because he's hungry."

Gayle couldn't help but notice that Clive had said "coming to see *you*" and not *"coming to see us"*, and it re-enforced what was going to be happening: there wasn't going to be an *us* for much longer. Clive hadn't noticed he'd said it like that, but he did recognise that Gayle's expression hadn't got any happier.

"Come here," he said extending his arms out for a hug.

Gayle reluctantly entered his arms as physical contact of *any* kind was something that they hadn't done much of recently. When he wrapped his arms around her, it felt nice. It felt familiar and warm; and she felt safe and somehow soothed and comforted. Clive closed his eyes and shared the same feelings: a pleasurable contentment that he'd not felt for a long time.

"Whatever we've done not so well," he began "There's one thing that we've done that's been perfect..... *Jack*! He's turned out *perfect*. You should be so proud of yourself."

Gayle pushed herself back slightly so she was still in Clive's embrace but could now look him in the eyes.

"*We* should be proud. We did it *together.*"

For a moment they looked at each other and smiled and both of them couldn't deny it: there was a little spark. A little feeling; a little reminder of how things used to be all those years ago, when there was no doubt that it was *true love*.

The clock on the wall began to chime, signalling that it was eight o'clock.

"Oh no, I am *so* late now!" said Gayle, pushing out of Clive's embrace and reaching for the front door.

"Don't forget the estate agent is coming round this morning."

"What time is he coming?" Clive asked.

"Whatever time you booked him to come!" said Gayle, shortly. "It was *you* that booked him!"

"*You* told me to book him" countered Clive "I thought you might have remembered what time I told you. It doesn't matter; I've probably made a note on my phone."

As I said earlier: Mobile phone = memory / brain replacement.

It's just like when calculators became affordable in the late 1970's meant that there was no need to learn mental arithmetic anymore –

17

something that everyone, with the exception of Carol Vorderman and Rachel Riley, have taken great advantage of.

Gayle opened the front door and stepped back out onto the pavement.

"Oh" she said turning round "Can you get us some bread and milk later, we need it to keep us going until I go shopping at the weekend?"

"I thought you were going yesterday?" snapped Clive.

"I didn't have time because I was cleaning this house until ten o'clock last night so it's ready for the estate agent! That's why I didn't get chance to have a shower last night and why I look like I've been dragged through a hedge backwards this morning."

Clive wondered why people were always dragged through hedges *backwards* and never *forwards*. Was that one of the rules you have to follow if you ever get the urge to drag someone through a hedge?

"Ok, ok." said Clive. "I told you we shouldn't have stopped getting those home deliveries, didn't I?"

"You know why we stopped – they kept sending weird stuff when they didn't have what we ordered. I mean a bottle of *Limoncello* because they didn't have lemon *juice*? It was pathetic!"

Clive nodded his head in agreement, whilst at the same time remembering the best Pancake Day he'd ever had. Mmmm alcoholic pancakes!

"But I'm going out later" Clive said. "I'm playing snooker with *Knobhead*."

Gayle shook her head.

"What?" asked Clive.

"There's so much *wrong* with that statement. First of all, a fully grown man still readily accepting a nickname of *Knobhead*? No matter how appropriate it may be, it's just plain *wrong*. And who the hell plays, or even *watches*, snooker? How bloody *sad* are you?"

Clive stood there dumb struck. He was unsure about how he could defend himself against any of the points that Gayle had made.

"Is it too much to ask for you to take a couple of minutes to get bread and milk when I spent, pretty much, the *whole day* cleaning yesterday?"

"*I* did some cleaning too" said Clive. "I spent a good hour and a half hoovering upstairs."

"Putting the hoover on for an hour and a half whilst you lie down on the bed watching the tele, *isn't* cleaning!" said Gayle. "What *were* you watching up there for all that time?"

"Snooker!" Clive said, a huge, cheeky smile growing on his face.

Gayle couldn't help but smile back; it was that cheeky smile that was one of the first things about Clive that she noticed all those years ago.

"Bread and milk!" she said as she walked out of the door. "See you later."

"See you later."

As his wife left the house Clive turned around and his eyes were drawn to the numerous photos on the ledge above the radiator. Most of them were of Jack in various stages of his life but there was one, behind all the others, that was an old school class photograph that had both Clive and Gayle in it. He picked it up and his mind was cast back. He was standing at the back, tall and proud while Gayle was sitting on the long bench on the front row, looking like she would rather be anywhere else on Earth. They both looked so young. He remembered that the photo had been taken not long after Gayle had joined his class mid-term after her and her Mum had moved to the area and she'd had to change schools; something she wasn't too pleased about. It was probably around about this time that they first began to get to know each other – *properly*. As he glanced around the various kids in their class, wondering why every new time he looked at it there was at least one extra kid he couldn't name anymore, and then focussed back at himself and Gayle, Clive worked out that the picture was now more than 20 years old. Wow, that was a *long* time ago, and it *felt* like a long time ago; in fact it felt like a *lifetime* ago. And yet strangely, at the same time, it felt like it could have been yesterday.

FOUR: *Love At First Sight.* (23 Years Ago)

Both Clive and Gayle remember the day as clear as anything. It was a Tuesday morning, in the springtime: the day that they first met.

Was it something resembling a scene from a classic love movie; was it *love at first sight?* Maybe it was on a crowded train station platform on a cold, rainy morning that their eyes first met? A connection that warmed and melted their hearts as cupid struck one of his perfect bull's-eyes? Did they both try to catch the same taxi cab? And after they'd both selflessly argued that the other should take it, they agreed to take it *together,* had got talking and had been together ever since? Were they two unfortunate, or fortunate, young people who got trapped in a lift? Thrown together into an inescapable, confined space; fate's unsubtle way of ensuring that two hearts that were meant to be together were given a dramatic first push? Did they catch sight of each other over the bananas and apples of the fruit aisle in a supermarket? Instantly and subconsciously associating each other with the healthy and naturally good things that life had to offer? Did their cars accidentally collide and, as they both got out to examine the damage and discuss who was to blame, their hearts all a flutter because of the collision, their eyes linked together with the instant connection of love? Was it.....

I should probably just tell you, right? Sorry!

It was around 11.30 a.m., certainly some time after the high school morning break, that Gayle walked into classroom B7 for the very first time. Clive was sitting at his usual desk on the right hand side of the room, by the window, where he liked to breathe on the glass and draw little doodles on the foggy condensation. On this day he was trying to draw a big rocket but was having trouble getting the circular launch jets underneath to look just right. Gayle and her mother had just moved to the

20

area after a messy divorce with her father which had resulted in her having to change schools. And this late start seemed to typify Gayle's, and her mothers, attitude to the importance of school.

She kind of swaggered into the classroom slowly but very loudly, completely interrupting Mr Jackson who was in full flow at the blackboard trying to explain the Pythagoras theorem for the umpteenth time, batting away jokes about Greek footballers and dinosaurs named Pythagoras Rex. The whole class turned to face Gayle's noisy entrance and Clive immediately noticed her slightly snarled lip, arrogant chewing and couldn't-give-a-shit, lethargic walk.

The whole class stared at her and she just stared right back. Clive knew right away that she was nothing but trouble. She was all attitude and huge, pink bubble gum. The clothes she was wearing, probably as far away from school uniform as you could get, were all black and baggy, and her hair was long, curly and big; *very big.* It was the sort of do that Kylie Minogue had inspired a generation of teenage girls to copy – albeit about ten years earlier. On that day though, it just completed the appearance of a girl who looked like she wanted to look totally different to everyone else. If her look was giving off any kind of sign, then it was a big two fingered salute to the whole world.

Yep, Clive knew straight away that she was someone he wouldn't get on with. She was probably a pampered Daddy's-girl who just had to stamp her feet to get whatever she wanted. She looked like she had no idea about how difficult *real life* can be sometimes; and she probably *didn't care.* No, Clive had made up his mind – he would attempt to avoid her like the plague.

Gayle remembered standing before the door of classroom B7 for a good two minutes before working up the courage to enter. She was hideously late because the old banger her mum had just bought wouldn't start and so she had to catch two buses to get to her new school.

The woman at reception had done nothing to calm Gayle's first day nerves and had rather curtly just pointed her roughly in the direction of her new classroom after giving her a huge pile of paperwork that needed to be "completed a.s.a.p." (When did people feel the need to speak in acronyms all the time? Is it any more difficult to say "as soon as possible" than it is to say "a - s - a - p"?)

Gayle remembered clearly taking one last deep breath before placing her hand on that door to classroom B7 and stepping forward, only to trip over the long black dress that her mother had made her wear and banging loudly into the door as it opened. She was faced with a room full of strangers all staring directly at her. It wouldn't have felt any different had it been the *whole world* staring at her. She began chewing her chewing gum as fast as she could, staring back so she wouldn't appear like the little, scared new kid; whilst all along just wishing that the floor would swallow her up. Why had her mum and dad split up? Why did she have to move and leave all her friends behind? Why was she *here*? Why was life so unfair?

As she continued to stare back at the room; the room of her new classmates, aware that her new teacher was standing a couple of feet away in front of a blackboard with a drawing of a huge triangle on it, there was something that caught her eye. Over on the far right side of the room, on a desk by the window, was a pleasant looking boy who, in contrast to everyone else, who were aggressively staring, was actually smiling softly at her and it made her feel a little better.

It's the little things in life that make all the difference in making people feel better about themselves; a simple hello, a nod of the head or, in this case, a soft smile that stood out amongst a sea of otherwise hostile faces.

Unfortunately, for Gayle, this moment of slight relief was very short lived as her eyes were drawn to the boy sitting next to the pleasant looking soft smiler. And she knew what *he* was straight away: *the class trouble maker*. The loud mouth. The cocky nuisance. The one person to keep away from *at all costs*. The type of immature, brain-dead person that spends entire lessons ignoring the teacher because he is too busy drawing large penises on the window. He probably came from a privileged house where he was allowed to do whatever he wanted. A spoilt brat who Mummy and Daddy threw money at all the time. Someone who had no idea about the realities and hardships of *real life*; the things that she was so painfully experiencing right now. Yep, she knew straight away that he was someone who would annoy her immensely and so she would attempt to avoid him like the plague.

FIVE: *Road Rage.*

This is exactly why Gayle didn't like leaving for work late. In fact, this was exactly why she *hated* leaving for work late. It wasn't the inevitability that she was going to arrive at work late, because she often finished work late and so arriving late now and again maybe compensated for that slightly.

No, the reason was because she hated feeling the way she felt right now.

And it always happened right here, at this exact point on the by-pass where the dual carriage merged into one lane and, because of the volume of cars at this time, became a traffic bottleneck.

All the semi-reasonable people in the world, who happened to be driving on the by-pass at this time, did the morally *proper* thing and joined the queue in the left hand lane, ready for the one-lane section of road. But every now and again someone decided that they didn't want to, or maybe shouldn't *have to*, queue up with everyone else; and so would speed down the, now clear, right hand lane to attempt to join the single lane right at the point where the road becomes one lane.

Not to attach labels to anyone but Gayle found that the cars doing this often had blacked-out windows and/or spoiler and skirt kits and/or ridiculously loud exhaust pipes and/or were playing hardcore dance tunes at a volume level that suggested they maybe thought they were DJ-ing in Ibiza.

And today's latest member of the *no-consideration-for-others* club?

Man in a suit in a navy blue *BMW 5 Series* who, despite the fairly dark nature of his windows, Gayle could clearly see was also chatting away on his mobile phone – that he was holding in his hand!

Hands free?

Not for me, I'm an inconsiderate arsehole who's much too important to abide by the law or to queue up with all you losers!

Gayle could feel her blood beginning to boil. *BMW Arsehole* was about eighty feet in front of her now indicating to join the left lane where she had been waiting, patiently, along with everyone else, for the last seven or eight minutes.

"Don't let him in, don't let him in, don't let him in, don't let him in, don't let him in, don't let him in, don't let him in, don't let him in, don't let him in..." she said out loud, trying to transfer her message of frustration to the six cars in front of her.

Gayle smiled as the first two cars, a silver Beetle and a red Peugeot, ignored *BMW Arsehole* and joined the single lane without letting him in. The third car though, a white Micra, didn't advance when a gap opened up in front, instead letting *BMW Arsehole* in.

"NOOOOOOOOOOOOOOOOOOOOOOOOO!" shouted Gayle at the top of her voice and immediately wanted to *kill* two people at once. *BMW Arsehole*, of course; but now also *Micra Knob/Knob-ess* for having the sheer stupidity and weakness of moral fibre of letting him in.

And this is exactly why she hated leaving for work late; because it can't be healthy wishing you owned a machine gun so large that only prime-era Arnold Schwarzenegger could realistically use it, can it? How can a bit of road rage turn you into wanting to commit murder in the blink of an eye? And if you kill *two* people you become a *serial killer* straight away. And for what? Because someone jumped a queue and someone else let them in? It can't be right, can it? She wished she could just relax and not get worked up about such trivial things because getting angry and wasting so much mental energy doesn't do anyone any *good*, does it? It would be so much better to just be cool, and more Zen, *all of the time*. (Or so she thought. She kept having these thoughts that being more *Zen* would be a positive thing in her life when, actually, she wasn't even sure what *Zen* meant.) But then again, if you *didn't* get worked up about things that are clearly *wrong* in life, are you even alive anymore? This was the type of debate that Gayle often had with herself, especially on a Friday morning after another *long week.*

Gayle wondered whether all this road rage escalation began when such incidents first started to get published more and more in the newspapers or shown on TV. There was no way that she wanted to commit GBH on any other road users until there were nightly news reports about people scuffling over things like differences of opinions over who had right of way on a roundabout. Before then there was probably no one in the land who had even considered putting chunky

DIY tools, golf clubs or baseball bats in their boot, you know, *just in case.*

Do most people who take up golf do it because they actually enjoy golf, or because they want to have a handy six-iron in the car to be ready in case they are caught up in any road rage-y incidents? Damn it, thought Gayle, what good was Clive buying that axe recently if it was just going to be left idle in the shed?

She took a deep breath and cleared from her mind the vision of herself screaming out loud as she ran down the bypass towards a white Micra and a navy blue BMW whilst wielding a large axe over her right shoulder. As she tried to calm down she also had to fight the thoughts that next time she was here, with similar, busy traffic, *she* would also speed down the right lane and jump the queue; because that wasn't right either, was it? If *everyone* in the whole world turns into an *arsehole* then the word arsehole would become redundant. Well except for when you were actually referring to the hole in ones arse.

Gayle wished Clive was sitting next to her. He could tell her one of his stupid jokes. She would probably groan rather than laugh, as usual, but she'd be laughing inside and it would certainly lighten the mood. Instead she turned the radio up and, irony of ironies, began to hear Cerys Matthews from *Catatonia* singing: *Road Rage.* What were the chances? Not of Cerys Matthews singing *Road Rage,* because did she ever sing any *other* songs?, but because she was singing it *right now,* in this road rage-esque situation?

Although you think that it may have escalated Gayle's already crazy-woman-on-the-edge sort of mood, her mind was pacified by the song immediately as, although she hadn't heard it for a while, it was one that she really liked and remembered well. She smiled as Cerys distinctively rolled her tongue around the "R's" of the title words in that special way that only Welsh people can as part of the unique way that they speak – especially when talking in their own language. Her smile turned into a little laugh as she remembered Clive's amusing assessment of the way that the "people from the valleys" speak.

"Welsh: A language invented for people who wanted to talk whilst, at the same, being able to clear catarrh and mucus their throats."

Gayle now felt much calmer as she again glanced around out of the window. Her eyes were immediately drawn to the cars that were passing by on the other side of the carriageway. (The side that was moving freely, without even the hint of any hold ups, which is always the way isn't it? If you are ever held up in a traffic jam, the final insult is that the cars travelling in the *opposite* direction are almost always free-flowing and carrying drivers who smugly smile at your gridlocked predicament. In fact..... sorry, now that Gayle has calmed down a bit, let's not aggravate things again.)

Instead Gayle focussed on the large house to the left of her and and, in particular, the "for sale" sign that stood at the end of the garden. She'd obviously seen the houses at this part of the road on several occasions, as she sat here motionless on her *leaving for work late days*, and knew that they were pretty big. Just how big though she hadn't been aware of until reading the "advertising shorthand" on the for sale board, that read: *Extended Dining Kitchen + 4 beds, 5 baths.* Would she want to live in a house like that? Probably not. Gayle hated cleaning *one* bathroom a week, let alone five. Although maybe a small downstairs toilet would be nice and handy. In fact, if you get to an age and condition that warrants having a stair lift fitted in your house, then a downstairs loo becomes *essential.* The benefits of a motorised seat that takes you to the upper floor of your house are clear to see but let's face it: they are not exactly blessed with the speed that can be required when you are desperate for a shit. And no house has ever been enhanced by having a permanent commode situated in the front room.

The thing was though, Gayle happened to like her (small) house on Percival Road. She and Clive had put their hearts and souls into making it a *home,* just the way they wanted it. Well, apart from the odd, hideous key rack and other similar, disastrous DIY-attempts.

Gayle looked the opposite way, to her right, and watched the free flowing cars shooting past and her attention was grabbed by a black cab that had red advertising along the side. Instead of speculating on just when and why black cabs had started pimping themselves out for advertising as she may usually do on one of these *plenty-of-time-for-mind-wandering* mornings, she instead focussed on the actual words of the advert.

Williamsons – Marriage Counselling Specialists.

Her thoughts were transferred back to around thirteen years earlier when she, more or less, *pleaded* with Clive to come to marriage guidance sessions with her or, at least, let them use some marriage self-help books. He had refused point blank though, reasoning that they were "pointless" and that they "should be able to sort out their differences" themselves; that the whole thing was "a money making scheme" and "too American." She knew back then that it wasn't that Clive didn't *want* to help save their marriage but rather that he was just being *too proud* and *too embarrassed* to talk about their problems to a complete stranger; he was probably being *too British.*

26

But the fact is by *not* going to some kind of counselling, or getting any help *at all*, their problems were never really addressed in a healthy manner. The fact that both of them felt trapped, unable to pursue things they may have dreamed of as children, meant that resentment inevitably grew. And from resentment, *bitterness* is inescapable.

So really, it was Clive's fault that things had led to this – the fact that they were now on the verge of splitting.

Or was it?

Would counselling have been able to save their relationship? Shouldn't they really have been able to save it *themselves* as Clive had said at the time? Gayle accepted that she must have been as much to blame as Clive. What is it that people like to say? *It takes two to tango?* They are probably right.

But *why* do they say that? First of all why have they chosen a dance analogy? It takes two to do a lot of things, so why choose a dance? Why not *it takes two to play chess*? Or *it takes two to ride a tandem*? And if you do have to use a dance analogy, then why choose the tango? *All* dances take two people don't they? Well ok, actually: NO. There are some dances that are done solo, and I suppose things like the *Conga*, or *Oops Upside Your Head* look pretty pathetic if only two people are taking part.

So maybe the tango has been chosen because of the alliteration of the "t's" involved? I suppose *it takes two to Cha, Cha, Cha* doesn't sound nearly as snappy. But then again, is this saying even appropriate for this context? Is the *it takes two to tango* saying really supposed to portray some kind of betrayal, in which one person cannot solely be blamed for an act of dangerous "tango"-esque passion, because it actually takes two to, well..... tango?

What the hell was Gayle thinking about now? Talk about spending *too* much time thinking – if it was possible she would love to take a holiday away from her own mind.

She cleared her thoughts and concentrated again on the music coming from the radio. As she hummed along to the, still playing, *Catatonia* song, thankfully almost all thoughts of the road rage, that had possessed her only moments earlier, were all but gone.

But her mind couldn't relax for a moment and another reflection instantly entered as Gayle remembered clearly that the song *Road Rage* was from way back in 1998. It was nearly as old as Jack, who had just left for university. Wow, where had all that time gone? And gone in such a rush? Everything seemed much simpler in 1998. Now, nearly twenty years later, she had no idea where her life was going. Although one thing was for sure, just like this traffic jam, even if time was speeding away from her, her life was going nowhere.

She glanced around and looked at some of the people in the other cars that were stuck in the jam, and she could see they all had exactly the same expression: *no* expression at all. They were all just staring away, blankly, into space. The minutes of their lives also just drifting away; between them hours and hours of completely *wasted time*. As Gayle focussed on the advert on the black cab again, she couldn't help but think: there has got to be something better than this, hasn't there?

SIX: *Three Little Pigs.* (12 Years Ago)

It is an indisputable fact that reading some books can be bad for you. (Not *this* book. *This* book is actually *good* for you, so carry on reading. You still here? Phew!) But some books, usually reference books that give you small insight into complex matters, can leave you with incomplete information that can be bad for you, or even *dangerous*.

Even worse, these days, is the internet. For example, if you are worried by a lingering discomfort and pain in your lower back you may take to the internet and come up with a fairly alarming self diagnosis – it turns out there's a fine line between degenerative spinal disorder and uncomfortable, but usually non-life threatening, mild lumbago.

For Clive the dangerous reading material was from a book that Gayle had borrowed from the library and was entitled "*The Three Little Pigs Guide to Surviving a Relationship*". When Clive had refused to attend marriage counselling sessions, Gayle had been advised to take out some "relationship guidance" books from the library and try to *reach out* and *connect* with him through them. ("Reach out" and "connect" = words that Clive believed were (two of many) used by professionals in various fields in order to justify *charging* us for something at some point.) The book that Gayle found most enlightening was the pre-mentioned "The Three Little Pigs....." book that, like many books, managed to fill 500+ pages with words that made up very little content. It was the type of book that relayed the same, simple principle in as many (slightly) different ways as possible. The "Three Little Pigs" concept was that relationships are a lot like building a house. Whilst things were going well, then you are building solidly with bricks; bricks that will stand your house in good stead for any uncertain futures ahead. When your relationship is struggling, then your house building is of lower quality, and is more like

29

building with sticks or straw. The key is to recognise these times and work hard to re-build the sticks and straw parts of your house with the far more sturdy bricks.

And this is essential because there are *always* times up ahead that are challenging. Circumstances beyond your control lead to arguments or difficulties that will test your house building to the very limit – the "big, bad wolf days". And when those days arrive and that big, bad wolf comes along, one of two things will happen. Either your house will be so solid, and made up of such small quantities of stick and straw, that the wolf will be completely wasting his time even visiting your house; or, it will be so badly made that, when he huffs and he puffs, he will blow your house right down. And it will be over. No more house. (You do know that I'm still using the house = relationship metaphor don't you? Ok, good – just felt like I maybe got side tracked by bricks, straw, sticks and wolves.)

Anyway, Gayle loved the simplicity behind this idea and, after plucking up the courage for a couple of weeks, one night she sat down with Clive and showed him the book.

"I'm worried about things" she said, once she had explained the concept of the book to Clive. "I'm worried about *us*."

Clive couldn't argue against anything she was saying. Their lives *were* becoming more separate. Having Jack meant that nights out *together* were near on impossible. They had no family to help with babysitting and they both hated the idea of *paying* for a stranger to come round and look after him. As such, almost all nights out, that either of them had, meant going out *without* the other. They also seemed to be spending more time than ever watching different TV programs on different TV's in different rooms. And pretty much going to bed each night at different times to each other.

When Gayle was pregnant with Jack their relationship had hit a defining point. It was maybe what most people would think of as a real low point: Clive's step mother, Sue, had just died, Gayle's divorced parents had pretty much disowned her and anyone else close enough to be called "friends" felt that they were wrong to be having a baby at their age and had also turned their backs on them. But for Clive and Gayle this somehow made their union *even stronger*. They almost adopted the *Space* song "Me and You vs. The World" and used the meaning behind it as their anthem.

They didn't *need* anyone else. They had *each other*. They didn't mind taking on the whole world, because they *knew* that they would win. Nothing could ever come between them.

The problem was: they hadn't accounted for the fact that maybe it wasn't *just* the whole world that they had to contend with. There comes a time when fighting together isn't the thing that is needed; but rather *living together*. And when the small, everyday practicalities of life become difficult to endure, then grand statements like "Me and You vs. the World" start to feel like old, faded memories.

There had been a time when they would always watch TV together – both making the effort to watch each others' shows, even if they didn't really like them themselves; but they did it because they were *together*. There had been a time when they *always* went to bed at the same time and would very often watch an episode from their X-Files box set. A box set they had bought, not because they were huge Mulder and Scully fans, but because they had both loved the cheeky sexiness of the song *The Bad Touch* by *The Bloodhound Gang*, and in particular the line ".....and we'll do it doggy style so we can both watch X-Files."

In fact one of them asking the other whether they wanted to watch X-Files was their code for asking if they wanted to get "jiggy with it", whether they wanted to "get it on", asking to "pour some sugar on me" and if..... well, you get it don't you? Just so we're sure – it's about *sex*. Good, you got it!

Those were the times that they would *always* go to bed at the same time and, very often, Clive would whisper the chorus of *The Bad Touch*: "You and me baby ain't nothing but mammals, so let's do it like they do on the discovery channel" as they would rip each other's clothes off and collapse onto the bed in each other's arms, kissing and tasting each other like they were uncontrollably addicted to one another. Sweating and steaming as they..... sorry, getting a bit *50 Shades-esque* carried away there.

Anyway, those days had gone.

Like so many people who have had children, that playful lust for life and sex had faded somewhat. Sexiness had been replaced by tiredness. They were both feeling burdened and unattractive due to the stresses and strains and *disappointment* of feeling trapped in jobs that they didn't want to be in. Dreams, that sparkle and shine in the ignorance of youth, had been replaced by a monotonous reality; and that had spread into their relationship.

As Gayle continued to pour her heart out Clive, though he knew she was right, couldn't help but be put off by all the sugary analogies that Gayle was quoting from the book. It felt like the counselling idea all over again; that almost *American* way of addressing your problems – in the most dramatic and public way possible.

31

Why did people want to "talk about their feelings" all the time these days? Why didn't they just *get on* with things? Why was Gayle now obsessed in dwelling on the fact that their relationship wasn't perfect? Whose relationship was perfect? And why was she getting books out from the library that emphasise the problems you're having and actually make them *worse*?

"I know there's a problem" said Clive after a long silence and much to Gayle's relief. "But this is like the counselling thing all over again. We don't need *this* kind of help. All relationships have tough times. We just need to make more of an effort with each other."

Clive reached out and took the book out of Gayle's hands, closed it and put it on the coffee table in front of them.

"We don't need books" he said pulling Gayle towards him and then loosely wrapping his arms around her. "We just need each other. Like we always have. We'll be ok. We'll be ok!"

Gayle closed her eyes and tried to stop herself from crying. She could hardly feel Clive holding her. His response had been the same as always.

She knew that, deep down, he wanted to try and fix things as much as she did, but he was too proud, too stubborn, too afraid; too *stupid* to do something *real* about it.

They would probably go to bed at the same time tonight. They may even "watch" an episode of X-Files. And for the most part of the next week or so they would be nice to each other, probably talk a bit more than usual; but then, after that, things would just revert back to how they were.

Their house was more sticks and straw than ever before and yet there was nothing she could really do about it. And it felt like that big, bad wolf was getting ready to blow it right down.

SEVEN: *The Things That Turn A House Into A Home.*

Clive marched back and forth along the same bit of carpet, wondering how the hell he could have been so stupid. He had checked the notes on his phone, seeing as he was another definite disciple of the phone-having-now replaced-memory-function generation, and found that he had booked the estate agent to come round "some time after nine".

Some time after nine.

How had he been so dim-witted to book something so open-ended? Even for those delivery slots in which you are given something a little more specific, like *between seven and one*, they usually turn up at least an hour late. (More often than not because of bad traffic on the by-pass.)

So, what sort of time will the estate agent arrive after leaving it *open-ended*? Midnight? Some time tomorrow? Some time next week? *All* those scenarios fall under the category of "sometime after nine".

Oh, how could he have been so stupid? That's the problem when something is left too *vague:* there is no pressure for things to be done properly or even logically.

It's like the movie *Gremlins* and the ridiculous plot point about *".... no matter how much he cries, no matter how much he begs, never feed him after midnight."*

Well, when on earth *can* you feed him? Technically *any* point in time is *after* midnight, one way or another. And that's the problem with being *vague,* how can you.....

Clive stopped himself. He was obsessing about the whole *Gremlins / Midnight* thing again, wasn't he? It was a good job Gayle wasn't here or she would have been saying that same thing to him again – "Will you just let it go? *Everyone* you know has had to hear you moan about the

Gremlins feeding thing at least a dozen times!" God, she didn't half repeat herself!

Clive began pacing again.

He was supposed to be meeting *Knobhead* for snooker at twelve o'clock but there was no way that was going to happen now, was there? Not now he realised that he'd readily agreed to an open-ended booking. He may as well phone *Knobhead* and cancel now. No, a leisurely afternoon on the green baize, whilst sinking half a dozen pints and talking uncomplicated nonsense to one of his oldest buddies, was completely out of the window. How could he have been *so stupid...?*

A knock at the door caught Clive's attention and offered that poor same stretch of carpet some much needed relief. Clive glanced out of the window and saw a car bearing the name of *Slater's Estate Agents* on the side parked out on the street. Thank the lord for that. He looked at his watch – it was one minute past nine.

Clive walked to the front door and opened it and knew that, because of his punctuality, he would like the estate agent instantly. As he opened his mouth to say hello he was met by the outstretched palm of a young, slickly dressed man who was busy chatting on his mobile phone. Clive changed his mind - he knew he was going to dislike this young upstart straight away.

Instead of even meeting eye contact with Clive the estate agent continued to chat away for the next thirty seconds; a conversation that seemed to have no relevance to estate agency in general, and certainly no relevance to this part of estate agency-ing: namely his visit to Clive and Gayle's house. (That is of course unless "meeting up with Sharky, Dean and the "pussies" at Nobbies house at eight" was actually estate agent code for valuing someone's house.)

No, instead of ending his, clearly personal, call *before* knocking on Clive's door, this young high-flyer decided it was ok to knock on that door and completely ignore Clive as he completed arranging his night.

He was wearing a, quite-possibly fitted, three-piece charcoal suit (unless he was one of those annoying people who were just the perfect dimensions that one of the off-the-peg sizes *looked* like it was fitted, whilst the rest of us look like we've either lost or put on a huge amount of weight since buying our clothes), shoes so shiny that you could most probably see them from the moon and had one of those ridiculously trendy long beards that seem to be all the fashion with young people right now. (Which are obviously one of those fashion statements that will be looked back upon in the years to come with the same kind of confusion and hilarity that shoulder pads and mullets are now.)

Clive gave thanks that his "cool" days were in the 90's during which fashion seemed to be having a fairly low-key decade and so future piss-taking may hopefully be kept to a minimum. (Of course it helped that he had burnt all copies of photos that captured him during the few years that he sported a ponytail. Praise Nikon and Canon, and all those other camera manufacturers, for delaying the introduction of digital cameras – you look like a twat *these days* and it's captured *forever*.) Do you remember when beards, for people that you actually *knew*, were the exclusive fashion choice for strange uncles? (And some, *even stranger*, aunties??)

Finally the estate agent hot shot finished his phone call with the phrase "later, bitches!" and glanced across at Clive.

"I'm Slade from Slater's, nice to meet you!"

Through gritted teeth Clive managed to speak,

"Slade? That's an usual name."

"Yeah, yeah, man. My folks are pretty out there. It's old English – means *child from the valley*."

Really, thought Clive. It doesn't actually mean *child conceived to "Cum On Feel The Noize"*?

"It's Clive, innit?" asked Slade, or *Slick* as Clive had renamed him in his own head.

"It's alright if I call you C, innit?"

"Err, yeah" said Clive, again through gritted teeth. He hated it when people he didn't really know felt like it was ok to use nicknames. Nicknames should only be used after earning them after several years; and then ideally for taking the piss in one way or another.

"Right C, if it's ok with you, I'll just take a quick slip round the house and make a few notes for myself."

He didn't wait for any kind of agreement and instead just walked past Clive and began talking into his phone, Dictaphone style, no doubt also unable to retain any facts in his own "memory".

"Access to front door directly from the pavement..... enter into fairly dark, pokey entrance hall..... might just be able to get away with calling it *quaint* or *cosy*..... some sort of weird key storage thing on wall, probably some school kids first ever CDT lesson effort..... advise vendor to take down..... and ideally *bin*..... decor on first impression..... *shocking*..... probably have to say in need of a little *TLC*....."

What the hell? Clive was standing right next to him as he muttered these damning words into his phone. *Right next to him.*

This pattern continued around the house and, as Clive reminisced about things like how he and Gayle used to watch TV whilst eating their dinner on trays in the front room, or about how they used to sometimes have sex on the lawn under the full moon of a summers evening, Slick would make comments about how "the kitchen / diner would struggle to seat a game of chess, let alone a family dinner" or how the "garden was hideously overlooked". Oops, seems like there used to be sex shows for free on Percival Road. (Maybe this was why Mr Dennis would regularly come round, wearing a dressing gown that allowed him instant access to his tackle?)

Clive chuckled even more as Slick inexplicably decided to make a comment about their CD and DVD collection being "horribly dated" adding "does anyone *really* like *Bon Jovi*?" and "who realistically owns a Jim Carrey collection or multiple X-Files box sets *these days*?" If only the young upstart knew the history behind those X-Files box sets he may not be quite so quick to criticise it.

Clive looked at the CD collection, music that that had been added to and loved for as long as Clive and Gayle had been together, and realised that the *Bon Jovi* effort that Slick was openly criticising was the album at the top of the stack: *This House Is Not For Sale*. It was ironic, and sad really, seeing as the individual who was disapproving of such a CD was actually the one who was here to *sell the house*. It seemed that Jon Bon Jovi's house was not for sale but Clive and Gayle's soon would be. And when that happened, not only would it be Clive and Gayle that were forced apart but all those CD's and DVD's, that had sat side by side for years, would have to be sorted through and would also be heading in different directions. Clive took a deep sigh.

As Slick from Slater's paused in the bath room and made some derogatory comment about how "the tiler must have had a bad day", Clive cleared his mind of all the house items that would need splitting and, potentially, arguing about and, instead, stopped and gazed into Jacks bedroom.

He ignored the comment about this room "not being big enough to swing a cat" and took a moment to soak in the memories. (Does anyone *really* ever "swing a cat"? Is this an acceptable and legitimate way to *measure a room*? Are there any other, similar historic ways of measurement? How long is your garden? About as long as you can kick a tortoise? Maybe not. But this isn't the only well known cat saying that is a more than a little concerning. As well as: "not enough room to *swing* a cat", there's: "put the cat *amongst the pigeons*", "more than one way to *skin* a cat", "like a cat on a *hot tin roof*" and "let the cat *out of the bag*". Should we really be *swinging* and _skinning_ cats; or even putting them *amongst the pigeons* or on *hot tin roofs,* or keeping them *in bags*, in this day and age? Maybe the RSPCA should look into *all* these things in some detail?)

The first bit of decorating that Clive ever did in his life was in Jack's room. When they moved in to this house the room was a strange mish-mash of different coloured squares, each about half a metre in size. It felt like what life would be like if you lived inside a giant Rubik's cube. Clive painted the walls blue and the ceiling white and then hand painted a lovely landscape scene with a large tree and a family of cute owls sitting on it. It was a perfect little nursery; a lovely room for Jack to begin his life. Clive smiled as he remembered their first few months with Jack as a baby and, in particular, those nights that all new parents go through in which you believe you may never, *ever* sleep again. Those nights when it seems that your baby was just born to cry; and cry and cry and cry and ..... oh, you know what I mean. (Anyone with kids *really* knows what I mean!) Nights when, through a cocktail of complete exhaustion, and the helplessness of not knowing how to calm a hysterical baby, a family of cute owls that you know are not real, because you painted them on the wall yourself, begin to occasionally wink at you. And then talk to you. And then fly down and begin to nibble at your toes.....

Clive snapped out of that particular, nightmare-ish memory and remembered Jack as he grew. The relief of being able to paint over those bloody, freaky owls and replace them with (his own collection of) Star Wars posters, and then football stars, and then scantily dressed women (again, mainly from his own collection; but shhh, that's a secret) and then different musicians and bands. The memories of a baby growing into a man, right here in one room told through the changes of colours and posters on the wall. Clive smiled again as he thought of Jack and the love he would always have for his boy that was now a man as he also wondered whether he had taken *all* of those scantily dressed women posters to university with him. He best probably check later by having a good look around.

"It's just the two bedrooms innit?" Slick asked Clive after he'd obviously felt like he had slagged the bathroom off quite enough. Can bathroom suites actually be *so* old that they "could have been similar to those on the Titanic"?

"Yep, just the two" he replied, knowing full well that Slick could criticise the house off as much as he wanted, but could never take away the years of happy memories that came with it being a *home*.

Back in the front room, Slick explained to Clive how he (not *Slater's*, but *he*; like he owned the bloody firm) would not just be selling a house but would be "providing a full service". This included advising on price and advertising strategy, constant appraisal of market conditions, expert advice on improvements and alterations should offers not be immediately forthcoming, professional assistance on finding their next house and blah, blah, blah, blah, blah.

Then came the final insult.

"These little houses in *this* area are great for first time buyers who have, what shall we say, *limited* budgets? What about you – I take it you're moving to a bigger, *nicer* one now?"

I think it was the emphasis on the word *limited* that struck the first cord with Clive and the fact that it was delivered as if it didn't have a "t" in the middle and by a jumped up little shit who had done nothing but insult him for the whole duration of his visit. Before he had arrived, Clive had assumed that he would be telling the estate agent about his and Gayle's impending split and asking for advice about the rental market for small flats in the area, but he wasn't going to discuss that with this young prick. A guy who walks into your house, holding his palm up to stop you talking while he finishes his private conversation with, most probably, friends of his that are every bit as rude as he is? A guy that walks around your house and criticises *every* aspect of it; maybe so that he can convince you to agree to a low selling price, increasing his chances of a quick sale? Ripping apart any DIY jobs that he notices, whilst probably knowing that the man who did the majority of it was standing right next to him?

OK, Clive *did* have, actually more-than-one, bad day when tiling the bathroom, but that wasn't the point. The point was, after Slicks behaviour and complete rudeness, there was no way that Clive was going to let him sell the house. NO WAY! Because someone like Slick couldn't notice *real life things*. The things about a house, that may not seem perfect to idiots like him, but are ultimately the things that turn a house into a *home*. THERE WAS NO WAY SLICK WAS SELLING THEIR HOME.

"Shall I take some photos now, save me coming back again?" asked Slick, completely oblivious to his own prick-ness. (I know that's not a real word, but it should be, so I'm sticking with it.)

"I know you phoned *me* first because *I'm* the best," he continued, ignoring the fact that Clive phoned *Slater's* first because they probably paid more money than anyone else and were at the top of the local estate agents search results on Google.

"Besides," added Slick, "you don't really want to arrange for other estate agents to come round and traipse around your house do you?"

Clive thought about it.

"Yeah take your photos now."

The young prick had a point: how many other young pricks did Clive want wandering around his house, insulting him? It was also such a faff having to organise people to come round, and then remember what time they said they were coming and then anxiously wait around to see if they're actually on time or not. It was much better to get things out of the way in one go; and then Clive could go and fulfil his date with *Knobhead*, the snooker table and the beer.

EIGHT: *Moving On.*

Gayle pulled into the car park and noticed straight away that someone had parked a rather shocking pink Smart car in her usual parking bay, C3. For God's sake, you set off for work a little late, drive yourself insane in a traffic jam, arrive a few minutes later than usual and the whole world thinks that they can just change the normal, and accepted for years, status quo? It just wasn't on. The nearest alternative bay she could find was E10 and meant that her walk into the building would take, at least, *seven seconds* longer. Ok she needed to calm down. She couldn't let her earlier road rage to morph into car park rage and cultivate any more unwanted, psychopathic thoughts; especially now she could see that so many people had parked *so close to other cars*. It's a wonder some people had actually been able to get out of their cars. Gayle took some calming, deep breaths as she got out of her car and began walking towards across the car park. As she did, the slight worry that the darkest clouds you could ever see in the sky meant the imminent arrival of some *severe* rain passed immediately as she saw a different sight that stopped her dead in her tracks. For parked up at the first loading bay was an *Aqua-Kool* delivery van and, yes, sure enough there was *Lee* getting ready to unload the company's latest delivery.

Damn it, there was yet another reason that Gayle should have made sure that she had time for a shower this morning. She quickened her step and headed for the reception at the main door. If she was quick she may just have time for a couple of minutes "freshening up" in the toilet before heading to her office and, hopefully, catching Lee as he delivered the huge bottle for the office water dispenser.

"Morning Lena" she said as she passed through reception. As usual she was ignored by the receptionist known as Lena (in fairness, her name) who was, as Gayle always assumed, *pretending* to be speaking to someone through the silly phone headset that she insisted on wearing. She didn't have time to wait and insist on, at least, a fake smile response from Lena because she needed to speed on quickly to the women's toilet. Once inside, Gayle realised that she needed a miracle to be able to "freshen up" to anything even close to being acceptable. Fortunately, these days, miracles are small enough to carry in handbags.

In less than a minute she had lined up her "scrubbing-up first aid kit" on the ledge above the sink: Her can of dry shampoo, her mini, non-stain, roll-on anti-perspirant, her travel-size Armani Diamonds perfume, her semi-posh-occasion earrings and her compact make up kit that consisted of two black mascara primers, her two favourite lip pencils, a rose powder blusher, a translucide compact powder, 6 power eye shadows and 4 different lip colours.

In just three minutes flat, Gayle had used all the items from her first aid kit, packed them away, and was triumphantly looking at herself in the toilet mirror. She had gone for the reddest of her red lipsticks without really thinking about it; the red she would only usually go for on a night out. She wasn't sure what that meant but she felt good about herself as she gazed into the mirror. She had even been able to re-work the dry shampoo miracle and release her hair from its tight ponytail; and it actually now looked quite nice hanging around her shoulders. She even thought that she may never wash it ever again.

Now that she was happy that she looked good there was only one thing left to do. She took a deep breath and forcefully yanked the wedding and engagement rings off the third finger on her left hand. It took quite some effort, maybe because her fingers were much thicker than they were when she got married all those years ago, but eventually she managed to pull them clear of her finger. She looked at her finger, now free of the golden rings, and the tell-tale band of pale skin that accounted for nearly twenty years of marriage. Would her finger always look like that, even if she *never* put the rings back on ever again?

She sighed a little as she twisted both rings around in the palm of her hand. They didn't look like much, very unimpressive really, but they had represented every penny that Clive could afford back in the day and used to mean the world to her. She sniggered slightly as she stared at the *two* rings and *not three*. Clive always promised that he would buy her an eternity ring that would sit on her finger next to the engagement and wedding rings; but he *never* had. She realised that it was much easier to *say* things, than actually *do* them, as she let the rings slide out of her palm and into the "secret" little section at the back of her handbag. She zipped them away and looked back at herself in the mirror, re-asserting some strength of mind making sure she didn't allow herself to cry again.

She was ready to go into the office and was now appropriately stunning to "bump into" Lee. (Well, as much as she could hope to be in three miraculous minutes.)

Lee was the man who delivered the water that supplied the twelve dispensers that were located throughout the warehouse and adjoining offices. Gayle had been responsible for ordering the water for the last ten years but, curiously, the company seemed to have been going through more and more water for the eighteen months or so that Lee had been supplying them. Strange really.

Lee was not exactly what Gayle would describe as her "typical type" but, then again, what was her typical type? She had only ever had a serious relationship with one man in her entire life and that was Clive. And Clive and Lee were just about polar opposites. Lee had a skin-head, tattoo sleeves on both arms and the kind of muscle-bound physique that only came from spending hours and hours at the gym. Clive still had the type of hairstyle that looked cool on the members of Oasis about twenty years ago, thought tattoos were for sailors and prostitutes and the only time you heard him mention anything close to "gym" was when he used to boast he had met Jimmy Saville in 1987 whilst being in the audience one Saturday morning on *Going Live*. (A "claim to fame" he had not used for quite some time.)

Gayle didn't really know much about Lee and, on seeing him for the first few times, his shaven head, tattoos and physical appearance had intimidated her somewhat. After a while, and a few conversations though, she realised that he was a nice guy and his "image" began to become a real turn on. He had that kind of Vin Diesel swagger and buff-ness about him and almost seemed thrillingly dangerous. Exciting. Electrifying. Exhilarating. He may not be as *cute* as Clive, but not many were. Anyway this wasn't about Clive.

Lee was in his early 40's, was divorced and had two daughters - ages of 12 and 10, and he and Gayle flirted every time he made his water deliveries. At least Gayle thought it was flirting, it had been so long since she had spoken to any male, who was not one of the brain-dead morons who worked on the warehouse floor, that she was possibly mistaking it for just friendly conversation. But the fact that her two fellow office workers, Jennifer and Janine, who were both considerably younger and, so Gayle thought, prettier than her, did not have the same kind of "chemistry" with Lee that Gayle did, did make her think that there was "something" there.

Gayle was "unofficially" the office supervisor and, as such, had to manage both Jennifer and Janine who, in a kind of "Jedward" way were referred to by the boys in the warehouse as "Jennine" or "Jannifer". They obviously thought this was clever but "Jennine" sounded a lot like *Janine* and "Jannifer" sounded a lot like *Jennifer*, and so when anyone would say Jennine or Janine or Jannifer or Jennifer it was unclear if they were referring to the pair of them or just one of them. I'm confused just typing this! As such, they were often also referred to as "the two J's".

Gayle's supervisory role was probably more of an informal agreement attained through longer service and age rather than anything you could actually "see", you know, in something like a pay packet. Before Jenny and Janine, a girl of similar age to Gayle, Tina, had worked there. She was probably the closest thing Gayle had to a best friend back then but she left about two years ago after finding a new job and Gayle missed her terribly. But that's what people do: move on to new challenges, better jobs and better lives. Well, except for Gayle who was still here, stuck in the same old rut.

Gayle walked into the office just at the perfect time, as Lee was picking up a new, full, water bottle; perfectly flexing his triceps as he did. He was replacing the old, empty one that he had obviously already removed. (No need to have seen that as the lightness of an empty bottle means no muscles are flexed whatsoever.)

"Hi Gayle!" said Lee as she walked in the room "You are looking as sexy as ever!"

Gayle could feel her cheeks reddening straight away.

"Oh please!" she flirted back regardless, "I was late up and didn't have any time to get ready properly..... I must look a right state?" (Yes this was spoken as a question that she wanted answering.)

"No way!" said Lee, just as she had hoped. "You look amazing!"

Gayle smiled at him as she walked around the room to her desk by the window. She felt that, as she had worked there the longest, she deserved to have the best desk by the window and, in an attempt to stop someone else using it every day, had purchased her own name plate to sit on the desk. Thankfully, despite her lateness, no one had been tempted to try and steal her desk this morning or put her name plate in the recycling bin – again. Gayle straightened her name plate as she got around her desk and shuddered slightly as she recalled the number of times people are amused when they mistakenly think that, instead of saying her name was *Gayle Ford,* she has actually said *Gayle Force*. Oh the endless humour that can come from marrying into a name that makes you sound very similar to a severe weather event.

Gayle looked over at the paperwork inbox and saw that it was almost overflowing with work yet to be processed. It seemed no one had been tempted into doing any work, despite the fact that Jenny seemed to be looking at her phone (she had regularly answered that she was busy organising her diary when asked if she needed some work to do) and Janine was painting her fingernails.

"Ok, just about done here!" said Lee, putting the empty bottle over his shoulder and looking as sexy as someone carrying a huge bag of ice in a Baileys advert.

"Ok, thanks Lee" said Gayle. "I'll speak to you in a couple of weeks..... when we need some more water!"

She laughed nervously after speaking, but without knowing why.

Lee walked towards her and gently sat on her desk. It creaked slowly straining under the weight of a gorgeous, skin-headed, tattooed muscle man..... who was sitting on Gayle's desk!

Her heart began to flutter.

"I don't want to speak out of turn" he began, as Gayle stared helplessly into his big, brown eyes. "But you've said before about splitting with your husband and Jenny just told me that it's happening *now*..... is there any chance that you'd let me take you out for a drink? Maybe Sunday night?"

Gayle knew that her mouth was wide open, probably capable of capturing large owls, let alone flies, but there was nothing she could do about it. At least it seemed that Jenny had done *something* productive today.

"Erm..." she started. "Ok. Why not? It sounds good!"

"Great!" said Lee. "How about the Farmers Arms on the village high street? It's just been done up."

"Ok. Why not? It sounds good!" said Gayle, knowing straight away that she had just completely repeated the six words from her last sentence.

"Shall we meet there then? Eight o'clock?" asked Lee.

"Ok.....Why not?..... It sounds good!" said Gayle, accepting that these may be the only words she would ever be able to speak for the rest of her life.

"See you Sunday then gorgeous!" said Lee winking, as he stood up and relieved the desk of his considerable mass.

"See you later Jenny..... Janine." He added as he walked out of the door.

"Bye Lee!" they both swooned after him before, once more, concentrating on their phone and nails respectively.

Wow, thought Gayle. She had a date..... *with Lee!*

She couldn't help but send a look over to "the two J's" that said "He asked *me* out, not either of you two. What do you think about those "happy, laughy lines" now?"; but they were both *too busy* to notice. Instead she thought about what this actually meant – the time had finally arrived that she and Clive said they were going to move on..... and she was moving on.

NINE: *Pretend Best Friend.*

Clive pulled his jacket tight together and squinted his eyes to prevent the sudden increase in the wind and rain intensity from rendering him blind. The last thing you need when walking through a busy shopping precinct is the inability to spot, and give a wide berth to, those annoying people wandering around with clip boards. You don't want to be the latest vulnerable individual who agrees to "answer a few short market research questions" that end up costing you a good hour or so of your life. No, you needed to see exactly where you were walking, especially with the increase in the number of weirdo's feeding pigeons and creating huge, potentially hazardous, feathered blockades all over the place.

But what was with this weather anyway? Rain and strong wind? Clive had watched the *official* weather forecast barely half an hour earlier that had promised of "fine, dry skies until early evening". (You know the legitimate forecast on TV, not just some random smart phone app that changes its mind every thirty seconds.)

Well it was still morning and it was, in Clive's admittedly non-professional opinion, pretty damn close to officially "pissing it down". What other job is there in the world, other than weather person, in which you can get things *so wrong* on a daily basis and still have a job to keep going to? Then again, maybe that's a bit harsh because I suppose predicting the weather is tantamount to being able to predict the future, and if you can predict the future then there's probably better things to focus your talents on. So I suppose anyone with the potential to be a half decent weather person gives up that particular career path once they have won the lottery a couple of times.

Clive continued to walk against the wind and rain and could now just about make out his destination, which was the front of the building which used to be *Woolworths* but is now the latest branch of the *WeLendAnyMoney.Com* to pop up in the town centre. It is also the building that is on the corner of the street that leads down to *The Cruciball* snooker hall. (Which was, until recently, called *The Crucible* snooker hall until a legal contest argued that the name was mis-leading and it could be mistaken for the famous *theatre* in Sheffield that hosts the Snooker World Championship – even though that one is nearly fifty miles away. It's a crazy world.)

As he got nearer, Clive could make out the distinct outline of his good buddy Robert Adshead - a.k.a. *Knobhead.* A nickname that had originally come from the rather sophisticated, playground thought process of Robert Adshead (if you take away the "ert" and "Ads") = Rob Head = Knob Head.

Ever since being assigned with his new moniker over twenty five years ago, and being baffling proud to receive such a label, Robert seemed to have made it his life's work not to waste a single second in living up to such a name. Right now he was standing amongst the tens of people who were queuing to borrow "anything between £20 and £2000" at something like a couple of million per cent APR.

Knobhead was tall; the kind of tall that made Greg Davies and Richard Osman seem like mere mortals. The kind of tall that made playing snooker with him foolish, because he could stretch so far over the table that he never needed to use the rest or the spider. Luckily, he was also partially colour blind and so having that reach advantage was usually negated by the fact that he would often hit the brown when thinking he was playing for a red.

Good old *Knobhead*; always there when he says he will be, never lets you down, reliable, trustworthy, salt-of-the-earth bloke. Clive realised that, even if was losing Gayle right now, he would always have *Knobhead.*

"Allreet there *Knobhead.*" said Clive as he got close enough, as always (but never knowing why) adopting a high pitch, stereotypical scouse accent to greet him.

"Fordy!" replied *Knobhead,* "How goes it dude?"

They embarked on some lengthy, elaborately choreographed handshake routine, the type of which probably seemed semi-cool about twenty years ago.

"Come on then lar, let's go and have some beer and play some snooker-ball." said Clive after the handshake formalities were complete.

"Dude, I can't make it today, that bird from the chippy is coming for a drink with me!"

"Which bird?"

"You know, Adele from the chippy on Smithy boulevard..... and she's a cert for a shag."

Clive scratched his head.

"Which chippy? Oh, you mean *For The Love of Cod*? You don't mean *Estelle* do you?"

"Yeah, yeah *Estelle*," said *Knobhead* "pretty close with Adele, wasn't I?"

"But *Estelle's* pretty old, you know? She's Tommy Dalton's *great auntie*. I think she's probably in her mid to late sixties!" said Clive, shuddering slightly.

"Hey, beggars can't be chooser's dude. It's been months since I've had my leg over."

Clive could appreciate that, and then some.

He cast his mind back to his and Gayle's red-hot, passion days and the cheeky sexiness of the *Bad Touch* song "...then we'll do it doggy style, so we can both watch X-Files". These days the heat was well and truly gone, and the last times he could remember having sex, instead of that *Bloodhound Gang* line, it was more like "... then we'll do it quietly because one of us wants to watch Emmerdale".

So maybe *Knobhead* was right to get it whenever he could; and maybe wherever he was taking Estelle for a drink may offer some kind of OAP afternoon special?

"But we're going for a quick game first aren't we? That's why you've met me here?" asked Clive.

"No, dude, no time. I'm just here hoping I can borrow sixty quid!"

"What, so it's just lucky I saw you here?" asked Clive feeling somewhat aggrieved "Why didn't you call me to let me know you couldn't make it?"

"Sorry dude, no credit on phone!"

Bloody idiot *Knobhead*; never where he says he's going to be, always lets you down, unreliable, untrustworthy, waste of space.

"Some other time dude." *Knobhead* added as he placed a cigarette between his lips and began passionately frisking himself to (hopefully) locate a lighter.

"When did you start smoking again?" asked Clive.

"Oh last week, dude. Those e-cigs started getting right on my tits. I was getting a mini-electric shock every time I took a blast. Having a smoke felt like trying to snog R2D2..... anyways, I've decided – life's too short. I could get run over by a bus tomorrow. There's a saying, isn't there? "Live life to the full - the way you wanna live"; that's my new motto!"

Clive nodded his head.

"It's a good saying isn't it?" asked Knobhead. "It's not like one of those stupid ones people throw about here, there and everywhere. *"The pen is mightier than the sword"* – that's all ok until you end up in a sword fight. What use is a bloody *pen* to you then? Fuck all! Then there's: *too many cooks spoil the broth* but *many hands make light work* – well *which* one is it? You can't bloody well have it both ways can you? And what about …"

Clive realised *Knobhead* may go on with this line of thinking for a while and so tuned him out. Anyway, the "could get run over by a bus tomorrow" argument for doing unhealthy and/or crazy things was one that Clive had heard many times, usually by smokers, and he didn't really agree with anyway. Clive always felt that, if you take great care when crossing the road, the likelihood of you *actually* being run over by a bus was probably pretty slim. In fact, he thought that if you looked at the statistics regarding people who were unfortunate enough to actually be run over by buses you may find that the majority of them were people who were *not* taking great care crossing the road – probably because they were too busy concentrating on lighting a fag.

"See you around then," Clive said rather bitterly as *Knobhead* stopped his "stupid sayings" rant to concentrate on shuffling forward in the *WeLendAnyMoney* queue. "Best of luck with Estelle!"

"Thanks dude..... laters."

Clive turned away and caught a face full of rain.

Great, what a day this was turning into already: insulted for the best part of an hour by an upstart estate agent and now let down by his best friend who would rather take his chances of sleeping with a woman old enough to remember the war (maybe even both wars) than stand by a pre-agreed day out.

But was *Knobhead* really his *best friend*? A man in his late-thirties who couldn't even speak a sentence without using the word: *dude*. What was *that* about? It wasn't still the late 80's or early 90's and, as far as Clive was aware, *Knobhead* wasn't a surfer, or a ninja turtle.

No, the more Clive thought about it, Robert Adshead wasn't his best friend; he was just a guy that he knew from school, who still acted like he was in school *now* – over twenty years later. He just met up with Clive now and again – when he didn't have anything better to do. Or anyone better to *drink* with; because every day, for him, was about *drinking.* Even now he was queuing up to borrow money so he could buy more booze.

It was sad really. *Knobhead's* idea of an *alcohol free* day was when he couldn't get his hands on any money and so had to steal a bottle of whisky instead of buying it. Clive realised that *Knobhead* wasn't really a *real* friend. Throughout the whole of his life, there had only actually been *one* person who Clive could ever have classified as being his genuine, indisputable, authentic *best friend*. And that was Gayle. And he was letting her slip out of his life. He tried not to allow his mind to think about Gayle and, instead, diverted his mind to thinking about the one thing that he and Gayle had got perfectly right: their son, Jack. He could feel some moisture in his eyes that, despite the profuse about of rain in the air, he knew was coming from the sad feeling that his *little boy* had just left home. Very quickly though the overwhelming cause of his tears was the immense love and pride he had for Jack. Through his blurred eyes, Clive saw numerous important memories as they skipped out of his mind like tiny moments of sunshine.

Jack's beaming smile as a baby, those initial wobbly steps as he began to walk and his first word: *"Jabba-Fool"* (Which everyone put down to the fact that the poor boy probably had to sit through the *Star Wars* trilogy (original trilogy, of course) and re-runs of *The A-Team* more times than was healthy for any toddler. In fact, more times than was healthy for *any* human being of *any age*.)

Clive smiled as the memories continued and reminded him of his efforts to teach Jack how to tie shoe laces, which didn't go *completely* smoothly. But, hey, what's the harm in wearing Velcro-fastening shoes until you're a teenager? That's what it was invented for, isn't it? His thoughts returned to Jack as a baby and he pictured him being held in Gayle's arms. He stared at Gayle in his memory as she beamed a look of love and joy at him as she held onto the most perfect little boy in the world. And that moment; that instance of his and Gayle's love expanding into a perfect little family, the thought that they all belonged to one another, felt like one of the happiest anyone could ever wish for.

Clive tried to clear thoughts of Gayle from his mind because, ever since they made "the pact", any thoughts he had about her, even the really happy ones from the past, ended up morphing into possible visions of the future. Most clearly, the thought that Gayle would end up belonging to someone else, and it made him feel sick to the stomach. It wasn't the idea of someone else kissing Gayle, and her kissing them back. Or even her touching someone else, and *being* touched back; not even her *sleeping* with someone else. Although all that was tough enough to think about, the thing that *really* tore him up was the idea that she would one day tell someone else that she loved them; and the idea that she would *mean* it. And that she would then love someone else more than she loved him; and perhaps love them more than she had *ever* loved him. It ripped his heart in two just to think about it and so he had just tried his best *not* to think about it, reasoning that was the best way not to feel hurt.

As usual, Clive knew it was best to deny his mind the opportunity to think about those kinds of things again. It was the best way to avoid feeling the hurt.

Instead, he squinted his eyes and walked back into the rain, wondering how the hell the rain always seemed to change direction and hurtle itself in exactly the opposite direction in which you are walking. The whole precinct was, of course, completely deserted. Who in their right mind would be out walking in weather like this? He began to head for the far side, towards Sainsbury's, where he could pick up some bread and milk. Maybe he would buy Gayle a bunch of flowers as well; this may be close to the end of their relationship but she would always be the mother of his son and he would always love her. Damn, he should have bought her flowers more often, he thought as he approached the orange painted supermarket.

(Isn't it weird how the major supermarkets have each adopted a different colour as their own recognisable image? Tesco = Blue = Reliable. Asda = Green = Safe. Sainsbury's = Orange = A bit different. Morrison's = Yellow = ? Last to choose their colour?)

Clive paused before entering because, through the driving rain, he had noticed a man not far from him walking around the precinct. That was weird. He hadn't been there a couple of seconds ago; it was liked he had appeared out of nowhere. He was a tall and skinny man who was wearing a black sandwich board. (Why are people who wear sandwich boards *always* tall and skinny? Do sandwich boards only come in one size?) Clive hadn't seen anyone wearing a sandwich board for absolutely ages and, although he realised these days it was probably an advertisement of some kind, he used to find some odd humour in reading about why "the end is nigh" in the signs you'd often see in the past. He couldn't help but feel drawn to it, just in case it was one of those profits of doom telling us just how the world was going to end. Would it be a huge comet that's path had aligned with the Earth and would be colliding with us imminently? Or would the end be caused by the wrath of God, who was sick of the amount of cheap blue, green, orange and yellow plastic bags, and now shopping trolleys, that he was seeing impaled on his trees and floating down his rivers?

As Clive had got closer he realised that his initial sandwich board assumption had been correct and this was just a man carrying an advert around and wasn't actually some morbid soul trying to suck any remaining happiness out of anyone who was lucky enough to have any left. But he couldn't help his eyes being drawn in by the, rather rough, chalk-written words that had been etched onto the black surface; words that oddly hadn't been washed off by the torrential rain. For this wasn't news of a buy-one-get-one-free muffin at a local café, or information regarding the "very last day" of a major shoe sale; no, this was something that Clive couldn't help but think may be of interest to him.

Is your relationship coming to an end? If it was <u>true</u> <u>love</u> then it shouldn't be! Before you give up on it let Love Is… *try and re-find it for you. Money back guarantee if we are unsuccessful**

TEN: *T.E.A.M.W.O.R.K.*

Gayle watched through the office window as the Aqua Kool van slowly drove out of the gate and past the security lodge. She still couldn't believe what had just happened and couldn't quite work out how she felt. She had a date, *with Lee the water man,* (if the date went well, she would probably need to ask him his surname) and it was in just two days time.

It wasn't *enough* time.

What would she wear? What *do* people wear on first dates these days? Maybe she could go shopping on Saturday for a new outfit? But *what* new outfit? She wondered if, at this short notice, she would be able to book in to get her hair done? It had been ages since she'd had it coloured professionally and it could definitely do with a good cut. What would she *eat* on Sunday? She definitely didn't want anything that might bloat her up before she went out at 8 o'clock so it was probably best that she had something light. But then again, Clive and Jack used to like to have a roast dinner on a Sunday. Maybe she could make one and just have a little bit? Maybe just some roast beef on a barmcake? Maybe one or two roast potatoes on the side? And maybe a Yorkshire Pudding? She did like Yorkshire Pudding. No, that would be too much. Besides, she realised, Jack wouldn't be there this weekend.

She stopped her mind making manic plans and just focussed again on the fact that her only son had now left home. It made her feel sad. Also, she didn't really need to be worrying about making Clive a roast dinner; very soon they would need to start sorting meals out for themselves; wherever they both ended up living. And how would Clive cope? He would probably end up having to live on nothing more than microwaveable ready meals. She began to feel some moisture forming in her eyes, but cleared her mind straight away. She had been over and over things like this in her mind more times than she would ever have wanted to, and cried enough tears over it to last a lifetime. No, this should be a *happy* moment; a moment that represented her first step into what could be a bright and exciting future.

Her mind was now tidied of negative thoughts and she thought it best to get on with some work. She stood from her desk and began walking towards the *In Tray* that stood on the filing cabinet by the door. As she walked across the room she allowed herself a little smile as she again thought about her date with *Lee the Water Man*. In a flurry of excitement and anticipation her mind began to pirouette across the room while *My Fair Lady's - I Could Have Danced All Night* echoed around her head, in quite a lavish number for this time on a Friday morning. By the time she got across to the paperwork that needed processing she felt quite dizzy and somewhat nauseous. How do these professional dancers do all that spinning around – and *for real*?

She took a minute to let her head calm down whilst wondering if the lack of any real breakfast this morning had contributed to the feeling of sickness brought on by her impromptu imagination dancing. Maybe she could go down to the canteen and get some of the famous sausage and bacon on toast?

What? When she had to prepare herself for a date that was less than fifty eight hours away? Not likely! Maybe she could have a banana? Or, more realistically, *half* a banana? Maybe a couple of grapes?

She realised eating would have to be very closely monitored for the next couple of days and so, for now, did a deal with herself that she would settle for no food in exchange of a much needed cup of coffee. She was just about to ask if the two J's wanted one when she noticed the full extent of the work that had *not* been done. Not only was there a mountain of paperwork precariously balancing on top of the tray, on top of the filing cabinet; but there was also probably between fifteen and twenty pieces that had fallen down the back of the cabinet. She looked over at Janine and Jennifer and watched, almost in horror, for a few seconds, as they continued to concentrate on their nails and phone respectively; completely oblivious to the work that needed doing.

Ok, it was time to flex her unofficial supervisor muscles and get some work out of the pair of them. She cast her mind back to a week last Thursday when they had all been sent on that teamwork workshop with the man who promoted his "own, copyrighted *positive mind technique*". Yep, *PMT!* What were the chances that Gayle would be sent on a mind-numbing "workshop", that dragged on and on, with an acronym of *PMT* when it was her own, personal "time of the month"? Chances must have been pretty good, seeing as *every single* training session she had ever been on, that turns out to be a tediously, monotonous waste of time and a challenge of concentration skill, coincides with Gayle's, shall we say, *least patient time of the month*?

"Ok, you two." She announced in a "clear but calm" manner. "We've got lots of work to be processed here. I'll split it into three and we'll be done in no time. Many hands make light work."

She took a deep breath before adding. "Remember what we learnt about TEAM and TEAMWORK last week? We are a TEAM and *Together Everyone Achieves More*, and good TEAMWORK is *Talented Employees Attaining Meaningful Well Organised Rewarding Knowledge*."

Janine looked up from doing her nails and gave Gayle the kind of look that, quite frankly, she deserved. It was a mixture of surprise and disgust; the kind of look usually reserved for if you ever see anyone on a motorway hard shoulder having a shit. Jenny just carried on intensely looking at her phone almost as if she was no longer able to hear anything.

Gayle felt a bit dirty. Not only had she had to sit through that meaningless training course, but she had actually listened enough to take some of it in, and was now *quoting* it. It felt like some kind of "career" low for her.

Thankfully Janine changed the subject.

"So, you're going out on a date with Lee?" she said while at the same time shaking her hands in a way that you would only do if you either wanted nail varnish to dry quicker or you were starting some kind of epileptic fit.

Jenny suddenly looked up from her phone, proving that she hadn't actually gone completely deaf.

"Yeah Lee..... lucky you! He's well fit and I bet he's a right good laugh when he's out-*out*. I bet he's really dirty in bed as well....." she added as a naughty smile grew on her face ".....and I bet he's got a *huge cock*! You'll be lucky if you can walk on Monday morning!"

Both her and Jenny smiled and laughed at each other and continued talking about Lee and speculated about how good he may be in bed and how well endowed they both thought that he would be. Gayle could feel her cheeks warming up and instead her mind diverted in a different direction.

When Lee had asked her out she hadn't thought that Sundays date could mean she ended up in bed with him; not right away anyway. The only man she'd ever slept with was Clive and, well, they were both kids really when it first happened; and they'd got to know each other really well before *anything* happened. These days though it appeared that people didn't mess around wasting time getting to know each other really well before jumping into the sack. She tried to think about how that made her feel. She was just about ready to accept going on a date with somebody new, was she also ready to have *sex* with them, *straight away*? Also, she could do with being able to walk on Monday morning; it was her primary way of getting around.

"WELL, GAYLE?"

She was brought back into the office by Jenny, who it appeared now had been trying to ask her a question.

"*When* is Clive *the loser* moving out?" she asked as both her and Janine stared at her smiling.

"He's not." Gayle said. "We're just going to sell the house and then see what to do. The estate agent is coming around this morning and..... wait, he's *not* a loser! He's a *good* man. We just lost *our* way, that's all. It doesn't mean I have to hate him. It doesn't mean we have to hate *each other*. We just....."

She looked up to see that Jenny had gone back to her previous state of mobile phone ignorance and Janine was beginning a second coat of nail varnish.

Gayle gave out a deep sigh before picking up the various pieces of paper behind the filing cabinet and adding them to the huge pile in the tray. She struggled to carry them back over to her desk; this time the journey across the room silent of any music within her head. She justified her actions thinking that, usually, she had to double check Jenny and Janine's work anyway. She may as well make sure that it was right *first time*.

Before she started though, she needed that coffee she had promised herself, which meant that she had best get one for *Jennine* as well. Couldn't expect them both to go to the brew machine whilst they were both so busy.

TEAMWORK eh?

As she left the office and made sure her bra was on properly, preparing herself in case there any warehouse guy "banter / abuse" as she walked to the coffee machine, Gayle wondered why she felt the need to stick up for Clive all the time. They were nearing the end so she didn't really need to do so anymore, did she? The thing was though: he *was* a good man. And things *were* pretty special; at least at the start anyway.....

56

ELEVEN: *The Pre-Dinner Snack Club.* (23 Years Ago)

Clive sat there at his usual desk by the window and watched as Mr Jackson paced back and forth past the blackboard as he always did at this time of day. It was 3.30 p.m., the official start of detention time which was exactly five minutes before he would disappear for thirty-five minutes before returning for the final five minutes of the "punishment forty-five". His pacing was probably brought on as he pondered the need to set thirty-five minutes worth of "token gesture" work that needed to be achievable with absolutely no supervision, whilst he went and spent over half an hour doing whatever he did for over half an hour with his favourite eighteen stone member of the after-school cleaning team. It came as no surprise that Mr Jackson could often be heard whistling Alison Moyet songs – he certainly seemed to have a preference for the *larger lady*.

Because of Mr Jackson's habit of disappearing, most detention sessions were largely unsupervised and so Clive actually quite enjoyed having them now and again. Being there felt pretty similar to the cool '80s movie *The Breakfast Club* but it didn't really warrant being given a similar title because *The Pre-Dinner Snack Club* didn't sound anywhere near as snappy.

It certainly wasn't any real punishment having to attend. There were no lines to be written on blackboards or in books, no chance of the cane or a ruler rap on the knuckles (it was the 90's – the decade of letting kids get away with anything) but rather it was a chance to sit for a while in a quiet and (usually) warm classroom either listening to music or chatting to any of the other "naughty" kids who fancied doing the same thing.

As such, there was almost an unspoken agreement between the detainees and Mr Jackson: he wasn't too bothered about whether anyone actually did any of the aforementioned "token gesture" work he had set (he certainly never checked it) as long as they didn't bring it to anyone's attention that he always volunteered to run the detention sessions because he was actually shagging the big woman who was responsible for mopping the main hall floor. (It was confusing that none of the other school staff had ever actually realised what was going on seeing as that hall floor was, more often than not, dirtier than the playing fields.)

Gayle pulled her bag over her shoulder and let out a big sigh as she pushed open the toilet door. She couldn't avoid it anymore, it was now slightly after 3.30 p.m. and she was already late for her first detention with Mr Jackson. She wasn't bothered about the fact that she would be late getting home, her Mum (if she was even there) probably wouldn't notice anyway, but it was the idea that she would have to spend forty-five minutes with Mr Jackson, possibly even *alone with him*, that concerned her.

He creeped her out.

Although that wasn't really saying much because *all men* creeped her out; because all men were bastards. But there was something about Jackson that was even creepier than all the other bastards – he had strange, vacant eyes that were either showing he was completely bored all the time or were a façade that concealed a dirty imagination. As such, as she walked towards the classroom she was juggling a strange mix of emotions. On one hand, she hoped that she wouldn't be alone with Mr Jackson yet, on the other, she couldn't think of one, single kid she had come across in her first week at this shithole of a school that she actually liked and might hope to also be in detention.

Oh well, she decided as she got to the classroom, it would, as usual, be left to fate to decide; so it depended on how cruel he or she was feeling today.

Mr Jackson finished explaining to Clive that he wanted him to look through pages 71–79 of the *Ancient Egypt History* book he had given him and "write 250 words on the construction of pyramids during the old and middle kingdom periods." He would "check it later". Clive nodded to let Mr Jackson know that he understood and that "he would do that". Both of them knew and accepted that none of this would happen.

Clive began to get his walkman out of his bag realising that this was probably going to be a solo detention. He was a little disappointed because *Knobhead* had promised the day before that he would try his best to also get detention. Bloody *Knobhead* – what a letdown.

Not even Kev or Dan looked like there were going to be there this evening - they were quite regular attendees; *or Stacey Wellington*. She had also been getting more detentions of late and was quite funny..... for a girl. And, actually, quite cute.....

Oh well, it would just be Clive and his music.

Just then the door opened and so Clive looked up. Had good old *Knobhead* made it after all? He hoped so; they'd had some right laughs together whilst in detention. Or maybe Stacey Wellington? Oh no, it wasn't either of them, but actually that new, arrogant kid with the big hair who had just started in his class: *Poodle Girl*.

Bloody *Knobhead* – complete waste of space.

At least he had his walkman with him; as long as *Poodle Girl* kept herself to herself it would be ok.

Gayle walked through the door and felt a little momentary relief as she noticed someone sitting by the window on the far side of the room; at least she wasn't alone with Jackson. Her relief soon died down though when she realised who it was, it was that weird guy from her class that liked to draw on the windows: *Penis Boy*.

She sat down at a desk on the opposite side of the room thinking as long as she didn't have to talk to him, then it would be ok. At least it wasn't just her and pervo Jackson.

"Ah, Miss Platt, you made it then? I thought I said to be here at three-thirty, on the dot?" said Mr Jackson. "Being late for the detention you got for constantly being late? That's not a good start is it?"

"I was just in the toilet, sir" said Gayle "You know, *women's* stuff!"

At first Gayle thought that playing the "women's stuff" card was the way to go, it certainly worked for most of the teachers in this school, but she should have known better than to use it with Jackson. The ridiculous look that grew on his face as his left eyebrow arched into a position that looked impossible, even for Roger Moore, made her wish that she had just told him that she couldn't be arsed getting there on time. How can someone make a statement about "women's stuff" seem almost porn-like? He was such a dirty, old perv.

"I can hardly check *that* can I?" said Mr Jackson.

He stared for much too long following that comment, his eyebrow arching so much now that it looked like it could tie itself in a knot, before turning to head towards the door.

"Very well, I'll let Mr Ford here..... *fill you in*....."

He also left this innuendo-laden comment lingering, smiling back at them as Gayle and Clive both looked at each other in disgust. He was obviously feeling a little frisky about the thought of his latest liaison with Mrs Mop.

He closed the door behind him and the room soon filled with silence. Gayle looked over at Clive and waited for him to let her know what work she needed to do while Jackson was, thankfully, away from the room. But he was just ignoring her, instead looking for something in his bag: he was *so ignorant*. As she looked at him Gayle noticed that he had a walkman sitting on his desk and cursed herself for not having her own with her. This ordeal may be something closer to bearable if she had *her* music with her.

As Clive looked through his bag for a tape for his walkman he couldn't help but feel Gayle staring right at him. What was her problem? She was *so rude*. Eventually he decided that he best let her know what was happening, it might just stop her staring if nothing else; *rude bitch*.

Finally, thought Gayle as Clive turned his head in her direction, he may just be letting me know what to do; *arrogant prick*.

"Jackson asked us to....." Clive started, but then stopped as he noticed Gayle snigger.

"What?" he asked.

"Sorry," said Gayle "It's just that you called him *Jackson* and not <u>Mr</u> *Jackson*..... just like I do."

Clive smiled. "Well I don't think he's ever earned enough respect to justify anyone using the *Mr* part of his name."

Gayle smiled at Clive.

Wow she was smiling, thought Clive, she looked so much friendlier when she wasn't scowling or frantically chewing.

"I think the only title he's ever earned is: *Pervy*." Said Gayle, still smiling. "*Pervy Jackson* – that's what I call him."

Clive laughed a little. "Yeah he's definitely *earned* that title!"

They both laughed and smiled at each other.

"Sorry," said Gayle "You were about to tell me what work *Pervy Jackson* has left us?"

Still smiling, Clive said "Well he asked us to read pages 71 to 79 of this history book and write 250 words about pyramids..... but we don't have to do it."

Gayle looked puzzled, so Clive continued.

"He never checks any *work* he gives us to do. He won't be back until it's time to go home. He'll be on his way now to see his favourite cleaner. *The big one*. You know, *big Bertha*..... I think he's shagging her!"

Gayle looked a little shocked. "Really? How do you know?"

"He goes to see her *every* detention. They meet by the vending machine near the canteen. He buys her a king-size Mars bar and then head off somewhere together. We've tried to follow them a few times but they gave us the slip; they're pretty good at being sneaky. I'm pretty sure though that they go to one of the science storerooms."

"Wow" said Gayle, not able to shake the look of disgust that she knew had twisted itself onto her face. "He really *is* Pervy Jackson. The science storerooms? I wonder what they do in there? I'm not sure I'll be able to look at a Bunsen Burner the same from now on!"

They both laughed again.

"And it's *always* the big one who's usually mopping?" she added.

Clive nodded.

"And is her name *really* Bertha?"

Clive nodded again as he smiled. "I think every woman of that size is named *Bertha*..... it's the law!"

Gayle laughed again.

"What are you listening to?" Gayle asked after a few seconds.

"Oh," said Clive, desperately trying to think of someone modern and "cool" to pretend he was listening to. He couldn't think of anyone so decided to go for the truth, besides he wasn't trying to *impress* Gayle or anything.

"It's an American band called *Bad English*. You won't have heard of them. They only did a couple of albums and broke up a few years ago."

Oasis or Blur!

Damn it, he could have said Oasis or Blur, that would have sounded more impressive. It didn't matter though he told himself again: he *wasn't* trying to impress her.

Gayle's eyes lit up.

"No way!" she said. "I *love* Bad English. I thought I was probably the only one in England who'd ever heard of them. *When I See You Smile* is my absolute *favourite* song of all time!"

"No way!" said Clive in exactly the same, excited way that Gayle just had.

"Is that the only copy of that history book?" asked Gayle, standing up and swinging her bag over her right shoulder.

"I think there might be some more....." Clive started saying, pointing towards the bookshelf by the teacher's desk, but Gayle spoke over him.

"Looks like I'll have to sit *next* to you then!"

She walked over to Clive's desk and let her bag drop to the floor as she sat down in the chair next to him. Clive got a scent of her sweet, almost fruity, perfume as Gayle positioned herself close to him and felt his cheeks reddening slightly, without really knowing why. He'd only really smelt perfume on Sue, his step-mum, before but Gayle's smelt and made him feel different. It was alluring, enticing; somehow seductive. He gulped deeply, as quietly as he could, as he moved the history book across his desk so that it was exactly half way in between the two of them.

"I thought you said we didn't have to do this?" said Gayle, picking the book up.

"Err we don't...." said Clive at the same time that Gayle threw it over her shoulder and on to the desk behind them.

He laughed again.

"So, how did you get to know about Bad English?" Gayle asked, shuffling her body side on to the chair so that she was fully facing Clive.

Clive reached up and touched his left cheek, half expecting that his fingers may well be burnt right off, before answering.

"I had a foster Dad, Jim, who used to record *Americas Top Ten* off the TV. It was on overnight in the, you know, night." He stuttered.

Gayle smiled at him as he struggled.

"He used to love all these American bands that were really big in the late '80's. I used to watch it with him. A lot of them were really good."

"Cool" said Gayle. "Sounds like a cool guy. Where is he now?"

"Don't know" said Clive shrugging his shoulders. "My Mum, sorry foster Mum, she had lots of male friends..... but none of them ever ended up sticking around. Too many kids to look after, I suppose. Bet they all felt like they were second best to us kids. Mum *always* puts us first. Sooner or later, suppose they didn't like that..... Jim *was* cool though!"

Gayle looked on intently. Clive had never seen her this close before and her brown / green eyes had a real warmth to them; it was like he was looking at someone that he had known for all his life. And she was actually very, very pretty. He carried on talking.

"Yeah Jim, he had long hair and used to wear brown leather pants quite a lot. He drove an old, blue Skoda, around the time that all those jokes about Skoda's were popular – but he didn't care one bit. He was *too cool* to be bothered."

Gayle looked confused. "What jokes?"

"You know," said Clive "like, what's the difference between a hedgehog and a Skoda? A hedgehog has the pricks on the *outside!*"

Gayle laughed.

Clive smiled, happy that he'd made her laugh. He may as well go for the full repertoire of Skoda gags that had always amused him and he'd somehow always remembered.

"Why do Skoda's have heated rear-windows? To keep your hands warm when you're pushing them! What do you call a convertible Skoda? A skip! What do you call a Skoda with twin exhausts? A wheelbarrow!"

Clive stopped there as Gayle laughed. He was sure there were more jokes than that – maybe he couldn't remember them all, after all.

"I always remember the Stan Ridgeway song *Camouflage* when I think of Jim's blue Skoda. He always seemed to have it playing." He said smiling.

Gayle looked a bit blank again.

"You don't know *that* song?" asked Clive.

Gayle shook her head.

"I'm sure you've heard it, it was on the radio, like all the time, for a while in the late 80's. It's about a mystical, superhuman marine – "camouflage", helping a stranded soldier out of a hopeless situation in the Vietnam War. It's probably a metaphor for *fate* or *salvation* or something. But it feels like *more* than a song. It's like *listening* to a film. It's really cool; I'll have to bring it in for you to listen to..... you know, *if you want?*"

Gayle nodded. She wasn't completely convinced by his song description but she liked the idea of Clive "bringing something in" for her.

"Yeah, sounds good."

She paused for a while before saying, with a cheeky grin.

"This Jim of yours, though, he doesn't *sound* very cool. Sounds like he dressed and looked like a woman and drove an old man's car!"

She laughed as she spoke, before adding.

"Sounds more like a *saddo* to me!"

"Ahhh" said Clive now turning his body in his chair to be face to face with Gayle and talking over her laughing. "That's where you've *misunderstood* what being cool is. A person isn't cool because they wear the clothes or listen to the music that *everyone else* does. You're cool if you do whatever you want to do – because you *want to*, regardless of whether others would *think* of you as cool. There's a massive difference between *acting* cool and *being* cool."

Gayle stopped laughing but continued smiling. She quite liked the fact that Clive had now turned to face her. Now she was seeing him close up for the first time she was surprised how good looking he actually was. She had always thought he was just a weasel looking boy who liked to draw penises, but there was a bit of a young David Bowie look about him. He had a really nice, and very attractively cheeky, smile; and his blue eyes, now she was right next to him, looked so familiar; somehow like she already knew him.

The two of them just sat there smiling at each other for a little while before Clive asked, "What about you, how did you get to know about Bad English?"

"Because of my Dad" said Gayle a little irritably. "He works for Sonic Media, an agent of most of the big record companies. He worked away a lot. Often went to America and he used to bring back advance tapes of all these cool bands that you never heard on UK radio, like Bad English and Skid Row and Warrant and Nelson and Damn Yankees and Poison and Alice Cooper and....."

Gayle stopped because Clive was nodding and smiling at her. "What? Are you making fun of me?"

"No!" said Clive. "I *love* all those bands. It's like you've just read through my record collection..... Just one thing though – Alice Cooper *isn't* a band, he's actually a *man*!"

Gayle smiled at him.

"I *know*!"

Whilst still smiling, she added:

"Of course, I *love* Take That as well. I mean, come on, *everyone* does, don't they?"

Clive was just about to say "NO!" as angrily as he could until he noticed Gayle was still grinning and looking beyond him, out of the window. She was clearly joking with him. She was pretty funnily.

Gayle frowned a little before looking back at Clive and saying:

"My Dad *wasn't* cool though, he was a complete *knob*. He cheated on my Mum and then left us both. I haven't seen or heard from him in months. At least he showed me the music that not a lot of people knew about. He left something that I could have that was *just mine*."

Her last words were followed by complete silence and the atmosphere in the room felt a little tense as Gayle again stared past Clive and out of the window.

"He does sound like a knob" said Clive after a while. "Just to be clear though, that music isn't yours, it's *mine*!"

Gayle looked back at him and mirrored the large smile that Clive was wearing. She gently pushed him in the chest before saying,

"Maybe we can share it?"

Clive kept smiling as he nodded his approval.

"Can I ask you something?" said Gayle. "There's something that I need to clear up."

Clive nodded a little suspiciously,

"….ok, then."

"Why do you draw pictures of *cocks* everywhere?"

Clive opened his eyes wide taken completely by surprise.

"I don't draw cocks..... *anywhere!*" he said defensively, feeling his face heating up faster than an angry *Yosemite Sam*.

"Yes you do." said Gayle "The first day I joined your class, you were drawing a big one on the window, just over there!"

Clive frowned as he thought about it.

"I was not!" he said, again defensively. After thinking for a while he added. "I may have been drawing a *rocket*?"

He reached into his school bag and removed his maths book, flicking to the last but one page on which he had drawn a more detailed rocket during another of Pervy Jackson's ridiculously boring lessons.

"Did it look like this?" he asked.

"Yes!" said Gayle laughing out loud. "There's another one you've drawn!"

"It's clearly a rocket!" said Clive as he stared at it, now realising that he probably shouldn't have gone for the pink and purple colour scheme.

"Damn" he added, now laughing along himself. "I knew I should have coloured it green."

After a good twenty seconds of laughing together, Gayle calmed down and said,

"I take it art isn't your *thing* then?"

"What?" said Clive in amazement. "You do know that's my art portfolio displayed in the corridor near the library don't you? I am the North West High School Artist of the Year this year! So, apart from penis-looking rockets, then art is actually *very much* my *thing*!"

"Oh my God" said Gayle. "All those paintings are yours? Wow, you're *really good.* You could probably make a good living out of doing art!..... Especially if there's a market for penis portraits!"

They both laughed at each other.

"Ok, can I ask you a question now?" said Clive.

Gayle smiled, looking like she was really enjoying herself. "Of course, *bring it on!*"

"What's with the big poodle..... the big, permed hair thing? Isn't it a bit 1980's Kylie Minogue-ish?"

Gayle sighed.

"It's my Mums fault. I wanted to try something different and she talked me into having *this* done. I feel like Cher sometimes! And there's no taming it, I've tried all sorts. I'm thinking the only thing I can do is chop it off and start again. What do you think?"

"No!" said Clive straight away. "I actually think it suits you. It's different to everyone else. It's unique..... it's feisty."

Gayle smiled.

"Are you flirting with me?" she asked cheekily.

As Clive's cheeks reddened once more, Gayle could also feel a little hot flush of her own coming on. They looked into each other's eyes for a few seconds before Gayle said.

"So that makes *me* cool then doesn't it? If I've got a look that's different to everyone else but I don't care because it's just the way I *want* to look?"

"No way" said Clive straight away. "You've just admitted that you look the way you do because you *Mum* told you to do it – that makes you the biggest geek in the school!"

They both laughed at each other again.

"Can I listen to Bad English for a few minutes please?" asked Gayle when they had both stopped laughing.

Clive had never let anyone listen to his walkman before, it was one of those "rules" that he had. Kind of like when your Dad buys a newspaper but won't let anyone as much as look at it before he has read every last word of it.

"Yeah sure" said Clive, finding that his lips had taken over from his brain when it came to making important decisions. What were his lips after?

"Let's listen together!" said Gayle after Clive had passed her his walkman.

She leaned over and gently put one of the ear buds into Clive's right ear before putting the other one into her left ear. Their heads gently touched to ensure that both buds stayed in ok, and it felt nice.

As Gayle pressed play on the walkman she said, "I never knew it until now - but I quite like detentions."

TWELVE: *Love Is…*

Clive sat at the small desk that had nothing more than an old fashioned telephone on it of the, seemingly, hastily put together "office" that was the head quarters of the Deanwater Way branch of *Love Is…*, "a brand new enterprise that will revolutionise and give new life to relationships in this country." (According to the words of the poster he was reading anyway.) He had hung his wet coat on the back of his chair and was now wondering if there was an actual medically acknowledged length of time for which sitting in wet trousers would guarantee the onset of piles.

Clive looked around and focussed on the numerous posters that hung on each of the four walls in a large room that was brightly lit by the two large front windows and the small sky light up on the ceiling. He had followed a man with a broad Brummie twang named Jason, who had been wearing the sandwich board advert for *Love Is…*, to this small, (albeit alarmingly bigger inside than it looked from outside) former shop down one of the tight alley ways off the main precinct. Clive had never been down here before and, quite frankly, didn't even know that this part of the shopping centre even existed. After a brief chat in the pouring rain, Jason had encouraged Clive to come and meet his boss, Jeremy, for a discussion about how *Love Is…* could help to find those lost feelings of love between him and Gayle. It had taken both Clive and Jason's combined efforts to get in through the "shop" door that could only be best be described as "a little stiff" and in need of "a drop or two of oil".

Clive had been sitting here for about five minutes now after Jason had gone into what he described as the "back office" to see "if Jeremy was available right now."

As he continued looking at the various posters on the walls, most of which wore a slogan describing exactly what "Love Is", Clive began to feel uncomfortable. Not just because this "office" used to be a *One Quid Bakery* store and the smell of stale cheese and onion pasties was overwhelming and really quite nauseating, but because he couldn't help but ask himself: were things not a bit *late* now between him and Gayle for him to be doing something as radical as this? Coming into the office of a business he had never heard of and thinking that they may somehow be able to miraculously wave a magic wand across his and Gayle's relationship; a relationship that had been breaking down for well over a decade, and fix it - just like that? The more he thought about it, the more ridiculous it sounded; and even more *American* than the idea of going to counselling all of those years ago. Maybe he should just get up and leave before this Jeremy arrived? He was almost certain that the main reason he was here anyway was the advertised "money back guarantee if we are unsuccessful".

God he was a sucker for money back guarantees, most of which were not anything of the sort anyway and were offset by confusing, lengthy small print that would have been much clearer if it had just stated:

Money Back Guarantee*

* - Under no circumstances is there <u>any</u> <u>way</u> in which you will <u>ever</u> get <u>any</u> of your money back.

Before Clive got the chance to further explore the possibility of skedaddling (a perfectly functional word that is grossly underused these days) the door behind him opened and a tall, thin man with a neatly-trimmed handle-bar moustache entered the "office" area. He walked slowly across the room looking like he was trying to minimise the squelching noise that his, clearly soaking-wet, shoes were making on the concrete floor. He smiled at Clive as he walked around the small desk and sat on the seat opposite him, his, also unmistakably saturated, trousers connecting with his chair making the sound of a wet towel being dropped onto a tiled floor.

He was wearing a yellow and red vertically striped shirt and a bright green bow tie; a clear *trying-too-hard-to-be-quirky* fashion statement that seems to be popular with a certain faction of society lately (you know, odd balls). Judging by the large name badge he was wearing that detailed: *Jeremy Corden. CEO. Love Is...*, Clive assumed that this was, indeed, the aforementioned Jeremy. Although he did share more than a passing resemblance to Jason who, as yet, had not re-appeared from the "back office area". (That may or may not actually be just a kitchen area that still had large industrial ovens that were once used to bake highly-saturated, luke-warm savoury snacks.)

"It's Clive, isn't it?" asked Jeremy in a thick, Australian accent as he reached a hand over the desk for shaking. "Sorry for the delay mate, I've been stuck in the office all morning on the blower, people trying to arrange appointments. You know how it is when you're busy, don't you?"

Clive smiled and nodded his head whilst coming to the conclusion that something didn't quite add up. Why would someone who had been "stuck in the office all morning" be as soaked as Clive was himself – someone who had been "stuck in the rain all morning"? And why did Jeremy, despite the fact he had a very distinctive moustache and spoke in a different accent, appear to be very, very, very, very, very (I think that's enough verys') similar looking to Jason?

"Jason tells me you want to discuss the possibility of us taking your case on?" said Jeremy in a kind of statement / question way and putting the sort of over-Australian emphasis on the word Jason that would make you think it must be spelt: *Jaiiii-sun*.

"Erm yeah. I just saw the advert that..... *Jason?*..... was carrying and thought it might be worth a go."

Jeremy nodded his head.

"This is what we do" he said, his arms stretched out wide to bring attention to all the different posters on the wall.

Clive took a few seconds to look around the room again and read some of the different slogans that he was being presented with.

Love is a Football Field.

Love can be your Best Friend and your Worst Enemy.

Love is like Oxygen.

Love is the Perfect View from the top of the Highest Mountain.

Any 3 Pasties or Sausage Rolls for £1. (Clive assumed this was a relic of the *One Quid Bakery* days, well certainly hoped it was anyway – otherwise it was a pretty strange love slogan. Mmm, 3 pasties or sausage rolls for £1 – even though they would make you feel sick as a dog, you would be powerless *not* to eat them all at once.)

Love Makes The World Go Around.

Love is like a Butterfly.

He stopped at one particular poster and felt like he had to ask Jeremy about it.

"*Love is like an old Boiler*? That's not particularly..... *poetic*?"

Jeremy smiled.

"That is one of my favourites, and is actually one of my own sayings; a real analogy that really fits. Old boilers are the best in the world, much better than the flaky, plastically modern ones you get now. But when they break down, they can be really smelly, and you start to wonder if they are past their best, maybe even obsolete, better off being replaced. But those babies were *really* meant to *last* and don't have much that can go wrong with them. When they do, it's usually something simple like the pilot light just needs re-lighting. And when it is re-lit then the boiler fires again, as good as new, and *rages* just like it used to – much *stronger* and *hotter* than any of these new ones can ever hope to."

He smiled as he spoke, his energy and enthusiasm really shining through, despite that rather large moustache that dominated most of his face.

"Is your relationship going down the dunny? Because maybe you just need someone to help *relight* the pilot light for you?"

"Yeah it is..... kind of has been for a long time....." began Clive, before noticing that Jeremy's handlebar moustache had begun to slump near the right side of his mouth. It was clearly a stick-on facial hair accessory.

"Ok, where were we?" said Jeremy, noticing that Clive had stopped talking mid-sentence. "Oh, before we go on, can I get you a drink of something? I know I've got a mouth like the bottom of a cocky's cage!"

Clive didn't say a word and instead just stared at Jeremy as his moustache was, very slowly, peeling away from his face like wallpaper from a wall that hadn't had enough paste applied. (Yep, memories from Clive's attempted decorating in the past.)

"Are you ok mate?" asked Jeremy after several more awkward, silent seconds.

"Erm, your moustache is coming off!" said Clive.

"Oh shit!" said Jeremy, instinctively reaching up and reattaching it to his face.

He spent the next minute or so stroking it firmly against his face trying desperately to re-attach it, whilst looking like a demented Bond villain. When he was finally happy that it was back looking as it should, Jeremy began to talk again, only this time in a brummie accent.

"As you can see it isn't real – it's something I bought when my attempt at joining in for movember got so bloody itchy....."

He stopped talking as he, again, felt the discomfort of Clive staring at him with complete incredulity. And then the penny dropped.

"I changed my accent again, didn't I?" he said in a, now, rather plain Cheshire accent.

Clive nodded his head.

"Shit! Look I am sorry. As you may or may not have guessed there is no Jason as well..... yep, that was me out in the rain carrying the advert around....."

Clive sat back in his seat feeling completely bemused but also a little satisfied. He had never had the ability to work out what was going on in classic TV crime mysteries, like *Sherlock Holmes* or *Poirot* or..... *Bergerac?*; and the board game *Cluedo* had been completely beyond him but, on this day, he had spotted what was going on right from the start. As was appropriate, he adopted a very *Angela-Lansbury-Murder-She-Wrote*-esque smug grin and contentedly leaned back in his chair.

Jeremy (if that was his *real* name) slowly removed the fake moustache as he continued talking.

"Business really hasn't been that great and so I haven't had chance to employ any staff yet. I thought by making it look like there was more than one person here, it would make everything appear a bit more *professional*..... I suppose I'm not really giving that image off am I?"

Clive slowly shook his head whilst wondering whether he was now ready to re-visit some of those crime TV shows or maybe even fish *Cluedo* out of the loft. He could possibly give Gayle a good run for her money if he could keep up this kind of detecting level.

"Sorry, I just got carried away." Jeremy carried on. "When I was younger I used to go to parties and speak in a different accent for every different person I spoke to. It was great fun at the end of the night, after a few drinks, trying to remember which accent I'd used for each person, it was my little way of entertaining myself..... haven't actually been invited to any parties for quite some time now....."

Clive began to revisit the idea of just leaving; he wouldn't even have to sneak out now, surely Jeremy would have to understand completely someone deciding to get up and head for the door given the circumstances.

"Look, I wouldn't blame you for walking out right now, God knows what's going through your mind, but let me just say this: I am really passionate about what I'm trying to do here, *really passionate about love*. I also arrange meetings between people, the *cupid branch* of the business I like to call it, but I really like to concentrate on this side of things. Situations like you're in, because I hate to see so many people throwing love away, just because they don't understand it properly. *So many* couples let *true love* get lost *forever*. If you and your..... wife? girlfriend?..... boyfriend?"

"WIFE!" said Clive quickly and with conviction.

71

"If you and your wife were genuinely, truly, absolutely, beautifully, wonderfully, *magnificently* in love, then I will find it again for you..... I *guarantee* that!"

Clive couldn't help but be intrigued by the enthusiasm and passion that Jeremy seemed to have. But, even though he wanted to believe what he was saying was possible, it was hard to accept that Jeremy would actually have any clue how to do it. Can you really believe a man who speaks in multiple accents and wears a fake moustache?

"Thank you for your time." Clive began, slowly standing. "I think I'm going to go home and think about it. I know where you are if I decide to go ahead with anything."

He stood up and began walking towards the door.

THIRTEEN: *It's All About Time.*

Jeremy remained seated as Clive walked away from the desk, a massive, almost cunning, smile growing on his face.

"*Time!*" he said loudly, before Clive had chance to reach out and wrestle with the door.

"You've hit the nail on the head!"

Clive didn't say anything but instead turned around and looked at Jeremy, frowning in confusion.

"Let me let you in on a couple of secrets, in case you didn't know them already. There are only two *currencies* in life that actually mean *anything*; that are actually *real*. They are *love* and, like you said, <u>*time*</u>. If you find love; *real love,* then you're one of the lucky ones and you need to do *everything* you can to hold onto it. But even love is nothing *without time.*"

Jeremy's grin seemed to grow even wider as he paused briefly before continuing.

"Do you know what? How often do you hear people saying things like: "where has all the time gone", or "doesn't time fly by", or even "isn't time dragging"? Well that's all just a *myth*. *Time is time*. A minute is exactly a minute, like it always has been and always will be. The trick is to not let it slip away from you. Always live in the *moment*. Nobody knows how much time they actually have – don't waste it by *thinking* about doing things; *just do them*! I used to do a bit of poetry when I was younger, what was the thing I did about time.....?"

As Jeremy wracked his memory, Clive walked back to his seat and began reminiscing himself.

"Gayle used to do a lot of poetry type stuff." He said out loud. "She was *really* good at it."

"It was something like this," said Jeremy, catching Clive's eye.

"Focus yourself somehow,
On only the here and now,
It's just the things in reach, you can touch and feel,
Yesterday is gone,
And tomorrow's yet to come,
Today's all that matters, only now is real."

Jeremy squelched around a bit in his chair.

"It was something like that anyway. Probably still a work in progress really."

Clive knew what it meant though and he agreed totally. Now was now; and now was the time to act. And this was why he had come in here, wasn't it? To give it a go? Sure, even though the last minute or so had shown that Jeremy maybe wasn't a *complete* buffoon, the jury was still pretty much out about him. But he wasn't going to walk away now and give up, *again*, without giving it a chance.

"Ok, what do we do?" asked Clive.

Jeremy smiled.

"A simple test, I'll just ask you seven questions, you answer as truthfully and in as much depth as you can. I will need to do the same for your wife, and then I will organise a bespoke range of handpicked activities for you to do together and, by the end of it, you will have those feelings of love reawakened."

As Clive sat there thinking, Jeremy pulled a diary out from a drawer on his side of the desk, opened it up, and moved to close the deal.

"If you can do it *this weekend*, I'll do it for a bargain..... 50% off the normal price!"

Damn it. Now there was a *bargain* being wafted in front of Clive's face; how the hell could he say no to that? He composed himself.

"I'm still not totally sure how it all works." he said.

"Ok," said Jeremy, shuffling and squelching in his chair. "Here's something pretty basic. Love affects *everything* around us. It surrounds us and penetrates us. It binds the galaxy together..... sorry if that sounds a bit Star Wars-y."

It sounded *Star Wars-y* because it was part of a quote *straight from Star Wars*, albeit it substituting the *Force* with *Love,* but it was enough for Clive; Jeremy could have stopped talking right then and he would have done the deal. Instead Jeremy continued.

"Love changes the way you look and feel about even the most normal, everyday things. And then these things can take you to other places and other times and stir *other* feelings and re-awaken memories.

Tastes, smells, sounds, sights..... anything and *everything*. Here we go, do you have a *song* that, whenever it is played, stirs memories or feelings about your wife and your relationship?"

Clive didn't have to think hard.

"Yeah, there's a song by a band from the late 80's, early 90's, *Bad English* called "When I See You Smile", it always make me think of how Gayle's happiness, back in the day, made me feel .... kind of special..... just to see her smile was..... kind of special."

"There you go then!" said Jeremy smiling. "It's *exactly* that type of thing. It's the same for me and my wife – only *our* song is "Smack My Bitch Up" by the *Prodigy*."

He sat there smiling, lost in his moment, before, once more, realising that Clive was staring at him in bewilderment.

"We actually *met* at a *Prodigy* concert – our eyes connected during that song. So that song, for me, always brings back *that* moment, *that* feeling, *that..... initial spark.....* you know, rather than any memories of me actually, you know, smacking *my* bitch up!"

Clive nodded along; as he did the look on his face didn't change one bit.

Jeremy decided to push things along.

"Ok. For some people love is like a jigsaw and it's about putting all those pieces, that have got mixed up over time, back together. For others it could be all about re-connecting with *one* specific element, or even moment, that could be classed as their *happily ever after* moment. For some, it's a combination of both. And it's up to me to find out how it would best work for you and your wife."

Clive nodded slowly as Jeremy continued to talk, becoming more and more passionate as he did.

"So it's about helping you to look beyond any changes that have happened to deflect those original feelings of love, and re-focus on things that made the love special in the first place. And it's just seven questions from me to find out all of those types of special *moments* and *memories* and *feelings* and..... *everything* else that makes up what is universally known as *true love*."

"What sort of *questions*?" asked Clive, his cautious nature again overruling his desire to be a seize-the-moment type person.

"Ok" said Jeremy. "This is *one* of the seven that I ask: Do you remember where and when it was that you and your..... you said *wife*, didn't you and not....."

"YES!" snapped Clive before Jeremy could suggest that he may have a boyfriend again.

"Do you remember where and when you and your wife first kissed? You know *properly* kissed?"

A slow smile grew on Clive's face as his mind took him back in time and to a different place.

"Yes." He said. "Yes I do. I'll never forget it. It was a Tuesday night and we were at the school youth club. It was the disco room. They used to play lots of cheesy 80's pop songs but also the odd chart rock song that me and Gayle liked. We were sitting against the wall on the stage and weirdly when we did kiss it was whilst that *Crash Test Dummies* song *Mmm, Mmm, Mmm, Mmm,* was playing. It wasn't a particularly favourite song of ours; it was pretty weird if we're being honest. But it was something I'll never forget. Gayle lips were so soft and just tasted like ....."

Clive realised that his reminiscing mind had let his lips start talking about things he wasn't sure he was ready to authorise.

Jeremy smiled.

"It's *that* type of thing that I'm looking for. We'd probably need to go into more depth; details about the venue and how you felt etc, but the fact that you remember *that* moment so fondly is a pretty good start. So what do you think? If you're in, and you can do *this weekend*, I will do it for the price of just £250."

Clive didn't say anything because he had no idea how much something like this was going to cost; was this the bargain Jeremy had promised or not? He moved his lips to say something but then thought better of it and stopped himself before the words could escape.

"What is it?" asked Jeremy straight away.

Clive took a deep breath and tried to articulate what he was thinking.

"Look, me and Gayle were..... *very young* when we first got together. I sometimes wonder if..... we were maybe *too young* to know what *real love* was. Or *is*. Or..... do you know what I mean?"

Jeremy smiled slowly.

"Some people do *mistake* what real love is. But let me guarantee you this: as long as it wasn't just a crush or lust or infatuation that made you get together; and it was something that you felt here, in your heart, and to the depths of your soul; then it was *real love*. It doesn't matter how young you are, or how old you are; *real love* is *real love*."

Clive smiled back and nodded.

Jeremy continued.

"From what you've told me so far, *I'm* in no doubt that it *was real*. And you're *here* aren't you? Telling a complete stranger all about your relationship and asking for help. That says something doesn't it? Let's cut to the chase: If you do this, I *guarantee* you will be *completely* in love with each other again by Sunday night..... or you can have *all your money back*. What is £250 and one weekend of your life in exchange for being in love, with the love of your life, *all over again*?"

Suddenly everything made sense. £250 was nothing if it meant him and Gayle feeling exactly like they used to. In fact, *all the money in the world* would be nothing. Clive reached into his pocket for his wallet.....

FOURTEEN: *Late Is The Hour.*

Gayle stood by the kettle as the pitch of the rumbling water inside got slowly higher. She *needed* a cup of coffee. One of the other things about setting off late for work in the morning and having to sit through the rush hour was feeling like you had to work later into the evening to make up for the lateness, and then having to sit through the rush hour with the rush hour morons all over again when coming home. Thankfully this evening she had made it back without wanting to kill anyone.

As she waited, staring at the wall, a movement up near the very corner of the wall and ceiling made her jump and squeal a little. *There was a spider.* Before she could instinctively call for Clive, she realised that it actually wasn't a spider but rather a daddy longs legs. Thankfully there'd be no need for Clive to use his "spider catching kit" of plastic beaker and Indian takeaway menu and humanely show it out of the back door, because daddy long legs were something Gayle could take care of herself.

Why is it that no one has any of the same kind of raw fear towards daddy long legs' as they do for spiders? Because, basically, daddy long legs' are pretty much spiders with wings.

Flying spiders.

Spiders that have a whole extra dimension in which to terrify you. And yet, they're not scary in the slightest. Very odd. Maybe, for Gayle, the reason for this was that she remembered daddy long legs quite clearly from junior school and, in particular, Phil Tipman who used to take great pleasure in catching them and pulling their legs off one by one. Nothing seems that scary when a laughing nine year old boy easily catches and sadistically dismembers it. What does that tell you about a persons' mental conditioning? Someone who takes great delight in doing such

78

cruel and brutal things? Gayle wondered what Phil Tipman was doing now? Surely he was in prison for committing the type of outrageous offences that you see on those Channel 5 shock-crime programs? Or maybe he was a politician?

As Gayle watched the daddy long legs haphazardly fly around, bumping into the wall and ceiling (it would seem that no flying lessons or test are required to be a daddy long legs) her eyes were drawn over towards the fridge. She began to scan the numerous "important" items that had been attached to the door with magnets. (The majority of which fell off, and needed replacing, every time anyone opened and closed the fridge.) There was a voucher for "bonus" nectar points "for your next shop" that she now realised was six weeks out of date and could be thrown away – obviously not now but whenever she had time to do it. Next to it was a scary looking green appointment card that informed her that she had an appointment in two weeks time with the dental hygienist. She shuddered as she recalled the last appointment, or rather "ordeal", with the hygienist – a harrowingly painful event that she wouldn't wish on her worst enemy. Surely the government would be best strapping any terror suspect who refused to talk to a dentist's chair and letting a hygienist give them a good clean and floss session – without a doubt they would tell them anything they wanted to know after that. What type of person *chooses* to study and train to become a dental hygienist, and inflict that kind of *legal torture* on people? Gayle was sure that those people could have a Channel 5 program of their very own. Maybe Phil Tipman was now a dental hygienist? It was ok, she reassured herself, there was plenty of time to *cancel* that appointment yet.

Next she noticed the car insurance reminder letter attached to the fridge but quickly closed her eyes and tried to think of anything else. She didn't want to allow thinking about car insurance to stir up perhaps her worst memory of all time. Instead she revisited her thoughts and realisations from earlier in the car when she had used the time stuck in traffic to *not* think about murdering anyone but rather the "date" she had arranged with Lee. Because what that also meant was the acknowledgement that her life was going to be moving on and therefore the beginning of the acceptance that things were *really* over between her and Clive.

Before this point, this was just something that was going to happen "one day", but now it felt different. It felt *real* and that made Gayle feel anxious and somewhat regretful. As such she was feeling mentally exhausted and really in need of that nice cup of coffee. If she wasn't so worn out she would have taken the extra few seconds needed to use the expensive espresso machine she had recently bought but not used that much; but the "specially selected" Colombian roast instant from Aldi would be quite adequate. She'd long given up on her "no caffeine after 6p.m." rule that was implemented to try and help her sleep better, seeing as it'd had no apparent effect on her sleeping success rate. She just had to accept that, these days, her chances of sleeping soundly all the way through the night were pretty slim. No matter what she tried before she went to bed; whether it be hot milk, Ovaltine, or even a mug full of rohypnol, she still couldn't sleep, so therefore there was no harm in having coffee at any time.

She poured the boiling water into the cup and wearily walked the three steps to the fridge to get the milk. She opened the door inevitably knocking off all the things held on by the magnets and, as the cool air gently caressed her face, she stared inside like a moth mesmerised by the bright light at the back of the top shelf. After several seconds of numb staring she realised that something was wrong: there was *no milk* in there. She snapped out of her almost trance-like state and walked over to the bread bin and removed the lid. It was empty: there was *no bread.*

"CLIIIIIIVVVE!" she shouted at the top of her voice.

Clive entered the kitchen holding the business card that he had been looking at when Gayle had arrived home. She'd assumed it was something that the estate agent had left behind in the morning and was going to ask him about it – *after* she'd made her coffee. It was weird that he was still looking at it.

"Where's the bread and milk?" she asked, her voice having calmed down to something close to its normal volume.

"Oh shit!" said Clive, confirming Gayle's worst fears that he hadn't got any.

"For God's sake!" she said. "I ask you to do one little thing but I suppose you were too busy getting pissed. Should've known you'd be unable to do more than *one thing*!"

Clive could see the disappointment on Gayle's face, a look he had caused way too often.

"God, I can smell the booze on you from here. Could you not have just taken *five minutes* to get some bread and milk? We've got *none* of either..... what am I going to put on Jacks cornflakes in the morning?"

Gayle processed the words she had just spoken and tears began to swell from her eyes immediately. She wouldn't be making Jack his breakfast the next morning, or any other morning, because he was no longer there.

It made her feel so alone.

She reached for the kitchen surface as she arched her head and shoulders forward as if unable to hold them up anymore. She couldn't, and didn't want to, stop the tears from flowing and the loud sobbing that accompanied them.

"I can't believe he's gone!" she tried to say through her heavy breathing and blubbering.

Clive stepped across to her and put his arms around her. He wanted to say something but couldn't find the words he needed. Gayle carried on crying and kept her left arm down by her side; she certainly didn't want to hold Clive back. She had defended him once more today, but why? He had, again, put his own interests before doing the one small thing that she had asked of him. It crossed her mind to tell him about the date she had arranged with Lee; to let him know that she was moving on with her life. She didn't though; instead she couldn't help her mind reverting back to its original thought: Jack had gone. Her baby was all grown up and he had flown the nest.

Clive held his arms around Gayle as her body shuddered in mini crying spasms. He couldn't blame her for not wanting to hold him back. As he looked down towards the floor he noticed Gayle's left hand and could see that she wasn't wearing her rings. He didn't say anything but, if he hadn't realised before, he certainly knew now that, as per those sandwich board messages he was thinking about earlier, *the end is nigh.*

Yep, late is the hour.

He couldn't stop that part of a quote from *Lord of the Rings* forming into its full sentence in his mind: *Late is the hour in which this conjurer chooses to appear.* But it made him realise something. Much like it was when Gandalf did appear in *The Two Towers*, the current situation appeared hopeless, and yet all was *not* lost. Gandalf was able to rescue the situation and Clive's visit with Jeremy at *Love Is...* was his attempt to do the same.

Clive grabbed hold of Gayle's, ring-less, hand.

"Come with me" he said, before leading her, reluctantly, into the front room. "Sit down."

She sat on the sofa, still crying, and looked at Clive who stood in front of her looking like he was desperately thinking of how to say something.

"I *haven't* been drinking today." He said finally, after kneeling in front of her and looking into her eyes.

"*Knobhead* let me down..... *again*; like he always does. In fact, apart from Sue, the only person who has never let me down is *you*. But I've let you down. Time and time and time again. I've let us *both* down. I didn't fight for you; *for us*, when I needed to. If I had, then things wouldn't have got to this. I never faced the fact that things were really ever going to get to this point. I always thought that things would be ok; that they would just sort themselves out. I always looked away instead of facing things the way I should have. This is all *my fault.*"

As he blinked his eye lids quickly, unable to stop the escaping of liquid from his own eyes, Gayle took a deep breath. Was it really *all* Clive's fault? Could she really let him take *all* the blame?

"I forgot the bread and milk because I got side tracked" Clive continued. "You are right; I can't focus on more than one thing at once."

Clive wondered whether he should tell Gayle that, before he was side tracked by Jeremy, he had planned to buy her some flowers. This would make her happier, wouldn't it? Seeing as it's the *thought that counts*? Of course he decided not to tell her. *No one* believes any of that "it's the thought that counts*"* shit!

Instead, he passed the card that he was holding over to Gayle. She wiped her eyes and focussed on the writing at the top. *LOVE IS ... RELATIONSHIP SPECIALISTS.*

"That's where I've been today. That's why I forgot the bread and milk. I met a..... fairly *strange* man named Jeremy who says he can "re-find" our love for us. I know late is the hour but I want us to try and do this. I don't know if it's *too* late but this is my way of trying to fight for you; to fight for *us.*"

For the next half an hour Clive told Gayle all about Jeremy (and his weird dressing up, impersonating other people and fake accents) and *Love Is...* and the deal he had made for the upcoming weekend. More than anything in the world he wanted them to *try* this. Gayle was completely taken by surprise by it all and, although she did feel that it was too little, (much) too late, she agreed that one weekend of their time was not too much to give up after all their years together and all the things they had gone through.

Clive then went out for the bread and milk he'd forgotten earlier and headed off to bed for an early night. He had to be up for work at 4.30 a.m. and said he wanted to be fresh for the busy weekend that they both now had ahead of them. Gayle spent what remained of the evening wondering what she had let herself in for. For starters she had the "pleasure" of an early morning visit from the, very strange, Jeremy that Clive had described to her in worrying detail. She had no idea what this "Love is" interview, and the weekend as a whole, would have in store but, the more she thought about it, the more she was apprehensive. It felt like nothing more than a gimmick; an easy way for this Jeremy to make money rather than a real solution for rescuing doomed relationships. And the more she thought, the more Gayle felt pretty low about it; and pretty low about life in general.

Around 11 p.m. she decided she would have one more cup of coffee, which would definitely be enough to make her think about the history of her full life instead of sleeping, before heading for bed herself. She also knew that, while she drank it, she wouldn't be able to stop herself thinking about some of the other "low points" that she'd experienced over the last few years.

FIFTEEN: *Thanks, But No Thanks!* (16 Years Ago)

Clive let out a deep sigh as he put the letter he had been staring at for the last five minutes on top of the other letters in the small shoe box on the coffee table. He put the shoe box lid on and closed his eyes. Come on, he thought, *out of sight, out of mind.*

It was a rejection letter advising that his art scholarship grant application to the Open Art Foundation had "regretfully" been "rejected". He had been "thanked" for sending in his work (the new art portfolio he had slaved over for the best part of a year, most afternoons whilst Gayle had been at work) and was "wished every success in the future". It represented the final response of the twenty four letters he had sent out to education councils, design firms and animation studios, that he hoped would open a door into a new world for him. The other twenty three responses were already in the shoe box and offered much the same "thanks, but no thanks" kind of sentiments.

He looked over at Jack who was still sleeping on the sofa, his red blanket covering everything but his face and keeping him snug and warm. He had been somewhat under the weather for a few days now. Assured by the doctor that it was nothing more than a seasonal virus ("a lot of it going around" apparently) Jack had slipped into a routine of sleepless nights and daily snoozes on the sofa, punctuated by doses of strawberry paracetamol and orange ibuprofen, as often as the dosage instructions allowed.

He looked so peaceful, comfortable and settled; unlike Clive who felt so anxious, troubled and so empty. He had always been of the belief that you have never, ever *failed* anything until you *give up*; until then you are still just *trying*. But he felt like he had tried to chase this "art dream" of his for long enough. It felt like it had passed him by; like it was nothing more than a fragile dream that had now been shattered into a million pieces. It felt like it was time to admit defeat and give up.

Clive picked up the shoe box and took it into the kitchen. He put it back into the tall cupboard, on the shelf above the potatoes, where Gayle couldn't see it. He had kept the fact that he was creating and submitting work hidden from her; probably for *two* reasons.

One, he wanted to be able to surprise her when he got his big break – she would be so proud of him.

And two, he didn't want her to have to see any rejections that he received – he didn't want her to see him failing again and again.

Clive walked back into the living room and sat down gently on the edge of the sofa by Jack. He reached out and tenderly placed his hand on his little boys' forehead while at the same time checking his watch. His temperature felt ok at the moment and, if he did wake up soon feeling unwell, then it had been over four hours since his last dose of medicine.

He smiled as he gazed at Jacks angelic face. At least there was one thing that was going right in his and Gayle's life. They had a beautiful little boy and were able to provide a roof over his head, and food in his mouth; and medicine when he needed it. And that little boy had a Mum and Dad who loved him more than anything in the world, and would do *anything* for him.

Clive looked out of the window and checked his watch again, which funnily enough told him the same time as it had two seconds ago. Where was Gayle? He had been expecting her back well before now. He just hoped that she would be bringing better news with her.

Just as he thought about this he heard a key in the front door. He instinctively looked up and saw the car was actually outside on the road; he just hadn't seen it pull up from where he had been sitting on the sofa. Gayle was home.

Clive stood in the middle of the room feeling even more anxious than he had before. He could hear his wife closing the front door and then hanging her coat up and removing her shoes; but it was all happening much more slowly than it usually did. Finally the living room door opened and Gayle walked in.

Clive didn't need to ask. Her face was red and blotchy and her hair was slightly sticking out of the neat up-do that she'd taken so long over "getting right" in the morning.

"How is he?" she said, walking over to Jack and, now, placing her hand on his forehead.

"He's ok." Said Clive. "He's been asleep for a good hour and a half or so."

Gayle gently stroked Jacks cheek for a few seconds before tucking his blanket even further under him around the edges.

She took a deep breath before standing up and looking at Clive for the first time since she had entered the room.

"The job wasn't even for a *label liaison*; it was just a secretary role." She said, her voice quiet and quivery "Answering the phone, typing, filing, getting tea and coffee..... and the *best bit*? They said I wasn't *qualified* enough for it!"

She couldn't hold her eye contact with Clive as more tears began to form, and she started to stare out of the window as she continued her hushed talking.

"And there was no sign of *Daddy Dearest* not *before* the interview anyway. He was there after though, oh yeah. He was there to make sure that he told me that he had never been more *embarrassed* by me. Apparently he didn't know I didn't have Maths and English GCSE's. If he did then he would never have got the interview for me. He said I should just stick to what I'm best at..... *having a baby*. He never even *asked* about Jack ..... or you! He just made me feel about one centimetre tall and then left....."

She continued to stare out of the window, the tears now streaming as fast as they had been when she had been driving home. She was not sure what she was *most* upset about. It could be that she had allowed herself to believe that maybe she did have a shot at landing a job that was somewhere close to her dream, or it could just as easily be the final words that her father had said to her; the words that she didn't want to repeat to Clive.

"You should just be thankful that you've got a job, because I have no idea how you ever actually got it. I suppose you must have worn a short skirt and flashed your eyelashes a lot!"

She was pretty sure that not every girl in the world was lucky enough to have her own father make her feel almost like a prostitute.

"I wish you'd never talked me into contacting him" said Gayle, weakly through her tears. "I never want to see him again..... *not ever again.*"

Clive huffed a little.

He knew somehow Gayle would turn this into being *his* fault. He was only trying to help; offer some small chance of her going for something that she really wanted to do. For most people who end up in these dream jobs, they seem to get their foot on the ladder because of *who* they know rather that what they know. He thought that Gayle's Dad might be one of those "who you know" types for her; he had no idea that he would still be the same twat that Gayle had always described him as.

As he thought, Clive stared at his wife who was slowly shaking as she continued to stare out of the window, still sobbing. He had never seen her looking so fragile and so broken. He realised that he had no idea how to "fix" her; or even how to make her feel any better. He wanted to hold her tight and tell her everything would be alright, but couldn't help but think that she looked *so delicate* that he might break her even more. He had no idea how to even hold her properly anymore; something that had been the case ever since the incident with the loan shark.

Gayle looked out of the window, focussing on nothing in particular other than the water that she couldn't stop flowing into her eyes. Why wasn't Clive holding her? He used to be able to make everything feel like it would be ok just by holding her in his arms. She felt like she needed him more than ever, *right now*, so why was he just standing there, *doing nothing*? She took a deep breath. Even though her Dad had made her feel like she was nothing, at least she had *tried*. It was more than Clive ever did. He was *so* good at art and always spoke about trying to do something with it, but it was just talk: he had never got around to actually giving it a go.

Clive licked his dry lips and prepared himself to say something to try and make Gayle feel better. He needed to tell her that she didn't need to take any notice of her Dad; he was just a loser and had *always* been a loser. Any father who hadn't taken the time to have such a wonderful daughter in his life was just a complete tosser, and she never had to see him *ever again*. She didn't need him anyway. She had a family of her own. They had a beautiful baby boy and had provided a house and a home for him. It wasn't perfect, but the three of them had one another. And she had Clive, who would *always* be there for her, because it would *always* be *Me and You vs. the World*; just as they had promised each other.

These words that he needed to say all jumbled up in his mind and he couldn't put them in any kind of logical order to force them out of his mouth.

"I'll go and put the kettle on." was the best he could find right now. He would work on how best to say everything else later.

Clive walked off towards the kitchen, hoping that the kettle would take so long to boil that he may have come up with the answers to everything, or that all their problems would be forgotten about, by the time that it had.

Gayle continued staring out of the window.....

87

SIXTEEN: *The Academy.*

Clive's alarm began to sound, pulling him out of one of those dreams that he felt like he was enjoying but would probably never be able to precisely remember what it was about. He contented himself that it was probably about happier times; times that, unfortunately, seemed like they were long ago now. At least it wasn't one of those *other* types of dreams that he often had; ones that seemed to focus on him being in an aeroplane crash, wetting himself in front of lots of people, having all his teeth falling out or being in an exam that he was hideously unprepared for. What were *those* dreams all about? Although he accepted that dreams of under-revised exams could also be technically classed as "memories". (And, unfortunately, the "wetting himself" ones also.)

He reached for his phone and, although tempted to switch it to snooze (for the next three hours or so), turned the alarm off. Even after all these years of getting up at 4.30 a.m. Clive still found it difficult; especially on a Saturday. The only thing that had changed over time was that, instead of wanting to throw the clock radio alarm against the wall, he now wanted to throw his phone against the wall. But it was an expensive smart phone and the house insurance company would probably wheedle out of any claim expressing that somewhere in their (never ending) small print it says that they do not cover items damaged in a fit of early morning don't-want-to-get-up rage.

Clive slipped out of bed quietly and headed for the bathroom, contenting himself that at least next Saturday would be his day off for next week. The beauty of a rolling day off meant that every six weeks you had the reward of a three day "long weekend". Unfortunately this also meant that you looked forward to, focussed on, and almost obsessed about these long weekends so much that you spent the vast majority of your life just wishing time away. As usual, Clive cleaned his teeth and had a quick wash whilst staring at himself in the mirror cursing the fact that, instead of the manly Sean Connery-esque hairy chest that he always wished for as he grew up, the chest hair he'd been blessed with made him look like a skinny, badly-shaved chimp. After the morale sapping few minutes in the bathroom he returned to the bedroom to get dressed in the dark, as he always did; so not to disturb Gayle. It was something that required great care and a certain level of skill because making mistakes getting dressed could have pretty severe consequences at work. The time he arrived wearing odd shoes (one trainer and one steal toe-capped boot) was something that was "hilariously" brought up every day for about two and a half years. Luckily for Clive, this unfortunate event seemed to be forgotten instantly the day that Burkey turned up one morning wearing his shorts inside out. (Even the fact that the cleaning instructions label was at the front and sticking out like a small, white, rectangular penis hadn't alerted Burkey to his wardrobe malfunction.)

Once satisfied that he was dressed appropriately, Clive quietly walked towards the door, glancing at Gayle as he tip-toed across the room. She was sleeping peacefully so he continued his hushed footsteps and moved out onto the landing. It seemed like a lifetime ago that he would wake her with a kiss because she had insisted on being woken before he left; and she would hug him and send him off on his way with the warmth that came from being told "*I Love You!*"

Clive paused before going down stairs as he realised that he could do with popping into the toilet for a "number two". He quickly changed his mind and began to descend downstairs reasoning that he would go to the toilet when he got to work. Just how much more satisfying is it to have a shit when you know you're also getting paid for it?

Clive left the house, got in the car and told himself that he had between ten and fifteen minutes (depending on the mood of the traffic lights) to enjoy sitting down and listening to the radio before having to start another, pretty much groundhog, day working as a postman.

He had been a postman ever since leaving school. Gayle was heavily pregnant with Jack and Clive felt like he needed to get a job straight away to begin supporting them and so needed to take something that was realistically reachable. His true employment desire always involved doing something that linked into his talent for art but his thinking, back then, was to begin earning some money as soon as possible. He could always *look into* his dreams *sometime later on down the line.* (Which, for Clive, would turn out to mean the same as it did for most other people who approached things in a similar way: *Sometime later on down the line* = never actually getting around to it; while the very memory of it eats away at you constantly.)

Clive had actually been drawn to look into being a postman by the fact that he'd had a foster parent, Billy, for a couple of years around the age of ten who was, at the time, a postman and used to speak about the position in such glowing terms.

"Out in the fresh air. The sun on your face. Able to work at your own pace with no management breathing down your neck. Being paid for exercising. Finish work around mid-day, with the afternoon free to do whatever you wanted."

These were just a few of the things that Billy would regularly say about the "utopia" that was being a postman. Of course Billy had never elaborated, and Clive had never picked up, on *the small print*.

"Out in the fresh air"? Yep, for most of the time with the emphasis firmly on the word "fresh" when it's used in its function as meaning "bloody cold".

"Sun on your face". In England? Maybe for a hand full of days a year, if you were lucky. For the rest of the time you needed to be able to handle the freezing cold (you know, "fresh") snow, frost, wind and rain; lots and lots of rain. And with lots of rain comes the need to explain/apologise to people why the letter they were expecting is now the ball of paper-mache that you are trying to force through their letter box with numb fingers. (Whilst trying desperately not to let those numb fingers themselves be pushed through even a millimetre – in case they have a dog that decides to try and bite one or more of them off.)

"Being paid for exercise" was technically true and a real positive if your exercise of choice is to walk as fast as you can for around ten miles, often up and down stairs, carrying bags that were so heavy they should really only be lifted by a crane.

And yes, you did indeed "*finish* work around mid-day", with the "afternoon free" to do whatever you wanted, but this was only because you *started* work at a time that the rest of the civilised world refers to as *the middle of the night*. So that "doing whatever you wanted in the afternoon" invariably meant going back to bed because you were knackered from starting in the middle of the night and then walking for around ten miles, often up and down stairs, carrying bags that were so heavy they should only really be lifted by a crane.

But Billy had neglected to tell *this* side of things, instead focussing on the other aspects of the job. Was he ahead of his time and showing a remarkably positive "glass half full" attitude long before people decided that glasses *always* have to hold liquid at 50% of their capacity so you *have* to decide if it's half *full* or half *empty*? Why can't glasses be *completely full* or *completely empty*, or somewhere else that's not exactly *half*? Sorry got a little side tracked there.

Anyway, rather than being a pioneer of positive thinking, there was another explanation for the way that Billy looked at things, but we'll get to that in a minute.

Remaining with the postman job thing, another reason that Clive was really interested in becoming one was because of Billy's portrayal of: *The Academy*. Which apparently was a boot-camp style training facility that had to be successfully completed before you were ready to be accepted as a postman. (And this was described as a proper *army* style boot camp and not a chance for Simon Cowell and co. to show off their fancy houses during an X-Factor style one.) Clive had been assured by Billy that getting into Royal Mail was more difficult than getting into Fort Knox; and that the academy was an SAS style selection process where only the best of the best, and the toughest of the tough, made it through.

For example, there were daily "marches" during which you would have to carry mail bags, often containing three or four bundles of letters and up to five parcels, over rough terrain for miles and miles. Those who couldn't keep up could pack their suitcases. There were regular sessions with professional whistling coaches to hone your skills because, when assessment time came, if you couldn't perform a perfect whistled rendition of the intro to the The Scorpions' *Wind of Change* or Otis Readings' *(Sittin' On) The Dock of the Bay* then you would be sent home instantly. Every day there would be ever-more complicated walking gauntlets, designed with the toughest of council estate delivery in mind, in which you must avoid on-the-ground obstacles whilst being able to, at the same time, sort through your mail while a dozen people chased you demanding their giro. These were colloquially known at the academy as the *Dog Shit Slaloms* – you stand in one sloppy canine turd, a hypodermic needle or an empty can of special brew, and you're out of there. Billy also reminisced to Clive about the hours and hours spent in the classroom with language experts who drilled you endlessly making sure that you could clearly articulate the complicated *key phrases* as if they were second nature.

"Morning love!"
"Nice day for it!"
"Got a parcel for you!"
"Sign here please!"

"Would you be kind enough to ask your dog to remove its' jaws from my around my ankle, please?"

All these phrases needed to be at your beckon call, whilst all the while you needed to be calm and cool enough to smile through gritted teeth during the numerous times each day that people would say to you "If you've got any bills you can take them back with you!"

And then, if you made it through all of that, there was, what Billy described as, "the most important part of the training", which was apparently "the part that more cadets fail at than any other": *The Sprinting Test.*

Day after day after day after day of running as fast as you possibly could and, even then, only the fastest few were selected to face – *the dogs*. At first you were given padded, protective clothing as you try to outrun these crazy dogs that, just like those in the "mean outside world", have evolved to, mystifyingly, despise the postman even more than they despise cats. At first the dogs *always* catch you and frenziedly gnaw away at your foam arms and legs; but you get a little faster as the days pass, and a little closer to the safety zone. (A waist-height fence that you must also learn to hurdle as if you were Colin Jackson.) If, after these initial tests you are deemed worthy, and you had "the balls" to do so, you could attempt *the final test* – to try to outrun the dogs *without* any protective clothing.

If you did try, one of two things would happen.

1. You will run faster than you have in your entire life, outrun the dogs, make it to the safety zone, successfully hurdle the fence and achieve the ultimate status – a pass from the postal academy.

2. You will get caught by one, or more, of the dogs and be sent home with nothing more than "the three T's" (Train Ticket and Tetanus shot.)

But there are always an elite two or three out of every group of cadets who do make it. And those special few, who entered the academy as boys, leave it as men..... *postmen.*

Of course, the reality of all this "academy" stuff was *slightly* different to how Billy had described it to Clive. The actual selection process didn't involve an academy at all and was just a rather simple test in which you had to complete "complex" number sequences, such as –

1, 3, 5, 7, 9, _, _, _, _ and

2, 4, 6, 8, 10, _, _, _, _.

If you could do this, you were in!

If, on top of this, you could also actually spell your name correctly, then you were put on the fast track to management.

So, going back to the reasoning behind why Billy looked at things the way he did, it turned out that he probably wasn't just an optimistic, positive thinker who was ahead of his time but, actually, there was a pretty good explanation as to why most people seemed to refer to him as *"Billy Bullshit"*. It was also more than likely that he *wasn't* able to balance a small elephant on his head.

SEVENTEEN: *The Love Doctor.*

Gayle poured the boiling water into her coffee cup and inhaled the release of the coffee aroma in through her nose. There was nothing more satisfying, to her, than a nice cup of coffee (or two) in the morning. (Or three – this was actually her third cup.) She smiled as thoughts of her morning, so far, gently swayed around in her mind. She had been looking through some of the boxes that Jack had left behind the previous day and her memories had, once again, been nicely shaken into life. The old Nintendo games systems and countless games that he used to love to play took up three large boxes. She smiled as she remembered numerous, memorable nights having Mario Kart grand prix events, just Jack, her and Clive. She was always pretty useless at it, and baffled by how Jack and Clive would zoom around the crazy circuits pressing, seemingly, random buttons at random times; but those nights were still great fun. Yep, they were fantastic times, with the three of them functioning nicely like a healthy family, despite what was going on with her and Clive.

She had also seen Jacks very first pair of shin pads in one of the boxes. He hadn't worn them for years, as they were much too small, but had always refused to throw them away. He was a bit like Clive in that sense: overly sentimental about basic, material things. Even now it was difficult to talk Clive into getting rid of anything; even things like socks that were so old and worn that he may as well have been walking around with bare feet – it seemed that it would break his heart to throw them away. Ridiculous! (He would be an absolute cert to end up on one of those sad hoarder TV programs, where people have rooms full of old magazines and other useless shit they've collected over the years, if she didn't keep up with throwing stuff away behind his back.)

94

Jacks shin pads were different though. For him it represented the first time he got to play *real,* eleven a side football with a real team and real football boots and, yep, those real shin pads. And, for Gayle, it brought back those Saturday morning feelings that always represented "her and Jacks time", because Clive was always at work.

Very often she was the only Mum standing out in the cold and the rain watching football training or matches. And she loved it. Isn't it weird how a "sport" (men running around aimlessly and *collapsing* every time they are faintly touched?!?) that you can detest most of the time, can become something so *enthralling* and engaging when your offspring is taking part?

Gayle smiled, and even laughed a little, as she recalled seeing the "X-Files: Complete Season One" DVD box set in one of Jacks boxes. She wondered if he'd "enjoyed" it as much as she and Clive had. She was pretty sure that if he knew the detailed history of *that* particular set, then he wouldn't have been as keen to have kept it in his room as long as he had.

Gayle put a splash of milk into her coffee and stirred it gently, before cradling it in her hands and carrying it through to the front room. She sat down and closed her eyes and let her body relax into the sofa.

DING-DONG

Gayle opened her eyes and looked out of the window and saw an old, maroon Volvo sitting outside the house. Wow, that was weird. She *always* heard cars arriving on the street outside. It was like this one had appeared out of nowhere. She stood up, realising that this must be the arrival of the "love doctor" and began to feel a little nervous; she had *no idea* what to expect. She walked through to the front door, checking her hair in the hall mirror as she always did. She ran her hands through it a couple of times but, as usual, had to settle for more of an "it will have to do" feeling rather than the "just stepped out of the salon" feeling she always hoped for.

Gayle opened the door and was faced with a tall man holding a brown briefcase. He was wearing a dark jacket and a black chauffeur cap and was putting what looked like a camera back into his pocket. What was he doing with a camera?

Over the road, Gayle noticed the familiar twitching of Mr Dennis' curtains. No doubt he was making a note about Gayle's early Saturday morning visitor and, by lunchtime, everyone who had visited Patel's mini-mart on the corner of Walker Street will know that she was having a "clandestine and hot-blooded affair with a man with a maroon Volvo".

"Good morning Mrs Ford" said the tall man with the briefcase in a strange South African accent. "I'm Henry, Mr Corden's driver. He has had to take an important phone call in the car, but will be with you presently."

Gayle nodded her head and wondered whether to invite "Henry" into the house, whilst she waited for "Mr Corden" to finish off his important call. Instead, after glancing at the maroon Volvo and being pretty sure that there was no one sitting in there, decided on a different course of action that she thought may "cut the bullshit".

"Please, call me Gayle. And are *you* actually Jeremy?" she began, feeling particularly straight-to-the-point. "Clive told me last night that you like to impersonate different characters."

"Henrys" shoulders visibly slumped.

"Guilty!" he said through an embarrassed little laugh, his accent turning instantly to something typically local.

"Sorry, I try to make a real, professional business impression because I think it'll impress people. If they realise it's just me on my own then I worry they'll just think I'm a bit of a loser."

Gayle opened her eyes wide, acknowledging the irony of what Jeremy had just said. Did Clive really think that *this* was someone who could help them in any way, shape or form? She stared at him as he now, rather bizarrely, turned his facial expression to one of mini-shock and walked past her into the hall. He quickly glanced at the pictures sitting on the radiator cover before bending down and reaching for something that appeared to be lodged behind the radiator itself.

"Sorry" he said, passing Gayle what looked like a poem in a small picture frame. "My eyes were drawn to this. I presume it shouldn't be hiding down there, out of sight?"

Gayle took it from him, confused at first but then realising what it was. It was the framed lyrics of a "love song", or poem, that she and Clive had written many, many years ago. She couldn't actually remember the last time she had seen it and, judging by the amount of dust that was on it, it appeared that it may have been stuck behind the radiator for quite some time. How strange that the first thing Jeremy should notice when he walked into the house was a long lost poem by her and Clive. What a curious character.

"Wow, I haven't seen that in ages" Gayle said, deciding that she should explain its origins to Jeremy. "That's something that me and Clive wrote together, back when we thought we could write songs. That one even related to something that happened to us; something that made me feel like our love was *deeper,* somehow, than just *normal* love.

Stupid really. In fact, it was mainly *me* that wrote it. I always thought Clive would be best designing *my* single and album covers – he was really good at art. But I used to think *I* was destined to be involved in the music business ... if there's a *next time*, I'll be a *rock star* ... *next time* I'll do it *all!*"

She paused as her mind was taken back. It was unclear if she heard Jeremy say, rather quietly:

"Sometimes what you've *already* got is better than it *all*."

After a couple of seconds of silent staring, Gayle added:

"... but I haven't done anything music related in a *long time*."

She realised that her caffeine buzz was kicking in and was making her chat, rather manically, to this stranger, but she didn't really care. There's no point fighting the caffeine buzz.

"That's actually one of the reasons that me and Clive first got together: *music*. We shared a passion for the same sort of music. He did turn out to be a bit precious though really and didn't think anything could be "cool" if it was too *mainstream*. Even now he likes to like *different* music from everyone else. His latest favourite band is *The Struts*. Oh, yeah and he says he loves *melodic rock*. He likes bands from *Scandinavia*, especially *Eclipse* and *H.e.a.t.* You ever even *heard* of *any* of them?"

Jeremy was taken aback slightly by Gayle asking a question out of the blue in the middle of what seemed like a pretty lengthy rant.

He slowly shook his head.

"Err, no..."

"Exactly!" said Gayle. "I mean they are good..... well, *really good*...... but that's not the point, is it?"

Jeremy again shook his head slowly, having no idea what Gayle's point was at all as she prepared to continue talking.

"Yeah Clive *likes* music, but music was my *life*; my *dream*..... but, come on, how can *anyone* *not* like *Take That*? Especially back in their prime; in their heyday. I know it's not quite the same now, what with Gary Barlow judging those crap TV singing shows, hob-nobbing with royalty and fiddling tax; and with Robbie being *in* then *out*, then *in* then *out*, then *in* then *out*, then .... well, you know ...... and obviously Jason's gone for good. Howard's still there and Mark – who's still singing like a child who's learning to talk, which used to be cute back then but now he's an old man – not so much so .... "

Gayle stopped again, this time realising that she was waffling on excessively, even for someone who had two quickly-downed cups of coffee pumping around their veins.

97

"Sorry" she said and gestured for a bemused looking Jeremy to go into the front room. He began talking again as he walked.

"What a lovely house you have here." He said, hoping to change the subject as quickly as possible.

"Thank you" said Gayle. As she spoke though she couldn't help Jeremy's compliment make her think about Jacks packed boxes again; and that made her realise that, very soon, there would be boxes all around the house with *all* of their stuff in it. And that this "lovely house" would not be where she lived for very much longer.

As Jeremy sat down Gayle smiled a little, as she tried to work him out. There was something charmingly quaint about him trying to make a positive impression and he did have an, almost, *vulnerable likeability* about him. Either that or his odd behaviour was because he was a *raving lunatic*? She did, though, find it quite amazing that he had somehow walked in to her house and immediately spotted a personal "love song" that had been misplaced for quite some time. *That* seemed quite spooky; but somehow good, in a *fate-y* kind of way.

Jeremy shuffled in his seat and composed himself before speaking whilst wearing a very serious expression.

"Now then Gayle, before we begin, I need to ask you an important question. Have you been *rail-roaded* into doing this? Because the process only really works if you're open-minded and if you really *want* it to work."

Gayle thought about the question. She had somewhat allowed Clive to talk her into it, and it had led her to this point: listening to a man who, quite frankly, wouldn't seem out of place being chased by men in white coats.

"Because I'll be honest with you," continued Jeremy. "I obviously met Clive yesterday and I think it's safe to say he's got *issues*. He also comes across as a bit of a *loser;* he's certainly not man-of-the-year material. I wouldn't blame you for thinking that your relationship's gone as far as it could. So, if that's how *you* think also, then it would save us both a lot of time if you say so now."

Gayle could feel her heckles rising.

Why did this strange man, this *clueless* man, who likes to *pretend* he's *other people* all the time, feel that he had the right to come into *her* house and insult *her* husband? Sure some of the things he said about Clive were true. He *did* have issues and wasn't particularly one of life's winners. He also *wasn't* man of the year material, but *who else* was, when there's George Clooney to compete with? And, despite all of those things, Clive was *her* loser and his issues were not just his, but they were *theirs*.

She sat up straight in her chair and put her coffee cup down in front of her so that she couldn't be tempted to throw it at Jeremy during the delivery of words she was lining up.

"Let's get a few things clear." she began in her most stern voice, which was usually reserved for when sending Jack to bed or letting Clive know that, after a heavy drinking session, he had urinated in the wardrobe again.

"Clive is *not* a loser. He is a lovely man who works incredibly hard and has made untold sacrifices to be a good husband to me and a great father to Jack. He was my childhood sweetheart and is my best friend. And he is the one who....."

She stopped ranting as soon as she saw the smile emerging on Jeremy's face. It had been a test. He had just wanted to see what her reaction would be to hearing someone openly criticising her husband. And she had felt the need to defend him, again, vigorously and absolutely, because she obviously *did* still feel *something* for him. Maybe Jeremy wasn't as completely clueless as he first seemed. Gayle couldn't stop herself from smiling too as she followed Jeremy's gaze, that was now fixed on the far wall; he was still smiling and was now looking at the big photograph that was the only picture taken during her and Clive's wedding day.

EIGHTEEN: *Nice Day For...*

Gayle's mind slowly made its way back to the very moment that the picture her and Jeremy were looking at had been taken. She remembered it very clearly. She and Clive had just been married at the town hall registry office and the assistant registrar, a nice man probably in his fifties named Terry, had taken pity on them. He had obviously realised that they had no one there to take any pictures, and so had kindly offered to take a photograph of them outside the rather grand looking town hall. They'd had no friends or family at the ceremony because the only person in the world who had offered them any support, Clive's step-mum Sue, had sadly passed away quite recently. Gayle's parents had, surprisingly, given their written consent to the marriage. But this wasn't done to support the two of them in any way but rather, seemingly, was a final gesture of them "washing their hands of Gayle". As such, the main registrar had successfully found two random "witnesses" (it seems that there are always people, with nothing better to do, who are hanging around registry offices in the hope of being called upon to be a wedding witness – perhaps feeling like they are doing their own bit for true love?) and the whole wedding had been completed fairly quickly and without much pomp and circumstance. Gayle had thought that Clive would maybe have wanted to postpone the wedding following Sue's death but he had insisted on it going ahead, even conveying afterwards that he had felt sure that she had been with them in some kind of spiritual way.

They had decided to go ahead with a speedy marriage because they both wanted it to happen well before their baby was born. Gayle had always been concerned that, on the day, she looked like she'd spent too much money on lunches at Greggs or had said yes too many times when being asked: "do you want super size?" at McDonalds, as the only white

/ wedding-ish dress (she *really* wanted to wear white – it just felt traditional and important) that she could find and afford was an outfit from a local charity shop that was, at least, two sizes too small for her.

As she looked at the photo now though, Gayle actually realised that she looked really nice. She looked a little pregnant rather than fat. She wasn't *huge* and totally showing, but that was ok because she *was* pregnant. She felt a little sad to think that this was one of the very few photos that she had of herself actually being pregnant. It was obviously back in the day that photos were not taken hundreds of times a day to document events and when it was memories and feelings that were relied upon to keep a record of life. She would perhaps have liked a few more photos though to be a visual reference of the time that she had *life* growing inside her. When she had Jack, her little boy that was now all grown up, developing into a baby - inside her tummy. It was just, back then, there were enough opinions and criticisms aimed towards her and Clive that had made her feel more than a little uncomfortable and embarrassed when, in reality, it was one of her happiest times.

Clive looked nice on the day in a dark blue suit, also purchased from a charity shop and, thankfully, from this front on-angle the slight iron burn to the back of his right trouser leg couldn't be seen. Gayle smiled as more memories of the wedding came back to her. The day before a lot of rain and fairly wild weather had been predicted but the day itself turned out to be very calm with quite a lot of sunshine. Not like those weather people to get it wrong, is it? Gayle and Clive had taken it as a good sign though. Although neither of them were particularly religious or spiritual the fact that their wedding day, that had been predicted to be a wild washout, turned out to be actually very nice seemed like a good start for them.

Gayle also remembered the other "small" thing that happened as they stood there outside the town hall that felt like the icing on the cake for them. Perhaps because of the need to practise, or maybe a test after some kind of repair, the church bells of St. James's church unexpectedly chimed out for a couple of minutes. And it somehow made the whole event feel more real; more *authentic*. Like their wedding had *really* happened and it had been endorsed by a higher power.

It turns out Clive had a slightly different outlook to what had happened. At the time he had initially thought it was the sound of a nearby ice cream van and had been excited that they may be able to celebrate their marriage with a *Mr Whippy '99*. Gayle sniggered to herself. That was the type of thing that he would always say to make her laugh. He would take a serious situation and turn it into something wonderfully whimsical and silly. She could never be sure if he was being serious about things or trying to be humorous, but that made it all the more funny. At least in the past anyway.

Gayle continued to smile as she gazed upon the most obvious feature of the photograph. It wasn't how young she and Clive looked, even though they did, it was how very *happy* they looked. She let that feeling of happiness radiate through her body as she, once again, subconsciously said thank you to Terry, the kind assistant registrar who was generous enough to take a photo from his own camera, have it developed, and send it through to them later.

Of course, in those days before digital cameras there was more than just an element of "in the lap of the gods" about photographs, but that somehow also made photographs more *real*. They weren't taken and then re-taken because someone wasn't looking or had red-eye or didn't like the way they looked. They were taken once, and they captured the *real moment* before life moved on. Fortunately for Gayle and Clive it had been a good photograph and, as such, was put up on the wall in the front room in pride of place – something to be proud of, and for the entire world to see.

Gayle stopped smiling as she realised that even though it had always been there she hadn't looked at it properly for such a long time. It's funny how you stop looking at the important things after a while, because you've lazily started taking them for granted.

NINETEEN: *Street Heroes.*

"Tell me when will you be mine? Tell me Quando, Quando, Quando?"

Clive stopped doodling on the notepad in front of him and covered his ears because, yep, George was singing again. It happened everyday; it wasn't a matter of if, but just a matter of when. Clive didn't cover his ears because George was a terrible singer; no, his rendition of the *Engelbert Humperdinck* version of *Quando, Quando, Quando* was actually quite tuneful, but rather in anticipation of the torrent of abuse that would always follow when George began to sing.

That was the thing about Clives' Royal Mail office, one day blended into another. Everything repeated itself in a kind of perpetual déjà vu. George would begin to sing, either "Quando, Quando, Quando" or "Love is in my Hair" (to the tune of "Love is in the Air" – ironic genius as he was completely bald) and the majority of the rest of the office would shout some kind of disapproving insult while all the while Pete would stand at his delivery frame in the corner muttering "dig a hole, fill it in..... dig a hole, fill it in..... dig a hole, fill it in....." as some kind of quiet commentary on the monotonous nature of life as a postman. If Bill Murray thought he had it bad in the film *Groundhog Day*, he should try doing a couple of days at Royal Mail.

Clive had been a postman now for so many years that he was used to the complete madness that was always going on around him. When he had started, though, the "culture" and general hap-hazard craziness and bizarre mix of characters had been something of a shock to him. So much so that, on his first day, he wondered whether Royal Mail was going above and beyond the required government quota of giving opportunities to, shall we say, *intellectually challenged* individuals.

For a start, there is so much obscene name calling and bad language randomly shouted out that a tourettes expert would have a field day. It's hard to explain, but imagine if there was ever a Muppets movie made about postmen, maybe *Kermit and the Royal Mail Muppets?*, and this would probably be a true reflection of Royal Mail reality.

Clive had arrived in full time employment straight out of high school and yet felt like he had been sent back to infant school, due to the rowdy, crowd-like heckling and immature comments that got shouted out with regular frequency. Over time though you get used to your environment, or perhaps become "institutionalised", and Clive often finds himself shouting out the same nonsense at the same time as everyone else. He is also able to sing along, word for word, to, not only every current pop song that is played to death in heavy rotation, but also to every radio advertisement that is played daily. This is something you can only hope to achieve once your mind has been completely turned to mush.

"*Love is in my Hair.....*" began George, probably to instigate the latest round of angry, echoing shouting throughout the office - because he loved to start things off.

George had worked there for much longer than Clive which fitted in with how things seemed to work in the life of a postman. There were two categories –

1.   The people who lasted no more than two days. (Some people had even been known to leave the same day as they started – often *escaping* through the tiny window in the gents toilets.) These people had usually had (any other) jobs in the past and so realised how crazy this particular environment was – and wanted to get out of there as quickly as possible.

2.   The people who were in it for *life*. Some because they enjoyed the school playground-esque banter. (Where else could you get daily debates about what were the best cartoons or pop songs of the 1980's?) Some because they actually enjoyed the early start / early finish, outside lifestyle that it offered. Some because they didn't feel they could do anything better. Some because they couldn't be arsed looking for anything better. *All* because they were *fucking crazy*!

"Tell me when will you be mine?" George started up again "Tell me Quando, Quando, Quando?"

"Shut it you little, bald, big-nosed twat!" came the first response, before the *real* insults began. George just smiled and carried on singing as normal, not bothered in the slightest that his nickname, that had probably been with him for decades, revolved around him being small, having no hair, a bigger-than-average nose, with any random and crude swear word attached for good measure.

With his hands over his ears, Clive looked across at Stevie Taylor and wondered whether he, too, should wear a pair of bright blue ear defenders to drown out the noise that bounced off all four walls – because they didn't make Stevie look crazy in the slightest! Clive remembered the day, about three years earlier, that Stevie had stormed out of the office, complaining about the "same shit everyday" on the radio, and returned a few minutes later wearing something that you would only usually see worn by someone guiding planes around on the ground at the airport. Since then he had been pretty much incommunicado which probably suited him *and* the rest of the office. (Incommunicado - a great word that, despite *Marillion's* best efforts in 1987 hasn't really ever become "mainstream".) As Clive watched him, Stevie stepped away from his work frame and pleaded with himself,

"Come on brain, come on. What's the matter with you today? COME ONNNNN BBRRRRAAAAIIIIINNN!"

It was not an unusual thing to see him do; he was definitely the sort of crazy, crazy guy that was best given a wide birth. For good measure, he also had a level of bad breath that even a dog would be embarrassed of.

He wasn't the only one around here that fitted that *crazy* description though, that was for sure. Clive began to look around the office, to give himself a little tour of the *eccentric* characters that surrounded him; his work colleagues that were part of the eyes and ears of the villages, towns and cities of this country. The primary squad of dedicated observers that become aware of petty crime, injustice, discrimination and prejudice and are the first to take action. They are the first line of defence. *The street heroes.*

What a worrying thought.

The office could only be described, at best, as "dingy". It was cold in the winter and hot in the summer; never in between at a temperature that may be considered normal. And certainly nowhere near a level that would pass modern health and safety laws. And it was also always dark. The only natural light came from a couple of small, heavily barred, windows that were high up on the back wall. There were two rows of very dim fluorescent strip lights but half of them flickered regularly which, each time, would make Clive wonder whether someone, in a secret room nearby, was being executed by electric chair. It was hard to imagine hell being much different.

Clive first looked at the next work frame along and at Mark Tipton, or *Tippo*, who was one of the *strangest* individuals you could ever wish to meet. He was a confusing mix of wannabe alpha male, and yet the only man Clive knew who was *always* sensitively talking about his feelings. In fact, he acted so rough and tough one minute, and then was so in touch with his feminine side the next, that you had to wonder if he had a detachable cock. And yet he was a constant source of good company and amusement; always playing pranks, waving at strangers on delivery or getting on his hands and knees and barking wildly back at dogs who'd had the audacity to bark at him. Completely bonkers!

Just past Tippo was Jason who, rather sadly, used to be known as *smiley Jason.* Unfortunately his perpetual smiling had been slowly worn away over the last couple of years of Royal Mail's ever toughening grindstone and the *smiley* part of his name had been dropped. I suppose it's much the same as, for most people, *the good old days* now seemed to be referred to as *the old days.*

As Clive looked around further he heard the first shouts of "Owww – for fucks sake!" and "Snapper! Another fucking *snapper!*" of the day. This meant that some in the office had started "bagging up" (preparing their mail for delivery) and had experienced their first snapped elastic band of the morning that, after breaking, had rapped them somewhere across their fingers or knuckles, like some kind of sadistic daily torture ritual.

Hopefully some Royal Mail purchaser somewhere got a nice little bonus by making a healthy saving on the huge number of elastic bands that the company uses – by doing a deal to buy bands that *do not stretch!* Every postman goes out on delivery each morning looking like they'd had a particularly bad day at the hands of some overly-aggressive, corporal-punishment obsessed Victorian school teacher and his trusty splintered ruler.

This is just one of the *new* challenges that faced the *modern postman* these days – how to stretch elastic bands that *won't stretch.* The traditional problems of *abysmal weather, aggressive dogs, giro-demanding smack heads* and *lonely, horny, under-sexed housewives* were issues that had been addressed, and mastered, over the years, but these *new* work puzzles were something else. For example: *mobile phones.* Not only does being in possession of a mobile phone mean that the boss can get hold of you at any time, there is also the potential catastrophe that is *posting your phone.* As such, you should never be tempted to deliver and text / browse the web at the same time. Because, whereas for the customer, receiving a mobile phone (that may or may not be viewing a "questionable" web page) is probably favourable to the latest Screwfix DIY catalogue, it's not ideal for the postman – especially when excessive knocking on the door you've just posted your phone through leads to a neighbour coming out and informing you that the occupants have gone to Torremolinos for a fortnight.

Clive shuddered, remembering not having his mobile phone for two weeks the previous summer and hoped that his own elastic bands ordeal today didn't lead to a snapped band striking him dangerously near his eye again. Eye patches look cool on some people and are often the result of extreme and dangerous shenanigans that provide an interesting story worth repeated telling. Losing an eye to a cheap, non-stretchable elastic band whilst doing a job that was painfully like some Groundhog Day hell would certainly not offer an account worth multiple renditions.

Clive's shudder turned into a sigh as the mundane nature of his "career" struck him again. As he began doodling on his pad again, to finish the sketch of the grim reaper he had started earlier, he couldn't help but think about the news article he'd just heard on the radio about the state retirement age being under review again. How many more times would the retirement age be increased before he would be eligible to take his well earned old age rest? Could he really live this humdrum life for another 25 / 30 / 35 years?

TWENTY: *The First Time.*

Gayle had now spent nearly a full hour with Jeremy and was completely and utterly baffled about what she thought of him. She had certainly never watched someone take five minutes to slowly rummage through, what she could now see was a vintage, *LA Law style* brown briefcase, unpack some papers, a budget writing pad and carefully line up *seven* pens on the table in front of him with the slow precision you'd only usually expect during a complicated set up from a domino rally professional. And why *seven pens*? Well, apparently, "you can be sure if one pen runs out of ink then two or three will quickly follow"! Why this should mean that you need to carry *seven* pens with you at all times was completely unfathomable.

Gayle had always prided herself on her ability to judge people almost instantaneously. She was able to suss out what a person was all about, very often, the first time she ever heard them speak. Of course, she was regularly very wrong and had to change her knee-jerk opinions of people at a later date, but that didn't really matter. What was so unnerving right now was that Jeremy had stirred up, pretty much, *every* emotion within her in under an hour. She felt that she liked him, and yet couldn't stand him. She was angry and yet she was calm. She thought he was quite intelligent and yet a raving lunatic. And the whole experience was exhausting. It was like watching an episode of *Big Brother*.

"Ok" said Jeremy, after writing down Gayle's response to his previous question. "Without wanting to sound like a pervert, I need you to tell me about the first time you and Clive had *sex*."

Gayle's confusion about Jeremy instantly cleared up: she couldn't stand him, she was angry and he *was* a raving lunatic.

"I beg your pardon?" she said defensively.

"I know it seems a little intrusive of me to ask that, but the fact is that the act of sexual intimacy is a major part of the connection between humans; none more so than the very *first time* it happens. I don't need a detailed account of the actual act; but the time, the place, the build up, how you felt etc. All these things are important parts of you and Clive falling in love."

Gayle calmed down.

That didn't sound too bad. As long as he didn't expect the intimate details, then she wouldn't have to recall ripped knickers, mistaken orifices and a nasty, naked roll onto stinging nettles.

"It was a summer's night." Gayle began. "Me and Clive were 15. We had started seeing each other, pretty much, every day. *All day, every day.* Clive's step mum wasn't too well and so wasn't around to check where he was, and *my* mum; well my mum had begun to forget I even existed. And so we had each other. And we didn't need anyone else. We used to go down by the stream walking, sometimes even swimming in there. When we first started dating we used to go to the cinema or to McDonalds like the other kids but over time we found that we just wanted to be somewhere on our own; somewhere away from everyone else. Then one time we climbed over the fence to the school grounds and found a place we'd never seen before, right away in the corner of the field behind the big oak tree. It felt like it was private from the rest of the world, that it was *our place*, almost our own private little desert island. We started taking an old tartan blanket and having late picnics there. They were made up of whatever bits of food we could find in each other's houses. Usually some cheap wafer-thin ham on milk roll, *Trio* chocolate bars and packets of those *Disco* crisps, that often had so much flavouring on them that you couldn't feel your tongue for a couple of days after eating a packet. We also thought it was cool, and maybe *grown up*, to take some mixed spirits in an old hip flask that Clive had. Little bits of any old bottles of hard booze – enough to get us a bit tipsy, but not so much that anyone would notice straight away. We would have one of our walkmans and listen to one ear phone each, sitting in each other's arms pretending that we were in our very own house, that we were grown up and in love. Clive sometimes used to attach pictures to the tree; hidden behind a small black towel he'd once received in a Lynx Christmas set. The one time he smelt good for a few weeks into the new year!" Gayle stopped and smiled at her own joke.

"It became a ritual. I would remove the towel to see what he'd put up there - post cards or pictures from magazines of scenic views, mansions, mountain tops or beautiful golden beaches. I'm not sure where he got them from but he found these pictures that we would stare at and pretend that we would go there one day; that they would be the perfect places for us to be together. Because we *knew,* back then, that we were going to be together, *forever.*"

Gayle paused for a moment, her eyes moistening as she recalled her yesterdays.

"But what did we know!" she added with a little snigger. "We were just kids!"

She composed herself for a few seconds before carrying on. Before she did, Jeremy furiously wrote something done onto his pad.

"Anyway, the night in question was the same. We were sitting on our blanket; I was lying on Clive's chest. We were sipping away at the hip flask, hideous really – probably a mixture of gin, whisky and sherry or something. But I remember clearly that a warm night breeze was slowly blowing through. My walkman started playing one of my favourite songs: *When I See You Smile* by Bad English. We started kissing, and it started just like usual; but somehow it grew into something *more.* We stopped and looked into each other's eyes and, for the first time, it's like our eyes were so big that we felt like we could climb *inside* each other. Because we could *see* what each other was thinking. And then, when we started kissing again, it was almost like the *best* kissing in the world just wasn't enough anymore. We hadn't planned anything but we just started taking each other's clothes off; we *needed* to be *together*, as *one*, and so....."

Gayle stopped herself as she had glanced over at Jeremy who was sitting at the edge of his seat smiling. Was he getting off on this? Was he just some, weird, raving pervert?

"And *so*.....?" asked Jeremy.

"And so..... you said you didn't need details of the *act*!"

"No, no, I don't." said Jeremy, suddenly realising that he was at the edge of his seat and somewhat thankful that his tongue wasn't hanging out. "But how did you *feel*? What happened *next*? These are all important parts of it."

Gayle stared at Jeremy for a little while wondering whether this was all just a waste of time. This didn't feel anything like how some counselling would be, like she had wanted all those years ago. This just felt like she was telling some fairly intimate details of her past to a *very strange* man. Her instincts told her that she had told *him* all she wanted to. The weird thing was, though, that she was actually enjoying recalling, out loud, stories of her and Clive; *this one* especially. She almost ignored the fact that Jeremy was listening and carried on.

"It felt really *good*" she started, letting her mind return to that fateful night. "It felt like we were *together*. We weren't two teenagers having sex; we were two young adults *making love*. And it was like the whole world wasn't there anymore; like the whole world was *ours*. There we were, under the night sky *making love*. Lots of stuff back then seemed to be us almost *living* some of the songs we loved. One of them was by Cher, called *Love on a Rooftop*, which has a line in that says "*we never stop to see the moon at night*". But that *wasn't* us. We said we were *always* going to stop and see the moon at night. We were *always* going to live "young and foolish lives". And, right then, during our *first time*, it felt like everything we had spoken about was *real*. And then, of course, I realised that certain parts of me were very itchy and really quite sore."

"What was that?" asked Jeremy, looking up from his latest note making.

"Oh nothing!" said Gayle, realising that the nettle-roll was not something that she had planned to recall out loud to anyone; *ever*. All she could think of was: thank God for dock leaves.

"Anyway, that feeling didn't last that long. As we were lying there, in each other's arms; ironically just after Clive had suggested that we actually sleep there for the night, we heard the caretaker shouting at us as he crossed the field. He must have seen, or heard, us there somehow while he was checking the grounds. We had to pack everything up really quickly, and then he chased us to the far end of the field where we had to climb over the back gate that led to the main road. It was really quite frightening and yet afterwards we laughed and laughed about it. It somehow made everything even more *eventful*. It had made our *first time* feel more monumental; somehow *dangerous*. We still went back to *our* place regularly and somehow hoped that he would spot us and chase us again, but it never happened ….."

Gayle stopped talking and looked again at Jeremy. He didn't acknowledge her because he was too busy jotting things down on his pad once again. She wasn't sure what he was writing, but he appeared very focussed and was wearing a large smile; so he must have liked what he had just heard. She smiled and left him writing away as she went back to the memory in her mind.

111

TWENTY ONE: *Get Me Out Of Here.*

Clive rolled his sleeves up, took a deep breath and focussed on "getting on" with things again. He smiled a little to himself as he noticed his own action of rolling his sleeves up symbolising that he was preparing to get *stuck into work*. "Roll your sleeves up" was one of those phrases that he'd often wondered about; primarily where it had come from. You probably rolled your sleeves up to prevent them from getting dirty or wet if you were about to embark upon some kind of manual labour, and yet Clive couldn't help but always picture someone who was clearing their forearms as someone who was preparing to assist in the birth of a calf. Nothing to clear your mind of your mundane, humdrum life than imagining that you are about to insert your arm into a cows arse. And why is it that there isn't a similar, but opposite, phrase to coincide with you having finished the need to be getting on with things? No one ever tells you to *roll your sleeves down* do they?

Clive's attention was (thankfully) grabbed by Colin Barber, who was walking past him wearing a very smug look on his face. Clive quickly turned away before any kind of meaningful eye contact could be made because he knew that Colin was looking for *anyone* to talk to. And that *anyone* that he spoke to would have to endure a conversation that went pretty much like this:

Colin: "Hey, how are you doing?"
Anyone: "Alright mate. How are you?"
Colin: "Yeah, good thanks. You're off next week aren't you?"
Anyone: "No."
Colin: "Oh, it must be *me* then!"

This was not really exclusive to Colin and seemed to be a conversation that *anyone* who was approaching any time off liked to have – as a kind of celebratory announcement that they didn't have to come into the mad house for a while. Clive particularly didn't want to talk to Colin about his imminent time off because he had already had similar conversations, at least three times, in which Colin had boastfully given Clive the full itinerary about the "holiday of a lifetime" Caribbean cruise he was about to embark upon.

Clive didn't want to listen to that again, thank you very much. Besides he had never really fancied a cruise himself anyway. For pretty much most *bad* situations that happen in life there's someone who'll always say: "never mind – worse things happen at sea". Well, what the hell *happens* at sea? Clive had always thought it was probably best not to find out.

Whilst turning to avoid eye contact with Colin, Clive did see the Nick, the (current) boss, approaching fairly quickly holding a piece of paper. The odds were in favour of the paper containing the details of a customer complaint and the boss heading over to two frames down from Clive to see Chris "Woodsy" Woods – the undisputed record holder when it came to customer grievances. Like when you see a police car and feel like you need to drive more carefully, Clive at least tried to make it look like he was doing some work as the boss approached.

"Alright boss? You're off next week aren't you?" said Colin after Nick must have foolishly connected eye contact with him.

"Piss off Colin!" said Nick nonchalantly walking past him before arriving next to Woodsy, as Clive had predicted.

Clive leant over and tried to listen as they talked because Woodsy's complaints were usually sources of great amusement.

".....Number 45 Oak Lane." Clive heard Nick saying. "She says she's got photographic evidence of you walking down the side of her house yesterday and urinating up against the wall. What do you have to say about that?"

"It was very cold!" Woodsy replied, quick as a flash.

Nick sighed deeply and shook his head.

"I don't think she contacted us to comment about the size of your penis! I think she's more concerned about you pissing on her geraniums!"

"Hey *Fordy*, look what I got!"

Clive was interrupted from listening any further by Dave Black who was approaching carrying a *redirection* instruction. It would have been nice to see how Woodsy got out of this one. He wasn't known as the *Teflon Garfield* for no reason – nothing anyone ever threw at him seemed to stick and he had more lives than a cat. Only last week he'd somehow managed to talk his way out of a serious complaint about him breaking a vintage glass vase, by delivering it through an open window – on the top floor of a townhouse! Judging by the fact that Nick seemed to be showing Woodsy something on his phone, perhaps the photographic evidence of his toilet break, maybe it wasn't something Clive wanted to see after all. Instead he turned his attention to the oncoming Dave Black.

Clive was referred to by the majority of his colleagues as *Fordy*, as most postmen only seemed to be comfortable using nicknames instead of real names. In contrast to Georges' nickname(s) then Clive had to be reasonably happy with his, rather unimaginative, modified surname one. Dave Black, on the other hand, had been known as *Blackie* for years until an overly pc-correct manager had deemed that this could be offensive to individuals of certain ethnic backgrounds. (Although, ironically, the only black man who had ever worked there during Clive's entire time was Nigel Whyte, who didn't seem to have any problem responding to the nickname: *Whytey*. How is it that political correctness can get it *wrong* so, so often?)

Following the banning of his *Blackie* nickname, Dave Black, has since been referred to by one of three nicknames. One, *Piss Head Dave*, was not because his head had ever, unfortunately, been on the wrong end of some urinating mishap, but because he constantly appeared like he would struggle to pass a breathalyzer test. The other nicknames were *The Cider Barrel*, which concisely accounted for the size of his chest / belly and his love for alcoholic apple juice; and *Sir Stella Artois*. Someone had once tried to incorporate a nickname that linked his surname (Black) to something Guinness-related, but it had been far too complicated and clever for anyone to take seriously, and so, most of the time, *Piss Head Dave* was his default nickname.

"A redirection for me? Great!" said Clive, knowing that another one to add to his twenty five or so, that already took *forever* to do (well, at least three or four minutes) could only make things *even more* difficult for him. Why do people have to *move* at all? And if they do have to move, do they really need their old postman to search through all the virgin media adverts going to their old address and forward them on to their new address? It was so unfair!

"It's not just any redirection," started *Piss*... (Sorry, *Dave - Piss Head Dave* is so crude, even by the standards of these potty-mouthed postmen.)

"It's for number 5 Atherton Lane!"

114

He was, remarkably, not slurring in the slightest for a man who was giving off such intense whisky fumes that he must be considered a fire hazard.

Clive knew exactly what Dave was going to say next, because he knew the address, 5 Atherton Lane, very well – it was where an old school friend of his, Stacey Wellington, lived.

"You know, 5 Atherton Lane, where your, hic, girlfriend Shhtacie lives, well her boyfriend, hic, FFFillip, is moving out..... and she is shtaying there!"

Thankfully he was hiccupping and slurring now just about enough to justify the way he smelt.

"I told you they were shplitting up! Now's your chance. And this is jusht, hic, when you and Gayle are finishing..... it's like Karma or shomthing..... or is Karma a chype of curry?"

Clive smiled, while at the same time taking evasive action as Kieran came walking past at great speed. Kieran, or *Runaround*, as per *his* particular nickname was very fast-talking and was fairly high-pitched; in fact he was the sort of bloke that should come with subtitles. The reason for Clive's evasive action though was that his *Runaround* nickname had been earned by his tendency to travel around the office with the speed of an Olympic power walker. He was also the owner of the sharpest elbows ever known to mankind and many postmen had been on the unfortunate end of accidental collisions during visits to the toilet or brew machine which had regretfully resulted in them needing to take a couple of weeks off work with suspected broken ribs.

Thankfully, Clive had stood back just in time.

"Karma" he said to Dave "means *what comes around goes around*. What you're thinking of is *fate*!"

"There you go then. You can't argue, hic, with the fate! And she's well-hot, and clearly fanshies you; you're always flirting with each other!"

"Saying "Hi" and having the odd chat now and then is hardly flirting."

"She talks to ya? I told you she fanshies you!"

"Look Dave, just because you're invited into someone's house now and again, it doesn't mean that they fancy you. I mean....."

"You've been in her house? You dirtchy dog!"

"No, it's not like....."

"EVERYONES" Dave shouted,

"FORDY'S BEEN, hic, SHHHAGGING THAT FIT BLONDE BIRD FROM ATHERTON LANE!"

"WAY HEY WHOA HEY WAY WHOA!!!"

The whole office erupted with the cheering of a few dozen juvenile postmen / Muppets. Clive hoped that if he didn't react to the hullabaloo following Dave Black's announcement regarding his and Stacey Wellington's fictitious "relationship", the ridiculous reaction would die down pretty quickly.

But far from it.

He was now contemplating asking Stevie Taylor if he could borrow his ear defenders because George, still channelling his Englebert Humperdink signing voice, had sparked an office wide sing-along of "*Clive and Stacey, sitting in a tree, Clive and Stacey, sitting in a tree, Clive and Stacey, sitting in a tree K-I-S-S-I-N-G!*"

Shit, thought Clive. I'm a postman..... get me out of here!

TWENTY TWO: *Thought Of The Day.*

BEEEEPP! BEEEPPP!! BEEEEPPPPPPP!!! BEEEEEEEPPPPP!!!!
"Out of the way, you bloody lunatic!"
Probably one honk of the Royal Mail vans horn would have been enough but Larry decided that four, fairly lengthy blasts was the only way to express his displeasure of someone getting in his way. In fact, Clive felt that *no horn* use would have been more appropriate seeing as the "bloody lunatic" in question was an elderly man, riding a mobility scooter. A more appropriate action may have been for Larry to actually *slow down* a bit, instead of sticking to his usual style of driving that felt like he was constantly practicing in case someone ever invited him to drive his Royal Mail van around *Brands Hatch.* To say he was a reckless driver didn't nearly cover his driving style. In fact, to say he was "reckless" was like saying Usain Bolt was "a bit fast".

Recently there had been several safety "team talk" meetings that stressed to everyone the need to wear a seat belt in vans *at all times.* This was one of the few things that Clive didn't need to be reminded about; when he was sitting in his van with Larry driving, if it was at all possible, he would also wear a crash helmet and hold a bible on his knee.

"It's bloody sickening, isn't it?" asked Larry "Have you ever, *ever* seen anyone using one of those bloody mobility scooters and not thought – *you lazy bastard*? And why do they insist on using the road and getting in your BLOODY WAY?"

BEEEEEEEEEPPPPPPP!!!! BEEEEEEEEEEEEPPPPPPPPP!!!!!
Another two aggressive blasts of the horn seemed to make Larry feel better, but touché to the man on the mobility scooter who punctuated these last two honks with a perfectly timed two fingered salute.

"Bloody geriatric lunatic!" Larry muttered under his breath, fairly ironically seeing as he was probably of similar age to the mobility scooter man himself and, in the days before certain labels were deemed inappropriate, would definitely have been a candidate for having his name on the census accompanied by the description "lunatic", "imbecile", "idiot" or "feeble minded".

Clive shared a delivery van with Larry and had done for the last three years since some bright spark in some Royal Mail warm office somewhere had decided that postmen should actually work in pairs. It was something that, in business bullshit speak, was described as "starbursting" and had been tried a couple of decades earlier only to be found to be an inefficient way of working. Of course, back in the day, it was known as "opal fruiting". (Sorry to anyone born after 1980, who has no idea what *opal fruits* were.) But obviously some university graduate looking at data and spreadsheets, and trying to justify a ridiculous salary, had decided that mistakes from the past are always worth revisiting and decided to bring it back.

Larry was one of the elite, older members of the Royal Mail workforce who was technically known, in postman's terms, as a *lazy bastard*. He had worked there for well over forty years (yet spouted life lessons as if he'd travelled the world multiple times) and developed, and skilfully maintained, a somewhat work-shy methodology. He probably could have retired by now but was stubbornly holding on to the belief that, after being there for so many years, the business owned it to him to offer some kind of redundancy pay off. Seeing as, so far, Royal Mail didn't quite see things the same way meant that Clive was stuck with him.

Larry, who *always* insisted on driving (probably mainly so he had access to the vehicles horn), parked the van at their usual first drop point on the corner of Cotton Road and Atherton Lane; thankfully avoiding the need to blast said horn at any further mobility-challenged individuals. They both walked around to the back of the van as Clive breathed in some fresh air with the same daily sense of relief. Larry often possessed the weird and (not so) wonderful aromas of a man who obviously left his work clothes on as he cooked his evening dinner and then wore them the following day. He most probably *slept* in them as well. (A stuffy, enclosed van always seems to enhance the rather offensive aromatic blend of chicken stir fry and night time excessive sweating.)

At the back of the van, Larry opened the door and he and Clive picked out the first bags they had for delivering. As per usual, Clive's bag was very bulky and should really require the carrier to be wearing a weight lifting belt of some description; whereas Larry's was around a quarter of the size and weight. ("One of the perks of being here a long time!" Larry would gladly advise if Clive ever complained.)

"It's amazing isn't it?" began Larry, easily slipping his bag over his shoulder as if it was filled with nothing heavier than candy floss "There's people out there who pay a fortune every month at the gym, and yet here we are getting *paid* for doing the same sort of exercising! We really are very lucky!"

Clive shook his head in disbelief as he struggled to hoist his own bag over his shoulder and around his neck, wondering how many of his back discs he was repositioning in the process.

"Ok, young man, time for the thought of the day." said Larry.

Clive rolled his eyes.

Larry had taken to giving him "life advice" through a series of "nuggets of wisdom" that he had "earned" over his "long and varied" life. Over forty years in the same, mundane job – you don't get much more "varied" than that.

"What was yesterday's nugget?" he asked before revealing his latest star drop of wisdom; probably through a mixture of wanting to test that Clive actually listens to him and the memory frailties of an aging and variety starved brain.

"It was the one about the snow!" said Clive, accompanied by a fairly audible sigh.

"Ah yes," said Larry smiling "*everyone* is warned about not eating *yellow snow,* but that *brown snow* is just as bad..... yep, *never eat yellow OR brown snow.* And I did warn you to be extra vigilant about *lemon sorbet*, didn't I?"

"Yes." Said Clive, disconsolately.

"Good, you can never be too careful. You know what those *funny bastards* at the Iceland processing warehouse can be like after a twelve hour nightshift!"

He took a minute chuckling to himself, obviously pleased with his "humorous" advice, before readying his latest thought.

"Ok, here's today's thought: *Never* take seriously, a man whose sideburns are different lengths. If he can't even be bothered to make sure his facial hair has equilibrium, does anything in his *whole life* have any credibility whatsoever?"

"Ok..... good one!" said Clive, his eyes glazed over about the same amount that they always were, each day, around this "thought of the day" time.

119

"Watch out when you're crossing the road" said Larry, pointing his finger towards the middle of the road about 20 metres away where there sat a huge pile of horse shit. "Bloody disgusting isn't it? Do these horse owners not get fined for leaving their shit behind – like dog owners do?"

Clive looked over at where Larry was pointing, before saying:

"They'd need one hell of a pooper scooper to pick all that up!"

He smiled and waited for Larry to laugh, but it never happened. His old partner was already on his way.

"Be careful out there young man!" Larry said, walking off spritely with his small bag.

Clive took a deep breath as he turned and contemplated heading down Atherton Lane. It was this part of the working day that was the hardest – knowing just how much walking was in front of you. It's like starting a big tiling job, or even starting to write a book; if you think too much about *how many* tiles you have to attach to the walls, or *how many* words you have to write or, in Clive's case, *how many* steps you have to take, before you are finished then it really freaks you out – and makes you feel like never even starting. But, like for everything in life, if you *walk in the right direction*, metaphorically and literally, then sooner or later you will *always* reach your destination. The thing is, though, Clive didn't want to have to give himself that philosophical inspiration *every day* because he wanted to be doing something else. Ideally something linked with art but, the more time he spent, walking those same steps *every day*, the more he felt like he wanted to do *anything* else.

He'd had the same "pubescent" dreams as most young boys in the past. The first thing he thought he wanted to be was a train driver, until *Thomas and Friends* took away the *Ivor the Engine glamour* and made that seem too *toddler-ish* – there was no shovelling coal, dirty faces or extreme bronchitis in sight. Being an astronaut also seemed cool until Clive watched a documentary on the training they have to go through. Constantly running to reduce muscle wastage, eating "food" out of toothpaste tubes and having to shit standing up before catching your floating turd with a fishing net before it floats off and slaps against the wall. No thank you! He'd also wanted to be a footballer for a while. Not a modern day footballer but back in the day when footballers lived in the *real world.* You know, before the obscene money; when they weren't obsessed with cash, world-wide fame, weird hair, beards and tattoos but were happy with hero status and a moustache and a perm.

Instead of next focussing on his real dreams of art-based employment, Clive began facing up to the mundane, physical challenge that lay ahead.

It had to start how it always started: with the *first step*. And then the second one, and then the third one.....

After nine or ten steps he was back into his rhythm.

He reached his first call, the greasy spoon, ironically named "Fresh Cafe", and they had a letter addressed to "The Chef". Do you qualify as a "chef" when you pretty much just fry eggs and bacon all day? Clive walked in and saw that there was no one in there and so just placed the letter on the counter. It wasn't unusual to be empty in there and Clive knew that the "chef" would probably be standing at the back door, as usual, smoking a fag. "Fresh"? There's irony for you. They either got through a lot of hand gel in that cafe or had bought their hygiene certificate from some Del-Boy Trotter type character.

Clive next went past another food outlet, the fairly newly opened and rather small shop that represented another branch of the slowly expanding, local *Klucky Fried Chicken* empire which, ironically, had replaced the independent "Good Health" shop that had obviously failed. (Good to see that, in these troubling austerity times, the nation has decided to say "fuck it" to dietary welfare.) Again Clive had no mail for this shop as well but couldn't help but focus on the big sign in the "fake-*KFC*" window which read: "We only use Grade A chicken".

Clive chuckled as he mulled over the thought – *I never even knew Chickens took exams!* That was a *good* one. He would have to remember that one to tell Gayle later. Or maybe not. She probably wouldn't find it funny.

He and Gayle used to love to make each other laugh, *all the time*. They would laugh and joke about everything and anything but, in reality, that seemed like a *long* time ago. And the really sad thing was, Clive wasn't sure why that had ever changed.

TWENTY THREE: *The Loan Shark.*

Gayle cast her mind back and let it focus on an event that she *never* liked to think about. She had just light-heartedly told Jeremy about the time that she and Clive had celebrated their wedding anniversary one year at a fancy tapas bar on the high street called *Picasso*. It had seemed so exotic and grown up and neither of them had ever had tapas before. Between the fact that Clive had managed to drop potato bravas sauce down his brand new white short sleeve shirt (the only time he *ever* wore it – only multiple "hot" washes with *Vanish* got *that* stain out, shrinking the shirt so much a garden gnome would struggle to get into it) and the fact that Gayle had admitted being confused about why a Spanish restaurant had been named after a Disney character (yep, she'd mixed up *Picasso* for *Pinocchio*) the whole evening had been one non-stop laugh fest.

Which was pretty much how most evenings, and most of their lives, were back then – they *always* seemed to be laughing. She had also just fondly recalled how, at one of the baby group meetings she and Clive attended not long after Jack was born, she realised they were a *real* family; and how she thought that they would all be *together forever*. But now she was just about to answer Jeremy's latest question that seemed a whole lot more serious:

GAYLE
Tell me about your relationship *low point*.

I remember it like it was yesterday; I know I'll remember it until the day I die. I've never been so scared in my life. It was a Wednesday morning, Clive was at work, Jack was still really young. He was usually always very calm in the mornings; attentive, inquisitive; almost right from the start. But this morning was different. He was agitated; very unsettled. I thought that maybe he was feeling unwell but his temperature was normal, he had fed well, the way that he always did, there was just something that he wasn't happy about. I've always wondered whether he knew what was about to happen.

It was about half-ten. There was a knock at the door. Not a particularly loud knock, but not a quiet one either, just a normal knock. I was quite relieved to hear it because it meant I had something different to do than pace up and down the front room gently bouncing a baby that would just not settle.

I knew it was possible that it was just Mr Dennis, from over the road, who may have been coming round to ask whether I knew who had stolen his milk that morning. (I think I was always number one suspect seeing as I had a baby. He didn't seem to realise that he'd annoyed so many people it could have been anyone from within a radius of about twenty miles.) But I didn't mind, even if it was him with his milk-theft interrogation, because I just wanted a break from trying to settle Jack.

When I opened the door though, still holding and rocking Jack, it wasn't Mr Dennis. It was a man I had never seen before; a man who sent a chill down my spine straight away. I later found out, from Clive, that his name was Andy Taylor, but he never told me himself. He was only of medium height but my first impression was one of intimidation. He was dressed completely in black; black shoes, black trousers and a longish black coat that was zipped up right to his neck. His head was shaved and you could clearly see five or six different scars on top of his skull. I could also see that he had a spirally tattoo that cascaded around the area of neck that wasn't covered by his coat. It was hard to make out exactly what it was but my guess is it was some kind of snake that was slithering around his neck. But the most striking thing about him was his eyes. They were also black. Black as coal; cold, almost lifeless.

He was very polite. He said he was sorry to bother me and he was looking for Clive Ford. I told him he was at work and asked if I could help. The strange thing was, as soon as I opened the door, Jack stopped crying. He was just intensely staring at this man who had knocked on the door. The man said I could help by getting the £250 that we owed him. I had no idea what he meant. At first he thought I was lying. His voice became a little aggressive, he said that Clive was two days late in paying him back and that he had come to collect: "one way or another". Four words that made me imagine all kinds of terrible things; four words that haunt me to this day.

123

It was then that I understood what had happened. Two weeks earlier Clive, on his day off, had returned from shopping with lots of brand new stuff for Jack. A new cot, which we desperately needed as all we had was the second hand Moses basket that we'd bought at the charity shop before Jack had been born. An electric monitor that we always said we were going to get as soon as Jack could go into his own little bedroom. Some new baby grows and quite a few, cute little toys. I'd asked him at the time where he'd got the money from and he said they'd got an unexpected bonus from work because their unit had been the top performers in the area. It felt like we'd got a nice little break, like you sometimes do in Monopoly if there's been a bank error or it's your birthday. But it turns out he'd actually borrowed the money from this …… loan shark.

It's no wonder Clive had looked so pale when I told him that the car insurance was due earlier in the week and that I had cleared our joint account and paid it at the post office.

Clive never said anything to me though. Ever.

And he never has.

Even after I told him about Andy Taylor's visit and how I'd agreed for us to pay the money back, he just acted like it was something and nothing. All I knew was that he had <u>lied</u> to me. He was the man that said he would always protect me, and Jack, and yet he had lied to me and left us in a position where this man was at our front door and threatening us.

I never really told Clive how terrified I'd been because I didn't want him to think I was weak. But Andy Taylor had scared the living daylights out of me.

He stood there, this man dressed in black, calling me a liar, and saying that he wanted his money <u>there</u> and <u>then</u>. If I continued to lie to him then he would come into the house and take £250 worth of goods. If he couldn't find £250 worth of goods then he would take it <u>some other way</u>.

He reached out to Jack and grabbed him by the hand. I started screaming for him to let go and Jack started crying again. This man said that he couldn't let people get away without paying him; his business would fall apart if he did. He said he may just have to take a "different" payment and that he sometimes accepted <u>fingers</u> instead of cash: "£100 per adult finger or £50 per child finger" – he said that as he stared at me - and held Jack by the hand.

I screamed hysterically.

This man was threatening to cut fingers off my baby's hand. I shouted that I would call the police if he didn't go, straight away, but he just stood there staring at me, those black eyes not showing one sign of emotion. I must have screamed and shouted at him for a good few minutes and yet not one of our neighbours appeared to hear. If you have your radio volume on higher than number 5 then people come round knocking on the door complaining; especially bat-eared Mr Dennis who was <u>always</u> complaining about something; and yet not one of them "heard" anything that morning, when I needed them.

As my screaming turned to tears, I begged this man to leave us alone; to take whatever he wanted but just to leave me and Jack alone. He pushed us back into the house, still holding Jack by the hand as he continued to cry, and came in after us.

I feared the worst. I told him the only thing of any value that we had was the cot and monitor that Clive had bought with the money he had borrowed. I told him to take them, and whatever else he wanted, but to please, please, please leave us alone.

And then something strange happened. He began to gently bounce Jacks hand up and down in the air.

"It's ok, little fella." he said. "I won't hurt you. It's ok."

His voice was different now. He was talking like someone who had experience of being around little children, his tones were soothing and Jack responded to them, and he stopped crying straight away. The man smiled as he continued talking gently. "That's a good boy; a clever boy. Who's a clever boy?"

After about a minute of playing with Jack he then looked at me.

"Do you know who I am?" he asked.

I shook my head, my face was sore from the screaming and the tears.

"You don't need to then." he said. "I lend people money. They pay me back..... one way or another."

He stared at me as he spoke, but his eyes had changed. They weren't black and cold anymore, but looked a bit more blue; a bit warmer.

"What's this little one's name?" he asked.

I told him.

"Hello Jack" he said bouncing Jacks hand up and down again. "I've got a little one just like you back at home."

He looked at me again.

"I'm sorry to have scared you. It's the business I'm in; I need to know if people are lying to me or not. I know now that you're not."

If I wasn't shaking so much I might have taken this as a personal insult; he had come inside our house and decided that we had nothing of any value in there.

125

"I have a reputation to uphold." he said to me. "An image to maintain. Without that I cannot continue to do what I do. Do you understand?"

I nodded my head.

"But I don't do what I do because I want to see young families suffering. I am not an animal..... well, not <u>all</u> <u>the</u> <u>time</u> anyway. You can call this an administration error, but I now believe I may have accepted that your husband could pay me back <u>weekly</u>. So, you will pay me back at ten pounds per week. I will come round on Wednesday mornings, for the next twenty five weeks, and you will be here, ready with ten pounds each time. If you fail to pay, <u>ever</u>, then I will be using the alternative collection methods I spoke of earlier. If I have to do that your husband may need some help writing a letter. Do you understand?"

I nodded my head.

"Also, your husband will <u>never</u> come to me again to borrow any more money and neither of you will mention this new agreement to <u>anyone</u>. If just one person finds out about how I am letting you pay....."

He didn't finish his sentence, instead deciding to look at me and letting me work it out for myself.

He bounced Jack's arm up and down one more time, gently saying, "I will see you next week little Jack, yes I will..... yes I will!" before nodding at me and walking back through the front door closing it behind him. I sank to my knees and began crying again. Strangely Jack didn't. He was now calm and happy.

I'm not sure why but I've never gone into that much detail before; not even with Clive. When he got home, just to see his face; I couldn't help but cry. I just about managed to tell him that I knew he'd borrowed the money, that I'd arranged a re-payment plan, and to call him a liar; before I needed to get away from him – before I hit him. Because for putting me and Jack through that, I wanted to hit him again and again and again ....

We've never really spoken about it ever since; because I can't face talking to him about it.

<u>That</u> was the low point.

And I'm not sure that things have ever really recovered from it.

Jeremy stared at Gayle, who was visibly shaking after reliving that "low point" moment with him. For a good few seconds he wondered whether there was anything he could say to make her feel a little better. After a while he realised he had no idea what words may help and so he looked down at his notes again to see Clive's rather short and somewhat different answer to the same question.

CLIVE
Tell me about your relationship *low point.*

The day Gayle burnt my oven chips.

TWENTY FOUR: *The Pact.* (8 Years Ago)

The stairs creaked, as they always did, as Clive tiptoed down them after reading Jack a story and tucking him into bed. Clive shook his head as he recalled the number of times that Gayle had implored him to do something about the groaning steps; to somehow "fix them". Who did she think he was, one of Nick-bloody-Knowles' crew?

"I've done your dinner – it's on the table." Gayle said to him as he entered the kitchen. "Did you get him off ok?"

"Yeah, he's sleeping like a..... *baby!*" Clive said, pausing on the word baby, seeing as his "little man" hadn't been a baby for a long time and seemed to be growing up faster and faster. How did *that* happen so quickly?

He walked into the small extension room behind the kitchen that doubled as the dining room and laundry drying area, picked up his plate, knife and fork and re-entered the kitchen.

"It's ok; I'll just have it on a tray in front of the TV."

Gayle shook her head; for two reasons. The "dining room" was hardly ever used anymore despite them promising each other when they moved into the house that, once the room was done up, they would eat every single meal in there. Also, despite her spending lots of time and effort to make a lasagne from scratch, Clive had come home from work, turned his nose up at it and proclaimed he "just wanted pie and chips". It brought back memories of the time when he had treated her to a Michelin star meal and then proceeded to complain about his sushi starter "not being cooked properly". It was like living with a bloody caveman.

Clive removed his cushioned tray from the cupboard, (*so comfortable* – why would you eat at the table when you can have padded luxury on your lap?) placed the salt and vinegar and brown sauce on it next to his plate and cutlery and walked through to the front room. He had been fantasising about this meal for the last couple of hours of his overtime at work. Sometimes, even when Gayle has made one of her famous, *delicious* lasagnes, your body just needs a good serving of stodge.

He turned the TV on and plonked himself down on the sofa, accompanied by that "oouughh" sound that you have to make when you finally sit down after fourteen hours at work.

Then he noticed it, right there on his plate: his oven chips, though pleasingly well numbered, were not that nice golden, yellow colour that you see on the picture on the bag, but *brown*. Not a light brown colour that you may see on a well varnished soft maple, wooden table, but rather a darker, dirtier brown that you may see on..... well, *burnt oven chips*.

How the hell do you burn oven chips?

You take your frozen chips out of the freezer and place them on a baking tray, put them into a pre-heated oven for twenty minutes, and then take them out – end of instructions. You leave them in the oven for twenty-five minutes and they are burnt. It's hardly bloody *Masterchef* stuff.

Gayle entered the front room as Clive crunched into his first chip, wondering if it may be best, before continuing, to make sure that he had his dentists' phone number on speed dial.

"Do you fancy opening a bottle of wine and watching a film when you've finished that?" asked Gayle wondering if she should tell Clive his chips were slightly over-cooked because the timer on the oven had broken *again*, despite Clive saying that he had fixed it earlier in the week; which was pretty consistent with everything else he *fixed* around the house.

Gayle decided not to mention the over-cooked chips and/or the broken oven timer; she didn't want to argue *again*.

"No, I'm going to bed soon – bloody knackered. Just going to watch last night's footy highlights and then head off." Clive said, again risking his teeth on another potato-less, rock hard chip shell.

Not bloody football again, thought Gayle, wondering if she should go upstairs herself and watch something a little less boring on the TV in their room. You know, something from the paint-drying or grass growing channels.

She took a deep breath and decided against it. She needed to make more of an effort. There was a time when they would always watch things *together* and not just things for both of them, like..... the *X-Files box set*. But no, Gayle would actually happily sit and watch football in the past, just to be with Clive. (And some of those multi-millionaire footballers were not too offensive on the eye.) And Clive would happily invest himself into things like the soaps and *Strictly Come Dancing* because Gayle liked to watch them. (Attractive female celebrities and dancers in short skirts and dresses did soften the mundane "entertainment" of the dancing.)

Instead Gayle stayed where she was and made another offer.

"What about tomorrow night then? Movie and wine? We could get a takeaway as well?"

"Oh, I can't tomorrow. I'm going out with *Knobhead*..... I told you, didn't I?"

"No, you didn't." sighed Gayle, disheartened by the fact that her husband spends as much time as he can with a man named "*Knobhead*" and, almost certainly, *hadn't* told her about it – again.

What followed was four or five minutes of silence, well apart from the loud chomping sound of neglected oven chips, and possibly shattering teeth, and the unfathomable ramblings of overpaid "pundits" obsessing about every little detail about men in boys' shorts running around after a leather bag of wind.

Finally Clive spoke.

"How was your day?"

Gayle was taken by surprise. She assumed that Clive, almost like her, had forgotten she was even there.

"Oh, pretty average as usual." she began. "I did have a heated run in with Tina though. Do you know she has started using red and gold *glitter pens* when she's marking up the paperwork she's checked? When you come to look for anything through the filing cabinets – your hands get completely covered in pen and glitter. And it doesn't just wipe off easily, you've got to go to the toilets and give your hands a good wash and scrub in hot water. Well, I've told her anyway – *no more*. She should just be using normal black or blue ink pens like the rest of us. We exchanged a few words but, hopefully, she's got the message now!"

What the hell was she talking about? Glitter pens and paperwork? Was this the *highlight* of her day? The only thing worth relaying in a story about the events at work? Bloody hell; this felt like a new low in Gayle's mundane, nine-to-five hell of a "career".

Wow, those "dreams" of a music career, even if they were just the immature longing of a child who had fallen in love with music, were more than a million miles away from the eventual reality. Even the back up plans of being a songwriter, or working in a recording studio, or even just working in a record shop; anything to be around music all the time, felt like long, lost fantasies.

To make a living out of doing something that you really love – that's the real key to a happy life isn't it? But now all of that seemed like distant memories; thoughts that Gayle had no real right to have ever been thinking. Of course, these days, there were shows like *The X-Factor* that allowed anyone and everyone the chance to go and try out for that dream; but did she want to be the next past-her-best, over-weight, middle-aged dreamer to be laughed at by one and all. No thank you.

"What about you?" she asked Clive. "Did you have anything as remotely interesting as that happen to you today?"

Clive smiled at Gayle's exasperated mocking of herself.

"No, not really. I can't compete with that! Well, it *was* pretty funny when Dave came back to the van and had walked in the sloppiest dog shit you've ever seen. And it stunk to high heaven. Well it was funny until we realised that he had climbed over the seats before noticing it, and got it all over the seat where I was sitting."

As Clive thought about it more, it wasn't actually funny at all. It took him ages trying to wipe his trousers clean, and the stench was at a level that would probably stay in your nostrils for a good couple of months. For Clive also, this was a moment of realisation that this, "highlight" of his day, was probably everyone else's idea of a worst nightmare.

How the hell had he got stuck in this *job*? Out all day, in all weathers, quickly damaging your own body with the work load and miles demanded of you?

And for what?

To struggle through life with hardly two pennies to rub together?

He remembered his dreams of pursuing his love for art. Graphic designer, children's book illustrator, *anything* where he was able to imagine and create. He had even daydreamed when he was younger of travelling around the world, maybe living on nothing more than the few coins you could make by chalking some pavement art in major cities. Just travelling when and where the mood took you; free as the wind and free of care.

Gayle sat staring at Clive, slowly realising that he was most probably smearing dog shit on her sofa – he certainly hadn't gone to the trouble of *changing his clothes*. It was like living with a *dirty, disgusting* caveman.

She was in her own house and yet felt more trapped than she ever had in her entire life; even more so than when she was forced to move as a chid, to a place and a school where she knew absolutely no one, and almost had to start her life again.

"We need to talk, Clive". She said, accompanied by a huge sigh. "We need to talk about *us.*"

"Oh, not tonight!" said Clive, feeling that he didn't have the energy for another argument.

"I think we need some help." said Gayle. "Will you think about us seeing that councillor that Tina recommended?"

"I thought we agreed that it would be a waste of time *and money*? These people are only interested in making you think that things are wrong so they can drag things on, have you going time and time again, so they can make as much *money* as possible."

Clive couldn't help but think that if Gayle was really serious about working things out then she would stop mithering him all the time. Instead of going on and on about things like little jobs around the house that didn't really need doing, it wouldn't harm her to focus on more important things. Not only had she burnt his chips tonight, but he'd also had better tasting pies as well.

Gayle sighed again as she focussed on Clive's words: "we agreed"; because *we* hadn't agreed about anything for a long time. More and more often Clive wasn't discussing things anymore and was just "agreeing" things by himself; this certainly didn't feel like a team anymore. Life was just drifting away, and they were letting it happen – separately.

And then Gayle just said something.

She hadn't really planned it, but it must have been lurking somewhere inside her.

"Sometimes I think that the only reason that we're here, *together*, is for Jack. Like we stick together because we both want to be sure that he doesn't have to grow up in broken homes … like we did. Maybe if he wasn't here, we wouldn't be together anymore?"

Wow, it felt like a bolt from the blue but somehow came as a relief, like the words had been eating away at her and needed to be released.

Clive was taken by surprise.

He knew things weren't great, but was Gayle really thinking about *breaking up*? He knew that this was the moment to say something really important; to find the right words so that she knew that everything was going to be ok.

But he couldn't find them.

He just felt tired.

And maybe she was *right*?

They had both wanted a lot more out of life than what they were getting right now and so it was hard to come up with anything that contradicted what she had just said. Taking him by surprise also, words of his own came rushing out.

"I think you're right. If it wasn't for Jack then I don't think we would carry on like this."

Suddenly the moment had changed from the everyday routine of one man watching football while eating rock-hard chips and smearing dog shit on the sofa while one woman watched on in disgust, to something that felt like it would be pivotal in their lives.

"Like I said" said Gayle, her voice trembling a little, and not quite believing she was going to say the words that she was about to. "I want Jack to have the safe, loving upbringing that comes from having *both* parents that love him, there with him every day."

Clive nodded his head.

"So let's make a pact." she continued. "We stick together and remain good friends for the sake of Jack. But when he is old enough to leave home..... we will go our *separate ways*. We will get on with our lives in different directions."

Clive could feel some tears forming in his eyes, but couldn't think of anything to say except for four words that just confirmed everything that Gayle had just said.

"Ok. It's a deal!"

Gayle left the room and headed upstairs towards their bedroom, tears flooding from her eyes and her heart beating probably faster than it ever had as a mixture of adrenalin, sadness, excitement, regret, fear and hope rushed around her body.

Clive remained on the sofa, staring at the TV through wet eyes, completely in a state of shock.

They had made *the pact.* An agreement that was never really spoken about again; but was always in their minds as morally binding and something that they accepted would happen one day.

And "one day" always arrives.

Usually sooner rather than later.....

TWENTY FIVE: *A New Path To Walk.*

Clive psyched himself up and jerked the heavy bag back onto his back after finding the small parcel that he remembered he had for number 3 Atherton Lane. He placed it with the couple of items of mail they also had, before knocking on the door and waiting with the kind of pessimism that comes early on a Saturday morning. There were two cars on the drive and the likelihood was that somebody was in, but the front window curtains were closed and that meant: *awkwardness.* Yep, when part of your job was to knock on peoples doors fairly early on a Saturday morning, it often led to *uncomfortable* encounters. Clive took three steps back* away from the door and waited for the outcome of the four most likely scenarios.

1.   He would have to wait for an excessively long and frustrating time (each new waiting process at each new house added to the frustration) before having to consider knocking again (louder this time). Then he would have to contemplate filling in a card to let the habitants know that their parcel delivery had failed - which usually results in someone answering the door just as the lengthy card-filling process is complete. Finally Clive could attempt to deliver the parcel to a neighbours' house. (Which is encouraged by Royal Mail – but is increasingly annoying neighbours, who were probably also sleeping in. This is now slowly turning whole streets of neighbours, all around the country, against each other.)

2.   He would see the curtains of the bedroom twitching before hearing some hasty putting-clothes-on attempt and loud and rapid stair decent before an effort to open the door without unlocking it leads to

someone shouting "I can't find the keys". This can then turn into several minutes of key searching during which, in Clive's mind, sofa seats are thrown onto the floor and contents of drawers are emptied onto tables, before someone eventually opens the door (often half naked – great if it's women, not so good if it's Mr Dennis-esque men) or, if the key search has proved unsuccessful, a small window is then opened through which you have to attempt to squeeze the parcel.

3.   Most awkward of all – someone opens the door, clearly unimpressed with having to get out of bed and wearing a look that thunders: "Why are you knocking on my fucking door at this time on a Saturday morning?" In preparation for this scenario Clive always readied his counter look that said: "It was *you*, not *me,* that ordered the fucking parcel!" Very often he could also prepare a second look that added: "It is *me,* not *you,* standing out here in the fucking rain!"

4.   Someone would open the door fairly quickly because they were already up but had not yet opened the curtains. This could actually turn out to be the worst scenario of them all because it often meant that they were having breakfast which, nine times out of ten on a Saturday morning, meant that you were likely, once the front door was opened, to be struck by the smell of cooking bacon. And when you are standing out in the cold and the rain, usually tummy rumbling with hunger, that scent of bacon is tantamount to torture.

*The taking of "three steps back" from the door was a precaution because, in any of these scenarios, the just-out-of-bed-and-dozy home owner can easily "forget" to shut an angry (and, most probably, in desperate need of a piss) dog away in a separate room leading to it charging out of the house right at you – endangering you to a potentially nasty bite and/or being urinated on.

Thankfully this morning, on this occasion anyway, the door was opened fairly quickly and Clive was confronted by a man who (judging by his Ken Dodd-esque hairstyle) had got out of bed fairly hastily, but had been successful putting on his (thankfully non-wind affected) dressing gown and was fairly polite and thankful about receiving his parcel and, most importantly, did not appear to have a dog and had not attempted to cook any bacon as yet.

After the fairly pleasant exchange of parcel and polite words, Clive carried on and flicked through his bundle of mail again as he walked.

135

Next up was a brown envelope, that looked like a gas bill (no-one was sure why but the utility companies had now started to favour sending out their payment demands on a Saturday morning – nothing like good news for people to start the weekend, eh?) for number 5 Atherton Lane.

His heart skipped a little as he read the name on the letter: "Stacey Wellington". He remembered the little rhyme that he and a few of his mates had made up about her back at school.

Stacey Wellington – she is so cute.
Stacey Wellington – she's no old boot.

Why hadn't he gone after a career as a poet?

Before he really knew it his legs had brought him right to Stacey's front door. He couldn't help but think about what Dave at work had just been telling him about her boyfriend moving out and the implied chemistry between her and Clive, followed by that, juvenile office-wide singing.

The whole office now thought that Clive was regularly going into the house and delivering more than what was just in his *postal* sack. But he wasn't sure how he felt about it. The likelihood was that, even despite this planned *Love Is...* weekend, he and Gayle were splitting up and, well, he had always got on well with Stacey, and she *was* very attractive – you don't come up with lines like "she's no old boot" for any average looking girl. The thought of being with another woman was scary and yet maybe a little exciting at the same time.

Clive was startled and his mind was brought back to reality by the front door opening. Stacey was standing there wearing a very sexy looking white silk dressing gown, her blonde hair hanging down on her shoulders and, damn it, there was that blast of bacon smell; what was she doing to him?

"Sorry, Clive!" said Stacey when she realised that he had jumped a little. "I thought maybe you had a parcel for me or something – you have been standing there a while."

Clive felt his cheeks getting a little hot.

"No, no....." he said, thinking fast for an excuse for loitering outside her house "I, errr..... was just wondering why gas bills are now sent out on Saturdays – not a great way to start the weekend, is it?" he said whilst waving the brown envelope at Stacey.

What the hell was that?

If and when he and Gayle did split up was this the kind of fast thinking, smooth chat up lines he had to look forward to?

"Great!" said Stacey taking the gas bill off him "Just what I wanted!"

Ok, thought Clive, now was the time to deliver something a bit more interesting than facts about the timing of utility bill delivery.

" .....have a nice weekend!" he said, turning away from the front door. His impending singleton status need not be alarming for the lothario's of the land.

"Wait!" said Stacey.

Clive turned around and noticed Stacey's face becoming a little red; she was anxious too.

"Do you fancy coming in for some breakfast? A bacon sandwich, maybe?"

Clive tried to ignore the screams coming from his stomach: *yes, yes, yes, yes, yes, yes, yes, yes, yes, yes, yes, yes, yes, yes, yes, yes,* because, even if he wanted to go inside and have something to eat, which he still wasn't sure about, he had to get on so he could go back and meet Larry.

"Erm, thanks, but I'll have to say no." he said, before watching her expression fall a little.

"Some other time..... maybe?" he added without really knowing what he meant by it.

"Wait!" said Stacey, taking a deep breath and composing herself. "Sod it – I'm going to go out on a ledge here."

Clive stopped and watched her prepare to say something that obviously looked like a struggle for her.

"As you probably know, Phil moved out a few weeks ago..... we haven't had any kind of relationship for a long, long time."

She paused, as if trying to choose her words carefully.

"I hope you don't mind me mentioning it, but my cousin, Jenny, works with your wife Gayle, and, she's a bit of a gossip, bless her, but she says that you and Gayle are splitting up..... and have been for a while. Please tell me to mind my own business if you want but I was wondering if..... you might like to come out for a drink sometime with me? No strings attached. Just two old friends going out for a drink? You always used to be able to make me laugh..... I could do with a bit of cheering up?"

Clive took a deep breath.

Although he had organised the whole *Love is* ... events and hoped that, more than anything, they could conjure some kind of miraculous recovery for his and Gayle's marriage, as things stood that marriage appeared very much over. Was this some kind of sign? Was this fates way of opening up a new opportunity for him; somehow like Dave had predicted back at the office? The possibility of a *new* path to walk? Clive reluctantly accepted that it may just be that.

"Erm, ok then..... yes!" he said a little tentatively.

Stacey smiled at him, but said nothing, and Clive wondered whether her saying that he used to make her laugh meant that she was expecting some kind of a joke *now*. Would the one he heard at work on Thursday about the girl and the darts team be appropriate? Probably not.

"How about tomorrow night?" asked Stacey. "It doesn't have to be a date or anything, we could just meet somewhere?"

"Ok..... yes!" said Clive, accepting that the joke he knew about the Pope and Father Christmas also probably wouldn't be fitting to the occasion.

"Shall we say..... The Farmers Arms in the village at around eight o'clock? It's just been refurbed – I think they've even got the blood stains out of the carpets!"

Clive smiled.

Did he know an appropriate joke about blood-stained carpets?

No.

"That sounds good" he said. "I best crack on..... I'll see you there!"

"Great!" said Stacey. "I best go and check up on my bacon, see you tomorrow."

Clive wondered whether asking for a bacon sandwich *to go* would be appropriate but Stacey had already closed the door.

Damn it!

He walked slowly back onto the street slightly in a daze about what had happened. He certainly wasn't expecting something like that to happen this morning.

Before he could think about it too much his "postman sixth sense" kicked in. Yes, his subliminal postman super-power alerted him about a hooded man (sorry, somewhere wearing a *hoodie*; I don't mean *Robin Hood*) who had just turned onto the street ahead of him. Clive sniggered. *Hoodies!* This generation's new breed of young yobs. They didn't scare Clive though. He had grown up when hooligans were *real* hooligans: the *skin heads*. These new pretenders didn't fool him for one minute. How tough and dangerous can they really be, compared to those thugs from the past, when they are even worried about their heads getting a bit cold?

The man was dressed in a red hooded top but was so big there was no chance of him being mistaken for Little Red Riding Hood. He also had a fairly large and aggressive looking dog with him and so Clive's subconscious sensation was actually doubled. Clive stared at them and he quickly noticed that the dog wasn't actually on a lead and could potentially make a dash for him at any second. His training kicked in and he quickly surveyed the area for potential escape routes, coming to the swift conclusion that his only realistic chance of avoiding any possible attack would be to leap over the hedge of number nine Atherton Lane and into the front garden. Fortunately for Clive, especially as the hedge was over six feet high and would have taken a leap Dick Fosbury would have been proud of, it appeared that this was actually a fairly lazy dog. Even though it, too, had obviously received its own sixth sense message alerting it that there was a postman near by, after looking up and seeing Clive, it decided not to charge at him. Not as fortunately for Clive, the dog decided to "strike" him in a different way – by vigorously urinating up against the post box, on the street corner, that Clive had to empty in a few seconds time. Even though many animal behaviour experts would have you believe that dogs cannot articulate through facial expressions, Clive disagreed with this completely. He had lost count of the number of times that dogs had "smiled" at him – usually right before they bit him. And this was not to mention the number of winks and raised eyebrows he had received from his canine adversaries. There was a cockapoodle, who lived on Birch Avenue, whose extensive facial expression repertoire made Jim Carrey look like he'd over done it on the Botox. And this dog now, who was urinating all over Clive's post box, was definitely *smiling* at him; in fact he was practically *laughing* at him.

Clive felt an anger bubbling up inside him. Surely the hoodie the dog was with must have also seen Clive and realised there was a good chance that he may have to empty, and therefore *touch*, the box that he was allowing his dog to piss all over? Would it not have been good manners, or even *expected* manners, for him to try to stop his dog or, at least, offer something in the way of an apology? But, oh no, like many of the youth today this hoodie was either oblivious to, or just unbothered by, what was actually happening. Clive had a good mind to tell the hoodie exactly what he thought of him but decided to say nothing – it may turn out that this large hoodie wasn't actually as soft as his "scared-of-getting-his-head-cold" image made him out to be.

Instead, Clive let his mind focus back onto the encounter he'd just had with Stacey. He certainly hadn't planned it, and he wasn't sure how he felt but, wow, he had a date; or at least a "*it-doesn't-have-to-be-a-date, date*", whatever that was.

TWENTY SIX: *Number Five, Percival Road.*

Jeremy finished writing down Gayle's latest answer and had a flick through his notepad to see what Clive had answered when presented with the same question.

CLIVE
Do you have a special <u>day</u> that you remember?

I think it might have been the day that we moved into our house. It was mid-December, and it felt like an early Christmas present. The <u>best</u> Christmas present ever.

Gayle was eight and a half months pregnant and had become an expert at it. You know, she would walk around looking like she'd stuffed a football up her top while at the same time being able to reach back with one hand, place it on her lower bag and say "oooohhh!"

She would rest cups of tea on her bump, or Jack as we now know him, almost jubilant that she didn't need a side table or to put them on the floor in front of her chair. When Jack was born he had a small red birth mark at the top of his right thigh – probably a result of having a hot mug being balanced on his leg every night.

I know it's a well used phrase when people say pregnant women are "glowing" but, for Gayle, it completely described her. Apart from a two week spell early on when she felt a bit rough and was sick a few times, she had sailed through feeling really well. And she wore the physical changes with real pride; by this point she was genuinely happy to be pregnant. And, as such, she <u>completely</u> glowed.

On the day we moved in we'd been told to be patient and that moving days, and the exchange of keys and everything, could drag on and on. As it turned out for us, everything happened really smoothly and we were in the house before midday. Of course we had nothing to put in the house except ourselves so, like most other people, we weren't waiting around for the big removal van to turn up and bring in box after box of stuff we'd managed to collect over the years. No, all we actually brought with us, on the day we moved in, was an old plastic patio table, two deck chairs, and a second hand travel bed. And the start of a cool CD collection.

The house wasn't completely empty though. The previous owner had been an old man, who had lived alone with his dog for many years. He'd moved out and gone into a care home. His son had dealt with the sale and agreed to leave most of the furniture there as part of the deal. There wasn't that much, but it was good that we had an old sofa and TV cabinet (although no TV), a double bed and an oven to start us off.

I remember that day really clearly.

After opening the windows to try and clear the smell of old man and, probably seldom-washed, dog (they stayed mostly open for about two months) Gayle and I just sat in the front room on our deck chairs. I think we were both a bit wary of sitting on the sofa until we had given it a good wash with a steam cleaner, no one wants to openly risk being a feast for a sofa potentially full of fleas.

But yeah, we just sat there <u>smiling</u>.

We finally had our own piece of the world, that we had paid for. (Or, at least were going to pay for over the next twenty five years of our lives.) We both knew the place wasn't a palace or a mansion, we probably hadn't even considered that we may still be there twenty years later, but it didn't matter; because it was <u>so much more</u>. It was <u>ours</u>. Our place. A place where we would be together, with our baby, as a family.

It would challenge and stretch our limits financially but, again, it was <u>ours</u>. It felt like we had just taken a step onto the first rung of a ladder that stretched high into the sky; up to the place where dreams exist. It seemed like <u>anything</u> and <u>everything</u> was possible.

It wasn't actually long before there was a knock at the door and we were introduced to Mr Dennis, from over the road, for the first time. He had come round, with a bit of a double-edged message, that said welcome to the street and warned us not to make too much noise. It didn't take us long to work out what sort of person he was. If every village had as idiot, then Mr Dennis could easily represent many villages; probably even the county. We managed to get rid of him within an hour or so – which probably stands as the record to this day. But when he'd gone we got back to sitting in <u>our</u> front room and smiling.

We promised each other that this house was just the start. I was going to work on my art and somehow make a living out of doing something I loved. Gayle was going to get into the music business once she'd had Jack. She, too, would find a way to make a career out of something she had always dreamed of. And, together, we promised each other that we would never stop dreaming. We would support each other and always encourage one another to <u>always</u> aim for the stars. If we didn't reach the stars then it didn't matter, we would always have each other. Always Me and You vs. the World. And if we did fall short when aiming for those stars, we may just make it to the moon instead. And if we made it to the moon, we'd always have cheese!

TWENTY SEVEN: *The Han Solo Moment.*

Jeremy was completely intrigued.

He had just asked Gayle if she remembered where and when it was when she realised that it was *definitely* love between her and Clive and, without any kind of hesitation, she had answered: "Oh yeah, 100%. It was the *Han Solo* moment. It was, coincidentally, also the moment that inspired that poem you found behind the radiator - *Echoes Through Time*."

What was this Han Solo moment that she so obviously clearly remembered? Gayle hadn't been referring to, perhaps the most famous Han Solo moment – you know the "Han shot first" controversy during his face off with Greedo in the Mos Eisley cantina? No, what Gayle had been referring to was a moment in *Return of the Jedi*; although when you watch it properly it doesn't quite go exactly as she remembers it. She explained to Jeremy that it was the scene when Han and Leia were fighting the Empire forces alongside the *Ewok's* (you know, those fighting, warrior *teddy bears*!?!) and Princess Leia was injured by a random laser shot to her arm. After fighting off a couple of Storm Troopers (after Han tells Leia that *he* loves *her* – losing all the coolness he earned in *The Empire Strikes Back* when Leia said to him: "I Love You" and he nonchalantly replied: "I know"!) they are cornered by an AT-ST walker and are surely doomed. And it is in this moment, as per Gayle's recollection, that Han, with no other thought than to protect Leia, selflessly steps in front of her to shield her from any further shots with his body; and therefore his life. The reality is that Han actually stands up and raises his hands rather than making the "laying down his life" gesture that Gayle remembers. But her mis-remembered version is what she means by the Han Solo moment and it links in with a much clearer memory in her mind.

"Ok then, the *Han Solo moment*? Tell me more." Jeremy said, as he leant back in his chair intrigued.

Gayle ran her hand through her hair and smiled gently as she let her mind replay some of the memories, ready for recalling for Jeremy.

It was a Friday in December, we had been let out of school mid-afternoon because it had been snowing; you know it was back in the day when it used to snow in December and not just freakishly in March like it does now.

I'm pretty sure it was one of the last Fridays before the Christmas holidays because we'd been allowed to dress in whatever clothes we wanted to in exchange for a tin of something to go in the raffle for the Christmas fair. I think the "lucky" person who won my "prize" at the raffle would have been treated to a delicious, out of date, tin of mandarin oranges in syrup.

It was back when it really snowed and everyone was really excited about it. Obviously when you get older and you have to commute or work in the snow then you realise that it's just a real pain in the backside. Just ask Clive; he says trying to deliver mail in the snow, with a big, heavy bag on your back is like auditioning for Bambi on Ice. Anyway, like I say, we were just school kids and so everyone was really excited about the snow – especially as we were being let out of school early to help us with our journeys home.

Of course, no one really wanted to go home – it was snowing like mad and the fields were completely covered. Massive, blank canvas's, just waiting for excited school kids to come and build snowmen and have huge snowball fights.

I had arranged to meet Clive on the field at the side of the sports hall and we were going to walk home together. I was wearing a pair of my Mums fancy brown leather, knee-high boots and this really nice black silky top that I'd "borrowed" from her wardrobe – what she didn't know, couldn't annoy her, right? I would just sneak them back into her wardrobe when I got home, as good as new, and she would never know. I'd got up early that morning and showered and even attempted to straighten my hair and it actually worked pretty well.

I felt like a million dollars.

Not even Mr Jackson sickeningly saying that he "liked my boots", as he almost licked his lips, could dampen my spirits. All I had to do was wait for Clive by the sports hall and then we were going to spend the afternoon together. I don't know why but he must have been running late and I was standing there for ages, getting colder and colder, desperately holding my little umbrella up so that the snow wouldn't wet my hair and make all my early morning straightening efforts a waste of time.

I watched as countless numbers of kids moved up and down the field, making all kinds of objects in the snow from snowmen and women to mini igloos, some were lying down and making "snow angels" and there was even an attempt by someone to make a large snow penis that, for a split second, I thought may have been Clive's idea of a joke; but wasn't.

All of a sudden there was a real increase of the number of people who were near to the sports hall and it soon became obvious why. A massive snowball fight that had been taking place on the tennis courts had spilled out of the gate and was now heading straight towards me. And it seemed like it was every man for himself; because everyone was just throwing snowballs randomly at anyone.

The first one to hit me struck me flush on the left side of my jaw, almost spinning me around and making me drop my umbrella. Before I had chance to clear my head and pick it up some kid had swiped it from the floor and was using it as a make shift shield as he ran through, what now seemed like, some kind of shooting range. Dozens and dozens of large boys, probably from the sixth form, were aiming snowballs at everyone who was anywhere near.

And it looked like they were well prepared - they all appeared to have at least two rucksacks of pre-made snowballs; it was a complete siege. I realised that not only was my hair now completely exposed to the snow and imminently about to return to its' unruly, curly style, but I was also a prime target for all those boys and their snowballs.

I made a decision and decided to try and run for the relative safety of the middle of the field. What I hadn't realised was just how difficult it would be to run in my Mums fancy boots. I barely made it ten metres before I had completely lost my footing and was flat on my back on the field. It may have appeared like I was attempting my own snow angel, albeit in the most ill-advised of all places, because I was soon confronted by two of the sixth-form boys who had obviously seen me fall.

For a split second I thought I may have been ok as one of them said aloud "shall we help her up"; but the hysterical laughing that immediately followed confirmed exactly what I was: I was a sitting duck.

I turned onto my side just in time to see them resting their bags onto the ground about five metres away from me and opening them, ready for easy access to their "ammunition". The first snowball that was thrown hit me on my shoulder and hurt like hell. The second, that came quickly

145

after, hit me on the knee and was twice as bad. I realised that these boys had probably made the snowballs earlier in the day and they were now pretty much made of solid ice. Another one came and struck me on the side of the head, immediately making me feel a little woozy and bringing tears to my eyes.

And they just kept coming and coming.

Each one feeling like I was being struck by a baseball bat. All I could see through my tears were my Mums brown boots, completely soaking wet and ruined and definitely not in a state of being able to sneak-them-back-into-her-wardrobe-as-good-as-new.

I was freezing cold, unable to stand or defend myself, and obviously going to be in big trouble when I got home. The big boys just carried on, throwing snowballs at me from no more than about five metres away, obviously having immense fun. Maybe they couldn't see that I was hurting and crying; maybe they didn't care. Who knows what goes through the minds of cruel boys? I wanted to stand up and fight back somehow but I felt tired of having to be so tough all the time. Or tired of <u>pretending</u>. I wasn't tough. I was just like every other scared teenager. Only I didn't have a Mum who would reassure me that things would be ok; and <u>hug</u> me whenever I needed it.

I remember squinting my eyes as another "icy" snowball hit me on the forehead and, even through the thinnest of watery slits, I could just about make out somebody running towards me.

I opened my eyes a little more, half expecting it was someone coming to drop a massive pile of heavy snow on top of me, and there he was: Clive. I have no idea how he had seen me lying on the field, covered in snow and being pelted by these boys; it almost felt like maybe he'd been drawn to me by my pain and helplessness.

I knew straight away that he wasn't going to be a traditional knight in shining armour who would be able to fight and scare these boys away, because he looked so much smaller than them. But that didn't matter, because it was obvious instantly that he was actually <u>so</u> <u>much</u> <u>more</u> than that.

He quickly came to my side and lay down next to me – completely in between me and the bigger boys, and the feeling of those hard snow balls smacking against me stopped straight away. Clive just held me and looked into my eyes.

"It's ok, now." He said softly.

And it was. <u>Everything</u> was ok.

And I looked back at him, through the tears that were stuck in my eyes, and I heard the bigger boys laughing once again, no doubt amused by Clive's act of chivalry and, I suppose, <u>love</u>.

And the throwing of snowballs started again, maybe even more now than were being thrown before. But I didn't feel a thing because Clive was now my shield. And I saw every wince of pain on his face as each new one struck him on the back, but he didn't say anything or even make a sound; he just took each blow silently. And, as he did, he looked at me, and smiled.

And nothing else mattered.

All thoughts of my Mum's ruined boots, and me being in big trouble when I got home, disappeared because all there was, was me and Clive, lying on the snow, looking into each other's eyes.

And that was it: the <u>Han Solo</u> moment.

And it was also the moment that I knew that I was completely in love with Clive. Because to be <u>completely</u> in love with someone, I realised that they also need to be <u>completely</u> in love with you; and I knew Clive was.

Years later, when I heard the Aerosmith song, Full Circle, I knew exactly what Steven Tyler meant when he sang "Love Is Love Reflected".

I knew in my heart that Clive would have, without a doubt, died for me in that moment. And I would have gladly done the same for him.

TWENTY EIGHT: *From One Angel To Another.*

Jeremy continued writing away on his note pad with his original pen; there had been no use, so far, for the other six pens that still sat neatly lined up on the table in front of him. Gayle came to the conclusion that Jeremy must be one of those "better safe than sorry" types of people – at least when it came to pen contingency anyway.

Maybe it was fair enough: there's nothing worse than having to search for a pen when you desperately needed one. It's nearly as hard as, when you are out somewhere for the day, trying to find a toilet because you desperately need a shit – no chance.

"So, the *Apollo Picture House*, that was the first time you went to the cinema *together* then?" he asked, after carefully re-lining pen seven neatly alongside the other six.

"Yep, on a Saturday night." Said Gayle before bursting into song.

"*Saturday Night at the movies.....*"

She regretted singing straight away and put it down to the fact that she was either trying to clear her mind of the sort of toilet-based, *desperately-need-a-shit* kind of thinking and reference that Clive would normally speak of; or the fact that she had spent too much time with Jeremy and was now teetering of the edge of becoming someone that could be referred to as: *barking mad.* Whichever way, she decided spontaneous, crazy singing should be avoided as she focussed on the answering Jeremy's question – in the hope that the quicker she answered his questions, the quicker he would leave the house.

"It was *The Mask* with Jim Carrey. The cinema was really small, maybe a little family run thing, but very cool. I'm not sure exactly what the deal was with them but they seemed to get films much later than the

148

big cinemas – sometimes years later. But it meant the *Apollo* seemed really unique; somehow exclusive."

Gayle smiled as she recalled her and Clive's visits to the *Apollo.*

"There seemed to be tiny, narrow corridors everywhere that had loads of black and white pictures of film legends from throughout the ages. The seats were pretty old fashioned but really comfortable. They were red velvet chairs. And there were red velvet curtains everywhere, where ushers used to stand with their torches; and from where the people wearing ice cream trays used to pop out from in the interval. Me and Clive always used to share a tub of "real Devon clotted ice cream". I don't' know if this is a little sad but I even remember the seats we sat in for that first time: 14F and 14G!"

Jeremy smiled as he, once more, carefully picked up the same pen and made a note of what Gayle had just said.

"I *love* Jim Carrey" Gayle added as Jeremy wrote "Well, I love all his *classics* anyway. *Ace Ventura, Liar Liar, The Truman Show*, even *The Cable Guy* – I know it got slated a bit, because it is pretty *dark*, but it's *so cool.*"

Gayle stopped as she realised she had embarked on a bit of a rant again, before *having* to add something that she'd missed.

"But his best film *has* to be *Dumb and Dumber.* In fact, we haven't watched it for a while, but it's mine and Clive's *favourite* film."

She paused as Jeremy stayed silent, instead just gently writing some more words onto his notepad.

"I suppose not everyone likes Jim Carrey, do they?" Gayle asked, hoping to see whether Jeremy actually liked him or not. It was another one of her tests in life that served as an indication as to whether she actually respected a person or not.

Jeremy looked up smiling slowly.

"He's a bit like Marmite, isn't he?" he said, through a smile that grew with each word.

"What?" asked Gayle "You either *love* him or *hate* him?"

"No" said Jeremy, his smile now at maximum capacity "he's brown and sticky and smells like shit!"

He began laughing as Gayle looked on, slightly confused.

"Sorry" said Jeremy, trying to compose himself "That's a little joke I like to do about Marmite. Everyone thinks you mean the love or hate thing but then you say: *brown, sticky and smells like shit* and they're not expecting it – that's why it's *so funny*!"

He looked at Gayle, who continued to sit there completely deadpan.

"It's a bit like when you're in the pub and the round gets to a particular mate who says "sorry I haven't got any cash on me", and you say "you're a bit like the Queen aren't you?", and he says "what, I never carry any money on me?" and you say "no, because you're like an old, grumpy woman!""

Again, Gayle sat there unmoved.

"It's funny, because no one's expecting it?" Jeremy stated / asked whilst still laughing.

Still. Gayle's deadpan expression remained mostly unchanged, apart from a slight hint of confusion. Jeremy realised that he would have to accept that his jokes had quite possibly missed the bull's-eye on this occasion. He was pretty sure it was the audience and not the jokes themselves?

"Ok then..... I think I *read* that second one somewhere....." Jeremy said, hurriedly trying to calm himself down, whilst trying to disassociate himself with the second of his attempted jokes. Because he was now contemplating that if Gayle was the die-hard royalist type, then his inclusion of the word "grumpy" when describing the Queen may well have completely pissed her off. ".....let me finish writing this down before we move on."

Before speaking to her again, in an attempt to diffuse what may now be a hostile atmosphere, he slowly flipped the pages of his writing pad back and glanced over one of the answers that Clive had given him the previous day.

CLIVE:
When did you realise it was true love?

It was just like any other day; well most of it anyway.

I'd been to school, spent a nice lunch time with Gayle and the bump. We had been advised to maybe give the bump a name but what do you call a bump? Seemed like the best name for it was bump, and so we just stuck to bump.

I had got home around the normal time and Sue wasn't there. But that wasn't unusual; I just assumed that she was at some appointment or other that I'd forgotten about. I must have spent about fifteen minutes or so flicking through different TV channels before the phone rang and I think I knew something was wrong straight away. The ring of the phone sounded different; somehow serious.

As it rang I also noticed that the heating hadn't come on and suddenly the house felt very cold. I answered the phone; it was a nurse from the hospital who said that Sue was "very poorly" and I should try to get to the hospital as quickly as I could. "It's Ward B3" were the last words she said to me before hanging up. I arranged for a taxi straight away. And I phoned Gayle, who said she would meet me there as soon as she could.

Things feel like a bit of a blur now and thinking about it feels like trying to recall an old film I haven't seen for years and years. I think the taxi driver was trying to speak to me about things but I couldn't really listen. I just wanted to get to the hospital and so kept asking him to drive as fast as he could.

I arrived at the hospital and was shown how to get to ward B3. I'd seen Sue in hospital loads of times and so walked through the door and scanned the ward expecting to see her smiley face, in one of the many beds, staring out towards to the ward door, probably waiting for my arrival.

But I couldn't see her.

It felt like I was looking up and down the ward for ages before a nurse walked over to see me. She asked who I was and then took me through to a little side room just off the main ward; as we walked I continued to look up and down the corridor at all the beds, but I still couldn't see Sue.

The nurse said some words, quite a few words, but the only ones I ever remember were: "I'm so very sorry, but Sue passed away a few minutes ago. She died very peacefully as she slept."

And it felt like there was a huge BANG!

A huge crash as the sky was ripped in two.

The nurse asked if I wanted to see her. I didn't even know what that meant but said yes. I was taken to a private room around the corner where Sue was lying on a bed, on her back. She looked peaceful enough, but very different. At the same time she looked like her, and yet not like her. She looked almost like what a waxwork model of herself would look like.

I touched her forehead and she was cold; almost ice cold.

Looking back now, I wonder whether she had actually already died before they had even phoned me, but I guess I'll never know.

All I could think of, as I stared at the body she had left behind, was that I never got the chance to say goodbye to her. And that thought crushed all the air out of me. I couldn't breathe, I couldn't even think.

Later, I realised that we had actually been saying goodbye to each other every day, for months and months. As her illness had got worse, Sue had taken more time to speak to me, about everything and anything.

151

I think it was her way of trying to pass her experience and the lessons she had learnt in life, on to me. She also took more and more time talking to me about the baby we were going to have. I think she wanted to be sure that I understood what having the baby would be like for me and Gayle; making sure that I understood the responsibilities that were in front of me. But also, I remember the talks we'd had when she had tried to make me realise what an exciting and fun time we had ahead.

Of course I was so young and hadn't seen what was happening. I was not ready to realise and accept the reality of the situation; the reality of Sue's illness and the inevitability of the outcome.

I'd never had anyone <u>leave</u> before. Sure, I'd known plenty of people who had come and gone in my life, but it had always been through choice, no one had ever left permanently because of the end of life.

As I stood there, just staring at Sue's body, I had never felt so alone.

I was lost.

I'm not even sure how long I'd been there before Gayle arrived. She said that she'd left almost straight away after I'd called her so it must have only been a few minutes, but it had felt like forever.

Gayle was also shocked and upset.

Sue was probably the only person in the whole world who hadn't judged us for the situation we had found ourselves in. She was definitely the only person who was happy for us and focussed on the positives of us having a baby and getting married.

Not long after Gayle arrived we were asked to leave Sue's body because she "had to be moved".

I didn't want her be moved.

I didn't want anyone to touch her; ever.

We were ushered into another, different small room and told that we "could stay as long as you like", "take all the time you need".

We sat down and held each other tight.

Although I was numb, I knew that I wasn't alone, and those feelings of being lost slowly began to fade. As we sat quietly, we could hear noise coming from the room next door that must have been the wards' TV room or something. There was music playing, albeit it quiet-ish and muffled, coming through the wall. It must have been MTV or maybe perhaps there was a radio playing.

The first few songs I couldn't make out, and they meant nothing to me and were even a bit of an annoyance; so much so that I wanted to go next door and turn the TV or radio off.

Didn't the people in that room realise what had happened? Didn't they understand that the world needed to be in silence?

But then a song came on that I recognised and actually quite welcomed. It was a song that Gayle and I both liked and had listened to countless times sharing the earphones on our walkmans.

It was Space: "Me and You vs. the World".

It was our song. Our anthem.

Gayle's family had abandoned us. My Mum had been "taken" from us. We'd never had many people at school that we could have called "close friends" but, even those that we may have loosely described as "mates" didn't want anything to do with us anymore; almost like they were embarrassed by our situation.

So we were on our own.

But it didn't matter, because we didn't need anyone else. We had each other and we weren't afraid to take on the whole world.

Sue had been taken from me but she had left me so much. I felt strangely happy right then because I realised how lucky I had been to have the years that I'd had with her as my "Mum". If it's true that you get sent Angels in time of need, then Sue was definitely the first one I had been sent.

She had given me a sense of stability and safeness for the first time in my life. My first few years, before being homed with her, had been nothing other than disruption. The sad tale of another young kid who'd been neglected and then passed around from home to home; until, fortunately, landing at the doorstep of someone special. Someone who was beautiful enough to let in, and love, another wayward soul.

Sue had taught me what love was; how it works, how to give and receive. She had taught me to just be me, and not need to try and be anything else. But to be the best me I could be. And not through material achievement, but through <u>happiness</u>.

She taught me that success isn't measured in pounds and pence or in houses and cars and other such objects, but in moments of joy and happiness. And she had done it to so many other kids before me; and it felt like her job was done.

It was her time to rest.

She was leaving me, but she was passing me onto my new Angel, Gayle.

From one Angel to another.

And we were ready to start our new life; our new family. I was ready to spend the rest of my life knowing and practicing what Sue had taught me. And Gayle and I knew, and would often remind each other, that it was Me and You vs. The World.

TWENTY NINE: *Echoes Through Time.*

Jeremy carefully put his budget writing pad and seven pens back into his fancy lawyer-esque briefcase. Gayle couldn't help but notice that as he performed this, rather slow and meticulous tidy up, he was wearing a very satisfied grin on his face. It was one of those contagious types of mini-smiles and Gayle found her own lips unable to resist the urge to curl and smile along as well.

"Are you ok?" she asked, curious as to why he appeared so happy.

"Oh yeah!" said Jeremy, slowly turning to face Gayle. "Oh yeah!"

She continued to look at him, hoping that the look on her face would persuade him to give her a little more information as to *why* he was so ok. Jeremy laughed a little to himself as he realised that she was fishing for more than just a yes/no type answer to her question.

"This is going to be easy!" he finally said. "There's so much for me to go on here..... I guarantee that by tomorrow night you and Clive will be head over heels in love again!"

Gayle felt her own smile fading slightly.

Why was Jeremy so sure of himself? She may have just told him two or three nice stories about her and Clive's past, and she had actually rather enjoyed reminiscing about their good times together, but that didn't mean that *everything* else between them *hadn't* happened.

The more she thought about it, the more she realised that there had been too much water passing under their bridge. Simply talking about a few nice things that happened many years ago can't compensate for years of relationship neglect and mediocrity. She couldn't help but feel that this whole thing felt like a big gimmicky, waste of time again. She wasn't sure how much Clive had agreed to pay for the privilege of all this (knowing him, it probably wasn't a lot) but she wondered whether

154

that money, and all their time, could be saved if she put an end to it right now.

"I've got quite a few things to organise" began Jeremy before Gayle had any chance to say anything "but I will be back to pick you and Clive up for your first event, or maybe *date*, at 3 p.m. sharp."

He added such an emphasis to the word: date, and again displayed such an annoyingly infectious smile, that Gayle was unable to stop herself grinning once again. Also she couldn't ignore the strange feeling that was building inside her because of Jeremy's, somewhat rather juvenile, stressing of the word "date".

Wow, she felt as excited at the prospect of doing something different with Clive, perhaps even something *romantic* with him, as she had the previous day about the prospect of going on a date with Lee. In the space of one second she had gone from feeling like everything was a big waste of time to actually feeling, almost nervously, excited about it.

What was going on?

Was she now experiencing some kind of hormonal, mid-life change to go with the onset of beginning to look and feel older?

Jeremy had packed his stuff away, had carefully triple-checked that *all* his pens were present and correct, and had walked out into the hall.

"3 p.m. sharp!" he added before reaching out for the front door. Before he left the house though, another of those smiles spread across his face as he took his time reading Gayle and Clive's "song" that had now been restored to its position on the radiator cover.

Echoes Through Time.

How did I know your eyes,
Before I'd ever seen your face?
And your smile, before we'd even met,
Always, somehow, brightened my day.

I thank the Earth for food and water,
I thank the sun that cuts through the frost,
I thank fate, fortune and destiny,
For the day that our paths did cross.

It's you and me against the world,
And they're shooting at us all the time,
I will always be your shield,
And I know, you'll always be mine.

155

Time and space collide,
Every time you're by my side,
Because Baby, You and I,
Got a love that echoes through time.

When we shared our very first kiss,
Fate made sure the stars aligned,
Because Baby, You and I,
Got a love that echoes through time.

The music will always play,
The words will always rhyme,
Because Baby, You and I,
Got a love that echoes through time.

So let the whole world keep on shooting,
I'll be your shield, and you'll be mine
Because Baby, You and I,
Got a love that echoes through time.

THIRTY: *The Maroon Volvo.*

Clive yawned heavily as he locked the front door behind him.

He usually arrived home from work on a Saturday a little tired and grumpy and looking forward to a nice siesta. Well he liked to call it a "siesta", trying to make it seem somehow European-ly sophisticated, but Gayle saw it for what it was. A nap *is* a nap, much in the same way that a lazy bastard who avoids the Saturday afternoon food shop *is* a lazy bastard who avoids the Saturday afternoon food shop.

They both got into Jeremy's car, a maroon Volvo that could very well have been manufactured in the 1970's, wondering where he was going to be taking them for this, the first of the weekend activities they had agreed to. (And were both regretting doing so, right now.)

Clive slid into the worn, dark grey leather seating of the back seat and closed the door gently, worried that he may damage it if he slammed it too hard. This was probably one of those cars that stood completely on the border line between old classic and old banger. Gayle got into the back via the opposite door and couldn't help but feel like she was getting into a taxi in a foreign country. One of those taxis that had been running for generations, passed from father to son to grandson; one of those taxis that you just pray gets you to your holiday apartment before you get bitten to death by the infestation of bugs that have also lived in the back seat upholstery for generations.

"So are we both excited for the first activity?" asked Jeremy, as he hideously over-revved his engine whilst setting off. The best Gayle and Clive could muster were half-hearted "mehs", as if Jeremy was trying to talk to two teenagers in the back of his car, playing on their i-pads. As such, he kept the conversation to a minimum. In fact, the only attempted talking involved Gayle or Clive trying different questions to find out where they were going, only to be answered by an excited Jeremy, who answered with an annoying: "You'll have to wait and see!" every time. After a few minutes they both got bored of trying to coax any information out of him and so sat back in silence.

Clive closed his eyes wondering if a "power nap" may make up for his need to forgo his siesta, whilst being concerned that any sharply taken corner may see him skid across the slippery leather seat and crash right out of one of the flimsy back doors.

Gayle couldn't help but focus on the fact that, the more she thought about it, the more she really *didn't* want to be doing this. It really did feel like a big waste of time for everyone involved. But she knew that she had to try and clear this negativity from her mind. Whatever lay ahead of her she needed to embrace it in the spirit that she had agreed to; it was the very least that she owed to her and Clive's history.

Before too long Jeremy announced that they had arrived at their "first destination". Gayle was relieved that it hadn't been so long that she had slipped into a negative frame of mind again. *Be positive, be positive, be positive*; she told herself.

Clive felt frustrated that his attempted power nap had ended before it had begun. Then again, who was he kidding? This new-found, Japanese-invented phenomenon wasn't really fooling Clive, like it may be doing the rest of the world. Just adding the word "power" to something doesn't mean you can completely change the rules. A "nap" is as old as time and, in Clive's humble opinion, needed to be at least an hour long to have any real beneficial effect.

Both Clive and Gayle looked out of the car window and noticed that they had arrived at a church. As Jeremy slowly turned into the car park Gayle couldn't help but wonder whether Jeremy had brought them here to be married in a church seeing as she had told him that their actual wedding had been at a registry office. Could he actually arrange a wedding at a church in just a couple of hours?

If so, she wished he would have told them – she really didn't like the idea of getting married to Clive in the black dress she had chosen to wear. In fact, she didn't like the idea of getting married to Clive at all. She was already married to him and, as things stood, was pretty close to the ending that marriage.

A church ceremony wedding didn't cross Clive's mind at all. Instead he again thought about church pews - that he may now be expected to sit on for some unknown length of time. He hoped beyond hope that Jeremy hadn't brought them to some kind of christening ceremony. There's nothing worse than having to sit on those arse-numbing wooden seats for hours on end when all you want to do is be somewhere comfortable and have a little sleep.

Clive was also confused as to why Jeremy had driven around the car park, ignoring at least half a dozen empty parking spaces, and had now decided to park in the yellow striped spot that said "loading only" by the side door. He laughed to himself as he wondered whether Jeremy was planning a quick getaway – perhaps they were here to break into the church safe and would be given tights to put over their heads any second now?

Gayle tried to breathe in and out slowly in an attempt to suppress her road/parking rage instincts. Why the hell was Jeremy parking here? There was bound to be a delivery while they were here and .... *ok, just breathe in, and out; breathe in, and out .....*

As they all got out of the car, Gayle and Clive saw what Jeremy was wearing properly for the first time. From inside the car they could see that he was wearing a black coat but could see now that, underneath the coat, was a green and yellow chequered jumper that clashed hideously with his bright blue trousers.

Gayle frowned as she looked at him.

Was he trying so very hard to *appear eccentric* or was he just as crazy as a fish tank of lemons? Clive was confused at first but then realised that the green and yellow colour scheme did make some sense seeing as though he was Australian.

Damn it, *he's not Australian.*

Now that they were out of the car, Gayle and Clive could see the full glory of that black coat; that was a long, leather *Matrix*-esque number. It looked pretty cool if you could ignore the yellow/green jumper / blue trouser combo, and the fact that he wasn't a martial arts expert in a dark, sci-fi classic movie but rather a weird looking Doctor Who wannabe arriving at a church on a Saturday afternoon.

Clive and Gayle followed Jeremy as he walked purposefully towards the large double doors of the side entrance to the church hall, aggressively swinging one open as if he was entering a *Wild West Saloon* and hoping to make an entrance of intent. For a split second his coat flapped behind him, almost in slow motion, hinting at that cool *bullet time* effect that looked so good in the original *Matrix*. (Before, pretty much every other TV advert attempted to copy the effect and made it appear pretty bland.)

Clive followed closely behind but watching his step, just in case Jeremy's entrance had wiped out a couple of poor old age pensioner church volunteers. Gayle then walked into the building, as Clive held the door for her, wondering what on earth they were actually doing here.

In the small entrance hall area things began to become a little clearer. For a start the noise from the main road was now muffled by the closing of the large wooden doors, and the zooming of speeding cars from the road outside was replaced by the unmistakeable wails of crying babies coming from behind an internal green door. Another small hint came in the form of the large posters that clearly read "*Bumps and Babies every Saturday 3 p.m. to 4 p.m.*" Jeremy had brought them to a baby group, similar to the one that they used to attend prior and post the birth of Jack.

Jeremy noticed that they were both looking at the posters and so knew that they now realised what was going on.

"I've arranged for you to join in this session today." he began "Hopefully it'll bring back some of those memories and feelings you had when your Jack was born. Seems like a good place for us to start."

He turned around and reached out for the handle of a green door before checking his movement and turning to add:

"Let me do the talking. You two just..... let me do the talking."

They both nodded.

Gayle was slightly confused by what he meant.

Jeremy obviously wanted to do the talking, which was fine by her, but did he mean that he wanted her and Clive to *not* do *any* talking? A bit strange!

Oh well, it didn't seem out of character for Jeremy, he was *very* strange and did seem to really like talking. If fact, he struck Gayle as one of those people who tend to talk *a lot*; so much so that a large percentage of it, inevitably, ends up being complete bullshit.

Jeremy pulled at the green door and opened up the sight into the room beyond. It was a large oak-floored room where there was a large circle of adults, sitting on the floor, most of whom were either holding a baby or had a baby laying in front of them on a colourful mat.

Most people turned to see why the door had just opened, no doubt intrigued to see why anyone was arriving now, nearly twenty minutes into an hour-long session.

"Can I help you?"

A loud, lone voice shouted out from the back of the room.

Jeremy immediately began to walk clockwise around the circle and headed for the woman who had just shouted out the question. Everyone else turned back to what they were doing and Clive and Gayle couldn't help but hear snippets of conversations that were uncannily similar to conversations they, themselves, had been part of nearly twenty years earlier.

"Yeah, the health visitor said: *get used to eating cold meals* and she was right. This little one seems to know exactly when I'm about to eat my meal and suddenly becomes a little crying machine!"

"Me and Liam have been alternating the night feeds while the other one sleeps in the spare room. One good night's sleep every other night is better than not sleeping at all!"

"What's the best way to make sure you wind her properly?"

"How many feeds is he still having in the night?"

"When you're breast feeding, do you get shooting pains in your tits?"

Gayle winced at this last comment as a sympathy déjà vu pain spiralled through her own mammary glands. Clive just smiled like a schoolboy because someone had said the word "tits" out loud. Both of them however couldn't help but be mentally taken back to the time that Jack was just a baby. They too had experienced the demands of a baby around your own meal times meaning that the microwave became the star of the kitchen appliance team. Meals were very often nuked five or six times of an evening taking the culinary phrase "it's a little dry" to a whole new level. Thank God for *Reggae Reggae Sauce*.

Clive looked over towards Jeremy and saw him putting what appeared to be some form of identification back into his wallet. He then pointed over to where he and Gayle were standing and proceeded to lead the woman he had been talking to over towards them. As they got nearer, Clive could see that she was wearing a name label that read: *Zoe – Bumps and Babies Leader*. What the hell was Jeremy up to?

161

THIRTY ONE: *Bumps And Babies.*

Clive breathed a tiny, and hopefully silent, sigh of relief as it became clear that Jeremy was leading Zoe towards Gayle and not him; hopefully this relief was also untraceable on his face.

Gayle began to panic a little as she realised that it was her who the "bumps and babies" leader was actually headed towards. Things were certainly not helped by the little grunt that Clive had just made and the ridiculous, childish look that was shining out of his face.

"Hello" Zoe said wearing a friendly smile and offering a hand for Gayle to shake as she and Jeremy got close enough. "I'm Zoe. Jeremy has just been explaining your situation to me and I just want to say *thank you*. People like you are so important to those children most in need. Just wait here and relax for a couple of minutes whilst we quickly do a group exercise, then I'll introduce you to everyone."

She reached over to shake Clive's hand and added "It's a pleasure to meet you..... *thank you so much*!"

As she walked off towards the circle of new parents, Clive and Gayle looked at each other, both clearly displaying "What the hell was that about?" eyes. They both instinctively looked at Jeremy who, either consciously or subconsciously, was fixing his own eyes on the far wall, and therefore had no chance of "noticing" Gayle and Clive glaring at him.

"Ok then everybody" began Zoe, effortlessly at high volume, addressing the circle of people she was now standing in the middle of. Some individuals are just naturally equipped to speak to large groups of people.

"We are going to do another get-to-know-you exercise. I want you to quickly go around in a circle telling us the name of your baby, and why you decided on that particular name. We'll start here with Freddie and Fanny and then go around clockwise. After we've all had a go, there's a couple of special people I want to introduce you to."

She finished the last part of that sentence looking and smiling over at Gayle and Clive which made Gayle feel even more uncomfortable than she had before.

What was Zoe talking about?

She looked over at Clive to exchange concerned looks again but could tell his mind was miles away. No doubt he was amusing himself with the fact that Zoe had just revealed that the attractive looking blonde girl she wanted to start this exercise was called "Fanny".

Who in their right mind, in this day and age, calls their daughter "Fanny"? pondered Clive, allowing his mind to chuckle like it belonged to a twelve year old school boy.

It beggars belief.

At least this Fanny must know what it's like to grow up with a name that's a sitting duck for the immature Mickey-takers in life (people like Clive) and so will have thought long and hard about giving her child a more sensible name. He looked over and, after careful deducing skills were employed, came to the conclusion that her babies pink baby grow suggested she was probably a girl.

Ok then, what would Fanny and Freddie have called their daughter?

Ooh this was fun.

He was going to have a guess at the name of each baby as they went around the circle, judging by what their parents looked like. He'd already seen a couple who looked like they were wearing horse riding gear who had a baby name of "Tarquin" almost nailed on.

Ok Fanny and Freddie may well have gone for a name beginning with "F" as well, so could it be *Florence*? That feels a bit retro-modern.

Faith? That's nice.

Freya? That's cool, if a bit Norse-Goddess-y.

Fionn? No, that's a bit odd.

Oh no, Fanny was standing up and about to reveal the name, Clive needed to be quick.

Felicity? *Faye*? *Farrah*? *Fiona*? *Salma*?.....

Salma?, that doesn't even begin with "F", what was going on? Oh yeah, Clive remembered that he didn't like to go too long without thinking about *Salma Hayek*. Ok, Fanny was about to speak; need to guess now.

Florence.

Clive was going for *Florence.*

Fanny cleared her throat and looked down to where Freddie was still sitting and smiled at him.

"Freddie and I decided to name our beautiful daughter after Freddie's late Grandma."

She reached down and picked her daughter up; who was staying remarkably calm despite several other babies deciding now was a good time to test out their crying skills in preparation for the night ahead.

Clive smiled in anticipation: she sure looked like she suited the name *Florence*.

"This is..... *Bertha*!" Fanny said with the seriousness of a deadpan comedian.

Bertha?

Was she being serious?

It appears she was!

Oh my, she would have been better naming her after herself and going for *Fanny the second*. Surely even "here comes our little Fanny" is better than the inevitable "Big Bertha" that poor child is inevitably going to have to endure.

What the hell were they thinking?

Clive looked at Gayle as the name Bertha reminded him of the nickname that they'd given the school cleaner that Mr Jackson had been so fond of; that, in turn, reminded him of that first detention that they had shared together that turned out to be the start of them getting to know each other. Gayle didn't notice him looking and instead looked around the group wondering if anyone else was in as much shock as she was.

Why would *anyone* call a baby *Bertha?*

Clive focussed back on his game and thought: *that's it; if people aren't going to take this seriously then I am no longer going to play anymore.*

Next around the circle were a couple introduced as Steph and Jim who appeared to be in their mid-twenties and looked like they were "cool". (When the word is used to describe those who are up to date with the latest fashions). They both had fairly long, dark hair, were both bare-footed and were wearing tight jeans that were severely ripped. So, like I said, they were either "cool" or had lost their shoes during what must have been a brutal tussle, and frantic escape, whilst they encountered a large tiger en-route to the baby group.

"This is Paris" said Steph, smiling as she looked down on her baby, who was adorably gazing back at her.

"We named her Paris," added Jim, stroking his long hair with an air of cockiness "because we're pretty sure we were in Paris when we conceived her!"

They both sat down, looking very pleased with themselves.

The rest of the group "oohed" and "arrgghhed" a little, but there was no shock or objection to the fact that they'd all just been given some "information" that, even just a few years ago, would have been labelled by, at least one person, as "too much". I suppose it's a sign of the times. Thankfully, for their daughter, she wasn't conceived in Scunthorpe.

The next couple along, Neil and Liz, looked about similar age but far less cool. (Or maybe, as per Clive's earlier logic, they were far "cooler" because they weren't *trying* so hard to *be cool* and were just wearing "regular" jeans *and* shoes.)

"This is a coincidence" said Neil, appearing a little nervous to be addressing the group. "We named our little girl Paris as well. Not because she was conceived there....."

Everyone in the group laughed a little.

" .....But because Liz and I both *absolutely* love....."

He began to cough, a little at first, but it quickly escalated into an out of control *coughing fit*.

Clive thought about it.

He and Gayle had been to Paris and it was a beautiful place, so if you were going to name your daughter after a City, then Paris was quite a nice choice really.

Neil carried on coughing for at least ten seconds before thankfully getting a little control back as Liz passed him a bottle of water she pulled from her handbag. Well, after removing a make-up bag, a small mirror, a mobile phone, a couple of pens, a box of headache tablets, a perfume bottle, some keys, a small leather bag (yes, a bag *within* a bag), a pack of tissues, a purse, several tubes of hand cream and lip balm, a small diary, some sunglasses, a hairbrush and a box of tampons. (How the hell do women get *all that* in a handbag?)

As Neil recovered from his coughing, and Liz prepared for the hour or so it would take to squeeze everything back into her bag, Clive couldn't help but think that Neil was only a couple of seconds worth of coughing away from someone needing to step forward and attempt the Heimlich Manoeuvre on him.

Clive felt a bit disappointed. He didn't know how to do the manoeuvre himself but felt like he would have wanted to try. Not because he wanted to experience the sensation of dry-humping a man whilst standing up, but because it must be pretty good for your "life CV" to be able to say you've saved someone's life. He also thought it was probably for the best that the manoeuvre was invented by Henry Heimlich, because *Heimlich* is a pretty grand name for such a life saving action; if it had been invented by someone named Henry Butterworth it wouldn't nearly have the same kind of *gravitas*.

The Butterworth Manoeuvre?

No way.

This life-saving musing led Clive to ponder things further. It was probably the reason that, whenever he and Gayle had gone anywhere on an aeroplane he had always tried to book a seat on the aisle of the emergency exit. Sure the extra leg room was a bonus, but he liked that idea that if the plane crashed, and everyone was lucky enough to survive, then *he* himself wanted to be the one to break open the emergency exit and inflate that big yellow inflatable slide. He would stand by the door helping everyone out, one by one, making sure the whole plane was clear before triumphantly descending the yellow slide himself – face first.

He used to have similar feelings when he would take Jack to his swimming lessons, all those years ago. He would watch everyone in the pool closely to make sure that if anyone was struggling, and it had somehow gone unnoticed by the swimming teachers, then he would dive in and rescue them himself. Of course you have that whole dilemma about how long to leave someone flapping around in the water before jumping in. Are they *really* struggling or just messing around? Can they rectify the situation themselves by calming down and remembering the swimming techniques they have learnt? Will one of the teachers notice and go to assist? (Which is a fundamental part of their job.) If after all those things you decide you *must* dive in to help, you are left with the biggest dilemma of them all. Would you look completely shallow if you take your time, before diving in, to remove your mobile phone from your pocket and find somewhere safe and dry to leave it?

Thankfully Clive's random, life-saving considerations were broken by Neil who had regained his composure and was once again addressing his audience.

"Sorry about that. As I was saying we named this little one Paris because Liz and I both *absolutely* love..... Paris Hilton!"

What?

Really?

You're happy to admit that? Out loud? *To people?*

Wow!

There really is no shame these days.

166

As the shameless Paris Hilton lovers sat back down, Gayle couldn't help but imagine her and Clive being next to stand up and introduce *their* baby to the group. Words began to spin around her head about what she may say if it was her turn to speak to the group about Jack. As they did, Clive's mind focussed on something else; he couldn't help but think about the actual day that Jack had been born.

THIRTY TWO: *Time, Love And Attention.*

It was probably the moment that Jack was placed into his arms.

That was the moment that made everything *real* for Clive; that was the moment that the world changed forever. Before that all the things that were happening around him felt almost surreal. Things almost felt like they could even be events and images that he was watching on the TV or at the cinema. Even everything that happened immediately preceding that moment had an element of dreamlike wonder to them. Of course it's not every day that you rush to the hospital and then watch your new wife give birth to your first child but, even so, Clive hadn't imagined that everything would feel so fantastical to him.

But at *that* moment; when Jack was passed to him so that Gayle could "take a minute" and be "patched up a little", Clive awoke from his dream. He was intimately introducing himself to his son. And as he walked slowly around the delivery theatre, trying to soothingly talk and even sing to help his little man settle down, something very profound struck him. He realised that, in his hands, he was holding the most precious thing that he ever had, and ever would, in his entire life. He was joyous, excited, energized; almost high with life and yet felt so very, very terrified.

He had *no idea* how to be a father. He'd not even had *one* single male figure in his life that may have come close to being what a real father was. But then again, maybe *that* was a good starting point. He maybe didn't know what to do, but he had a pretty good idea about what *not* to do. He tried to clear any fear from his mind because he knew that his overwhelming emotion was pride. He felt so very lucky and blessed to be holding and talking and (successfully) soothing his baby that his pride overshadowed everything else. And as he soothed him, although Clive was pretty sure he couldn't really focus on anything, Jack seemed to be contently *looking* at him. And he seemed to be smiling and happy.

Clive remembered also looking across at Gayle and feeling so happy himself. There was his wife, the mother of his child, the love of his life; and together they were a *family*. Of course that lovely little moment didn't last long as he unfortunately saw more of the doctor stitching Gayle's "lady area" than he would have ideally liked. They had been told that she required "a couple of stitches" to bring things back together because "she hadn't experienced anything of that size coming through before"; even though Clive was pretty sure, that something rather big *had* been in contact with that area before, thank you very much!

Clive had been told by Shaun at work, in jest he hoped, to keep a close eye on what any midwifes and doctors were doing to Gayle after the birth. He had reasoned that his own wife had somehow been subjected to "extra" surgical procedures on the day she first gave birth. Most noticeably she'd received a *personality transplant* and a *sense of humour bypass*.

Clive knew he needn't worry about Gayle; she wouldn't change. But keeping an eye on things "just to be sure" had subjected him to the sight that he wished he hadn't seen. It was almost as if he'd watched one of those Animal Hospital programs and had just seen a vet repairing the damage that some cruel individual had caused by giving a particularly gruesome *Chelsea smile* to a catfish.

Some things you just cannot *un-see*.

Clive's thoughts made him feel content again as he concentrated, instead, back on that moment of him walking around the theatre with Jack in his hands. Just the two of them as the rest of the world got on with whatever they were doing. He couldn't remember exactly what he said, or sang; it was probably all nonsense – he was good at that – but he just remembered that feeling of thinking that Jack was happy.

And, thankfully, that was something that had continued for the rest of his life. He has always been a happy person. Clive contented himself by accepting that he and Gayle had always maintained a happy and stable home for him to grow in, and it had helped to let him to develop as a cheery, jovial and delightful young man. They perhaps hadn't been able to give him as many fancy gifts or holidays as some of his friends but Clive realised, as he grew into his role as a father, that it *wasn't* about that. It wasn't about giving *things*, it was about giving *time*. It was about giving *time* and *love* and *attention*. Money isn't the most important currency in life; because money fades into insignificance compared to *time, love* and *attention*.

THIRTY THREE: *Baby Group Poker.*

Gayle was ready.

She had organised her words and was all set to (imaginarily) speak them to the group.

This is Jack. She began in her mind. *Clive and I haven't got anyone in the family named Jack, in fact there weren't that many Jacks who were well known around the time he was born. There was Jack Straw but, no disrespect to him, he is hardly someone who has ever inspired you to name your baby after him, is he? There was Jack Dee and, although he's a funny guy, is it only me who gets a bit bored with the same "grumpy old man" comedy routine all the time? Does he get bored of having to be grumpy? Has he acted being grumpy for so long that it has now become mixed up with his real self and this almost manically depressed humorous view of the world is now actually him?*

Gayle began to wrap up her imaginary introduction.

Jack was a name that Clive and I had agreed upon because it was a good, sturdy, classic name. It seemed to instil a level of integrity, seriousness and almost timelessness – which was everything we wanted for him. Everyone knows a Jack and, more often than not, I bet they refer to him as "good old Jack". Have you ever heard of a Jack who hasn't been spoken about in such high regard? Well, I suppose there was Jack the Ripper! Damn it, I knew we should have gone for the name David. Suppose it's too late now. But another thing we thought about with the name Jack was that it had never really gone out of popularity; it's been a name that's always been around. Some names come and go, in and out of fashion, but Jack seemed like it would be around forever.

As Gayle continued her imaginary introduction of Jack to the group she couldn't help but reach out and hold Clive's hand. He jumped a little, surprised by her actions, but looked across at her, smiling back as she smiled at him. Both of them, now, couldn't help but be taken completely back in time to when they, too, were in exactly the same position as the people sitting around this circle: a young couple who had recently left the hospital with a little person of their own to look after.

There was no manual, no step-by-step guide about how to do anything, no "parenting *for dummies*" books. (The *"...for dummies"* books are ones that Clive finds himself seeking out more and more these days for some reason. Although that "pancakes *for dummies*" book unfortunately didn't have a chapter talking you through how to best scrape pancake mixture off the ceiling.)

And for Clive and Gayle there were no grandparents available to pop round and give assistance and advice etc. Sure, because of their situation and young age, they were given additional support from social services but that only equated to an extra hour visit from a health visitor every two to three days and, other than that, they were on their own.

But it didn't matter because they were on their own *together*. They were at the start of a brand new adventure, in their new house, with their new baby – a brand new family. There were feelings of excitement and possibility and, more than anything, feelings of *love*. So much love.

As they smiled at each other those feelings were slowly coming back to both of them, almost like sunshine slowly peeking its head around one of the clouds after an obscene amount of time when there had been nothing but rain. (You know – most of the time in England.) And it felt good.

Gayle squeezed Clive's hand gently as he continued to warmly smile at her. She looked around and allowed those memories and feelings of early parenthood to slowly glow inside her. It was such a special time.

She also sniggered a little as she watched most of the people who were holding the babies right now, because they were handling them as if they were made of glass. Life feels much better after you've got your first few *drops* out of the way. You are absolutely mortified at first but, when you realise that babies *do* actually bounce (most of the time); you do feel better in the long run. Unless, Gayle recalled, one of those first drops was because someone had taken their eye off a baby on a bed because he was too busy watching tennis on TV!

Clive watched as the last couple sat down, wondering why, all of a sudden, Gayle's nice smile had now turned into an angry frown that was being aimed right at him. The way she had been gently holding his hand was also now feeling a little like having your hand slowly tightened in a vice. What was Gayle thinking about now? Fortunately, Clive's attention was grabbed by group leader Zoe who had stepped forward to address the whole group. She beamed a big smile at Gayle and Clive as she noticed them holding hands.

"Ok, everyone." She began with that loud-haler voice. "Now we've been around the circle and introduced our babies to everyone – very well done to all of you – I've got a little introduction of my own to do. I bet you're wondering who these extra people are here today? Well, I'm about to introduce you to a *very special* couple, who I feel very honoured to have here today."

Clive and Gayle looked at each other, mirroring looks of confusion.

"First of all, though" continued Zoe. "This is Jeremy from the *AP Panel*, and he has brought us an extraordinary couple to meet – Gayle and Clive."

Clive's mind began spluttering out questions right away. Why was Zoe referring to him and Gayle as *special* and *extraordinary*? Why was she *honoured* to meet them? And what was this "*AP Panel*" that Jeremy was part of? The *Australian Pretenders Panel*? The *Absolutely Preposterous Panel*? Or, God forbid, seeing as they were here watching and listening to people talk about babies, the *Anonymous Paedophiles Panel*? What the hell had they got into here?

Zoe continued talking.

"Gayle and Clive have just had their final interviews and been given clearance to begin the process. After years of hard work the *Adoption Process Panel* has approved them for adopting a baby. They are here today to, hopefully, get a feel for the things that are ahead of them and hopefully pick up a few tips. Come on; give them a round of applause."

As the group began clapping loudly Clive felt a sense of relief to learn that *AP Panel* stood for *Adoption Process Panel* as he was just contemplating whether the *Anonymous Paedophiles Panel* were a group well know to the police and whether he and Gayle had unwittingly joined their numbers.

Gayle, on the other hand, couldn't help but feel like a rabbit caught in the headlights. As she glanced at Clive she could tell that he hadn't yet grasped the situation they were in, but she knew that those headlights she was staring at were going to continue speeding right towards them. As such, she shot a very disapproving look at Jeremy. He looked back at her with an almost apologetic look that said "sorry, but please play along".

"I'm so excited for you guys," added Zoe when the clapping had died down. "I know how difficult it is going through the adoption process. Tell us all, how do you feel?"

There it is, thought Gayle, sensing those headlights getting ever closer and waiting for the inevitable crush, fearing that she would never eat another carrot ever again.

Oh no!

Clive now realised what was happening. He quickly glanced over to his wife, who looked in no fit state to say anything and had strangely allowed her two front teeth to extend over her bottom lip..... very odd. He then looked over at Jeremy who was still displaying his "play along" face. Clive had to take control.

"It's been very, very hard" he began, repeating all the melodrama he had put into a school play he remembered when he'd had to perform a Shakespeare soliloquy.

".....and there were times; many, many times actually, when we didn't think we were going to make it. But when we found out a few years ago; well many years ago; many, many years ago, that we wouldn't be able to have children of our own, we were so desperate to become parents that we felt we *had* to do this. And it was those thoughts that kept us going through the many, many hard times during those many, many years."

Gayle and Jeremy stared at Clive in disbelief, not knowing what to make of his "performance" and completely unsure how Zoe and the rest of the group were going to react. There was certainly no sign of any feedback so far; everyone was just sitting there, staring.

Had he got away with it? Or had he gone too far over the top? *Many, many, many* times over the top? I suppose that..... wait a minute, he wasn't finished.

"And it was also the thoughts that we may be able to give a little baby a loving home, when he or she maybe otherwise wouldn't have that, that also was a real incentive for us. We've got so much love to give..... and we've now got the opportunity to give that to a little baby who'll need us."

There were some "oohs" and "ahhs" from the circle and a couple of people were visibly wiping tears from their eyes (including long-haired Jim, who a couple of minutes ago was boasting about where he and Steph had been shagging – unbelievable) and a fairly healthy ripple of applause. Jeremy nodded a very approving nod at Clive while Gayle looked around to see if there was a bucket nearby – it was very likely she may just have to throw up.

"That's beautiful!" said Zoe, her own eyes also looking a little moist. "Are you getting a girl or a boy?"

Gayle decided to take over this time, hopefully stopping Clive starting on another vomit inducing, waffling speech. Unfortunately Clive was still in the "zone" and they both spoke at the same time.

Clive: "Girl"

Gayle: "Boy"

Oh no!

Gayle stared at Clive trying to pass some words through her eyes and into his thick skull.

We had Jack. Jack is a BOY!

Clive understood what she meant and realised he should really have said boy himself but, with all the emotion he had stirred up inside himself during his speech, felt like, for this particular moment and this particular charade, it would be quite nice to pretend they were getting a girl. He couldn't really articulate all of that in one look so instead just scowled back at Gayle.

Zoe stepped towards them slightly, a look of suspicion clearly growing on her face.

"I used to work for the Adoption Panel" she began somewhat methodically, "Each new parent is pre-approved for either a girl *or* a boy. So which one is it?"

They both stood there frozen.

Gayle realised that the car that had hit them before was now reversing over them to make sure they were definitely roadkill. They were probably driving a pick up truck, had a shovel in the back to scoop them up with, and would be taking them home to eat for dinner.

Clive felt like they were robbers caught inside the church "vault". They had been stuffing extra wads of cash down their trousers because their bags were already full when the cops had turned the lights on and were now surrounding them, pointing guns their way and shouting things like: "On the floor", "hands where we can see them" and "you'll get it bad in prison, pretty boy". (It's strange which people think of themselves as "pretty boys" who will be targeted by the frustrated homosexuals / by-sexuals / just-want-sex-uals in prison.)

It was over. They were either squashed and dead on the floor or busted and caught red handed.

Jeremy could see they had given up the fight and so stepped in.

"It's a unique situation. They've actually been pre-approved for *both*." He said rather coolly. "We're just waiting now to see what becomes available …. Sorry, *who* becomes available, I mean *who*."

Zoe wasn't buying it.

"They've even been pre-approved for twins" Jeremy added, maybe hoping a bit more bullshit may just persuade Zoe, ".....And triplets. But not quads though. There's a whole extra level of criteria for parents who are suitable for looking after four babies."

"That's unusual" said Zoe, after a couple of seconds of allowing Jeremy's lies to echo around the room. She certainly didn't look as impressed as he did by the fact that he knew that *quads* meant four babies. "That never happened while I was working there!"

"You didn't mention earlier that you used to work for *us*." said Jeremy, somehow not losing any of the cool that he displayed when he first entered this exchange.

They both stared at one another for a couple of seconds as if they were deeply involved in a high-stakes game of poker. By the looks on both their faces it was hard to know which one of them was holding a royal flush and which one was bluffing. Well, obviously it wasn't difficult for Gayle and Clive who both knew the truth – that Jeremy was standing there holding nothing more than a pair of twos. (The way Gayle and Clive were both feeling, it was possible that they could easily produce a "pair of twos" of their own.)

Jeremy *raised* her.

"The rules on approval have been amended recently. For the right, outstanding candidates, the options are left as open as possible."

Zoe scratched her ear before *calling* him.

"That's odd. My sister and cousin still work for the panel and they have not mentioned to me that the criteria has changed in any way."

What did Zoe scratching her ear mean? It was obviously a *tell sign*, but did it mean she was bluffing too, or was she now just moving in for the kill?

Gayle could feel her cheeks reddening.

Clive could feel his arse twitching.

Zoe decided to *raise* – she was going *all in*.

"Could you tell me who your boss is at the Adoption Process Panel..... and I best take a look at that i.d. again, please!"

Jeremy removed his wallet from his trouser pocket slowly. Did he have one last play? Perhaps one last card up his sleeve? As he began to remove some papers from the front of the wallet he whispered, out of the corner of his mouth, towards Clive and Gayle.

"Quietly, but *quickly*, make your way out of the building."

No – he was *folding*.

Zoe began to walk towards him.

"In fact" Jeremy added, his whisper turning into a shout in the space of two words. "RUN FOR IT!..... NOW!"

Gayle and Clive instinctively reacted and quickly began running towards the door, with Jeremy, and his flapping coat, following close behind. Gayle couldn't quite rationalise what was going on but still ran with the intensity of someone who, after camping and queuing overnight, had noticed the doors were now opening for the Primark sale.

Clive got to the first door the quickest and flung it open whilst realising now why, and being thankful for the fact that, Jeremy had parked his car in the loading bay. That quick getaway that he amused himself about them needing – well they needed it right now.

THIRTY FOUR: *The Youth Club.*

Just the mere sight of the buildings was enough to begin the stirring of memories long passed. Warm and sunny days when there wasn't a care in the world and also cold, rainy ones when life seemed so complicated and the last place you wanted to be was actually *here*. It's funny how most clear memories work that way: either really good or really bad – there never seems to be much that is in between.

Here was Chestnut Street High School that Clive and Gayle used to attend and they were here tonight to specifically visit one part of it: *the youth club.* As part of Jeremy's "masterplan" to help them rekindle their love, they were here to return to the scene of their very first kiss.

The youth club was a small, one storey brick building that stood next to the main car park and somehow felt detached from the rest of the school that was mainly made up of multi-storey blocks that seemed to tower above it.

Jeremy's car turned into the school car park while Clive and Gayle tried hard to, as per instructed, "Let their minds wander back to that *fateful night*".

For Gayle that wasn't too difficult as her mother used to drive her to the youth club; well, on the nights that their car could be bothered starting, anyway. That combined with the fact that Jeremy had somehow got a copy of *Now That's What I Call Music! 19*, that was now playing *Should I Stay or Should I Go* by *The Clash* through his maroon Volvo's *cassette player*, meant that her approach to the youth club was very much how it had been all those years ago.

For Clive it was slightly different. His days of visiting the youth club had always started with a fairly long walk to get there, usually with the same one or two school pals. Jeremy had, at first, insisted on trying to

177

make "each and every detail as close to the original event" as possible, but admitted defeat on this occasion when he couldn't track down the whereabouts of one Robert Adshead. Clive suggested that seeing as, after he had met him the previous day, *Knobhead* was probably in possession of, up to, sixty pounds in cash, a "live for today" attitude and a horny pensioner, it may be several days before he once again appeared on the grid. So, for Clive, the actual arrival at the youth club felt new to him.

However the whole setting and, somehow, *mood* of the evening, so far, did feel strangely familiar. What was also probably helping was the couple of glasses of "champagne" that they had both drunk on the way here, courtesy of Jeremy insisting that the *Love Is...* service is "V.I.P. all the way." (It had certainly made both of their heads a little fuzzy, but Clive was more than a little suspicious of this particular sparkling wine from that elite area in France seeing as the label on the bottle appeared to be hand written and actually said "Shampagne". He thought it best not to show Gayle, as she too might wonder whether they were actually drinking something that was *meant* to be consumed rather than something that could very well have been produced for washing hair.)

One thing that was totally different about the night though was that, back in the day, youth club was *always* on a Tuesday whereas here they were now attending on a Saturday night. But maybe that was just a sign of *progress* and *forward thinking* by the organisers of the club – by running it on a Saturday night it gave teenagers something to be doing rather than having to go to the park and drink way too much alcohol and be sick everywhere.

Jeremy pulled his car into a car park space and his headlights, that appeared to be stuck on, illuminated a young boy in the bushes in front of them – he was being sick and looked like he had drunk way too much alcohol.

So much for progress.

The three of them got out of the car and it was only then that the true, nostalgic sensation of being there manifested itself inside Clive. The whole place looked, sounded and smelt *exactly* the same as it had over twenty years earlier. If he wasn't actually stepping out of a "vintage" Volvo then Clive would not have been surprised to find himself stepping out of a Delorean, while Huey Lewis blasted out *Power of Love* on the radio. He took a long and slow turn around; viewing the school in slow motion like it was the Coliseum in Gladiator, before settling on looking towards the youth club where there was a fairly long, snaking queue at the entrance. Clive zipped his coat up, out of habit rather than because of the weather as it was actually a very mild night, hoping to hell that the catchy *Clash* riff wasn't now going to be continuously stuck echoing around in his head for the rest of the night. It was a cool song but one of those that had the potential to drown out anything else up in your head that you may need. You know, for example: *thinking.*

Gayle took a slow look all around her and breathed in the air. She had absolutely *hated* and *resented* this place when she had first arrived here and yet, now, actually felt quite happy to be back, almost as though she had missed it.

"Before I forget." said Jeremy, removing a white envelope out of the inside pocket of his long black coat "Again, let me just say I'm profoundly sorry about the unfortunate incident at the church earlier. Now, these are the instructions for tomorrow mornings activities."

Gayle gave Jeremy a look that she hoped said "the "unfortunate incident at the church" was a complete nightmare, so apology *not* accepted" before taking the envelope from him. She read the hand written words on the front.

Sunday – 10 a.m. 221 Deanwater Way. Do Not open until arrival.

She held it up for Clive to read before placing it into her handbag. Clive quickly recognised that 221 Deanwater Way was the address of the *Love Is...* "office", in the shopping precinct. What could Jeremy have in store for the next day that meant going there?

"Ok, let's go." said Jeremy as he started walking towards the youth club. "Let me do the talking!"

Gayle and Clive immediately looked at one another. Why did "Let me do the talking" instantly remind both of them of the fiasco of the afternoons events, that had also begun with those same five words.

Oh please, not again.

Jeremy ignored the queue and headed straight towards the entrance door. He noticed Gayle looking at the queue and, perhaps expecting a question and deciding to pre-answer it, said: "We're not queuing, we're going straight in. I told you, V.I.P. treatment all the way!"

Gayle looked at Clive and rolled her eyes. She had a feeling that it would almost certainly not be the last time she would be doing that during their "adventures" with Jeremy.

A few steps later they were alongside a woman at the entrance door, who was standing by a small, makeshift desk that had a book and money tin on it. She looked exactly like the women who used to run the youth club back in the day. She had what, back then, seemed to be a typical "social worker" type of look - a bright red flattop hairstyle, baggy green jumper and Doc Martin boots.

It was hard to hear exactly what Jeremy was saying as he was speaking quietly and pretty much right into her ear but, after a few seconds of saying whatever he said and in God knows what accent, the woman appeared happy to let him, Gayle and Clive in.

"Ok, you'll have to sign in the book, and I'll give you visitors pass each." She said, passing Jeremy a pen, pointing to the large exercise book on the desk and then reaching for some blank, white stickers underneath.

"What did you say again? Health and safety and..... where, are you from?"

Without hesitation, Jeremy answered.

"Certified records and bursary services. They merged several departments together during the latest budget cuts. We'll be making the school dinners as well before you know it!"

The woman at the desk laughed along with Jeremy before he looked back at Clive and Gayle and offered a congratulatory, sly wink. Gayle rolled her eyes once again as she wondered, through a mixture of bemusement and confused admiration, how certain people are gifted with endless front and are fluent in complete bullshit.

"Jeremy, Clive and Gayle?" checked the woman on the desk, as she began writing on the white stickers in thick, black marker pen.

"That's correct" said Jeremy as he finished entering their names into the exercise book.

"Health and Safety, Certified Records and Bursary Services?" she asked next.

"Correct again!" said Jeremy, a bit over-smarmily to not be cringe-worthy.

"That's a bit long for the passes, so I'll have to just put the initials on."

"That's not a problem" said Jeremy. "We won't be long anyway; just a check of the interior of the premises and then a quick word with yourself and some of your marvellous colleagues out here about any health and safety concerns and..... record keeping..... and services and..... things."

Thankfully Jeremy's rambling dipped in volume towards the end of his sentence and the woman at the desk was more interested in peeling off the back of the stickers than actually listening to his mumbo-jumbo. She then attached a sticker to each of them, after rather embarrassingly asking Clive and Gayle which one of them was Clive and which one of them Gayle. No wonder she had fallen for Jeremy's ridiculous cover story.

"Thank you very much Hayley. We will come back to see you when our inspection is complete." Jeremy said, with a smile, to the flat-topped woman; somehow in a way that made a very normal sentence sound like outrageous flirting. But it appeared that his charms had worked a treat on Hayley who with a smile of her own, and reddening cheeks, said:

"I'll look forward to it. Take as long as you need."

Gayle watched in a state of confusion. Is this what passed for *flirting* these days in people of a certain age? She was now also of *a certain age* and was nearing the stage that she would require to be fluent in flirting herself. The thought of acting like this make her feel a bit sick.

Jeremy walked towards the far corner of the entrance room. Gayle and Clive followed; Clive feeling like he needed to give Jeremy a piece of his mind. Especially since he and Gayle had been gracious enough to accept his "sincerest" apologies about the afternoon events at the church baby group, and his "guarantee" that it "would never happen again".

"What's going on *now*? Are we actually going to go anywhere that we are *allowed* to be?" he snapped at Jeremy in a quiet but sharp voice. "And where the hell are we supposed to be from? Health and safety and bursary and *something else* records?"

Jeremy put his hands out in front of him and gently rocked them up and down, making a silent *calm-down* kind of gesture.

"Health and safety, certified records and bursary services." He said calmly. "I find that the more details, and more *extreme* you make an untruth, the more likely it is to be believed..... and how else do you expect me to get you in here?"

"How else do we expect you to get us *in here*?" Gayle interjected, her own anger bubbling away inside. "We didn't *ask* you to bring us here. If it turns out we're *not allowed* to be here, then maybe *not coming here* would be a better option?" she added with extra sting at the end of her sentence.

"Calm down." Jeremy said, his own voice remaining quiet and really rather soothing. "*This* is an important place in your history – we *need* to be here. Anyway, it's rather exciting isn't it? Doing things that you're *not* supposed to be doing?"

Gayle looked at Clive as he slowly smiled and cheekily raised his eyebrows. He *was* enjoying this. Without wanting to, she couldn't help but smile back as a small sensation of butterflies gently erupted in her stomach. She wasn't sure if it was the awakening of some thrill-seeking passion, and she would soon be trying out bungee jumping and sky diving, or if it was just the Shampagne talking, but she found herself reluctantly agreeing.

"Ok" she said, trying to keep any excitement out of her voice. "I suppose we're here now, we might as well do it. What's the plan?"

Jeremy flashed a massive smile.

"That's the spirit! You two have a look around, try and look a bit *official* as you do, and I'll come and get you when I've got everything ready."

After speaking those words, he was gone. He disappeared into the main youth club hall and out of sight before either Gayle or Clive could react.

Clive looked at Gayle and smiled again.

"Shall we?" he asked holding his hand out.

Gayle reached out and grabbed his hand and they, too, walked away from the corner and headed out into the main hall.

"This is so weird" Gayle whispered under her breath. "It's like nothing has changed."

Clive nodded his head in agreement.

Just as they both recalled from the last time they had been here, in the main hall stood a rickety, old trampoline that, every time the person on it bounced, groaned like a proud, wooden boat being battered in a severe weather storm. There was a queue of about fifteen kids waiting to have their go and risk the danger of jumping up and down on a contraption that seemed out of date 20+ years ago, and was surely going to give up and collapse at any given moment. A female youth club volunteer stood at the front of the queue, holding a stop watch, staring at in blankly, and looking like she had completely given up the will to live.

Against the side wall there was a game of badminton in full swing and beyond that, in the corner, there was a small arts and crafts table set up that had about half a dozen kids huddled round, making things.

As Gayle had said, it felt like *nothing* had changed whatsoever; everything was just as it had been back when she and Clive were at school. Gayle smiled a little as she noticed a line of people standing along the corridor to the right of the main hall that lead to the tuck shop that was by the small bar / kitchenette area. In a world in which everything is changing at such a rapid rate, it felt somehow comforting that some things hadn't changed one little bit. Kids were still handing over loose change in exchange for sweets and panda cola bottles.

Meanwhile, Clive had been gazing through the window that looked into what used to be a rather basic gym / weights room back in the day. It appeared like that room, too, remained pretty much unchanged and he could clearly see a couple of dozen, mostly big, lads in rugby shirts lifting weights, arm wrestling and pushing one another around; no doubt trying to impress the handful of girls watching on with their "macho actions".

Clive remembered venturing into that room a couple of times in the past before realising that weights *weren't his thing* and being "asked to leave" by some of the bigger, more muscled lads. Thank God Gayle never seemed to be impressed by this brainless act of strapping on a large leather belt and attempting to lift your own body weight in cast iron. Bloody Arnold Schwarzenegger had a lot to answer for back in the 80s / 90s.

As he realised that he still hadn't actually found out *what* *his thing* was in life, Clive watched on as a younger looking lad, who was just wearing a t-shirt, began to drink the contents of a large glass that Clive had seen one of the bigger lads fill up with beer from a can, what looked like cigarette butts and had allowed *all* the other lads - to *spit* into. He wretched a little as this young lad struggled to down the vile cocktail, as the male members of the room chanted something very loud. Clive realised it was some kind of initiation ceremony and the younger lad was trying to prove he was worthy of joining this rugby top wearing elite crew – by drinking cigarette butts and flem coughed up from the deepest areas of the throats of over twenty, probably germ-infested, teenagers. After a few seconds he lifted the glass high into the air in triumphant fashion before turning it upside down and placing it on top of his head. Loud cheers blasted out of the weights room, even threatening to be louder than the creaking trampoline in the main hall, as the young lad, who looked like he would have to go home immanently and spend a week in bed vomiting, was presented with his very own rugby shirt. Lots of the other lads began some strange celebratory actions which, to Clive's annoyance, including a lot of "dabbing".

Clive had no understanding of what this dabbing craze was about and, even at the risk of being exposed as a sad, old, out of touch, fuddy-duddy, found it completely got on his nerves. It summed up the youth of today – attention seeking and completely weird. His only explanation about where it had come from was that someone, at some time, had sneakily tried to check themselves for possible body odour, outstretched an arm as they did so and inadvertently, and randomly, started an unfathomable craze in the process. Probably similar to how most unfathomable crazes begin.

THIRTY FIVE: *Rubik's Cubes, Millennium Falcons & Tracey Islands.*

Clive tried to clear his mind.

It was wrong that he was allowing himself to become annoyed about *dabbing* once again. Although it *is* weird, and has robbed a legitimate way to clean something gently with a cloth or paper towel of its exclusive meaning, it is just a weird trend and is one of those things that has become fashionable; will be for a while before it gets replaced by something else – probably something even weirder and *even more annoying.* (Fidget spinners / flossing?)

As Clive tidied the irritation from his mind he couldn't help but smile as he remembered one of these "trends" from his own youth. It was when kids, mostly girls who liked Bros, used to wear those removable Grolsh bottle tops on their shoes. He laughed at how strange that seemed now but also remembered how annoying he had also found that at the time. Thankfully the fact that strange trends used to annoy him in the past, as a child, meant that Clive *wasn't* just a sad, old, out of touch, fuddy-duddy now. Of course it could *actually* mean that, *as a child*, he was a sad, old, out of touch, fuddy-duddy.

Hmm, was he an angry, Victor Meldrew like character when he was a young boy? Probably best not to open that can of worms. Instead Clive focussed on the stranger fact that, although these trends come and go, while they're "here" pretty much everyone goes crazy for them.

The first one that came to mind was when Jack was six and he was desperate for (in fact, he *needed*) a Tamagotchi pet. And the reason that he *needed* it? The fact that all his friends had one. And so, driven by Jack's *Emperor's New Clothes* like obsession to follow the crowd and the fact that Clive and Gayle could afford it, they bought him one. What followed were a few obsessive days of hatching, feeding, playing, walking and generally caring for a "virtual" pet by pressing buttons, at the right time, on the front of a plastic, egg-shaped electronic device attached to a key ring. (Who wants to do all the above with a *real pet* when you can do it at the touch of a button with a Tamagotchi?)

Unfortunately Jacks first Tamagotchi sadly passed away within a week due to being over-fed, and the plastic, key-ringed device quickly followed suit and made its way into the dustbin. The bin men will have taken it to the tip before it went into a land-fill site where it would have joined the millions of Rubik's cubes, Millennium Falcons and Tracey Islands and all those other, invariably nearly-impossible to get hold of (genius marketing strategy?) "must have" things. Things made of plastic that will never decompose and will sit there as a visual souvenir of mankind's stupidity long after we have obliterated ourselves.

Clive had read somewhere that dabbing had actually originated from a dance, which fits in with other boogie inspired trends over the years; from the *Birdie Song* to the *Macarena*, from the *Moonwalk* to *Gangnam* style. For someone who had been so annoyed by it, he had certainly done his research. And his research had led him to a pretty clear conclusion: all these dance trends, and maybe *all trends* as a whole, had annoyed him - the (pretty much not in dispute any more) Meldrew clone. He just couldn't really understand how things become so popular and how so many people seem to be completely powerless to do anything *but* become completely obsessed with them also.

As he thought more, Clive was happy that Jacks Tamagotchi fixation, and his keenness of "virtual" things in general, had been nothing more than a fleeting phase because he remembered all those outdoor and "real" things that they had done together over the years. Jack had certainly never been one to sit in his bedroom and play on a games system, all hours of the day. Many of his friends may have wanted to play FIFA on their Playstations or Xbox's but Jack had always preferred to play for *real* on the park. And more often than not it would be with Clive – something that suited him perfectly and had created many, many happy memories. Clive wondered about the kids who seem to play on their computers, in their dark bedrooms, all the time; especially those who don't play in the same room as the *other* kids they are playing against - because they play online. It had always amused him to wonder whether the people who had invented online gaming had done so because they finally got completely pissed off with their mates farting too much during all night sessions of Tekken.

185

Maybe there was something else that Clive needed to contemplate. Why is it that, whatever subject he begins to think about, nine times out of ten his thought process leads him to a joke that has something to do with somebody farting?

THIRTY SIX: *The First Kiss.*

Clive cleared his mind of any further flatulence related gags as he turned away from looking at the weight room. He slowly counted to ten to also steer his thoughts away from unruly teenagers and obscure trends in an effort to bring himself back towards some level of calm. He was certainly glad he wasn't a teenager nowadays feeling like he had to impress girls, and a bunch of macho morons, by drinking other peoples' cigarette butts and bodily fluids and, worse still, constantly dabbing.

Bloody dabbing.

As he looked across to Gayle he found her with a slightly sad and confused look on her face.

"What's wrong?" he asked her instinctively.

"Just feel a bit out of place here now." She said under her breath. "A bit *old* you know? We're a bit *old.* Everyone who walks past seems to be sniggering at us!"

Clive shook his head.

Sure they were *a bit* older than the teenagers here but he didn't believe that *everyone* was so rude as to be sniggering at a couple of people, who may well be here to help or, as per the ruse they were pulling, were actually carrying out some kind of safety inspection. He had to change his mind after a group of three girls were quickly followed by two boys and two more girls, all of whom looked him and Gayle up and down and did indeed snigger at them. In fact, snigger didn't cover it, the majority of them were almost laughing in their faces.

Bloody youth of today!

Just because Clive had his cagoule on (rain had been forecast) and Gayle didn't look like she'd drawn on her own, ridiculously thick, surprised-looking eyebrows (what's *that* all about with young girls these days?), it didn't mean it was acceptable for these youngsters to laugh at them.

Clive looked across at Gayle and looked her up and down just as the girls and boys who had just walked past had. His own involuntary laughing told him straight away that the kids weren't actually laughing at them because they were older, or because of what they were wearing, or the fact that Gayle's eyebrows looked pretty *normal*. No they were actually laughing because of a different fashion item Gayle was wearing.

"Where are we from again?" he asked Gayle whilst still chuckling.

"What?" said Gayle in confusion and frustration.

"Where was it? *Health and Safety, Certified Records and Bursary Services?*"

Gayle looked a little confused for a second before realising Clive was repeating where Jeremy had said they had come from.

"Wow, how did you remember that?" she said, impressed with Clive's rain-man like memory.

"It's written on your badge." Clive said still tittering. "Well the *initials* are anyway!"

Gayle looked down and read the white sticky label that Hayley had stuck to her chest: *GAYLE HAS CRABS*

What the hell?

Had Hayley not realised what she was writing when she did the labels? And how had she perfectly put a space between the initial for "safety" and the one for "certified" to make a clearly readable, highly embarrassing label?

Clive couldn't help but laugh even louder as he saw the look of horror on Gayle's face, that got even worse as he laughed even harder. He could only stop himself after he noticed Gayle looking at his own chest which transformed her distressed look into a fit of laughter of her own.

Wait a minute.

He "worked" at the same place as Gayle. He quickly looked down at his own chest and, yep, sure enough: *CLIVE HAS CRABS*. The lettering on his "id" badge was also perfectly spaced to warn of his own pubic lice infestation. He quickly forgave all the kids who had passed by and laughed at them; there was nothing wrong in laughing at people who had been suckered into wearing a sexually transmitted disease warning label.

Bloody Jeremy.

Had he done this on purpose?

Clive ripped his own label off and took hold of Gayle's too after she also removed her own – carefully trying to make sure she didn't pull her chiffon cardigan. He walked over to the large bin that was overflowing with bottles of Rola Cola and Panda Orange, thinking that sugar-fuelled teenagers were probably just as hazardous as alcohol fuelled ones, and stuffed his and Gayle's labels into it. He contemplated for a moment about how inappropriate it would be to join the queue for the trampoline, he'd always been a sucker for trampolines and bouncy castles, but thought better of it as he noticed Jeremy coming out of the side corridor and back into the main hall.

He was sweating fairly heavily and looked generally hot and bothered as if he may have spent the ten or so minutes away from them having an intense weights session / rugby mob induction of his own in the weight room. Clive thought about giving him a piece of his mind about the childish and pathetic name label gag but realised straight away that Jeremy had probably been completely oblivious to it, as he was still wearing his own label that also perfectly read: *JEREMY HAS CRABS.*

After they had walked over to where Gayle was, Clive motioned his head towards Jeremy's label to bring it to Gayle's attention and they both spent a couple of seconds of childish, snorting laughter as Jeremy looked on in complete confusion. He waited to be let in on the joke but neither Gayle or Clive had any intention of telling him, not when it would most likely amuse them completely for the rest of the night.

"That took a bit of sorting." Jeremy eventually said "But everything's ready now. Follow me!"

Clive and Gayle followed him across the main hall, down the corridor and towards the small room at the back of the building that they both remembered to be the disco room. As they got closer to the door a few disgruntled looking teenagers left the room alongside Hayley from the front desk. Gayle heard one of them mumbling ".....dunno, fire alarm test or summit, think she said" as they passed them and began to feel a little guilty that these kids were being kicked out of the disco room for them. They were three people who were too old to be here, had actually lied about *why* they were here, and two of them had already had their turn of being here many years ago. They really shouldn't be here.

She had no opportunity to air her views as, once at the door, Jeremy quickly ushered them into the room and stuck a piece of paper of the outside of the door before shutting it closed behind them.

Wow.

The feeling hit both Gayle and Clive completely and instantly. It felt like they had just walked through a door that had taken them back in time. Whereas the main areas of the youth club certainly had a similar look and feel to them as they had in the past, this small room felt *exactly the same*. It was dark and smoky and had the same array of blue, green, yellow and red lights spinning and oscillating and piercing through the foggy atmosphere. The only other light in there was the faint green glow that signalled the fire exit door on the far wall. The tiny "stage" area where teenagers used to sit and snog was still there along the wall to the left hand side. Clive and Gayle could almost picture these kids as they sat in a row, in their pairs, and had some kind of unspoken contest to see who could snog for the longest, without having to come up for air.

This room was also warmer than the other parts of the youth club, exactly how it used to be, and still had an aroma that you couldn't quite put your finger on; a fairly smokey but yet pleasant smell that was completely unique to the youth club disco. It was like this tiny room had somehow been sheltered from the rigours of time, like a lost world island that still had dinosaurs roaming around on it. (Although, admittedly, this wasn't an island because it was just a room. And (hopefully) there weren't any dinosaurs roaming around or this *would* be a night to remember.)

Jeremy disappeared into the DJ "booth", which was still a flimsy, wooden structure, probably begrudgingly thrown together by a previous school caretaker when the idea of a disco room was first hatched. Out of the silence came the Kylie and Jason "classic" (depends how you like your "classics", I suppose) *Especially For You*, and that completely sealed the deal – Clive and Gayle were instantly taken back to their previous encounters with this surreal, small room.

It felt, to them, exactly like that strange phenomenon when a specific set of individual memories, usually stirred by numerous senses, align to create something of a wormhole of feelings that transport you to another time and place. Maybe like the way the dying light makes the sky look on a warm summers evening, aligned to you sitting outside with your skin tingling following the kiss of the suns warm glow that day; and there's the smell of freshly cut grass and the taste of warm marsh mellows that have been toasted on an open fire. (Ok, that may just be a *little* too unique to be applicable for *everyone*, but you know what I mean don't you? Several déjà vu sensory moments coming together to create specific memories.)

Clive and Gayle were now in a completely different time; a time from the past, a time when their feelings for each other were growing to their absolute strongest. They began to smile at each other and sway a little to that mechanical, manufactured, but ultimately ear-pleasing, *Stock, Aitkin and Waterman* backing track.

Then there was dancing.

And it wasn't time-appropriate to the song, but rather the dancing that they always used to do for every song back in their days of the youth club disco. Hands behind their backs, slowly swaying left and right, with that undisputedly cocky *Manc swagger* as if they were members of *Oasis*.

The music then changed and the second record Jeremy played was *In These Arms* by *Bon Jovi*. Gayle clapped her hands above her head in excitement, not worrying one bit that she looked like a deranged, hungry seal, as Clive smiled and looked over at Jeremy in the DJ booth. This was one of Gayle's favourite tunes, a song that he also liked and they had enjoyed together, so Jeremy had certainly done his homework. Clive reached out and grabbed Gayle's hands and they began a very loose, but energetic romantic waltz type dance together – just like they had in this room in the past. They both laughed and smiled and gazed at each other as they sang out the last couple of lines of the first chorus loudly " .....*I'd love you 'til the end of time, If you were in these arms tonight.*" For the rest of the song they continued dancing and laughing and singing and spinning – something they hadn't done for at least ten years.

The record then began to fade away and Clive slowed his dancing a little and naturally pulled Gayle into *his arms*. Still beaming a huge smile Gayle allowed herself into his embrace and fitted perfectly back against his chest; just like she always used to in those days gone by.

A new song began and the intro was a slow, distinctive acoustic groove that they both recognised instantly: it was the song *Mmm Mmm Mmm Mmm* by *Crash Test Dummies* – the song that had been playing in this very room when they shared their first kiss. Without needing to speak to each other or even make a conscious decision about what they were doing they both slowly walked towards the tiny stage to the left of the room. They stepped up whilst still gazing at one another and then turned to sit down, backs against the wall. Clive put his arm around Gayle's shoulder and they just sat there for a few seconds, cuddling and taking in the music, exactly like they had done many times in the past as teenagers. Of course their previous experiences like this had been accompanied by other couples; other teenage "boyfriends and girlfriends", sitting in a row and snogging in that over-enthusiastic youthful way that must inevitably end in severe facial injuries for many of them. But it didn't feel any different because even though they weren't alone in the past, it had always *felt* like they were anyway.

191

Sitting against this wall, listening to the music and gazing at each other, the whole world had always just disappeared.

And it was disappearing right now.

Clive and Gayle stared into each other's eyes as the song headed into its titular chorus and couldn't deny that some feelings, that seemed like they'd been missing for a long, long time, felt like they were slowly awakening. Both of them naturally wondered whether they should be tilting their heads and allowing their lips to slowly introduce, or re-introduce, themselves to each other.

And then it happened..... BANG!

The door was barged open and in stepped a large teenager wearing a rugby shirt. He flipped on the main lights, almost blinding Clive and Gayle, and shouted at the top of his voice:

"WHAT THE FUCK IS GOING ON IN HERE?"

Clive and Gayle both held their hands up to their eyes to shield them from the bright lights. The big guy looked at them and asked, still using his voice at the top end of the volume scale.

"WHO THE FUCK ARE YOU TWO? AND WHO THE FUCK PUT THIS SIGN ON THE DOOR?"

Clive could just about make out the sign that the big teenager, who he now recognised as one of the loudest of the crew he'd seen earlier in the weights room, was holding. It was obviously the sign that Jeremy had stuck on the outside of the door a few minutes earlier. It read: *"KEEP OUT. Room unsafe – electrical testing going on inside."*

Jeremy stepped out of his booth and began one of his rambling speeches in an effort to calm down this large young man.

"As per the sign you are holding, you *really* shouldn't have entered this room. We are testing the electrical systems and it is really rather dangerous for anyone else to be in here right now. If you can ...."

The rugby-topped youth had heard enough.

"WHO THE FUCK ARE *YOU*? ELECTRICAL TESTING MY ARSE – THESE TWO DON'T LOOK LIKE FUCKING ELECTRICIANS."

Clive was now regretting throwing away his visitors sticker. It was the closest thing to "credentials" that he had, that he could have shown to the young guy. Then again, thinking about it, maybe he wasn't. Bloody *CLIVE HAS CRABS!*

The lull in conversation was filled by the *Crash Test Dummies* who were still singing in the back ground.

"Once there was this girl who,
Wouldn't go and change with the girls in the change room,

But when they finally made her
They saw birthmarks all over her body."

"WHAT THE FUCK IS THIS MUSIC?" asked the big, rugby youth, again at top volume. It was hard to argue with him, in this context the music did seem a little, well, *odd.*

Jeremy stepped over to the young guy and spoke to him in a hushed voice, as if he was sharing some big secret with him.

"Look friend; just give us a few minutes will you? We're trying to create a *moment* here?"

"I'LL GIVE YOU A MOMENT" he responded, again as loud as possible. "A MOMENT TO FUCK OFF BEFORE I GET THE WHOLE RUGBY TEAM IN HERE!"

"What a lovely way you have of using the English language," Jeremy said, seemingly a little annoyed himself now. "Did they teach you that at *this* school? If they did then I know where *not* to send my kids."

The rugby-topped guy seemed unfazed by Jeremy's words and instead just stared at him before asking: "Have you got fucking CRABS?"

Jeremy looked confused before looking down and noticing his name label. He ripped it off, fairly aggressively, before he and the rugby guy continued to stare at each other.

The situation that looked like it could get extremely tense, especially if the big guy carried out his threat to bring his other, obviously also large, rugby buddies was brought to an end by Hayley who had also now arrived at the door, holding a piece of paper.

"What's going on?" she now demanded, thankfully at a lower volume and without the potty-mouth expletives inserted by the rugby youth. "I've just been through our health and safety file and we actually had an inspection six weeks ago when I was off. We only ever get inspected once every twelve months, so could I ask you for some identification, please?"

Oh dear.

Gayle and Clive looked at each other and then looked at Jeremy, who looked a little flustered as; hopefully, he worked on some plan regarding what they should do next. Behind Hayley there was quite a gathering of teenagers who had all come to see what all the commotion was. From feeling completely alone in a different place and time it now felt like the whole world was watching them.

Suddenly Jeremy made a move. It seemed like whatever plan he had worked on was about to come to fruition. He stepped towards Hayley and started to take his wallet out whilst saying,

"Of course, let me show you my council ID card."

In an attempted whispered voice towards Clive and Gayle, to which you would think almost everybody else in the youth club could probably hear anyway, he said

"You two, fire exit. Run! I'll catch up with you!"

Gayle's mind worked instantly and decided she wouldn't be running for the second time today. For one, like earlier in the day, her natural response to *any* offer of any kind of running is: *thank you very much, but NO. I'd rather boil my own eyeballs.* But secondly she decided that she and Clive had not really done anything wrong and so they should just explain the situation, sort things out, and then go home – in a *non-running* kind of way.

Clive's mind was a split second slower but once he had analysed the situation he made a slightly different, more panicky-headless-chickeny, decision. He grabbed Gayle by the arm, pulled her to her feet, and dragged her across the dance floor to where he slammed open the fire exit. An internal alarm began to sound as Clive pulled Gayle into the night air and urged her to run with him. She now knew she was left with little choice but to run once more.

Oh the joy!

And this time, it was very likely that there may well be a pack of huge teenage rugby players hot on their heels. What a day.....

THIRTY SEVEN: *Midnight Feast.*

Clive's mind instinctively travelled back in time and reminded him exactly what to do in this kind of situation. He had been chased through the school playgrounds countless times in the past and so his brain guided his limbs, almost muscle memory-esque, around the small alleyways and courtyards that led to the school field. It was something that he'd had to get pretty good at when he was at school. When you are being chased by dinner money thieves, and therefore your prospects of being able to eat lunch on a given day are at stake, there is a survival instinct that kicks in; enhancing skills you may otherwise not require. Anyone following tonight, especially testosterone-fuelled, freakishly large, potty-mouthed, rugby youths who are always looking for an excuse to hurl people to the floor or gouge out the odd eye here and there, would struggle to keep up. (Finally there seemed to be a payoff to being chased by those dinner money thieves and, oh yes, those other bullies that liked to pick on you for having the unfortunate privilege of wearing long trousers that were so short it seemed you were constantly mourning a cat. Sorry Clive!)

"Where are we going?" gasped Gayle in between trying to take in large gulps of air.

"Onto the field" replied Clive as they, well, ran out on to the field. "We'll go to *our* corner and we can get our breath back."

They carried on running for the extra forty metres or so that it took to reach the large oak trees that led round to the area of the school field that was hidden out of sight; the area that they both used to refer to as "*our corner*". Once there, they both tentatively looked behind to see if there was an unruly rugby mob, in both their minds carrying fiery torches and pitchforks and accompanied by angry, foaming-at-the-mouth hounds from hell, chasing them down. Fortunately there wasn't and so by quickly stepping behind the largest tree, out of sight, it seemed that they were in the clear.

Gayle bent down, breathing hard, and placed her hands on her knees in that way that many athletes do after a grueling 10,000 metres or marathon run. Not because she was feeling athletic in any way but thinking that if and when she was sick then the splash back would be minimalised the closer she was to the ground.

"Ok," she said after about a minute, standing upright and feeling thankful that she hadn't followed her urge to consume as many (shockingly priced) cola bottles that any loose change she had could have bought her. "Where the hell did you find this *Jeremy*? And why is he making us run like lunatics all the time? And please, tell me, there is no way we are *ever* going to do anything else he says?"

Clive, feeling a little less out of breath and putting it down to the fact that his job forced him into running around like a lunatic *every day*, nodded his head in agreement.

"He had things planned for tomorrow, but I think we're done aren't we?"

Gayle nodded her head vigorously, she had never been more certain of anything in her life. As she did she turned her head to the left to look towards "their area" and her eye was drawn to a slight, flickering light that was coming out of the darkness.

"What's that?" she asked Clive.

"What's what?" he asked back, just now looking in the same direction and also noticing the flickering light.

"Is there someone in *our area*?" asked Gayle, a little angrily. Yes it was just a small secluded part of a school field and so, of course, they had no claim to it but she couldn't help a sense of ownership and protectiveness growing inside her. It was a special place for *her and Clive,* forged by special memories made by *her and Clive,* so what right did anyone else have of even knowing that it existed?

She couldn't help herself. She needed to go and see who was there.

"Gayle!" Clive whispered loudly, in that way that people speak to each other during tense moments in horror movies before something really bad happens to them both, as she began to head round the corner to go and take a look. Should he follow her? In that way that people follow other people in horror movies towards something scary that ultimately ends in something really bad happening to them both? Damn it, his legs were already moving.

As he walked around the tree, half expecting to see Gayle facing the corner of some room before receiving a fatal blow to his head, Clive was pleasantly surprised. The flickering light was coming from a single candle that was softly illuminating a picnic that had been set up on a blanket on the grass.

Gayle's smiling face turned around to look at Clive.

"Did you set this up?" she asked excitedly.

Clive still a little bemused about what was happening said, "No..... No, I didn't."

He looked down at the spread of food, and noticed a couple of packets of salt and vinegar *Discos*, some *Trio* chocolate bars and a Tupperware box that looked like it had some milk roll sandwiches inside. Clive smiled as his first thought was how Sue *always* used to buy milk roll as her preferred bread, and she would *always* refer to it as *milkloaf*. This always amused Clive as he couldn't help but think that *milkloaf* sounded like the lame name of some shit cover band, you'd find at your local pub, who played the entire *Bat out of Hell* album. As he took everything else in though, including the fact that everything was sitting on a huge tartan blanket, that had been placed exactly where he and Gayle used to have their picnics all that time ago, that feeling of déjà vu again washed over him. He and Gayle smiled at each other.

"Come on." Gayle said excitedly, grabbing Clive's hand and walking him over to the blanket. As they sat there, Gayle felt her heart beat a little faster as her subconscious was completely transported back to when she and Clive had made love for the very first time. Right at this place, on a night that felt very similar.

Clive sniggered to himself as his memory was tweaked by the sight of a large silver-looking hipflask that stood at the far end of the blanket near the candle. His body shuddered slightly as he remembered the volatile cocktail of mixed spirits that he would pilfer from Sue's alcohol collection (a little bit from each bottle he could find) and bring to these picnics. He and Gayle would sip away from it feeling that blend of light intoxication and nausea that came from teenage consumption of hard liquor.

Gayle smiled as she looked at Clive and breathed in the moments; both now and from the past. Jeremy must have been listening closely to her earlier in the day and had really been able to set up something that felt so similar to the past. He had really done his homework. How did he know that she and Clive would actually *run* here though? Was the whole interruption in the disco room set up so that they *would* run here? Perhaps she had mis-judged him a little? Although Jeremy was clearly

197

bonkers, Gayle wondered now whether there was a small part of him that was quite possibly brilliant.

"Look!"

Clive had just noticed that there was a small black towel hanging on the large oak tree just like he used to put up there hiding pictures of exotic places that he used to find. Gayle looked over and even more nostalgia surrounded her. Those pictures of golden sandy beaches and mountain tops and exotic castles and mansions in the middle of nowhere – the places they dreamed that they would go to and maybe even live. Jeremy had even recreated this. They both wondered what picture he had chosen to put behind the towel.

Gayle stood up and walked over to the tree, preparing to remove the towel, just like she would have in the past. Clive sat on the blanket and waited, also like he would have in the past, only this time he also had no idea what "special" place was hidden under the towel. When she got to the tree Gayle stopped and looked around at Clive smiling.

"Go on!" he said, just as excited as her to see what Jeremy had put up there.

Gayle waited a few more seconds letting the anticipation build up. It is something she had always tried to do with Jack when he was younger by insisting on things like them having breakfast before he opened birthday or Christmas presents so to add to the excitement; because once things are open they are open and the anticipation is gone. Clive never understood this and his philosophy was to have the surprise revealed as quickly as possible.

"Go on!" he said again, even more animated this time.

Gayle gave a cheeky smile for a few more seconds before finally reaching up and carefully removing the black towel.

They both looked, confused at first, at the picture that was staring at them from the tree. It wasn't a post card or a picture of scenic views, mountain tops or beautiful golden beaches; it was just a photograph of a simple, terrace house. It was number five Percival road. It was *their house.*

Gayle felt a tear form in each of her eyes as it slowly hit her what this was. She had explained to Jeremy that Clive used to put pictures of places that they could dream to visit or even live – and this was another one. It wasn't some exotic fantasy that was never going to be achievable but it was a picture of *their* home. The house that she and Clive had bought together; and put their hearts and souls into *making a home.* The place where they had brought up Jack. The place where lots of love had lived. And maybe still did? Was Jeremy right? Did they just have to *re-find* it?

Clive smiled as he too realised the message that Jeremy was trying to get across. It *had* been their dream home; a place where they had grown older and brought Jack up together. A place where a family had lived; a place where *love* had lived. He couldn't help but focus on the picture though because it felt like a photograph that could have been taken by an estate agent. It looked to him like a photo that you see on the internet or in an estate agents window because the house is for sale. It was their home, but like a lot of important things in Clive's life, it felt like it was slipping away. Maybe very soon another young couple would be moving in. A young couple with the same ambitions, aspirations and dreams, and *love* that he and Gayle had when they moved in. Hopefully they might be more successful.

"Look!"

Clive looked across to see that Gayle had sat back down and was now holding the hipflask in her left hand (that she'd maybe just noticed) and a small, black walkman in her right hand (that Clive had not previously noticed). She patted the blanket and, although feeling like he was a dog who had been summoned by its' owner, Clive shuffled over to be right next to her.

They both looked at the walkman and the long ear-bud headphones that were attached to it. It had been a long time since either of them had seen one. In the days before streaming and MP3's were even dreamed of, and probably even before CD's had become popular, the humble walkman, with its cassette tapes, had seemed like the height of technology. Now it looked like it belonged in a museum somewhere. Gayle flipped the cassette holder open and saw that there was a tape in there although, after inspecting it, noticed that there was no label attached to advise what was recorded on it.

Gayle took a small sip out of the hipflask and then passed it to Clive as she grimaced because of the harshness of the taste. She was no longer an expert on hastily put together mixed spirits but could certainly taste some vodka, whisky and sherry and, as Clive took a swig from it himself, could almost feel her stomach lining being stripped away by the lethal liquid straight away.

"Wow, that's ...... *horrendous*!" said Clive reacting to his own intake of the mysterious liquor.

Gayle smiled. Even though she completely agreed she couldn't help feeling the alcoholic warmth in her tummy reminded her of their previous times here in their "special place".

199

"Don't be such a big girl!" she said, taking the hipflask off him and taking another, larger swig.

She passed it back to him as she extended the ear-buds. She placed one in her right ear (after, of course, checking that it was the one marked with the "R" on it) and passed the other one to Clive. He took another mouthful of the mixed spirits, this time making sure that he kept any "big girl" reaction comments to himself, before accepting the second ear-bud and placing it in his left ear. To make sure that neither of their buds were pulled out they had to bring their heads tight together, just like when they had listened to music in the past. Clive waited patiently, knowing that Gayle would soak in the moment for an open-ended amount of time before pressing play. He closed his eyes and, after trying to ignore the foul taste in his mouth, started to enjoy the warm feeling in his own stomach as he waited for Gayle to start the walkman.

After a good thirty seconds of sitting there, her head almost leaning against Clive's, Gayle was ready and so pressed play on the walkman. It clunked down in that familiar way after needing a good, hard press of the thumb. She closed her eyes too.

Immediately they both recognised the soft keyboard melody intro to one of their favourite songs: *Bad English – When I See You Smile*.

As John Waite began to sing the opening lines Gayle said "hold me" and she snuggled into Clive's arms, just like she used to; comfortably where she fitted.

Sometimes I wonder how I'd ever make it through,
Through this world without having you,
I just wouldn't have a clue.

Clive tightened his arms around Gayle and breathed in her sweet perfume and, after not feeling like this for years, now had that special and content feeling again just like he had in the youth club disco about fifteen minutes earlier. He could feel butterflies in his stomach again. Maybe it was because his stomach was seriously contemplating ejecting that cocktail of spirits or, more likely, because of the excitement of the moment. He held Gayle tight but knew that very soon he was going to turn his head to face her, even if it meant their earphones coming out, because he wanted to kiss her; he *needed* to kiss her.

Gayle let the music fill her head and allowed the moment to take over her. It was amazing, again, how a song, in the right circumstances, can completely take you to another time and place. All she could think of was her and Clive in love and, specifically, the first time they'd had sex;

200

right here. She was almost breathless, excited at the prospect that it might just happen again. She *wanted* it to happen again and knew that it would feel just as special as that first time; *all over again.* (Of course she would probably take the time to check for the nearest doc leaves *first* this time.)

Clive decided he would let the first chorus play out and then would "make his move"; a thought process that made him feel like an awkward teenager all over again.

When I See You Smile,
I Can Face The World,
You Know I Can Do Anything,
When I See You Smile,
I See A Ray Of Light,
I See It Shining Right Through The Rain,
When I See You Smile,
Baby, When I See You Smile..... At Me.

This was it.

Clive rather awkwardly moved his body to get his face in range of being able to kiss Gayle. He caught her by surprise, making her jump, and she jerked her body sideways, leaving her well out of the reach of Clive's lips and removing both their earphones in the process. They both laughed at each other as Gayle being startled had, in turn, startled Clive, before staring and smiling at one other. It felt like a pleasant and warm moment. Before any thoughts of resurrecting an attempted kiss could develop however, Clive's attention was caught by the muffled sounds of someone shouting, that was slowly getting louder.

Clive and Gayle looked at each other a little puzzled before slowly getting up, walking around the corner and peeking out from their special place. Gayle was fairly thankful that her thoughts of sex had not resulted in the removal of any clothes just yet. As soon as they both looked across the field they could make out the sight of Jeremy moving quickly towards them, a torch in one hand flashing a light vigorously around as he moved in an almost comedic running style that John Cleese would have been proud of. He was still shouting something, but they still couldn't make out what it was.

"I also told him about the caretaker nearly catching us that night!" said Gayle, realising what was going on.

Clive laughed.

"He could have given us a few more minutes, don't you think?"

Gayle laughed as well.

It felt like typical Jeremy. He had set something rather special up but had then spoiled it by doing something silly.

As he got closer, they could finally make out what he was shouting.

"QUICK! GET OUT OF HERE!"

Clive and Gayle looked at each other, still laughing.

"ARE YOU THE CARETAKER?" Clive shouted back as he got closer. "CAN YOU COME BACK IN A FEW MINUTES?"

Gayle laughed as Jeremy finally got to where they were standing, slapstick run over and breathing heavily.

"What?" he asked, in between taking in huge gulps of air.

"Are you the caretaker?" Clive asked again.

Jeremy looked confused.

Gayle chipped in.

"I told you that the caretaker had chased us away from here once..... you're *being* the caretaker, right?"

"No!" said Jeremy, at last understanding what they were saying. "Quick, get out of here, the police are coming!"

Clive and Gayle looked back out over the field again and saw that there were some bright blue lights now flashing at the edge of the car park.

"Someone called them" Jeremy said still panting heavily "reported three weirdo's sneaking around the youth club..... quick, let's get out of here!"

Jeremy started running again; full Cleese mode reactivated, and headed off towards the fence by the main road.

Clive looked at Gayle.

"One weirdo and two gullible *idiots*!" said Gayle, preparing to run.

If nothing more, this day had been good training in case she ever lost her marbles and decided she wanted to run a marathon.

THIRTY EIGHT: ~~Saturday Night~~ *Sunday Morning At The Movies.*

Clive had just walked through the same stiff door (which required the same aggressive push to open), down the same side alley off the main precinct, that he had just two days earlier, and yet he had stepped into a room that looked completely different. Although the *Love Is...* "office" that he had encountered on Friday was somewhat sparse; there wasn't a single trace of it to be seen. The "inspirational" posters had all been removed from the walls (including the "love is like an old boiler" poster and the old "3 pasties for £1" One Quid Bakery advert) and been replaced by black and white photos of movie icons. Marilyn Monroe, Marlon Brando, James Dean, Audrey Hepburn, Robert De Niro, Morgan Freeman, Julie Andrews, Tom Cruise, Miley Cirus, Harrison Ford....

Wait a minute, Miley Cirus? On the same wall as these other, *genuine* acting "legends"? I think Jeremy would have been better leaving the "love is like an old boiler" poster up. Maybe even the "3 pasties for £1" poster?

Also the front windows had been covered in black sheets and even the small sky light had been covered, meaning the only light in the room was coming from the overhead lighting. The office desk had been removed, replaced by two, comfortable looking, leather armchairs that were facing the side wall, where a large screen had been erected.

The only other things in the, otherwise empty, room were what looked like an ice cream counter and a keyboard and stool over to the right hand corner. Gayle smiled as she looked around, realising that Jeremy had tried to set things up to resemble the old picture house on corporation street where she and Clive had shared their first *real* date; a

203

visit to the cinema to see Jim Carrey in *The Mask*. And it wasn't a bad effort really for someone who had never been there.

As they both stood there taking in their new surroundings Jeremy, who had obviously heard the latest struggle and physical battle Clive had just had with the front door, emerged from the back / office / kitchen area of the shop, wearing a dark suit and what looked like an old fashioned bus inspectors hat.

"Good, good" he said, checking his watch "Right on time, excellent. Are we both well this morning?"

They both looked around to face Jeremy.

"Yes thanks" they said in unison.

"Nothing like a bit of burnt bacon to get you going on a Sunday morning." Added Clive, smiling at Gayle as he said it.

She aimed a playful punch on his arm.

"Make it yourself next time."

Jeremy smiled. This good humoured interaction between them was something he hadn't seen before and he took it as a good sign that he was making some progress.

"Now then" Jeremy said. "If you have your tickets please, I will show you to your seats."

Clive and Gayle looked at each other.

"Do you have the tickets?" asked Clive.

"No I thought you had them." replied Gayle.

"Every time! You always…" Clive stopped mid-sentence and realised that the argument that they usually have about which one of them should be to blame for forgetting tickets to events was actually not relevant in this situation. They didn't have any tickets.

Clive looked around at Jeremy who pre-emptied anything that he was going to say by staring, wide-eyed, at the envelope that Clive was holding.

"Ahh," said Clive, opening the envelope.

He pulled two tickets out and quickly read the printed, black writing on them that said: *SEAT 14F* and *SEAT 14G*.

He showed them to Gayle who smiled and looked at Jeremy with approval: he had remembered what she had said to him about the seat numbers they'd had for that cinema visit all those years ago.

"Sir?" said Jeremy, prompting Clive to show him the tickets.

"Yes, this way please." He said leading them over to the two chairs in the middle of the room that, also displayed the numbers 14F and 14G. What were the chances!

"Here we go" said Jeremy gesturing that they should sit on these two (only) seats.

Clive began to sit on the right of the two seats until Gayle loudly cleared her throat to catch his attention. That was 14G, did Clive not remember? She sat in 14G all those years ago because "G" obviously stands for Gayle. How stupid is he still?

"Your refreshments sir and madam." Jeremy added, passing them both a red and white stripy paper bag.

They both immediately realised that, as they were at the "cinema", they must be getting some pic'n'mix sweets.

Gayle waited for a few seconds before being unable to resist opening her bag - with the zest of excitement that wasn't appropriate for someone of her age. Clive was a bit cooler; taking even longer to see what was inside. Although he enjoyed these types of sweets, his excitement for them had waned in recent years thanks to two reasons. One, he found that too many sugary sweets tended to give him a headache and, two, he had read an article about how gelatine was actually *made*. The fact that most of these (admittedly delicious) jelly sweets are made using the unused parts of animal carcasses, namely bones, horns, skin, cartilage and, most alarmingly, *testicles*, had, shall we say, *concerned* him a little. There's nothing that puts you off eating gummy bears like the thought that you will probably get a severe headache coupled with the fact that, at least some part of those bears, were once probably horse bollocks.

Gayle squealed a little with joy as she removed a little red sachet of fizz wiz and a silver can of cream soda from her bag and showed it to Clive. He smiled at her as he now began to remember back to what snacks they'd eaten at the Apollo picture house during their first "official" date. He opened his own bag and saw that, he too, had some fizz wiz and cream soda. Further down the bag there were also some white mice, pink shrimps, cola cubes and a couple of those large red and green *happy cherries* that did, worryingly, already look like red and green battered and swollen horse testicles. He shuddered slightly before ignoring the pic'n'mix element of his bag and removing, just like Gayle, the fizz wiz and cream soda. They giggled at each other as they realised they would both soon be setting off explosion parties of sugar and e numbers in their mouths.

All of a sudden the lights began to dim slightly and, from out of the back room, Jeremy appeared wearing a sparkling golden jacket. He walked over to the corner of the room and sat on the stool at the keyboard. Without any hesitation he began playing and filled the room with the nostalgic sounds of the cinema from a by-gone age. His keyboard was obviously set to organ mode and he, very impressively, began his way through a medley of tunes that you would be treated to / made to endure* (*delete as appropriate) at the cinema many, many years ago. As he played he swayed from left to right and, as he did, the sequins in his golden jacket were captured by the faded lights and danced around like tiny fireflies. As Clive smiled along to this really impressive performance from Jeremy he couldn't help but wonder whether he had hired this jacket especially for this performance, whether he actually owned this jacket or whether he had somehow been able to borrow it from Elton John. He realised the smart money would probably have to be on him owning it – it was probably his favourite "going out" jacket.

Gayle opened her fizz wiz and gestured to Clive to do the same. He did and, laughing, they both poured a large amount of popping candy into their mouths and together joyfully experienced those tiny detonations of delight along their tongues. To enhance things they both took sips of their cream soda making whirlpools of popping pleasure that couldn't help but make them remember that first date oh so clearly. As Gayle took another "swig" of fizz wiz she couldn't help but wonder where Jeremy had got it from, she certainly hadn't seen it anywhere for ages. It did then cross her mind whether he'd maybe somehow got hold of some "old" stock and wondered whether at was actually in date, or was maybe a couple of decades or so past its "best before".

Instead of worrying about potential stomach upsets and / or horrendous fizzing diarrhoea, Gayle focussed on how Jeremy had taken those words she had spoken to him about her and Clive's first date and turned it into this rather special moment. After spending most of Saturday disliking him and thinking he was a complete idiot, she was now beginning to think he was really rather clever. As she was thinking this, his organ playing began to fade in volume and, as he continued to play one last, decreasing melody with his right hand, he turned to wave with his left hand, just as that man from the Apollo had done during their first date. When his music had completely faded to silence he stood from his keyboard and quietly walked behind Gayle and Clive to where his projector was set up. They smiled at each other again, both a little numb-jawed and secretly relieved that they had finished the popping candy, as the faded lights faded even further into total darkness.

Jeremy started his projector and the screen instantly turned blue and displayed the words: Pearl and Dean presents. Then the room was filled with sound, playing a jingle that neither Clive nor Gayle had heard for many, many years and yet was instantly familiar and pleasing.

206

"Pa-Paa, Pa-Paa, Pa-Paa, Pa-Paa, Pa-Pa-Pa, Pa-Paa, Pa-Paa, Pa-Paa, Pa-Paaaaa-Pa".

What followed was at least ten minutes of "retro" adverts in "classic" low picture and sound quality. (From adverts back before anyone had invented cameras that could capture audio and visuals in anything like real life, and so they had that "fuzzy" quality to them.) And yet those words: "retro" and "classic" manage to make everything ok. Yep, it's accepted that they were a bit shit but they offer that nostalgic feel about the way things were; and that's the thing about nostalgia, it usually brings back any pleasant memories and feelings that you had from those days, as you are being *nostalgiasised.* (I know that's not a *real* word, but I like how it sounds.)

Those ten minutes didn't offer exactly the adverts that would have probably been playing back when Gayle and Clive were in that cinema on their first date, but they still had the desired effect of feeling like they could very well have been.

The two of them watched on in delight as a fat, semi-naked, orange man ran around slapping a man, two-handed, across the face as he took a swig from a can of orange pop, before the delightful catchphrase "you know when you've been "tango'd" was displayed. Of course the authorities banned that advert though, as children in playgrounds across the country were hospitalised after being slapped / tango'd. A few perforated ear drum injuries and those in charge go a bit overboard!

Clive and Gayle also watched a group of well dressed cartoon crows singing "I'll be your dog" as they followed a young man drinking Kia-Ora and then three frogs, with different croaks, eventually combining to promote *"Bud-Weis-Err"* (Did anyone ever check the mental state of, or do drug-testing on, the advertising "hot shots" back in those days?) They also sang along to that ludicrously catchy Potato Waffles song, as they were reminded that they were "waffly versatile", before watching Gold Blend and Renault Clio (Nicole! Papa!) adverts that presented themselves back then as ongoing stories, which were like gripping TV series, that you couldn't wait to see the next instalment. You don't get that from adverts anymore do you?

By the time they had Pa-Paa-ed along to that Pearl and Dean theme again, Clive and Gayle felt exactly like they did as teenagers in the Apollo picture house, eagerly awaiting the arrival of Jim Carrey and his mischievous mask of *Loki.*

They heard Jeremy switching discs behind them and Clive reached across and held onto Gayle's left hand. She reached over and cupped their two hands with her right hand and leaned over to him, gently placing her head on his shoulder. Behind them Jeremy smiled as Clive contently tilted his head against his wife's whilst thinking to himself that, despite coming across as a complete buffoon (perhaps an Oscar worthy act?), it actually appeared like Jeremy knew what he was doing. He hadn't felt this comfortable with Gayle for a long, long time.

THIRTY NINE: *Belong Together.*

Clive sat there quietly and contently as his mind was pulled out of the *Love Is* "cinema room". It wasn't taken to one specific time or place though but rather took a little tour through his and Gayle's history. This feeling of being comfortable and at ease with his wife, though sadly unfamiliar in recent times, was also something that was, in the past, completely natural.

They used to sit, or lie, intertwined with each other for hours at a time. His memory reminded him of times on the beach, lying with each other on a small towel, or just in each other's arms, gazing into each other's eyes, on the blanket in "their place" on the school field. At a party, or event, where Gayle would happily sit on Clive because they had to share a chair; or at home sitting together downstairs on the sofa or upstairs lying, as one, in bed.

They may have been dressed up in fancy party clothes, in comfortable, casual don't-need-to-make-an-effort lounge wear or totally naked. In didn't matter because they were totally happy and relaxed with each other. And the main reason for this was because they just *fitted* together. They both used to joke that it was as if they had been *made for each other*. Gayle just fitted perfectly into Clive's arms. Her body shape fit naturally into his as if they were two adjacent jigsaw pieces; perfectly cut so they would snugly fit *together*.

As he thought about it further, Clive remembered another one of the poems / songs that he and Gayle had written that was all about them belonging together, even if there were things about them that were different.

It was incredible that, after all this time of *not* feeling that way, all it took was actually being close together again to *completely* feel the same way. Like those two jigsaw pieces, perhaps lost under the sofa for years, when you try to put them back together again; they still fit.

And the reason for that?

Because they *belong together.*

Belong Together.

Your toothbrush is pink,
My toothbrush is blue,
But they belong together,
Next to the toothpaste tube.

You listen to pop music,
I love the sound of guitar,
But our CD's sit side by side,
In the glove box of the car.

You are Five Foot five,
I am Six Foot One,
But you fit snugly in my arms,
Because together we belong.

You like a trendy cocktail,
I'll choose an ice cold beer,
But we always drink together,
Right until we can't see clear.

It's like we're always holding hands,
Hearts side by side forever,
We will never be apart,
Because we belong together.

FORTY: *The Mask.*

They sat there for a few more seconds, completely happy cuddled together, before Jeremy had prepared the film and it began to play on the big screen in front of them. It was Clive who noticed first; he had seen *The Mask* more times than it should be admitted and straight away knew there had been a mistake. For, as the movie-preceding film studio logo appeared on the screen in front of him, Clive knew that *The Mask* had been made / distributed by *New Line Cinema* and yet the logo appearing in front of him was that of *Universal.*

He had always prided himself on his cinematic knowledge and wasn't going to miss something as obvious as this. He looked across at Gayle but she seemed blissfully unaware that anything was amiss. Clive decided not to mention it to her; she looked so very content and he didn't want to bring her world crashing down before he had to. He did, of course, realise that something as simple as a mixed up movie should not be enough to, as his own mind had suggested, bring someone's world "crashing down", but he didn't want to ruin his own sense of thoughtfulness on a mere technicality and so continued to say nothing.

The screen faded to black and, as it slowly brightened up again, the sound of gently tweeting birds was set to the background of a rather dramatic looking mountain side. Clive glanced down at Gayle, who still seemed oblivious to the fact that *The Mask* actually started with some rather forbidding music and a scene underwater in which the titular *Mask* is accidentally released from an ancient looking treasure chest. Should he tell her now that it was the wrong movie? She'd probably want to know, wouldn't she? Again, he decided to let things play out, instead trying to guess which movie Jeremy had actually set up.

Some white words softly appeared on the screen, announcing "A Martin Starger Production" as the camera slowly panned across to show an American highway. The words faded before being replacing by new ones: "Peter Bogdanovich's". In the space of a micro-second Clive's mind recognised *Peter Bogdanovich* as an actor and director but his vast archive of film knowledge could not recall any of the movies that he may have directed. What film, distributed by Universal, produced by Martin Starger and directed by Peter Bogdanovich, could Jeremy have possibly mixed up with *The Mask*. Think, think, think, think, think, think....

He was put out of his misery fairly quickly by the next word that was presented on the screen: *Mask.*

It appeared that this was the film "Mask" and not the film "The Mask".

Oh, that made a lot of sense.

Jeremy had actually got the film *Mask,* a rather heavy drama starring Cher and Eric Stoltz, in which a boy, suffering from a rare cranial disfigurement condition (who Clive now remembered may have been called "Rocky") struggles to be accepted by society, instead of *The Mask* – a (very) light live action / animation comic book-inspired comedy in which Jim Carrey is a cartoon-like "superhero".

Quite different really.

Clive wondered if he should tell all this to Gayle. He again looked at her, but she *still* seemed oblivious to the movie mix up. What the hell was wrong with her? If he did tell her though, she'd probably make some kind of derogatory comment about him being a *movie geek.* Gayle noticed Clive looking at her and quickly licked her lips, getting ready to say something.

"I think Jeremy's got the wrong film. This is *Mask,* not <u>*The Mask.*</u> This is that film with Cher in it. I thought *you* would have picked up on it – you always go on about knowing about films!"

Clive gritted his teeth and grinned.

The lights came back on and Jeremy walked into the room pretty quickly and looking a little flustered.

"Sorry, sorry, I must have burnt the wrong film. This isn't *The Mask,* it's actually <u>*Mask*</u> - the film with Cher in it."

Gayle raised her eyebrows at Clive in a kind of "told-you-so" way. Clive continued to smile through gritted teeth, mumbling away in his mind that he'd never miss an opportunity to use his superior knowledge and intelligence again in the future.

Jeremy carried on talking.

"It's not particularly romantic having to watch that odd-looking, weird face on a big screen."

Gayle couldn't help but think that was a bit harsh and over the top, even if Cher *was* a bit bizarre looking.

Jeremy held up a second DVD in his hand.

"Lucky, I've got another film. It's a different one but I think you'll like it. I've always had this motto in life: *it's best to be prepared for a big cock up.....*"

Gayle looked up at Clive, while still keeping her head rested on his shoulder, expecting him to comment on Jeremy using the words "big cock up". He didn't say a word but, instead, sat there with a strange clenched-teeth look on his face. She gave him a little carefree smile, suggesting she wasn't too bothered about what movie they were about to watch; she was just happy to be there. Clive finally released his gritted teeth and gave her a smile back and softly kissed her on the forehead. He, too, was enjoying this rare, tender moment that they were sharing.

"Ok, we're good to go." Said Jeremy "Sorry once again. Hope you enjoy *this* movie."

After speaking and inserting the DVD, his gentle footsteps could again be heard heading towards the back shop area before the black screen in front of Clive and Gayle turned a touch blue and the logo for *New Line Cinema: A Time Warner Company* appeared in front of them accompanied by their signature soft music. Clive's mind began to do somersaults. As a serious *movie geek*, despite Gayle doubting him, he had an obligation to himself to guess which film Jeremy had now put on.

With it being *New Line,* maybe it *was* The Mask after all? But Jeremy had said it *wasn't*, unless this was a *double bluff* which was, of course, possible with Jeremy. Clive's mind thought that if it wasn't then Jeremy would probably pick another film that came out roughly around the same time as *The Mask*. It was dangerous trying to predict what may come out of the mind of Jeremy but it was the best he had to go on.

So what films, from *New Line Cinema,* came out around the mid-90's? Would Jeremy have gone for something like *Seven*? Great film, but hardly romantic. The whole *gluten* murder would surely put them off their pic'n'mix as well.

What about *The Long Kiss Goodnight* with Samuel L Jackson? (How many films has Samuel L Jackson been in? Does the man *ever* take a break?) Maybe.

Or it could be one of the *Austin Powers* films? They were around the right time and very funny. As he thought about it, Clive hoped that if it was *Austin Powers* then he wanted it to be the original. If it was ...*the*

Spy Who Shagged Me then he couldn't guarantee not fixating and drooling over Heather Graham/Felicity Shagwell – again. Clive's mind reminded him of the life size poster of Felicity Shagwell that he'd received with a film magazine back around when the film was released and he wondered whether Jack had taken <u>that</u> poster with him to University. He'd best check that when he got home. He realised it was best to quickly clear his mind before other parts of his body took control of the thinking.

What about *Blade*? Not really appropriate.

Rush Hour? Very funny!

The Wedding Singer? Pretty romantic – in with a good chance.

Any of *The Lord of the Rings* films? Great films, but *very* long.

He glanced at Gayle and smiled. She wouldn't be doubting his movie knowledge / geek status if she'd been able to hear all of that speedy thinking!

Clive's one and a half second tour of mid-90's *New Line Cinema* movies came to an end as the black screen in front of them lightened up into day light and focussed on a green street sign with white lettering that said *HOPE ST.*

Clive should have known.

Should he tell Gayle quickly what film it was and restore his movie-geek status? No, he could tell right away that she also knew what it was already.

As a black limousine passed a bus stop before stopping and reversing back to be level with the attractive red head standing there, Gayle sat up and smiled at him. Jeremy's "preparation" for his "big cock up" was only to have their favourite film standing by: *Dumb and Dumber.* Even though they hadn't seen it in a while, and certainly not together, it felt exactly like it had in the past when they had cuddled up on the sofa wanting to watch a film they could both have a good laugh at. As Jim Carrey, complete with ridiculous bowl haircut, leaned out of his limousine window they both began to mentally act along with his opening lines. "....Austria? Well, g'day mate. Let's put another shrimp on the barbie!"

Clive smiled as he now wondered whether maybe Jim Carrey / Lloyds attempt at an Australian accent was actually the inspiration behind Jeremy's attempted Ozzie drawl when he had first seen him here a couple of days earlier; it was certainly ridiculous enough.

For close to the next hour Gayle and Clive smiled and laughed along to their favourite film, holding hands and eating their pic'n'mix as they watched Harry driving the "mutt cutts" van, and the diner / "kick his ass

Seabass" burger honking scene, the beer bottles, "are you a camel?", urinating moment and, especially, Lloyds kung fu fight montage part.

Clive even ate his *happy cherries*. If they *were*, in fact, battered and swollen horse bollocks then he didn't care – they tasted great. In fact, they were so nice, it was hard to know what all those celebrities on *I'm a Celebrity* ... were always moaning about.

Dumb and Dumber continued, re-awakening lots of feeling from the past as they laughed and sang and hummed along to the great sound track; and then, just before the hour mark, something neither Clive nor Gayle were expecting happened. After Lloyds mistake of driving the wrong way all night had left them with no petrol and no money and "in a hole", and with Harry infuriated with him and proclaiming "I'm walking home", Jim Carrey's quivering-lipped Lloyd emotionally crying "Forgot you never made a mistake" line had an unforeseen effect on Gayle and Clive.

Watching two best friends emotionally angry with each other and seemingly lost, no matter that they'd seen it numerous times before, somehow seemed to strike a big chord with them; maybe because of the memory excavating weekend they were having. The fact that it was being accompanied with an extract of their "first kiss" song: *Mmm Mmm Mmm Mmm* made everything even more intense.

Clive looked over to Gayle, who had already turned towards him with tears in her eyes, and saw clearly the girl that he had taken on a first date to the cinema and first kissed at the youth club.

He had missed her so much.

The Crash Test Dummies extract only played for about 40 seconds before Lloyd triumphantly returned to Harry having swapped the "mutt cutts" van for a mini bike, but it was more than enough. Gayle wondered whether Jeremy's "cock up" had been on purpose. Had he planned it all along that he would make it *feel* like their first date at the cinema but always intended that they would, instead, watch their favourite film that just happened to include *this* moment in which a snippet of their "first kiss" song was also played? If he had, then it had worked perfectly because, as she stared at Clive, with all those thoughts furiously rotating in her head, Gayle felt the pulse of excitement, almost like electricity, flowing all around her – which was *exactly* how she had felt at the moment of that first youth club kiss.

Clive, although again feeling the nerves of a naive teenager who had *never* kissed a girl *ever*, *knew* that *this* was the moment. They both naturally moved their heads towards each other and embraced the fact

215

that the world would change forever, once again, as their lips gently collided.

BANG!

The front door was slammed open and Clive and Gayle's heads automatically jolted towards the sound to see what was happening. An old-ish looking, unshaven man stood at the door.

"Hello?" he said, perhaps confused as to what he was looking at now the door was open. "Have you got any cheese 'n' onion pasties left?"

Gayle looked at Clive and began laughing; Clive laughed too. The "moment" of their kiss had passed again, this time interrupted by a man hungry for a luke-warm, unhealthy savoury snack.

Jeremy appeared from the back room, almost tearing his hair out, and turned the lights on.

"I'm sorry sir" he said with an almost demented, attempted calmness. "The One Quid Bakery is no longer here. As you would have seen if you had read the sign above you, this is now the headquarters for the Love Is romance company."

"What's going on in there?" asked the man, still staring at Clive and Gayle who were sitting on leather seats, inside this former bakery shop, now watching Jim Carrey and Jeff Daniels riding on a motor bike that wasn't even big enough for one of them.

Jeremy, obviously aware that things probably looked a little odd, but certainly not feeling like he needed to explain anything to this man, ignored his question.

"Are you in a relationship that's having problems, sir?" he politely asked instead.

"No" said the man.

"Then fuck off!" said Jeremy, his coolness leaving him abruptly as he slammed the front door.

"Sorry about that," he said, turning to face Gayle and Clive "now, where were we?"

Gayle and Clive looked at each other and smiled. The interruption had actually been a funny interlude to their favourite funny film and they both quickly felt like they had a few minutes earlier. As Jeremy subtly disappeared from sight and turned the lights off again the two of them slouched back down in their seats, oblivious that Lloyd and Harry had finally made it to Aspen because they were too busy still staring at each other; maybe the moment hadn't gone after all.

BANG!

The door opened again.

216

Clive and Gayle chuckled to each other once more. What this time, thought Gayle, someone wanting an apple turnover?

But this time was different.

Jeremy again raced from the back, looking angry as he turned the lights on again.

"I should've locked the....." he began, but then stopped mid sentence as he noticed who had barged in on Gayle and Clive's moment this time.

Two large men, dressed in black stood in the doorway.

"Hello Mr Corden!" one of them said as he stepped into the "cinema area". "We're here for Mr Garnett's money!"

Gayle glanced over towards Jeremy and noticed the colour quickly draining from his face leaving him looking as white as a ghost.

The second large man, actually now noticeably larger than the other one, walked into the room and addressed Clive and Gayle directly.

"Are you two anything to do with this "business"?" he asked, adding particular disdain to the word *business*. Gayle couldn't help but notice that his eyes were almost black, reminding her of her first meeting with Andy Taylor. "If you're not anything to do with this "business", it's time to make yourselves scarce."

Both Clive and Gayle instinctively looked over towards Jeremy. He still looked pale but tried to look as if nothing was wrong, speaking to them in his usual, enthusiastic manner.

"It's ok but it's probably best that you go home. I need to speak to these two gentlemen about some ...... business."

He appeared to mutter something like "so close" under his breath before continuing: "Yes, so go home, get yourselves ready because I'll pick you up at 2 p.m. – on the dot. And it's the *big one*. I promise it will be *the one!*"

Clive stood up from his chair and reached out for Gayle's hand. They both walked around their "cinema seats" but moved slowly; they felt awkward to be leaving Jeremy in what now felt like a very tense situation.

"Come on, hurry up" said the first man who had entered the shop and, now they could see him closely, looked a bit like a shaven-headed Steve Bruce, with a nose that looked like it had been broken more times than he'd had hot dinners. "We're here to collect what Mr Garnett is owed, whether it be cash, jewellery, or anything else of value. We don't mind taking it off of you two if you're not quickly out of here. We're getting what he's owed..... one way or another."

Gayle immediately let go of Clive's hand; the use of those four words again stirred up that memory in her that she'd long since tried to forget.

They both headed to the door after one final glance at Jeremy who had given them a nod that covered a thanks for their concern and a reassurance that everything was OK.

Once out of the shop the door was quickly closed behind them. Gayle felt a shiver run down her spine that was probably a combination of concern for what may be about to happen to Jeremy and her inability to be able to shake off the thoughts of fear, helplessness and anger towards Clive that those four words had reawakened in her. *One Way or Another:* four words that the rest of the world would hear and immediately have that snappy *Blondie* tune playing in their head but for Gayle they were four words that took her back to the day she met Andy Taylor and they scratched away at old scars and re-inflicted old wounds.

Clive reached out to hold Gayle's hand, ready for them to walk back home, but she allowed her hand to just brush past his as she began walking without him. Clive looked back at the old One Quid Bakery and wondered what was going on inside. Should he go in and offer to help Jeremy? Probably not "physically", but he could see if a little money could help? Then again, Jeremy seemed to know what he was doing. Even if he had no money or valuables to give these men, Clive was pretty sure he could talk his way out of it; he was the type of person who could talk his way off an electric chair. Instead, Clive faced the other way and quickly walked after his wife.

FORTY ONE: *Confronting The Past.*

Gayle had been sitting on the sofa and staring out of the window for, at least, thirty minutes now, her eyes unfocussed and fairly glazed. She wasn't sure why but she had taken to looking out of the window, at nothing in particular, more and more lately.

Clive walked back into the front room and saw that his wife was still staring out at nothing. As always, he knew that it meant she was in a downbeat and contemplative mood and he wasn't sure what to say to her.

"We best think about getting ready." He said. "Jeremy will be here fairly soon..... that's if he's still in one piece!"

He realised that the second half of his sentence, that he hoped would be light hearted, was actually a little in bad taste. When they had last seen Jeremy he was in an awkward situation. To make a joke about it, without knowing if he was ok or not, was somewhat ill thought out.

Gayle turned away from the window and looked at Clive.

"I think we should give this afternoon a miss" she said through wet but determined eyes. "We gave things a go but we need to accept that we're too far gone for silly little games. *It's too late.*"

Wow, Clive hadn't really seen that coming. Although this weekends events, or as Gayle put it: "games", had indeed been silly, he thought that they had actually made some progress. He looked at Gayle as she still stared at him and could see that she was shaking slightly. He sat down next to her and placed his hand gently on her knee.

"What is it?" he asked. "What happened earlier? You were in such a good mood and then..... what happened? You're shaking."

Gayle had never really spoken to Clive in any detail about that first visit from Andy Taylor, the loan shark. She had always been worried that he may have thought she was exaggerating what happened or was blowing the whole thing out of proportion. Looking back, maybe she and Jack were never actually in any *real* danger but Andy Taylor had wanted her to feel that way, and it had worked. She *felt* like her and Jack's safety was at risk and the whole thing was Clive's fault for lying to her; and that much was still true. Now, at the end, she no longer felt like she had to hide those feelings from Clive and so began talking; getting more and more angry as she spoke.

"It was what happened back there to Jeremy. It made me remember that visit I had from Andy Taylor; you remember him: *the loan guy*? It made me remember the visit me and Jack had from him!"

Clive lowered his head. He remembered the loan incident very well. He had been trying his best to provide his family with things they needed and wanted, but had gone about it completely the wrong way. It certainly wasn't his finest hour.

Gayle continued talking.

"That big one today, he had the same eyes as Andy Taylor. Cold. Calculating. Emotionless. He looked like he could do someone some *real* harm, and would probably *enjoy* doing it. And it reminded me of the day that *he* came around here, because he was the *same*. He *forced* his way into the house and made me feel that he would enjoy doing me some harm and, worse still, Jack some harm. *Baby Jack.*"

Tears began to flow out of Gayle's eyes but she continued talking, the passion being stirred by each new word she said.

"And it was all because of *you*. Because you had borrowed money from him and not paid him back. And you had not told me about it. You *lied* to me..... and then put me and Jack *in danger*. And you weren't here to protect us."

The tears now exploded and she stopped talking. She moved Clive's hand off her knee and stood up and walked to the window, staring outside and once more focussing on nothing.

Clive could feel tears of his own meandering down his cheeks. He had no idea that Gayle had ever felt like this. When they had spoken about Andy Taylor's "visit" and her agreeing to pay him at ten pounds a week she hadn't spoken about *any* of this.

He stood up quickly and joined her by the window. He grabbed her by the shoulders and turned her body so that she faced him. When he began talking his voice was broken and trembling.

"You never mentioned *any* of this to me. You told me that a man had come round and you had agreed to pay him at ten pounds per week. You never said that he'd come *into* the house; that he'd threatened you..... that he'd threatened Jack. I'd never do anything on purpose to put you or Jack in danger. If I'd known he was going to come round I would have never left the house that day. It was a stupid, stupid thing to borrow that money but I did it for you and Jack; *for us.* I knew I was working the overtime and would be able to pay him back straight away and so got excited and bought the cot and the monitor and those toys – because they were on *sale.* Mikey S, at work, had told me about this "good" guy you could borrow money off for a week until you got paid, and it seemed like a good idea. I should have known his idea of a "good" guy meant a thug – Mikey S is a bit dodgy himself. I had no idea that you would clear the bank account before I could get the money out to pay him. I know how stupid it was now, but I was trying to make our life *better.* The look on your face when I brought the stuff home made it feel like a good idea at the time. I shouldn't have lied to you, but I know you would have disapproved and I thought I was doing the best thing I could – *for us.*"

Gayle continued to stare at Clive as he carried on talking, almost rambling, at high speed, his voice still shaky.

"If I'd have known the car insurance was due I would have sorted it as a monthly payment, as we had always done, and I would have paid Andy Taylor his money back from the account, as planned..... and everything would have been ok. After you said you'd cleared the account, I tried *everything* to get some money. I asked everyone I knew if they'd lend me it to me for a few days, but everyone said *no.* I offered to work my days off at work for anyone who'd lend me a few quid; but nothing. You kind of find out who your friends are, or *not,* at times like that. When you said Andy Taylor had been round and that everything was sorted, I felt ashamed that I had lied to you. I'm still ashamed of myself and I have *never* lied to you since. *Never about anything.* But I felt relieved that everything was ok, because you told me *everything was ok.*"

Gayle wiped the tears away from her face and watched as Clive's own tears rolled uncontrollably down his face. She had only ever seen him cry on a couple of occasions and didn't like to see him like that. He looked so vulnerable.

"I should have told you *everything.*" She said. "I was *so* angry with you but I didn't want to tell you everything because ..... I don't actually know *why* I didn't tell you everything. But I think I've let it eat away at me *all this time.* I should have told you everything and got it out in the open..... I'm sorry."

"*You've* got nothing to be sorry about. I let you down *big time*; and I've been letting you down *ever since.* I honestly have *never* lied to you after that day, but I've never been totally honest with you either. I've never told you, enough times, how much I love you; how you're my best friend and *my world*. I have seen things slowly breaking apart between us but never been honest enough, or *brave* enough, to face them..... I let you down back then and have *continued* to let you down. It's me; I'm the one who should be sorry. It's *my fault* and I'm so *very* sorry. If it's too late, then it's *my fault*."

It was Clive's turn to look out of the window.

He too, wasn't particularly looking at anything but rather letting the words that he and Gayle had just said to each other spin around his head. And it was two particular words, ones that both he and Gayle had said, that were in the forefront of his mind: *too late.*

Realistically things *were* too late; much too late. This whole "love is" effort over the weekend had been a little desperate and really quite ridiculous. He took a long, deep breath and accepted the inevitable. Just two days ago Jack had moved out and that had signalled the end for him and Gayle; that was what had been agreed for so long now. Nothing had changed.

Clive took a deep breath.

He then blinked his eyes quickly and focussed on the houses across the road and something cleared in his mind. To think nothing had changed was wrong. *Everything* had changed. This weekend had been pretty weird but on Friday, during his original meeting with Jeremy, *everything had changed.* For the first time, in a long, long time, he had realised what he needed to do. He needed to *fight* for Gayle; fight for their relationship.

Why was he letting that defeatist attitude return now?

Gayle watched as Clive looked out of the window. He had just taken full responsibility for the breakdown of their relationship, but that wasn't really fair. She had been frustrated by his attitude towards her counselling idea but that wasn't the sole reason for things going the way they had. She, too, had let things drift. She, too, could have done more to avoid this situation. Maybe being more open and truthful about the way she felt after the loan shark incident would have cleared things instead of allowing them to eat away at her for so long. He had been ridiculously stupid and dishonest with her but hadn't *meant* to put her and Jack in any danger. If she'd made him realise what had happened, and maybe even *hit him, a lot,* so he shared some of those feelings of danger, then maybe the situation would have been resolved and wouldn't still affect her. She realised that it had secretly eaten away at her; and at their relationship, and it would have been best if they had spoken about it, *properly,* when it had happened. She knew deep down that what he said was true: he did love her, and they were best friends.

Clive turned to look at Gayle.

"We should finish what we started." He said. "We *agreed* to do the *full weekend*, we shouldn't stop now!"

Gayle smiled at him.

"I agree" she said, reaching out and holding his hand. She wasn't quite sure that she *totally* agreed, but felt that if this *was* to be the end then the least they could do was have one last event together. Besides she felt too tired to argue any more, both mentally and physically. Probably because of all the bloody running she'd had to do so far. What were the chances the "final" event would be some kind of outdoor fell run or something?

Clive was expecting to have to try to convince her a little more. He had some rough words ready about something only ever being over, or having failed, when you stop trying; until then you're just *still trying*. He was going to ask her if she could honestly tell him that she hadn't *felt* something this weekend. A spark? *More than a spark?* He was, though, quite relieved that he didn't have to say anything.

They both now began to stare out of the window. Both, this time, focussing on the street that had been their home for the last twenty years.

FORTY TWO: *The Last Supper.*

"What do you think we'll be doing?" asked Gayle, knowing full well that Clive would have just as little idea that she had; how do you anticipate the moves of a lunatic?

"I think it's fair to say that Jeremy hasn't really pushed the boat out financially yet, isn't it?" began Clive as Gayle nodded furiously in agreement. "He did say that this was *the big one*, so I'm thinking that it could be a meal or something. I did mention to him about that fancy food we had at *Picasso* on the high street, for our 5th wedding anniversary. Do you remember?"

Gayle smiled as she recalled.

"Of course I remember." She said. "I told Jeremy about that as well. I think you could be right."

Gayle opened her wardrobe and began looking through for something to wear for a fancy meal.

"I suppose it will be worth going if it is a fancy meal!" she said to Clive smiling.

He smiled back.

"Yeah don't worry about our last chance to re-find love, as long as we get a nice meal...." he said light-heartedly.

They both laughed a little.

She looked at Clive and put her hand gently on the side of his face.

"I want you to know, whatever happens, you'll always be my *best friend.*"

Clive smiled at her but, as he looked into her eyes, couldn't help but feel that Gayle had resigned herself to the fact that things *were over*. Maybe she was right. Maybe too much water had passed under their bridge. He felt sad but had a little twinge of positivity: he knew she would always be in his life, in one capacity or another.

Gayle walked over to her wardrobe and pulled her fancy black evening dress off one of the hangers.

"Let's get dressed up!" she said, her eyes widening as she continued to look upon the entirety of her clothes collection. "I may even wear my Kurt Geiger boots!"

She even let out a tiny excited yelp as she reached for the brown boots that she'd impulsively bought about eighteen months earlier. Footwear, that she had treated herself to and declared they would only be used "for best", that had only ventured out of her wardrobe twice since purchase. Once for a christening, one of those catholic types that seem to last a full weekend and then, later that year, for the office Christmas do that lasted 1 hour and 25 minutes before the *two J's* declared themselves bored and decided to head into town. That's the trouble with labelling something that's "for best" only – you may as well label it as "probably never wear / use".

Clive pulled the black suit from out of the back of his wardrobe that only ever made the light of day for weddings, christenings and funerals and, for all the use he had got out of it, may well have spent the majority of its time in Narnia.

For the next half an hour Gayle and Clive got dressed in the same room, at the same time, something they hadn't done in ages, and laughed and joked about... *complete nonsense.* Anything and everything. Just like they used to.

By ten to two, Clive and Gayle were sitting in the front room, ready for the arrival of Jeremy. Clive's suit looked ok despite not being dry-cleaned for the best part of ten years and the worrying dusty creases had miraculously cleaned and ironed out so you almost couldn't see them. With his best "formal" black shoes and the freshly ironed white shirt and "best", red and gold, tie he was looking pretty good. Gayle had chosen her cream "party frock", had styled her hair into a sophisticated half up / hair down do and was wearing her most dangerously red lipstick. Her Kurt Geiger boots had been slipped on nicely, and relatively easily, not giving away a hint of the *feel-like-they've-been-in-a-clamp-for-a-fortnight* feet she thought she may be facing later. Both Gayle and Clive were feeling great, especially as each of them had remarked on how good the other was looking. Gayle had even suggested that Clive didn't have the shave he was about to have as she liked how he looked with a couple of days' worth of stubble; something she had *never* mentioned before.

As Gayle sat there admiring her boots but now recognising the early signs of *tightening*, and wondering whether she would ever be able to walk properly ever again if she wore them all afternoon, Clive stared at her and thought to himself that she had never looked better. She really was the most beautiful woman in the world. How had he not told her this each and every day? He wondered, once again, how the hell he had let things get this far; this *desperate*.

"Are you hungry?" Gayle asked, perhaps noticing that Clive was almost drooling.

He nodded his head.

DING-DONG.

They both looked out of the window and noticed that unmistakeable maroon car parked outside, before looking at each other, shocked.

"What the.....?" began Gayle. "Did you hear the car arrive?"

Clive shook his head as a look of confusion grew on his face.

"How does he do *that*?"

Half an hour of driving later, Jeremy advised them both that they were nearly at the "final destination"; thankfully adding that there was nothing to fear as he hadn't meant it as "any kind of reference to the film series" – something that he had amused himself with greatly. By the way they were headed, out into the countryside; Gayle pictured a table for an afternoon lunch in a fancy country hotel; or maybe a quaint little pub, with an intimate table for two by a large open fireplace. They were maybe both a little dressed inappropriately for that but it didn't matter. If this was to be her and Clive's last supper; then a table for two by an open fire seemed as nice as anywhere. But actually, Jeremy hadn't said they were overdressed so perhaps it was more likely to be the country hotel? Maybe they were going to have a meal and a treatment at a fancy spa or something?

Very nice.

Oh, they were about to find out because Jeremy had set his left indicator going and they were headed towards a turning with a gravel path and a large sign. As the sign became readable though, it wasn't quite the "welcome to country hotel and health spa" type of thing that Gayle was imagining. It actually read: *Whispering Woods Paintballing and Go Kart Centre*.

What the hell?

Gayle felt her stomach lurch in horror. Had she really allowed herself to think that, with Jeremy in charge of proceedings, they may actually be headed to something that wasn't completely *weird*; something that may actually be *nice*? She realised that she was a complete fool and only had herself to blame.

Clive felt his stomach continuing to rumble and couldn't initially process anything beyond the thought that there must surely be a snack bar wherever they were headed. After he had reassured himself with the hope that there would, at the very least, be a lay-by type portacabin that served greasy burgers, and had a fake hygiene certificate on the flimsy back wall, he begin to wonder whether they were actually going to be paintballing or go-karting.

Which one would he actually prefer? He had been paintballing twice before and it was pretty painful when you got shot. He had also, both times, been given a gun that didn't shoot straight. So, initially, he hoped that it would be go-karting. Then again, he had been go-karting at least half a dozen times and, although it was always fun, he had always seemed to be unlucky enough to be given the car that was considerably slower than all the others; so maybe paintballing would be better?

Clive soon stopped his mind debating the pros and (mostly) cons of which of the two events Jeremy may be headed to because he noticed the look of disgust on Gayle's face: she looked like she had realised that she had mixed up a hand full of raisins for a pile of rabbit droppings but was trying not to spit them out. Before he could think of anything to say to her to attempt to make her feel better, Jeremy had turned down a left fork off the "main" gravel path. As they bumped along this new route, testing out "antique" Volvo suspension to the max, the mystery of what they would be doing was solved, for as they turned they had passed a large sign reading "*Whispering Woods Paintballing. Enter at your own risk.*"

Gayle stared out of the window as, even better still; a few spots of rain began to spatter against it. She watched as the trees, getting thicker and thicker, flickered past her eyes with the look of someone about to enter a gladiator arena. She was either getting herself psyched up for the battle ahead or was completely pissed off. Clive realised the probability of it being the latter was as close to 100% as you could get and so decided against saying anything to her.

About a mile down the path and into some really rather dense woodland a small car park emerged to mark the end of the road. Jeremy and Clive got out of the car while Gayle remained seated, the same, intense look that now seemed like it would be in place forever, etched onto her face.

"*Ta-da!*" said Jeremy to Clive, his arms stretched out wide and a huge, beaming grin on his face. "Here we are!"

227

"Paintballing?" Clive asked now feeling the rain falling steadily onto him; and his best suit.

"Absolutely!" said Jeremy.

"But we've never been paintballing..... not *together* anyway. In fact, I'm pretty sure that Gayle has *never* been at all!"

"*All* will become clear in time" said Jeremy, his impossibly large smile somehow becoming impossibly larger.

He walked around the side of the car and opened the door where Gayle was sitting.

"Madam" he said, offering his hand to her.

She reluctantly took it, after the short thought that if she had a meat clever to hand she would have happily chopped it off, and was helped out of the car by the smiling buffoon.

(She wasn't sure if the desire to chop Jeremy's hand off was the result of watching too much *Game of Thrones* or just having spent too much time with him.)

"What......?" she asked as she looked around, settling for a one word question because she couldn't be bothered making the effort of adding the four extra words of "...are we doing here".

"All will become clear in time." Jeremy said, echoing himself from before. "I promise though, *this* is *the one*. You give me just a couple more hours and I'll give you your love back!"

With that he began, almost skipping, towards what Clive could now see as a small cluster of prefab buildings just to the right of the car park, where there were also a handful of men, mostly wearing camouflage clothing.

"Follow me!" he added as Clive pictured that greasy burger once more in his mind.

Before he could follow Jeremy, though, Gayle had grabbed his arm.

"We're not doing *this* are we?" she asked, squinting her eyes slightly as the rain fell a bit heavier. "We don't *have to* do *this*. We can just make him drive us home?"

For a split second Clive couldn't think beyond the potential, food-poisoning inducing burger that his mind had promised his rumbling tummy, until he saw the bigger picture.

"This could maybe be the last couple of hours of us doing anything together. The last couple of hours of *us*. We agreed we were going to do *anything*, didn't we? Let's not give up now!"

Damn it, thought Gayle.

This was *so* different to not wanting to do something like counselling, and yet how had she allowed Clive to make it somehow feel like it was pretty much the same thing? She reluctantly nodded her head. She *had* agreed to do *anything* no matter how foolish that seemed right now.

But paintballing?

Had she had any remote hint that it may be paintballing then there's no way she would have made such a rash agreement. She could not think of anything, *at all*, that she would rather not do than paintballing. Well, maybe apart from get covered head to toe in bees. Why do people do that?

Clive grabbed her hand and gave her a little sympathetic smile.

"Come on" he said, and they both began to follow where Jeremy was headed.

Gayle let out a big sigh and cursed herself for not having an umbrella with her. Those twenty minutes spent using her *BaByliss Volume Waves* curling iron, the first time she'd ever had even semi-success with it, were going to be a complete waste of time; those carefully created curls were going to be a frizzy mop inside a couple of minutes.

Looking towards where they were headed Gayle could see several men hanging around the few small buildings and, in fairness, none of them had an umbrella. They were just standing around – *in the rain.* Then again, she accepted that these men, who come to the woods to play their war games, may just spoil the image they wanted to convey if they did happen to be holding an umbrella. *This* wasn't an umbrella type of place. She had to accept that she was going to get wet and that just added to the overwhelming feeling that she was being led somewhere she didn't really want to go.

Strangely, Clive felt something very similar. This feeling of taking Gayle's hand and walking her towards somewhere she was, he realised, *reluctant* to go made him think about the first time he had taken her to see Sue. Obviously, back then, she was a nervous teenager who was going to meet her boyfriends "parent" for the very first time but this, somehow, felt very similar. As they followed Jeremy, Gayle's mind no doubt focussing on the forthcoming ordeal – *in the rain,* Clive couldn't stop his own mind travelling back to the first time he took her to meet Sue, all those years ago.

FORTY THREE: *Never Let Her Go.* (22 Years Ago)

It was after Gayle had gone home that Clive remembered most – and yet he had somehow let those memories fade of late. He had just taken her home to meet Sue for the first time but the actual meeting felt like a blur of memories. He remembered some of the things that happened *before* they met. Like how Gayle had dressed rather conservatively for her – choosing to wear a rather plain, mid-length, grey dress that was completely different to the loud, vibrant colours that she had begun to wear. Even her big hair seemed..... *smaller* somehow. Her palms had been sweaty as she stalled at the front door for as long as possible, asking multiple questions about whether she looked alright and what Clive thought she should talk about.

During that first acquaintance, well things were more blurred. Clive remembered Gayle's initial nervousness easing fairly quickly as her and Sue bonded over conversations that repeatedly revisited music. It was a meeting that he thought would last around half an hour that somehow saw three hours pass by in the blink of an eye as the two of them really hit it off, as the conversation meandered through all aspects of life, aspirations and, embarrassingly, *love.*

But it was after he had walked Gayle home that Clive remembered *really* clearly. When he returned back home, Sue looked different. Sometimes with her medication she could look really withdrawn; like somehow the *real* her was not there. There were many times that it seemed like she had been replaced by an imposter who was standing in for her. An imposter who was dealing with the situation she was in: the pain, the horror, the need to carry on and fight, even though the fight seemed so hard, and the *will* to fight was so hard to maintain. But, after meeting Gayle, Sue was definitely there, 100%, and she was *beaming.*

She always prided herself in "knowing about people" and had always encouraged Clive and made him believe that he was one of life's "beautiful souls". He remembered Sue's first reaction to Gayle was that she was also "beautiful" with a "good, pure, heart" and that Clive had *done well.*

"She loves you, you know?" he remembered her saying as clear as day. "And I can see that *you* love *her*."

Clive smiled as thoughts of Sue warmed him from head to toe. But it wasn't just him thinking about his "mother" that was making him smile. It was him recalling Sue's instinctive fondness for Gayle that was just as important. His eyes began to moisten as he recalled one of the last things that Sue ever told him about him and Gayle. And not because it was just more compliments about how nice she thought Gayle was, but because it included some advice she had left him with. He realised now that they were words of guidance that he had very nearly allowed to slip away.

He held tighter onto Gayle's hand as they walked, following Jeremy, and told himself, again, *why* they were here and why, *right now*, he needed to fight more than ever. As he did, Sue's words played out in his head just as clear as they had been on the day that she'd spoken them.

"Some people will tell you that you're too young to know *real love*. But love doesn't have *any* boundaries. Age, sex, religion, race..... *none* of those things can get in the way of *real love*. You've heard me talk about my Steve before haven't you? What we had was *real*. There were other men after he'd died, quite a lot of other men, and I probably loved most of them to some degree; but nothing was ever like it was with Steve. What you and Gayle have - that is *real love*. You've done very well, son, – never let her down. *And never let her go*."

CHAPTER FORTY FOUR: *Into The Arena.*

Gayle slipped her left arm into the big camouflage onesie thing she'd been given and zipped it up the front. As she did she caught a glimpse of herself in the large mirror on the far side wall of the stinky port-a-cabin and let out a big sigh. She had looked a million dollars earlier when she left the house wearing her sophisticated cream party frock, now she looked like one of the mothers she often saw dropping their kids off at Talbot Street school, round the corner from them, who appeared to have not been bothered doing anything with their hair and to still be wearing their nightwear. After slipping her boots back on she walked back out of the "changing hut" and across to where Clive, already changed into his adult action man gear, and Jeremy, were standing.

"Don't you think you could have mentioned that we were going to be paintballing earlier when you picked us up?" she aimed towards Jeremy. "Maybe then we could have dressed a bit more *appropriately?*"

"What, and spoil the *surprise?*" said Jeremy with a grin. "Besides, you've got these overalls to wear haven't you?"

"I'm not sure if you've ever worn overalls *over* a dress" said Gayle, leaving those words lingering a while because she thought she wouldn't actually put it past Jeremy. "Because it's not actually *that* comfortable. And if I knew what we were going to be doing I wouldn't have worn *these boots*. They'll get ruined if they get wet!"

"I think you'll be fine." Said Jeremy smiling. "It's good you're wearing those boots. Besides it's pretty dry out there. And there's not a *lot* of rain predicted for today."

Gayle wondered what he meant about it being *good* that she was wearing her best boots. How could it possibly be *good?*

"Dry out there?" She asked, focussing on the *other ridiculous* part of his sentence. "We've had more rain than a Manchester test match!"

Gayle shook her head. Had she just made a cricket-themed joke? Yep, she'd chosen this moment, when the last thing she was *feeling* was amused, to make her first *ever*, and hopefully *last ever*, cricket-themed joke. What the hell was wrong with her? She looked over at Clive who was chuckling away seemingly amused, and impressed, by her subject choice of gag, which somehow made the whole thing even worse.

"David..... David..... DAVID?"

A shout from a man near one of the other buildings caught their attention and all three of them looked over to where it was coming from. Jeremy held his arm up and shouted back

"Over here! I'll be right with you."

He began walking towards this man, while looking back at Gayle and Clive and explaining to them why the man was calling him David and not Jeremy. It was the sort of explanation though that was not meant to be understood as he spoke in a low mumble of nonsense using words that had no significance to each other. Clive and Gayle hardly noticed though. They had got used to Jeremy's strange ways and were not surprised or looking for an explanation at all.

"Does it hurt when you got shot?" Gayle asked Clive, with a concerned look on her face, once they were alone.

"Erm, I'd probably say it *stings* more than *hurts*." Said Clive, in an ambiguous tone.

He felt happy that Gayle looked a little relieved by his response as he, in his mind, went into further detail. *The sort of "sting" you may get from a deadly scorpion.*

"You still think we need to go through with this?" was her next question.

Clive nodded slowly and gently stroked her on the arm, whilst actually thinking that if they *did* leave now then he may be able to go somewhere and get something to eat. How was it that there was a perfectly good looking "snack bar" hut here, that "wasn't open today"? Unbelievable!

"Clive..... Gayle..... this way please!" Jeremy's voice called.

Gayle attempted, unsuccessfully, to take a big gulp from her dry mouth as she and Clive responded to Jeremy's (or David's, or Jason's or Henry's or whoever the hell anyone else knows him by) call, by starting to walk towards him.

Ten minutes later, their camouflage onesie's had been accompanied by face masks and helmets and they had just listened to a safety briefing,

233

given by a man wearing camouflage trousers and a hi-vis jacket. (Come on mate, make your mind up!) Following his talk, he had made them sign a piece of paper that forfeited them to any compensation claim should they be hideously injured (or worse) by any unfortunate accident or, probably, gross negligence by the paintballing company. They had also met the other people who would be joining them for the imminent war of paint and pain, this last activity that, to both Gayle and Clive, seemed completely inappropriate for a "re-finding" love weekend.

The people joining them were six large men who were wearing a variety of uniforms from those who were completely covered in professional looking camouflage gear, including jackets that appeared to be made of leaves, to two guys who looked like they may just be about to go to a fancy dress party as the "Frog Brothers" from the *Lost Boys*. They were even wearing red head bands and had black make up smeared under their eyes. What all six men did have in common, though, was that they all looked intensely serious; all of them had <u>cold eyes</u>. They were cold-blooded killer wannabes who were looking for a legitimate, legal way of shooting people – in real life. (Before probably going home, once it got dark, and doing it all again, virtually, on *Call of Duty*.)

There was also actually a seventh guy who was holding a large camera. He had said that he was nursing an injury and wouldn't be able to take part but would be taking pictures. He had smiled sadistically as he spoke; no doubt he took great pleasure in capturing the looks of fear and pain on people's faces, as they were being shot at by any of the other cold-eyed assassins.

Gayle sussed him as a definite daddy long legs leg remover as a child straight away. She was fairly worried now though about how she seemed to be wanting to label every new person that she met as either a daddy long legs leg-remover or a non daddy long legs leg-remover. Damn you Phil Tipman and those newly remembered horrific, animal-maiming childhood memories. This was such a change to when Gayle was able to just instantly label new people as "nice" and "potentially new friend" or "not so nice" and "potentially someone to bitch about".

It wasn't long before the "rules" of the days paintballing had also been explained to everyone. There were to be two teams. The first one would be just Clive and Gayle and they would go by the name of "Team: Me and You". The second team was basically everyone else and they were called "Team: The World." The complete "game time" would be an hour and the objective was for Team: Me and You (Clive and Gayle) to make it across the game arena to the large flag pole and raise the red flag. If they could do this, without being shot more than five times, then they

234

would be victorious. If either of them was shot five times or more they would have to leave the game arena, via the yellow exit gate, and it would be up to the other one to continue.

Team: The World had to defend their flag pole and make sure that neither Clive nor Gayle could raise the red flag. Each of their players though would have to leave the game arena immediately if they were shot just once. The PA system would let the gamers know how long was left in the game by giving out a "remaining game time" announcement every five minutes. It would also signal any "kills" by letting out one blast from the fog horn for a Team: The World "death" and two blasts for any Team: Me and You "deaths".

As the "death" signals were demonstrated by the fog horn being blasted through the, very tinny, PA system Gayle couldn't help but notice Clive, and one of the "Frog Brothers", sniggering fairly loudly. She shook her head. True, the noise did sound uncannily like someone letting out a particularly raspy, loud fart that they'd probably tried to hold onto for too long, but it always amazed her how some people were overly amused by noises that sounded, in any way remotely, like flatulence. It was usually men who had never grown out of finding toilet and, especially, fart humour so hilarious as little boys.

Some last minute advice about the game arena, including good places to hide etc., and a short demonstration about how to use the paint guns (aim and shoot) came and went quickly and, before they knew it, Gayle and Clive had walked *into the arena* and were sitting in a wooden shack about 40 metres away from the flag pole that they had to reach to achieve victory. Their six opponents (the enemy) had initially headed towards the flag pole but had all now, worryingly, camouflaged into the background.

Clive looked at Gayle and couldn't help but think that the goggles she was wearing were making her eyes appear somewhat magnified and that it made her look a little like *Eddie the Eagle*. He thought it was probably best not to tell her. It wouldn't be the greatest compliment in the world and, given their current situation, they would both be best focussing on positive things. He slowly moved his head higher so that he could see out of the "window" hole at the front of the wooden shack. About ten metres in front of them to the left was another shack but, still disturbingly, as he looked around the flag pole area, and even further around the game arena in general, there was no sign of anyone else. Where *were* they all?

He sat back down and looked at Gayle in preparation for telling her that he thought they needed to try and make it to the next shack in front of them. Before he spoke, though, he couldn't help but notice Gayle smirking at him.

235

"What?" he asked.

"Nothing, really" said Gayle. "It's just that your goggles make your eyes look funny. You look a bit like Benny Hill!"

She laughed a little.

"You look like Eddie the Eagle!" Clive snapped back at her instinctively.

They both looked solemnly at each other before bursting out laughing.

"What the hell are we doing?" laughed Gayle. "I thought we'd be eating a fancy meal by now but we're crouched down in a dirty, old, wooden hut. You've not even been able to buy a greasy burger or anything."

Clive stopped laughing and remembered that his stomach was still acting like it was doing somersaults on a trampoline. He hadn't even mentioned to Gayle that he was hoping to buy a greasy burger; she had obviously read it in his eyes. You spend enough time with someone and they know you inside out.

"Fifty Five minutes game time remaining"

The PA system had crackled and a tinny, Scottish voice had indicated the amount of time left that they had to endure.

Clive raised himself to a squatting position, wondering whether it was another of Jeremy's *wonderful* accents drifting through the air.

"Come on. We can do this!" he said, focussing on their predicament.

Gayle looked at him strangely; her Eddie the Eagle magnified eyes, quite clearly, saying: *I don't want to.*

"Come on" started Clive again. "We're here; we said we'd go through with it. Let's make the most of it. Try and enjoy it. It could be fun!"

The look on Gayle's face changed slightly but only because she wanted to add more emphasis to the "don't want" part of the sentence she was emitting. She continued to stare at Clive, as he once again said "Come on", before having to smile a little as she couldn't look at him without the *Benny Hill* theme tune playing in her head.

Derrrr-der-der-der-de-de-de-der-der-de-de-de-der-de-de....

(Sorry, you can't really write the Benny Hill theme tune in words.)

Gayle watched as Clive, once more, slowly raised his head and looked out of the wooden shack. She then couldn't quite believe it as her legs also moved themselves into a squat position, blindly following Clive's orders. Was she really going to do this?

"Ok, no sign of anyone..... think they're either dug in around the flag or are trying some kind of stealthy flanking manoeuvre to attack us.

236

Either way, we need to try and move to the next cabin, about ten metres across no man's land." Clive said, lowering his head back down.

Dug in? Flanking manoeuvre? No man's land?

Gayle mystifyingly looked at Clive as he used these detailed, technical war terms, half wondering how he knew them and half wondering whether he was actually *enjoying* this now.

"Are you ready?" he asked. "Stay low and follow me!"

Gayle found herself nodding her head somehow even though, inside that head, a voice was screaming *no, no, no, NOOOOOOOOO!*

Clive slowly raised himself to his feet, while keeping himself slouched down, and then carefully walked towards the open doorway of the wooden shack, where they had entered a few minutes earlier. He leaned his head out in a deliberate and measured manner, once again scanning around the area for potential cold-blooded killer wannabes. Again he saw no one.

He looked around at Gayle and whispered: "After three?"

She nodded.

"One, two…"

"Wait" snapped Gayle, in her own whisper. "*What* after three?"

"We run to the next building" whispered Clive pointing to the other shack in front of them.

Great, more running thought Gayle.

"One, two, *three!*" whispered Clive again, only on *three* he headed out of the shack. Gayle quickly followed him and soon, side by side, they were running the short distance between one wooden shack and the other. Just before they got there an outbreak of multiple gun shots could clearly be heard, accompanied by the flurry of paintballs splatting against the wooden walls of the shack they were entering.

Duh, duh, duh, duh, duh, duh, duh, duh, duh.

As they made it to the relative safety of the second wooden hut, Gayle took a hit to her right upper arm.

"JESUS!" she screamed out in pain as the paint ball struck her. It felt a little like a mosquito landing on her and gently biting – before someone attempted to squash it by smacking her with a sledge hammer!

She instinctively rubbed her arm vigorously while saying.

"Oh my God, that hurts like hell!"

Clive pushed her gently against the wall and slid her down to a sitting position rubbing her upper arm, that was now covered in green paint, as he did.

"It's not bad" he said. "It could have been worse. I think you'll live."

"Not *fucking* bad?" said Gayle, tears streaming down her cheeks "It hurts like *fucking* hell!..... Just *how* could it have been worse?"

Clive paused, thinking.

"Well, it could have been *me*." He said smiling.

From out of a frown an unauthorised grin spread on Gayle's face.

"You stupid fucking..... *cock drawer!*" she said beginning to laugh before Clive joined in as well.

"It was a *rocket!*" he said with fake disgust as they both continued to laugh.

They sat down with their backs against the wall for about a minute, both smiling and breathing heavily after their short, semi-successful sprint. Clive continued to rub Gayle's arm with his left hand as he put his right arm around her shoulder and held her close to him.

"Does that feel any better?" he asked.

"Not really" said Gayle. "It feels like someone's squashing my arm in a clamp. There's going to be a hell of a bruise there. I thought you said being hit just *stung* a little?"

"Yeah, I may have *slightly* understated how it hurts."

Gayle pushed him away a little and aimed an aggressive look at him.

"But it was a long time ago that I did it and..... I think the upper arm is a particularly *bad* place to get hit..... anywhere really fleshy is bound to hurt..... and....."

Gayle interrupted him.

"Anywhere *really fleshy*? What do you mean about my arms?"

"Well they're not *really* fleshy. I mean, *everyone's* upper arms are *fleshy*. You've got normal arms..... well, *beautiful* arms..... and....."

Thankfully, for Clive, the tinny Scottish accent spoke through the PA system again, interrupting his get-out-of-the-hole-you-dug-yourself attempts.

"Fifty minutes game time remaining."

Clive and Gayle looked at each other.

"Fifty minutes?" said Gayle "I'm not sure that..... Wait a minute! I'm *out* aren't I? Oh thank God for that! Now where's that yellow gate?"

She began to stand up but Clive pulled her down again.

"You're not *out*. You're only out if you get shot *five* times." Clive said, shaking his head, wondering how Gayle ever had the nerve to accuse him of not listening to things.

"Five times? I've got to get shot *five times*? There's no way I'm going through pain like that another four times..... *no way!*"

Gayle closed her eyes and wondered whether she would cope with *this* pain once more, let alone *four more times*. Then again, it's not like

238

this was the first time she'd had to endure extreme pain. She was a mother after all.

FORTY FIVE: *All I Ever Needed.*

Gayle began rubbing her own arm and, although it hurt like hell, she decided that this obviously *wasn't* the worst pain and discomfort she'd had in her life. For one, she'd sat in the dental hygienists chair on a couple of occasions whilst an evil woman, with a pain-inflicting fetish, had squirted, scraped and flossed at her teeth and gums until they severely bled while, at the same time, spraying enough water down her throat to make sure that breathing was near-on impossible. Do *all* dental hygienists also have to pass an exam in extreme water-boarding before they are fully qualified?

And then of course she'd had a baby for God's sake. And *nothing* could ever remotely come close to *that* pain. The thing about having a baby though is that, even though the pain and discomfort is worse than anything you could ever imagine (even *two* hygienists having a go at you at once), when it's all over every single second of it was totally worth it.

Because you have a *baby*.

And an instant bond and feeling of love and attachment that is greater than anything you could ever imagine possible.

What would she have following this particular paintball-inflicted intense pain? Nothing. Well, apart from a bruise that would, quite probably, be around *forever*. It would certainly be one of those "deep" bruises that takes it's time to change into each colour of the rainbow before turning yellow for a few weeks and then (possibly) disappearing after several months.

Gayle smiled to herself as she ignored the thoughts that she would have to wear long sleeves for the next couple of months and, instead, focussed on the day she gave birth to Jack. It *was* painful, but it was also pretty quick. Not quick in the traditional sense of the word, but quick in relative, baby-delivering, terms. She'd heard tales of women being in labour for *days*; ordeals that must leave severe psychological scars. For Gayle though, she'd been "in and out" of delivery within three and a half hours and always remembered one of the mid-wife's telling her that she'd been faster giving birth than an average man takes running a marathon. She'd given birth to an actual, real, living baby quicker than it takes a man to run a few miles. That had always felt like pretty good going.

She smiled as she remembered being handed Jack for the very first time. Just holding him close to her and looking at him was definitely one of the best moments of her life, and even though he was "out of her" she couldn't help that feeling of knowing that he would *always* be a part of her.

Gayle continued to smile as she then remembered another image that would stay with her forever. As she was required to receive "a couple of stitches" in her "sensitive" area (thankfully not feeling a thing – but feeling woozy just thinking about it to this day), Clive took Jack and walked him around the room trying to stop him crying. He spoke quietly to him and sang a few soothing songs and Jack soon settled and looked so serene and comfortable.

And there they were: her new, little man in the arms of her other, bigger man.

Father and son.

Bonding.

The two men in her life; *her family.* And she felt *so happy.* Before that moment she'd not felt like part of a family for *so long.* Obviously her parents splitting had changed everything and, after that, she could count the number of times she'd seen her father on one hand. Her relationship with her mother had also changed, and become broken and strained, following the split. And then it fell apart completely when she told her she was pregnant with Jack.

Gayle could feel the tears forming in her eyes as she remembered *that conversation* with her mum. She wanted to stop her mind thinking about it and not give her mum the satisfaction of upsetting her once again but she couldn't. Instead she forced her memory to show fragments of it; just the images and raw emotions.

Her Mum just staring at her with no particular reaction. No joy, no happiness, no delight, no empathy; not even any shock, or surprise, or any level of being upset.

Not even any *disgust.*

It was like she did not care, in the slightest, about anything that was being said to her. The conversation ended with Gayle's mum announcing that she should leave home as soon as she could. And that was almost a relief. It was over. She didn't need her mum anymore. She had a baby coming and she had Clive; and Clive was the *only* thing that she ever needed anyway.

FORTY SIX: *Run For It.*

Gayle's thoughts came back to the present and she couldn't help but look at Clive and smile at him. It felt good to be back with him and not thinking about her mum and *that* most unpleasant moment. Although the sound of the rain, and the feeling of the wind, reminded her very quickly just *where* she had come back to. She was paintballing and people were *shooting* at one another. She needed to find a way to put an end to it before one of those people began shooting at *her – again.*

Clive put his arm back around her.

"*I* know" said Gayle, sitting upright, a moment of inspiration striking her. "We can just surrender, can't we? That'll put an end to it. We *can* surrender, can't we?"

"No" said Clive "......we're not *French.*"

Gayle ignored the question in her mind: was Clive's comment *racist* or just harmless, albeit lazy, *traditional English humour*; that *had* made her smirk a little? She had more pressing things to worry about it so, instead, took a deep breath and thought hard.

"I don't want to go through that again. It was awful. Do you think we can just run for the green gate that we came in through?"

"I suppose we could" said Clive. "But they would probably just shoot us again. We could just wait here for the game time to run down and hope that they just want to protect that flag. Of course, they could just wait until a couple of minutes before the end and then just charge us anyway."

He stroked his chin as he thought. As he did, he noticed that Gayle's eyes had begun to moisten and the look on her face was one of dread; any traces of the earlier laughter had long gone. She really wasn't enjoying this and she was obviously scared of being hit again; and she was in this position because *he* had insisted on it. Although she was displaying a distinct lack of backbone about a bit of a sore arm he did feel guilty.

"Ok, I've got a plan" he said, trying desperately, but failing, to not use the usual *Hannibal Smith* impression he did whenever he spoke about any kind of plan.

"I will go for the flag. You stay here and hopefully you won't get shot again. I will try my best to raise that flag; if I do, it will be over."

Gayle smiled at him through her glazed eyes.

"This is important. If I get stuck somewhere, I will wait until there are twenty minutes to go – I'm pretty sure that they won't leave where they are until there's just a few minutes left. So, when you hear the announcement that says twenty minutes remaining then you run for the green gate as fast as you can. I will make sure that, at that point, I *completely* have their attention and so you will be able to make it out without any of them noticing. You understand?"

Gayle nodded and gave Clive a hug, feeling a little better about things straight away. But then another thought entered her head; a much clearer and more important one.

"No!" she said, trying to sound as resolute as possible. "We need a different plan. Because we should do this *together*. We are team *You and Me* for a reason. This is our chance to prove it. Let's do it *together*."

Clive smiled as a warm glow grew inside him. He felt good, and knew that was because Gayle's words made him feel like they really were *together*. But he felt like he needed to prove something.

"Let's stick to my plan." he began, talking quickly so that Gayle didn't feel like he was dismissing her plan lightly.

"This is something I want to do. For you; *for us*. I always vowed that I'd always protect you and keep you safe, something I now know I haven't always done. I *need* to do *this* now. *Please*."

Gayle could see the genuine warmth shining through Clive's eyes and, despite the wind and rain, felt the same warmth growing inside of her. Maybe it was nice, possibly even important, to feel like someone is going to save you every now and again.

"Ok" she said quietly, giving Clive another hug. "Thank you."

It felt nice that Clive "*needed*" to do something noble, almost heroic and selfless; and all for *her*. As he began to stand up, she pulled his face down and kissed him on the cheek.

"Good luck!" she said.

244

"Remember," said Clive "On the twenty minute announcement, *run for it.* I'll make sure that everyone else is too busy to shoot you!"

With that he slowly looked around the wall of the shack and quickly ran across to a big tree that was just a couple of metres away. There was no sound of shooting guns, so it seemed that he had sneaked out unnoticed.

Gayle watched him as he passed out of sight and sighed heavily. She had a strange mix of emotions; happy that Clive was going out to fight for her and yet worried and regretting that she had agreed to let him do it. Perhaps she should have insisted even more that she went out with him, and that they should have fought *together.* She also regretted now just giving him the little "good luck" Princess Leia-esque kiss on the cheek; the least he deserved was a *real kiss* before he had left.

Clive carefully looked around the tree; feeling buoyed on by Gayle's rather cute kiss and "good luck" combination, and straight away his attention was caught by one of the enemy slowly crawling towards the wooden shack. Those leafy jackets really did blend in well with the leaves on the floor, but were a dead giveaway when someone was crawling; you don't see many patches of ground for which some leaves stayed still as others, that were also considerably higher, moved at a slow but purposeful pace. He gripped his gun tight and took a deep breath.

Wow, he felt like the character in the Stan Ridgway song *Camouflage*, as the enemy were "*moving in close outside*". What he'd give right now for his own mystical, heroic, ghost-marine to help him out of this situation. He resigned himself to the fact that one probably wouldn't show up to help him and so he had to handle things himself. As quick as a flash, in his mind anyway, he stepped away from the tree, aimed his gun at the moving leaves and pulled the trigger. Unfortunately the moving leaves were slightly quicker and a man emerged and fired a faster shot at Clive that, ironically, also struck him on the upper arm. He flinched in pain and quickly spun back behind the tree.

"Shit!"

Clive glanced back around the tree to see the man standing upright; clearly sporting the red paint of Clive's shot across his right shoulder.

Clive had got one!

The man slammed his gun to the floor in disgust with himself and turned around to make the walk to the side of the game arena and his yellow gate of shame. Clive then manically grabbed hold of his upper arm and began rubbing it intensely.

Damn, it *did* hurt like hell. Maybe he'd been a little hasty and harsh in his diagnosis that Gayle was missing that all important backbone. The crackle of an imminent PA announcement could be heard before a long, tinny blow of the fog horn sounded making Clive chuckle to himself once again.

PAARRRRRRP

Gayle's attention was grabbed by the sound also. She though resisted the temptation of laughing and, instead, waited to hear if there would be a second blast. After a few seconds of silence, she realised that there wouldn't be another, long fart sound, and *one* blast meant: Clive had got one!

A huge smile exploded onto her face as she again looked through the glaze of watery eyes. This time though it wasn't through fear or pain but because of pride. *Her* Clive had got one!

As she smiled, she looked down at her boots, and in particular the mud splashes that gave them a strange, almost *Inkblot* test look about them. Instead of employing some business-like, psychology bullshit about what the shapes of the splashes could represent though, Gayle just accepted that she looked like someone who'd had the bottom of their legs swapped for those of a wet cow.

As well as feeling more and more tight and painful, (although nothing like as bad as her arm that was still intensely throbbing) she also realised that her boots would need to be given a good clean when they got back home.

Clive was in charge of cleaning shoes. He would take multiple pairs out into the back garden and somehow take forever with them; although they did always come back looking sparkling and new. She would have to ask him to clean the boots later because she had planned to wear them later for her date with Lee.

Oh shit!

Her *date* with Lee.

She hadn't even *thought* about that for at least twenty four hours. Should she still go on it? She wasn't even sure if it felt right to be going on it after what she and Clive had been doing over the weekend. Or, at least, what they'd been *trying* to do. Then again, could a day and a half of silly events make up for years of letting a relationship crumble and die? Had she not got used to the fact, and accepted, that *this time* had been coming for a long, long time? Now that it was here didn't she need to *embrace* it, and get on with a new start no matter how scary it seemed?

Why was she asking herself these same questions *again*?

PAARRRRRRP

The PA system playing out more tinny flatulence pulled Gayle's mind back into the shack. Wow, that was quick. Clive must have bumped into someone else really quickly. But what had happened? Would there be another foghorn blast to follow? She held her breath and waited. As she did she could feel her heart almost beating out of her chest. She waited and waited and waited and waited and..... there *wasn't* any other sound; just silence. The silence that meant that Clive had "killed" another one, and that, more importantly, he was still "alive". He was out there fighting for *her* and he was *still alive*!

Clive slowed his breathing and stepped back behind the big tree. Wow, that one was much easier. That guy hadn't even seen him. He had just wandered into the wrong part of the arena and Clive had been able to shoot him, bull's-eye on the chest, before he had even noticed he was there. And his gun had definitely shot straight. Finally, he had been given a gun that worked properly! Hopefully next time he went go-karting, he may just be lucky enough *not* to be given the slow car. Clive felt happy and knew that he had just removed the second of the enemy six whose sole intent was to hurt his Gayle.

It seemed like maybe the enemy were sending troops out one by one to try and locate and destroy *Team: Me and You* so, if he just stayed right where he was, he may just be able to take them out as they crossed the arena.

Clive shook as head as he thought about the random team names that Jeremy had assigned to them both. *Team: The World* and *Team: Me and You*? What weird names. If he could have named his own team he would have gone for something a bit cooler, like *The Sharpshooters* or *The Armageddon Squad* or *Clive and Gayle: Natural Born Killers*. But he supposed that was Jeremy all over – always doing the unexpected and weird thing. The team names rotated around his head as he gripped his gun with *Al Pacino*-in-*Scarface* menace and glanced out to see if any more of the enemy had come to *say hello to his little friend*.

The World and *Me and You*. *Me and You* and *The World*. *Me and You*..... versus *The World*. He smiled as the penny finally dropped: *Me and You vs. The World*. Jeremy had done it again. He had put him and Gayle in a desperate situation and linked it into how they had felt about things in the past when they had felt in similar situations in *life*. It was *their* song, and *their* motto – *Me and You vs. The World*. Unfortunately they had both somehow seemed to have forgotten to live by it of late.

CRACK!

Clive instinctively looked around the tree and, sure enough, he was right – the enemy had sent another one out into no man's land. This one, one of the oddly dressed "Frog Brothers", had just stepped on, and snapped, a pretty big twig and was frozen rigid, obviously wondering

247

whether he had given his position away. Even though he had now sunk to his knees and had moved slightly to the left, behind a large bush, Clive *had* spotted him.

"*I See You!*" he said in his mind, mimicking that *Mac* line from *Predator*. Clive seemed unable *not* to link his situation to every film he had ever seen that felt even remotely similar. He began his slow breathing ritual and brought his gun slowly up ready for making his next kill.

Gayle heard the giveaway crackle of the PA system that maybe meant another blast of the fog horn was coming.

"Forty-five minutes game time remaining"

She let out her breath.

It was just the announcement of time rather than another.....

PAARRRRRRP

Gayle quickly held her breath again and couldn't help but be reminded about the scenes from *The Hunger Games* films in which, similarly, gamers' deaths were announced by a large sound echoing around the arena. Of course in those films the sound was a much more impressive and dramatic canon shot rather that a tinny release-of-gas type noise, but the effect was evocative of those scenes. She again waited for that dreaded second blast and again ..... it never came. Clive had done it once more. She felt so happy and relieved and, even though she now realised that he was probably going to be *talking about this forever*, was so proud of Clive.

Wow, *Team: Me and You* were actually putting up a pretty good fight of it. Gayle smiled as her own personal penny dropped. *Me and You vs. The World.* That's what this was. Her and Clive in a battle that, in all reality, they *couldn't* win and yet they were putting up a damn good fight. This is how things should have been, in life, all along. *Gayle and Clive vs. The World,* just like they had promised each other all those years ago. Gayle began to cry again.

Clive stood still; leaning against what he had now decided was his favourite tree in the world. Or certainly his joint favourite tree – the tree that stood on the school field, the location where he and Gayle used to have their late picnics, was one close to his heart also. As such, he had decided to give this tree a name: *Tree-ie*. Not the most imaginative of names but it certainly seemed to suit him. Every few seconds he would slowly lurch his neck around and look out, beyond *Tree-ie*, and into the no man's land area that had been the site of his three kills.

Yep, *three kills*.

Not a bad afternoons work so far. And that last one had been the easiest yet. The Frog Brother had basically walked over to Clive and presented himself to be shot; he had practically killed himself. Well, either that or Clive was actually getting *pretty good* at this.

Each time Clive looked around for more of the enemy coming through the same way and then returned his head back to resting against *Tree-ie*, that was *so much* more comfortable than you would expect from a tree; he would focus on an area of grass and bushes to his right that looked perfect for someone to hide in. If he had been in command of *Team: The World* he would have probably tried to send someone to get to *that* area rather than keep sending them up through the middle of the arena - that was certainly more open and exposed.

Maybe he should have been a military strategist? Was it too late to change professions? Are the army looking for potential new generals who have twenty-plus years experience as a *postman*? Possibly not.

Clive again slowly looked out to no man's land and scanned the area. Again, there was nothing to be seen between where he was and the flag pole area where, in fairness, he had not spotted any movement whatsoever. As he returned his head back against *Tree-ie* and gazed upon the area of grass and bushes once more, something looked different. There was a different shape amongst a couple of the bushes. A shape that almost looked like a man in a squatting position. Clive's brain processed the information in less than half a second. The shape *was* actually a man. A man who had sneaked up upon him without him realising. A man who, even though he had adopted a squatting position and looked like he may be taking a shit, was actually pointing his gun at Clive. A gun he was about to shoot.

BANG BANG BANG BANG BANG BANG BANG BANG.

He fired multiple shots at Clive, one of the first ones luckily, or unluckily striking him on the lower abdomen – about three inches above being totally catastrophic. What it did mean though was that Clive naturally collapsed to the floor, in complete agony, and involuntarily did a forward roll that evaded most of the other paint balls and returned him to facing his squatting ambusher whilst still holding his gun.

Duh, duh, duh, duh, duh, duh.

It sounded like the majority of the paintballs had missed Clive but had struck poor *Tree-ie* behind him. Clive, in total panic, squeezed his trigger and covered the whole area of grass and bushes in the red paint of his exploding pellets. Fortunately he managed to strike the enemy during his flurry of bullets. The man, in true dignified fashion, stood up, nodded his head and accepted his death graciously. He walked off towards the yellow gate not even seemingly bothered about the pain he must have been feeling due to the large red paint mark around his right knee. A paintball to the knee cap? That *must* have hurt. But he didn't show it; war-weary hard bastard.

In contrast, Clive struggled to the relative safety of, a now green paint-spattered, *Tree-ie* almost crying. The pain in his stomach was probably the worst pain he'd experienced in his life and was easily twice as bad as having a baby. As he rubbed the green paint, wondering whether it *was* paint or whether *he* was actually a *Predator* and was now bleeding, he also noticed that he had been shot on the left thigh and somewhere near his right hip as well. He could hardly feel any pain from those "wounds" at all. Maybe it was the pain from his stomach that was masking that or maybe he, too, was becoming a bit of a war-weary hard bastard?

What he had also noticed during this encounter was two of the enemy; actually now the *last two* of the enemy, were hiding behind a small wooden storage box right next to the flag pole. They had only been visible for a split second and had quickly hidden when they had seen what had happened between Clive and the squatting tough guy, but he had seen them. He knew where they were. Unfortunately he had now been shot four times and so any more and he would also be "dead".

PAARRRRRRP

Gayle let out an excited little laugh once she realised that there, again, was not going to be a second blast of the fog horn. Clive had killed another one. There were only two left now. He had already killed four so the last two should be a piece of cake, shouldn't they? Was she letting herself believe that they were actually going to *win* this? Would there be a trophy that could sit on the shelf above the TV in the front room? And, more importantly, was she actually going to be able to walk out of here without having to take, even one more, of those ridiculously painful shots? (Why the hell did people do this; and do it in the name of *fun*?)

"Forty minutes game time remaining."

Clive slid down *Tree-ie* and rested his bottom on the ground in between two large roots. He felt quite snug wedged in between, what felt like, two big protruding wooden arm rests; it was almost as though his new forest friend was giving him a big hug. Ahh *Tree-ie*, Clive felt like he wanted to take him home with him if he could; and he would try and clean off all that green paint that had unfortunately covered him. It looked like Banksy had mysteriously turned up and tried to create another of his anonymous "masterpieces". Poor *Tree-ie*. Clive hoped that he wasn't allergic to paint; otherwise this would be the start of a bad few days for him. He settled down and decided to rest his aching war wounds for a while. He was feeling good about his efforts so far, but also he was full of dread about the last little push that was in front of him. It reminded him about how he felt the day that he told Sue that he and Gayle were expecting a baby. He closed his eyes as his mind took him back.

FORTY SEVEN: *Unconditional Love.*

Clive remembered the exact moment with crystal clear clarity. As he approached Sue she was sitting on her new chair that allowed her to rock slowly forwards and backwards. She used to laugh at the irony of her buying a "rocking chair", even if it wasn't one of those traditional, wooden ones you see out on wooden verandas in old American TV shows, because she had promised herself that she would never get old. And so this, three piece suite arm chair that rocked a little, seemed like the *reluctant acceptance* of someone getting old.

Maybe not wanting to get old was part of the reason that Sue had fostered and adopted so many kids over the years. Maybe being a "parent" to kids who needed help was a way of staying young.

Clive remembered that she looked quite content, rocking away, as he approached her. Her latest round of treatment had left her feeling more positive and, in turn, more healthy. He had no idea what he was going to say to her; he certainly had no plan anyway. He was fifteen years old and popular opinion suggests that he should have been concentrating on playing football with his friends at the park or, perhaps, annoying *real* old people by recklessly riding his BMX on the pavements. But here he was, having to tell his step-Mum that his girlfriend, who was also fifteen, was *pregnant*.

He and Gayle had already spoken at great length and had both agreed that they would *definitely* be keeping the baby; that much was not going to change. But Clive had been absolutely dreading telling Sue.

Had he let her down?

Would she be angry?

Would she maybe feel like *she* had let *him* down? Would she feel like she had failed in her job because she maybe felt like part of that job was to steer him away from situations like this? The last thing he wanted was to make Sue feel like she had failed him in any way, shape or form. She had been the *only* constant he had ever known before he had met Gayle. She was also obviously very poorly and shouldn't be having to deal with any further problems.

"There's no easy way to say this," were the first words that came out of Clive's mouth after Sue had noticed him slowly walking towards her. "Gayle is pregnant. We are going to be having a baby."

He winced and got ready for Sue's response.

He heard all the possible things she may say flooding through his head: "You can't possibly keep it!" "How could you both be so irresponsible?" "You will be ruining your childhoods and, ultimately, your lives!" "You are too young." "You are not ready for this."

Sue took her time though before saying anything. She took lots of deep breaths and continued rocking, although slightly slower than she had been before. When she finally spoke, it was quietly and calmly.

"I take it, it wasn't planned?" she asked in an almost hushed voice.

Clive shook his head.

"Come and sit with me." Sue said, patting her hands on her thighs.

Clive sat on her knee, which was something he hadn't done for years and, although he felt like he was too big to do so, and may actually *hurt* her, doing so felt comforting and reassuring.

"Life is strange." Sue said after stroking Clive's hair for a couple of minutes. "It works in ways that we cannot begin to try to understand. Maybe a responsible parent right now would be advising you to have an abortion, but I *won't*. You must do whatever you think is right, whatever you *and* Gayle think is right, and I will support you. If you thought a termination was the best thing to do, then I would support you. If you think keeping the baby is the best thing to do, then I will support you …."

She paused for a while, obviously deciding what to say next. Clive thought she was maybe waiting for him to say something else but he just wanted to listen; he had said everything he wanted to say for now.

"You are both *so young* and *so unprepared* for something like this," Sue said after a silence that felt like it could last all day. "But, then again, I'm not sure that *anyone* is ever prepared; not *fully* prepared anyway. As you know I was never able to have children of my own and so find it hard to accept that anyone should just be able to frivolously pick and choose *when* they should or *shouldn't* have children. Life will decide what and when..... about *life*..... and *death*. And *new life* is so *beautiful*. The only thing that anyone really needs to be able to care properly for a child is *love*. That's all. Just *unconditional love*. Everything else will sort itself out. The society we have means that there is financial help for those who need it. If you and Gayle have decided that you are going to keep the baby..... then everything will be ok. Just love that baby, like you love one another, and *everything* will be ok."

Clive continued to sit there on Sue's knee knowing that he didn't need to say anything. He should have known that he had nothing to worry about before telling her about the baby. She had made all the fear and dread go away completely, just like she always did. He knew that if he could make his baby feel half as special as she made him feel, then he would be doing ok.

FORTY EIGHT: *This Is It!*

Clive opened his eyes and felt refreshed by the memory that had just played out in his head. It's funny how, in any situation he found himself in life, he could recall some of the wisdom and love that Sue had given him in the *past*, and he would instantly feel better about things in the *present*. It was almost as good as having her with him to help him out in person. God he missed her so much.

Ok, he thought, get your mind back on track. He'd had a little rest and was ready to face what was in front of him. There was a job to do and he needed a plan.

Within a couple of minutes he had decided on what he was going to do. He was going to keep his eye on the wooden storage box by the flag pole in case one of the remaining enemy decided to meet him head on; although he didn't think that would happen. The two of them had probably decided to stay where they were and protect their flag - by waiting for him. It made strategic sense not to risk either of them, especially since they had lost four of their comrades already. Yep, thought Clive, he'd wiped out two-thirds of their entire army; *all on his own*, and he was pretty sure that the remaining enemy would now wait things out; at least until much closer to the end of the game time.

It was also pointless him trying to advance any further towards the flag, with them dug in like they were he would be a sitting duck trying to get any closer; it would be suicide. He had begun to get a little excited about the thought of maybe raising that flag but that last paint blow to the lower stomach had eased any crazy thoughts of trying anything too recklessly heroic. No, this current state of play meant that his earlier plan of waiting until twenty minutes were remaining and then charging the flag, while Gayle escaped the game arena unharmed, should work quite well. Until then he just had to relax and wait things out, keeping an eye on the storage box, making sure that neither of the remaining two enemy did anything unexpected.

Gayle carefully looked out of the open shack window but, just like the others times she had tried, saw absolutely nothing at all. Well, nothing apart from the rain that had now been bouncing down for close to ten minutes. ("No rain predicted for today" my arse!) It had been too long since she had seen or heard anything that related to Clive. At least no blasts of the fog horn meant that he was still alive but, by the same thinking, no blasts of the fog horn meant he had not managed to kill either of the last two of the enemy. She tried to tell herself that, as per the well known saying, "no news is good news"; but she'd actually never believed that crap. In reality "no new is - *no news*". All that she had heard was the bouncing rain and the three announcements that had indicated *thirty-five, thirty* and then *twenty-five* minutes of game time remaining, and now she knew that Clive's plan was going to be happening any second now. She had been hoping that Clive may have finished things off so that she could have walked out of the arena in a leisurely, *Sunday-ly*, manner; but that didn't look likely now, so she grabbed her gun and got ready to make her move.

Clive continued to gaze at the wooden storage box as the rain crashed down around him. Fortunately he was mostly sheltered from it by *Tree-ie's* umbrella like branches, but he realised that he would have to run out into it any second now. He couldn't help but become the character in the song *camouflage* again and, as such, couldn't turn off the voice of Stan Ridgeway echoing around his head. *"Whoa Camouflage, things are never quite the way they seem, Whoa Camouflage, this was an awfully strange marine."*

Clive wasn't sure if this musical accompaniment was going to be a help or a hindrance, but he did know that he'd had been staring at the same thing for the best part of twenty minutes now and his Benny Hill eyes were feeling tired. He wasn't even sure that anyone was actually over there anymore; he might have been gawping at nothing.

"Twenty minutes game time remaining"

The Scottish voice again escaped through the PA system and entered the game arena. This time there was a real hint of disinterest about the announcement, maybe everyone outside the arena were completely bored by the lack of action for the last twenty minutes.

This is it, thought Gayle, standing up and walking to the shack door. She took a deep breath, hoped like hell that Clive knew what he was doing and began running towards where she remembered the green arena exit to be.

This is it, thought Clive. *Blaze of Glory* time. He grabbed his gun tight, gave *Tree-ie* a little "thank you" pecked kiss (that felt like he may have sustained a splinter injury to the lip – bloody tree) and began running into no man's land. A loud shout of *"FOR GAYLE"* rang around his head as he pierced the falling rain and headed for the flag pole. He wasn't sure whether he was imagining himself running in movie-like slow motion, with the puddles artily splashing as he crashed each new step into the sodden ground on the way towards his inevitable death, or whether he was so bloody knackered that he was actually just running like a geriatric sloth.

As he got about half way to the flag pole, his heart beating through his chest, Clive finally saw some movement from behind the wooden storage box. Two men, in perfect synchronicity, slowly stood up and pointed their guns at him. Clive raised his own gun and pointed it towards the man on the left side of the box while, in his mind, congratulating himself that he had been right all along about the enemies tactics; they *had* been hiding all that time – too afraid to face him. Clive pulled his trigger and two paint balls meekly fell out down by his feet. Bloody typical – he *did* have a broken gun after all. He tried to squeeze the trigger again, but nothing happened. He was out of ammo. He had already shot his load. It was over; his time had come.

BANG, BANG, BANG, BANG, BANG, BANG, BANG, BANG, BANG, BANG

The sound of paint pellets being shot his way overwhelmed Clive again. And this time it was in stereo as the two men behind the box fired in unison. The pain arrived immediately and, this time, wasn't restricted to any one part of his body. He felt blows all over him, including at least one that, unlike his earlier lucky escape, struck him full on middle wicket. If this was a test match then the instant tears in his eyes would let everyone know where he'd been struck – there would be no need for a *Hawkeye* review on this occasion.

Clive collapsed to the floor in agony, spatters of green paint colliding with the falling rain as he hit the wet ground. He lay for a few seconds, battered and broken, thankful that the sound of guns being fired had stopped and happy that he'd occupied the last two guys for a while, as planned. Gayle will have made it out safe and sound. He slowly stood up; pain throbbing all over his body and green paint spattered across his goggles, and looked around. He wiped his goggles and saw the yellow gate about twenty metres away and began a slow, struggled walk towards it. There was no sign of his executioners anywhere.

Gayle continued to run through the rain, towards where she thought the green exit gate was, her goggles were wet and steamed up, making seeing much very difficult. She squinted as she looked towards the fence at the back of the large opening she had just entered, and there it was: the green gate.

She was nearly there.

As she moved though, she noticed a huge muddy puddle directly in between her and her escape route to freedom. She would have to go around, she didn't want to ruin her boots anymore than they already were and, besides, she wasn't *Peppa Pig*. She began to run around, the surprising lack of needing to do *any* running during the morning activity was certainly being made up for now. As she ran, she heard that tell-tale crackle through the PA speakers.

PAARRRRRRP

Clive had done it again! Amazing! And if he'd got one he would probably get the other, and there'd be no need for any more running at all.

PAARRRRRRP

Oh no!

That was a *second* blast.

For a split second Gayle hoped that it meant that Clive had actually killed the remaining *two* enemies, but she quickly accepted what it *really* meant. There hadn't been two single blasts of the horn; there had been *two blasts of the horn*.

She stopped dead in her tracks.

Clive had failed.

He hadn't killed the last two.

They had killed him.

Clive was dead.

She felt an uncontrollable sense of sadness and loneliness. It had only been twenty minutes or so since she had last seen him but she knew that Clive had been out there, fighting for her, but now she knew that she wouldn't see him again. Her eyes welled up as the realisation that she would *never* see him again struck her.

Wait a minute!

Clive wasn't *really* dead. They were just *paintballing*! And this was part of his plan so that she could escape unharmed, and she was standing here, completely still, while there were two gun-wielding psycho's still out there. She looked again towards the green gate; it wasn't far at all.

258

Sod it, she thought, she was going to run *through* the muddy puddle. Maybe she was *Peppa Pig* after all!

She started running again and made four or five fast strikes across the mud, splattering it high and wide, before she heard a loud "squelch" noise and felt her left leg exiting her boot. She stopped, walked back and stooped, grabbed and heaved her boot, like some weird, expensive footwear tug-o-war, until it was released from its muddy captor. She squeezed it back on and began running once again.

Now she was out in the open she could properly feel the wind that was really quite wild. It blew the heavy, cold rain right into her and it stabbed away like icy little needles. Not far now, got to keep going, she said to herself, as mud splashed all around her and she fought against the cruel elements. Suddenly she noticed two figures approaching quickly from her left.

Oh no, they had caught up with her.

She raised her gun and blindly pulled the trigger hoping beyond hope that her random aiming in their direction may actually hit them. They both dropped to the floor, not hit but rather taking evasive action, until all of Gayle's pellets had been used. Her shots had gone nowhere near them and now she was out of ammunition. She dropped her gun into the mud and started to run again. Two massive squelches straight away told her that her little pause in the mud had been enough to get both of her boots stuck. She felt both feet slip out of the boots but didn't care; she would leave them there, she didn't have far to go – only about ten more steps.

She only made three more though, before being struck by a paint pellet on her upper left arm. She was spun around and fell into the mud. As dirty liquid splashed up and over her she grabbed for her arm and screamed out. This one felt even more painful than the first one had somehow. It was like having her BCG injection from school all over again – only, this time, like the doctor had administered it through a spear. She rolled around in further pain as a second pellet struck her on the back.

"Arrrrrrrggggghhhhh!"

Clive stopped just in front of the yellow gate as he heard a loud scream fight against the howling wind to echo around the game arena. His heart sank. It was Gayle. They had got to her. She hadn't made it; *they* hadn't made it. He heard her scream again as he, dejectedly, reached for the handle of the door, ready to leave the arena.

"Arrrrrrrggggghhhhh!"

Gayle tried her best to screw up into a ball to try and protect herself from the pellets that continued to be fired her way. Both men had now walked in front of her and were shooting at her from no more than about five metres away. What was wrong with them? She'd had at least double the five shots that had been needed to kill her. And where was that double fog horn blast? It should be over. She just wanted to go home. She closed her eyes tight and tried to cancel out the wind and the rain and her throbbing head from her tight helmet.

And the pain of the pellets; so much pain.

Instead she tried to focus on somewhere else that she wanted to be. It was home. Home in front of the fire. Or, better still, home in a nice, hot bubble bath. Home in a nice, hot bubble bath drinking champagne. (Ok, Cava. Who was she kidding?) She may even put a strawberry in it, like you see people doing on TV. She'd never had a strawberry in fizzy wine. She didn't know if she would like it, she didn't even know *why* people did it, but she felt like she wanted to try it. As she smiled slightly about her bath and Cava vision, tears continued to stream from her eyes as the shooting continued. She could hear each individual shot, followed by the burst of pain.

Pain after pain after pain after pain.

This was now, without doubt, one of the *worst* moments of her life.

Why wouldn't it end?

She even noticed one of the guys re-loading his gun as his partner continued to fire. It wasn't fair; she and Clive hadn't been given any "back-up ammunition". She closed her eyes again and re-connected with the rhythm of shot then pain, then shot, then pain, then shot, then pain…

Although it was only paintballing and the shots being fired were only paint pellets, Gayle couldn't help but feel like this is what it must be like for some people "at the end". It felt like, very soon, she would be having visions of her life flashing before her eyes.

And then something strange happened. The rhythm was broken. The shots continued, but there was no pain. Was she so sore that she couldn't feel *anything* anymore? She opened her eyes slightly but everything seemed darker than before. It took a couple of seconds to focus but then she realised why.

It was Clive.

He was lying next to her. The pain had stopped because he was shielding her from the shots. Through her tears she could see each grimace on his face that followed the continuing sound of the guns firing.

"It's ok now." Clive whispered.

And it was.

Everything was ok.

Gayle closed her eyes and she *did* start to get visions flashing before her eyes. But they weren't visions of her life, chronicling what may be the end for her, they were visions of the last few days: the events at the baby group, the school disco room, the picture of "their" house on the tree in the school field – which she now realised *is* her and Clive's dream place to live. The briefest version of *Dumb and Dumber* and, now, even visions of this paintballing afternoon – *her and Clive vs. The World*. These were visions that were announcing a brand new start, opening a brand new, blank page for the future for her.

For her and Clive.

She opened her eyes again and stared at Clive.

He stared back.

They no longer looked like Eddie the Eagle and Benny Hill but just themselves; only with magnified eyes. Eyes, finally, big enough to climb into once more.

Gayle grabbed hold of Clive and squeezed him as tight as she could. The PA system crackle sounded but this time there wasn't an announcement in a bored Scottish accent or the farting sound of a fog horn but rather the tinniest, crackliest version of *Space: Me and You vs. The World* that had *ever* been played *anywhere* in the world. It was so tinny that you could hardly even hear the trademark "crunch.....crunch, crunch.....crunch.....crunch, crunch" drum sound of the chorus.

It was certainly the worst version of the song that Clive and Gayle had ever heard and yet, somehow, it was the *best*. It was *their* song, playing at exactly *their* moment. And Gayle knew, all over again, that Clive would gladly die for her and that she would gladly die for him; because *Love is Love reflected.*

Clive smiled contently, even more so when the shooting stopped because what had seemed like a never ending supply of ammunition appeared to have come to an end. He was completely covered in green paint and was sore all over. He knew that he would be battered and bruised from head to toe, and his eyes, perhaps from having to squint from behind his face mask all afternoon, were stinging more than they had in his whole life; but he was *happy*.

His line of sight followed the two "victorious" paintballer's as they headed out of the green gate, mumbling something about wishing they had more paintballs. He was *so* thankful that they didn't. As they exited the game arena, Clive noticed that Jeremy was standing beside the green gate, staring at him and Gayle and smiling. In fact *smiling* didn't cover it, he was positively *beaming*. Maybe because he realised that he wouldn't have to give Clive his money back or, more likely, because he had succeeded in what he had set out to do. He had been able to help them *re-find* their love. He was a clever, clever man; a stark-raving, certifiable, outrageous lunatic, but a clever, clever man.

In fact, had the whole weekend been a *master plan* working up to *this moment*? Were all the interruptions on purpose, so they would get a little taste of everything that Jeremy thought they needed? Was their "first kiss" gate crashed by the foul-mouthed rugby guy planned so they would run off to their "special place" on the field? Was their "cinema date" even interrupted by design so that he and Gayle would go home and talk about the "loan shark" episode that had subconsciously cast a shadow over them for all these years? Were Zoe from the baby group, Hayley and the rugby thug from the youth club, the debt collectors from this morning and, even, all these paintballer's *all in on it*? Was everything set up flawlessly so that the weekend would climax in this most *perfect* of endings?

Maybe.

Or maybe not.

Perhaps fate, luck and circumstance had leant a helping hand as well?

Clive supposed that he'd never really know for sure. What he did know is that he would forever be thankful that he saw Jeremy, standing in the rain with his sandwich board, on one fateful Friday morning.

Jeremy slowly nodded his head as he saw Clive looking his way and then winked at him. Clive nodded back before having to blink his sore, stinging eyes a few times. When he was able to re-focus on the green gate, Jeremy was gone. Clive sniggered to himself as he recalled another line from *Camouflage* in his head: *".....he just winked at me from the jungle and then was gone....."*

Wow, Jeremy was *their* "Camouflage".

He had been sent to rescue him and Gayle from their own hopeless situation and now his job was done. Clive looked back at Gayle to tell her but her eyes were closed and she had a contented smile on her face. It was probably best he didn't tell her anyway. She, inexplicably, never really liked the song and, well the more Clive thought about it, the more ridiculous it sounded.

Or did it?

If they were to go back to that old *One Quid Bakery* shop, hidden down that obscure alley way in the precinct, would the *Love Is...* "office" actually still be there? Was it *ever* there? Maybe it had always just been an establishment where you could purchase reasonably priced savoury snacks off the beaten track? Clive thought he should try and remember that for next time he was at the shopping centre.

Clive cleared his mind and, instead, closed his own eyes and held Gayle even tighter. He was lying in the cold mud, freezing, sore, wet and humiliated and yet he never wanted this moment to end. This was his and Gayle's *happily after ever* moment, and it had made everything feel perfect again, just like Jeremy (or *Camouflage*) had predicated when he had first met him.

FORTY NINE: *Love On A Rooftop.*

Gayle moved her body slightly as she was getting uncomfortable after not moving for quite some time. It was only a couple of inches but it did the trick, and she also managed to stay comfortably in Clive's arms, wrapped up together under the tartan blanket on the sofa, where they had been for the last hour or so. Her eyes were closed and resting, yet thoughts were still uncontrollably spinning around her head. But they weren't manic, unsettling and unwelcome thoughts. They were pleasant thoughts that fluctuated from repeating events from the last couple of days, and replaying bits of the conversation that she and Clive had just had, to offering optimistic and bright visions of the future.

They had been home from their paintballing event for about an hour and Gayle hadn't had that hot bubble bath she had promised herself yet because, instead, she and Clive had just collapsed into each other on the sofa and were so comfortable just tangled up in each other's arms. They had spoken about how each of them almost felt like they had when they were first getting to know each other and how, right now, felt like the chance of making a brand new start. They had even confronted the last decade or so and it felt like, in doing so, they had exercised many, many demons and, right now to Gayle, that whole period felt like some, strange, unwanted bad dream.

The main aspects of their conversation though had centered on a brand new set of promises to each other that were ruled by two main points.

One - From now on they would *always* be open and honest with each other and,

Two - They would make sure that life was *fun* again.

264

They would laugh and they would joke and they would be silly.

They had allowed life to make them too serious and, in turn, too distant with one another. They promised to make sure things felt more like they had in the past. They would make time for doing things that they both wanted to do; *together*. They *would* stop to see the moon at night; they *would* make *love on a rooftop*. (Obviously not literally. Unless you could find a *flat roof*, it would be *completely bonkers*. But certainly *metaphorically* they would.)

For Gayle, she felt *alive* again, almost re-born. She felt a rush of inspiration running through her veins and even had a great idea about how to finish her poem / song "Next Time" that she had discussed with Jeremy the day before; and looked forward to being able to put it on the radiator cover next to "Echoes Through Time". But with this whole "being open and honest" with each other promise she also realised that she would need to tell Clive about the date she had arranged with Lee.

Clive allowed his body to move gently as Gayle wriggled around. His eyes were also closed and his body happy to be resting in the embrace with his wife. He couldn't help but think about the hot, bubble bath that Gayle had described on the way back home from the paintballing. He did feel warm and snug under the cover on the sofa but he had just spent a large amount of time out in the freezing elements, and a majority of that being sheltered by nothing more than a large tree. (Ah Tree-ie! Is it wrong to miss a tree so much and feel like you *need* to go back and see it again? *Very soon*?) Clive refocused on the fact that he felt like he had been chilled to the very marrow of his bones and would very much like, more than anything, to experience that hot bath. It didn't really go with the tough guy image that he had just worked hard for though, did it? He had just gallantly laid his life on the line (again, *metaphorically*) and then rescued Gayle in her hour of need, to tell her he wanted to go for a bubble bath would probably blemish all that a little. As such, he decided it best that he didn't mention it and to try and cling on to this new, tough, green-beret, animal aura for as long as he could. (He knew he was only one stubbed toe away from reverting back to himself.)

Clive, too, was feeling rather good about life and, especially, the future right now. Just sitting here with Gayle, after experiencing what they had over the last couple of days and having possibly the most truthful and sincere conversation they had *ever* had, made everything feel great. And it made this house, their *home*, feel more like home than it ever had. Clive smiled to himself as he thought about the opportunity he

265

would have to phone "slick", the estate agent, and tell him he could shove his services up his arse: *This House Is Not For Sale.*

He did, however, feel a little bit uncomfortable about something else. He wasn't sure whether he should tell Gayle about his planned date / *it-doesn't-have-to-be-a-date,* date, that he had arranged with Stacey Wellington. It felt weird now that he had even agreed to it but back then, a whole day and a half ago, *everything* felt so different. He and Gayle were calling it a day and so he shouldn't *really* have anything to feel guilty about. He couldn't help but feel cautious though, everyone knows what happened and the trouble that was caused by the whole Ross and Rachel "we were on a break" *Friends* thing. He didn't want that kind of scenario popping up and certainly didn't feel like he could handle reading a letter that was eighteen pages long (front and back.) Sorry to any non-Friends geeks out there! But they had just made a promise to be honest and open with each other and so he knew that he had to tell her.

"I've got something I need to tell you." He began, appropriately for someone who had something that they needed to tell someone.

Gayle fidgeted again on the sofa, this time moving so that she could look into Clive's eyes.

"Ok. But before you do, I just want to say something quickly."

"Ok" said Clive, looking back into her eyes.

"On Friday, a guy who comes into work asked me out for a drink. Back then, I had no idea *this* was going to happen. I was supposed to be meeting him tonight at the Farmers Arms but will obviously cancel it. Just thought I'd best tell you."

Damn it, thought Clive.

Gayle was already making dates with other men – as soon as Jack moved out. This was just about..... wait a minute, a little perspective here. She had done nothing different to what he had done. In fact if she had made her date on Friday then she had done it before she even knew anything about the whole *Love Is...* events, whereas his "date" was made *after* he knew that they were going to be trying these weekend events.

Hmm?

That made things a little awkward. But hold on, he *hadn't* made a date; he had made a *it-doesn't-have-to-be-a-date,* date, which surely was *totally different.*

Wasn't it?

Should he still tell her? She'd kind of stolen the thunder on this one anyway.

"Ok" said Gayle. "What did you want to say?"

266

"I'm sorry, but I've come to realise that I'm actually gay!" said Clive, completely not thinking through *why* he would say that, other than to try and be funny.

Gayle just stared at him in confusion.

"Don't tell me, you and *Knobhead* are getting a place together? You've been *at it* for years!"

They both burst out laughing.

Gayle wondered about a couple of things as she laughed. Firstly, if this was the kind of weird thing that Clive would be saying from now on then maybe she shouldn't have agreed to them being more funny and silly with each other in the future. Also, more alarmingly, Clive had been laughing for several seconds now and had not said a word; he certainly hadn't *denied* it yet. Imagine being dumped by your husband because he'd fallen in love with someone like *Knobhead*. That's probably the kind of blow you never recover from.

Clive continued laughing realising that his "date" news was now going to come across as even more strange seeing as he had tried to make the mood so light hearted with his ridiculous attempt at humour. He had to tell her the truth though and quickly because the way her face was changing it appeared she might actually be wondering if the whole *coming out* gesture might be real.

He tried to make it seem like something and nothing.

"How weird is this? I'd also arranged to go out tonight for a drink with someone. Do you remember Stacey Wellington from school? I saw her the other day and she asked me if I wanted to meet her – tonight as well, at the Farmers Arms – how strange – for a quick drink. Obviously I didn't know *this* was going to happen as well."

Gayle suddenly felt a little sad.

Wow, Clive was planning to get on with his life as well. She couldn't help but feel a little angry and jealous as well and yet quickly realised that this was a good thing. It meant that she *did* care. And she couldn't really be angry because Clive had only done the same thing as her – just reacted to a situation based on what they both thought was happening to their relationship just a couple of days earlier. She just felt incredibly thankful that they'd spent this weekend doing Jeremy's increasingly *crazy* activities, because without them, as Jeremy had said to both of them; they would be another couple just letting true love get lost forever.

Gayle realised something and so began to think out loud.

"I haven't got Lee's number or anything. I suppose he'd get the message if I didn't show up..... or maybe I should go and tell him to his face?"

Clive thought about it, before adding.

"I haven't got any way of letting Stacey know either. Maybe we should go *together* and tell them both..... *together*."

Gayle slowly nodded her head and smiled.

"Yeah, we'll do it *together*. Me and You vs. The World".

Clive pulled Gayle close to him because he needed to kiss her. And he kissed her like he was going to kiss her for the rest of time.

FIFTY: *Turns Out...*

"Are you ready?" Clive asked as he reached out and grabbed the handle of the front door to the Farmers Arms.

Gayle took a deep breath and nodded, fairly unconvincingly.

"I suppose so." She said as Clive opened the door.

She hadn't felt this nervous for as long as she could remember. She and Clive were only here to tell Lee and Stacey that they were actually giving their marriage another go; and they were here to do that *together*. What the hell would she have been like if she was arriving for her actual date, on her own?

As they walked into the pub, Clive grabbed hold of Gayle's hand and leant over and whispered into her ear.

"Did I tell you how gorgeous you look tonight?"

"Yes!" said Gayle, a little snappily, those feelings of nervousness, if possible, intensifying as they walked into the pub.

Clive frowned a little.

He had been thinking that he would tell Gayle how fantastic she looked on a regular basis, like he always used to, but if she was going to get ratty with him if he did it too often, he may have to re-think his approach.

He took a look at his watch as they walked in. It was eight, thirty-three and twenty nine seconds. (Sure digital watches are a bit 1980's but they give you so much more accuracy) Ok, good, he thought. Just as they had planned, they were half an hour late. As they had been getting ready, Gayle had suggested that they arrive a little late. She had remembered a conversation between Jenny and Janine at work in which they had both agreed that a good way to begin to break up with someone was to turn up late for a date because, straight away, it makes them a little pissed off with you. So, when the actual breaking up comes along, it's less likely to be greeted with an over-emotional response. Of course this situation was different to that, but seeing as both Clive and Gayle had never broken up with someone before, or even got *together* with anyone before (apart from each other), this seemed like the closest thing they had to any advice on how to handle things.

After agreeing to this plan, Clive reassured Gayle that she didn't need to *aim* to be late, she just needed to get ready as usual and that things would fall into place. And it had: thirty three minutes and twenty nine seconds of waiting for someone was surely enough to piss anyone off.

Gayle searched around the pub looking for Lee, the stocky water man. It was weird that two days ago she was excited about going on a date with him and yet now she felt nothing like that at all. She just wanted to find him, apologise for not being able to have that drink with him, and then, hopefully, be able to calm down and relax again. After intensely scanning the pub a couple of times, like a Terminator on a mission, Gayle first came across the ungainly figure of Clive's "good" friend Robert Adshead, a.k.a. "Knobhead", talking to an old-ish looking woman near the exit to the "beer garden" (the overgrown area where the smokers huddled in the cold next to the faulty patio heater). If she was a Terminator he'd be the first person on her list to be terminated. After that her robotic searching succeeded in its mission and she located Lee in the far corner of the pub, at the end of the bar. He was wearing a tight, white t-shirt that showed off his bulging arm muscles and he had a half-drunk pint in his right hand. He didn't look like someone who was anxiously waiting for someone who was running late and was actually chatting, and laughing, with a rather tarty looking blonde girl in a red top who was sipping away at a glass of white wine.

Clive continued to hold Gayle's hand and could actually feel the rhythm of her heartbeat through a pulse coming through her palm. He realised she was completely uptight about being here. They needed to find their "dates" quickly and get this over with. He thought that maybe if you were waiting for someone you may stand by one of the doors and so, first, focussed his eyes over to the beer garden door. There was no instant sign of Stacey but he did see the towering figure of *Knobhead* chatting up another woman who looked odds on to be a pensioner. He looked more like Peter Crouch than ever and, ironically, had to crouch to avoid wiping some hair gel onto the relatively low ceiling on that side of the pub.

Clive checked all the potential exit doors and toilets before changing his search to the bar area and, sure enough, after following it to the end, there was Stacey. She was near the corner, drinking white wine and talking to a rough looking meat-head in a white t-shirt that was clearly three sizes too small for him.

Gayle and Clive looked at each other at exactly the same time and said:

"There he is / there she is"

It only took them a split second of following each other's eye line to realise that their "dates" were at the end of the bar – *talking to one another*. Wow, how strange was that?

"Ok," said Clive. "Maybe they know each other? Oh well, two birds with one stone then, isn't it?"

He couldn't help but contemplate his own question: *did* Stacey and Lee know each other or was it fate that they had just met each other here tonight? Or maybe they had been introduced by someone they both knew before he and Gayle had arrived? Then again, is that the same thing as fate anyway? He cleared his mind and looked at Gayle, who now had the look of a small child being forced onto a ghost train ride at the fair for the first time.

Clive looked into Gayle's eyes.

"Come on, let's get it over with. Do you want me to do the talking?"

Gayle nodded and gave him a soft but warm smile.

"Ok then." He said, squeezing her hand gently in a reassuring manner.

As they began walking towards the end of the bar, Clive now processed the situation. He was openly heading towards the biggest, most muscular and scary looking guy in the pub and was about to tell him that he'd stolen his date for the evening. Of course, *his date* was actually Clive's *wife* and so, technically, Clive had the moral high ground on this one, but having the moral high ground means diddly-squat if you're confronting someone who could clearly kick the living shit out of you with half of one of their little fingers. As such he began to feel a little nervous as well. He couldn't also help but contemplate why Gayle had arranged a date with this guy; this *Lee*. Was this the type of guy that she would want to end up with if they were to split up? He was completely the opposite of him. What did that actually mean?

As they got nearer to Lee and Stacey, Gayle couldn't help but wonder why Clive had arranged a date with Stacey Wellington. She was always loud and annoying at school. (Which, in fairness to Gayle, could have pretty much been a description of the way she felt about most of the girls at school.) And look at her now – dyed blonde hair, wearing so much

271

make up she could make a Batman villain jealous, and just looking completely *false*. It was also odds on that she'd probably had a boob job by now; she was *that type.*

Gayle realised that maybe she was reverting to the teenage bitchiness that comes naturally to school girls and knew that she needed to rein it in a little. (Not a lot, just a *little.*) She also realised that dying you hair blonde may also be an easier way to hide the fact that you've got quite a bit of grey coming through and that maybe she should look into that herself. But was this the sort of girl that Clive would go for if he was single now? She was pretty much the total opposite of her. What did that say about things?

About ten feet away from Stacey and Lee, Clive was still unsure about exactly what he was going to say to them. One thing he did know though was that he was going to use the "three steps back" technique that he used whilst out on his postal delivery. It was usually employed to be sure that you were prepared for any dogs that may speed out of a house to attack you but it would, hopefully, be equally effective in staying out of range of potentially angry, burly water delivery men. Also, if this Lee did take a swing / came after him at least the last few days had proven that Clive still had a nice turn of pace.

Both Clive and Gayle intently stared at the two of them as they got closer, and something completely unexpected happened. Lee whispered something into Stacey's ear that made her laugh out loud. Clive couldn't help but feel that if he was coming on a date with Stacey then he would have been completely unprepared. She had told him that he used to make her laugh and yet here he was showing up without a single, appropriate, joke to tell her. He would need to look up his Bob Monkhouse joke book, just in case any future situations in life demanded some classic, clean humour. Lee then whispered something else into Stacey's ear only this time she didn't laugh. Instead she just stared at Lee as his face slowly moved towards hers before their lips connected and they began kissing.

What the hell was going on?

They were supposed to be sitting there waiting for individual dates and yet they were now snogging – with each other. And right in front of Clive and Gayle. Admittedly probably *unaware* they were snogging in front of them, but they were snogging never the less. Clive wondered what it was that Lee had whispered into Stacey's ear because whatever it was, it must have been pretty smooth.

Clive then looked at Gayle and she looked as surprised as he was.

What was going on? Was this what happened in pubs these days? People just snog each other within a few minutes of meeting?

Both Gayle and Clive quickly contemplated whether, if they had come on their individual dates, they would be kissing Lee and Stacey, respectively, right now.

Wow, *crazy*.

They both then looked at each other and couldn't help but laugh. This was actually a *good* thing. There would be no need for any awkward conversations about why they didn't want to go through with the dates and maybe feeling like they had to explain the whole weirdness of the weekend. It actually also felt quite nice that Lee and Stacey looked like they had turned what could have been a disappointing night into something that could maybe be the *start* of something for them. Maybe the start of *something special*, who knows? Most importantly for Clive he didn't need to find out whether Lee was as short-fused as his meat-head look suggested he might be, and whether he may actually be much quicker than a man of his bulk looked like he would be.

The whole situation felt a bit surreal, but both Clive and Gayle couldn't help but feel like something had lent a helping hand. It was almost like fate had intervened and brought Stacey and Lee together, for a reason, whilst they were waiting for Clive and Gayle to arrive.

Suddenly a cool blast of air shot through the pub and a man in a long black coat passed in between where Clive and Gayle were standing and where Lee and Stacey were kissing. Neither Gayle nor Clive got a look at his face as he moved too fast to focus on and almost floated across the room and round the corner and out of sight. They looked at each other as if maybe they had seen a dark-figured apparition of some kind. Clive shrugged this off as one of those weird, unexplainable things you sometimes see and, as he looked at Gayle, he was happy to see that she no longer looked as anxious as she had when they walked into the pub. As he turned his head to face her, Gayle placed her hands at either side of his face and pulled him into her lips. If there was kissing going on round here then she wanted in on the action as well.

After a good few seconds of their own snogging, Gayle pulled away and she and Clive smiled at each other.

Wow, that felt good.

Gayle glanced across at Stacey and Lee and felt a bit miffed that they were actually *still* snogging. It didn't matter though. This wasn't the youth club more than twenty years ago (or even last night for that matter) and so they were not involved in any kind of snogging contest.

Gayle looked around, and saw that *Knobhead* was still standing by the bar, before looking back at Clive.

"Are you going to go and say hello to your boyfriend Robert ...... I mean, *Knobhead*?" she said, grimacing as she used the nickname that she disliked so much.

"No." said Clive straight away.

"You can do, you know?"

"I know I can. I just don't want to." Said Clive, before moving his face closer to Gayle, coolly bobbing his head slowly up and down, a bit like he imagined George Clooney smoothly would if he was in this situation, before he spoke some more.

"I've spent too much of my time *not* concentrating on you. It's not going to happen anymore."

Gayle smiled at him, while wondering why he was strangely nodding his head up and down like some freaky nodding dog on the back shelf of a "classic" ford escort.

"Do you fancy a drink?" Clive asked.

Gayle looked at Lee and Stacey, who were *thankfully* not snogging anymore, but were now chatting and laughing and still hadn't noticed that she and Clive were there. She quite liked the idea of not having to speak to them because she just wanted to be with Clive; with no complications or awkwardness.

"We could just go home?" she said. "We've got some Cava and strawberries in the fridge; we could snuggle up and watch a film or something?"

Clive was a bit confused about why Gayle was saying they had strawberries in the fridge, but he liked the idea of the Cava and the snuggling up. He smiled and nodded his head.

"What do you fancy?" Gayle asked. "We could watch *The Mask* – seeing as Jeremy cocked that up? Or the whole of *Dumb and Dumber*?"

Clive nodded before putting his own suggestion into the mix, with a playful grin.

"I'd watch either of those .... or maybe we could watch some *X-Files*?"

Gayle couldn't help smiling.

She knew exactly what Clive meant and it had been quite some time since they'd *properly* watched some *X-Files*.

"Ok then." She said, speaking through her smile.

Clive reached out for Gayle's hand as they both took a sideways glance at Lee and Stacey, who were still chatting and smiling at one another and appeared to be having a good time.

As they began walking Clive leant into Gayle and whispered: "You and me baby ain't nothing but mammals....."

Gayle squealed out a little laugh and put her arm around Clive as they walked. Clive smiled to himself thinking that Gayle/Stacey's' Lee may be smooth..... but *he* was smoother!

Just a couple of steps away from reaching the front door a slim girl with medium length brown hair fairly rudely barged past them as she headed for the exit at great speed.

"Mandy!"

A desperate cry came from a fairly stocky, ginger haired boy who was also approaching them fairly quickly.

"Go to hell, Jake!" said the girl, apparently named Mandy, as she stopped by the door. She removed a ring from her finger, throwing it towards the boy, apparently named Jake, adding "It's over" before leaving the pub.

"I'm sorry" said Jake, fortunately finding the ring on the floor straight away. "Don't give up on me" he shouted towards the, now, closed door. "I love you!"

He also squeezed past Gayle and Clive, showing a bit more in the way of manners as he muttered a quiet apology before heading out of the pub and after Mandy. Clive couldn't help but think that this Jake was probably punching slightly above his weight but, in truth, he probably felt that about most men that were in relationships. Also, these days, thanks to Ron Weasley, those ginger kids seem to be more in with a fighting chance.

Clive and Gayle looked at each other but before either of them could say a word, a third person barged past them at high speed. Another blast of cool air hit them, which may or may not have been caused by the front door being opened twice in quick succession, as that mysterious man in the long, black coat became the latest person to quickly go by. His apology was much louder and both Clive and Gayle clearly heard the words "Sorry, excuse me .... duty calls", spoken in an almost shouted, and rather fake, *Australian* accent.

Gayle and Gayle instinctively looked at each other.

The pub door opened and closed quickly as he vanished out of sight.

"Was that.....?" began Gayle.

"I don't know." Said Clive, not needing to hear the rest of what she may have been going to say.

After a couple of seconds of staring at each other they both turned and quickly made their own way to the front door. It was fairly dark outside now and as they both frantically looked around outside there was no sign at all of any of the three people who had just barged past them. They both continued to look and listen but there was nothing to be seen and only silence to be heard.

Very strange.

"Look!" said Gayle after a few more seconds of scanning the area.

She was pointing into the pub car park where, right in the far corner, where the lights on the side of the pub didn't quite reach, there was a car that looked like it could possibly be a maroon Volvo.

"Shall we go and have a look?" asked Gayle.

Clive shook his head.

"There's no need."

Gayle felt confused. Why would they *not* go and check to see whether that was Jeremy's car or not. Did Clive not want to know if that was him in the pub, carrying out more "Love Work" in an almost supernatural way?

As Clive smiled at her she realised what he was thinking. He was right - there was *no* need. Whatever and however it had happened was irrelevant, what was important was that it *had* happened. She and Clive had re-found their love; and *nothing else mattered.*

She smiled back at him.

"Come on" said Clive. "Let's go home."

They both started walking, comfortable in the knowledge that there were certain things that they would never know for sure. But there was one thing that they could be *totally* sure about. For Clive and Gayle, Jeremy had been completely correct; because, for them, it turns out, Love *is* usually where you left it.

Next Time.

Next time I'll be a rock star,
Next time I'll write a symphony,
And I'll forever be at number one,
Yeah, next time I will make history.

Next time I will go travelling,
See every country in the world,
I'll learn every single language,
And meet every boy and every girl.

Next time I'll climb a mountain,
And I'll swim the deepest ocean,
Next time I'll change the world,
Yeah, I'll invent perpetual motion.

Next time I'll be an athlete,
I'll break every single record,
Running, jumping, throwing, sprinting,
I'll do it 'til I'm bored.

Maybe I'll fly up to the moon,
And I'll see all of the stars,
Yeah, next time I'll be an astronaut,
I'll be the first to walk on Mars.

I'll go right to the end of the Earth,
Next time I'll admire the view,
But I won't admire it on my own,
Next time I will take you.

Next time I'll live a million dreams,
But this much will be true,
Next time won't be as good as this time,
Unless I'm loving you.

Gary Locke

Love Is Usually Where You Left It is the culmination of various ideas; the seeds of which slowly cultivated over the past couple of years. The tone was always meant to be light-hearted and at times almost farcical, with lots of observational humour, hopefully resulting in an easy, undemanding and entertaining read.

Yet, as those ideas grew, I realised that sitting at the heart of the book is a really relevant and strong message. Everywhere you look you can see relationships breaking down and, for many of them, you have to ask: *why?* I believe that love; *real love*, is *eternal*. But like everything that is good in life, it doesn't always run smoothly. If this book can, on any level, make anyone realise that love needs to be cherished, constantly worked on and, in times of desperation, *fought for*; then bringing those various ideas together has created so much more than a light-hearted, farcical tale.

Thank you to all my family and friends and to everyone I've known and loved past, present and future.

This book is dedicated to my three girls – *Sharon, Ella-Louise* and *Hazel*.

You are my everything.
xxx

Also by Gary Locke:

Congratulations…..you're having ~~a baby~~ *twins!*

! – For when full stops aren't enough and question marks aren't appropriate

The Paul Day Chronicles Comedy Series -

The complete days of 2006 –
Paul Day Chronicles – Happily After *Ever!*

Short Stories from 2006 –
Paul Day Chronicles – Love Is Like Fireworks!
Paul Day Chronicles – The Stag Do.
Paul Day Chronicles – Football Is Like Sex!
Paul Day Chronicles – Fate… Bloody Fate!

The complete days of 1992 –
Paul Day Chronicles – Goodbye B.M.X., *Hello S.E.X.*

Short Stories from 1992 –
Paul Day Chronicles – Love for the Very First Time.
Paul Day Chronicles – Dead Legs, Exam Dreads and Fun Behind the Bike Sheds.

Cling and Grow Publishing

Copyright © Gary Locke 2019

Cover Design by Andy Tiplady – Freelance Graphic Designer

Printed in Poland
by Amazon Fulfillment
Poland Sp. z o.o., Wrocław

50787095R00171